The Kitchen Maid
Jenny secures a job as kitchen maid in a grand house in Beverley – but her fortunes fail when scandal forces her to leave. Years later, she is mistress of a hall, but she never forgets the words a gypsy told her: that one day she will return to where she was happy and find her true love . . .

The Songbird
Poppy Mazzini has an ambition – to go on the stage. Her lovely voice and Italian looks lead her to great acclaim. But when her first love from her home town of Hull becomes engaged to someone else, she is devastated. Will Poppy have to choose between fame and true love?

Nobody's Child
Now a prosperous Hull businesswoman, Susannah grew up with the terrible stigma of being nobody's child. When daughter Laura returns to the Holderness village of her mother's childhood, she will discover a story of poverty, heartbreak and a love that never dies . . .

Fallen Angels
After her dastardly husband tries to sell her, Lily Fowler is alone on the streets of Hull. Forced to work in a brothel, she forges friendships with the women there, and together they try to turn their lives around. Can they dare to dream of happy endings?

The Long Walk Home
When Mikey Quinn's mother dies, he is determined to find a better life for his family – so he walks to London from Hull to seek his fortune. He meets Eleanor, and they gradually make a new life for themselves. Eventually, though, they must make the long walk home to Hull . . .

Rich Girl, Poor Girl
Polly, living in poverty, finds herself alone when her mother dies. Rosalie, brought up in comfort on the other side of Hull, loses her own mother on the same day. When Polly takes a job in Rosalie's house, the two girls form an unlikely friendship. United in tragedy, can they find happiness?

Homecoming Girls
The mysterious Jewel Newmarch turns heads wherever she goes, but she feels a longing to know her own roots. So she decides to return to her birthplace in America, where she learns about family, friendship, love and home. But most importantly, love . . .

The Harbour Girl
Jeannie spends her days at the water's edge waiting for Ethan to come in from fishing. But then she falls for a handsome stranger. When he breaks his word, Jeannie finds herself pregnant and alone in a strange new town. Will she find someone to truly love her – and will Ethan ever forgive her?

The Innkeeper's Daughter
Bella's dreams of teaching are dashed when she has to take on the role of mother to her baby brother. Her days are brightened by visits from Jamie Lucan – but when the family is forced to move to Hull, Bella is forced to leave everything behind. Can she ever find her dreams again?

His Brother's Wife

The last thing Harriet expects after her mother dies is to marry a man she barely knows, but her only alternative is the workhouse. And so begins an unhappy marriage to Noah Tuke. The only person who offers her friendship is Noah's brother, Fletcher – the one person she can't possibly be with . . .

Every Mother's Son

Daniel Tuke hopes to share his future with childhood friend Beatrice Hart. But his efforts to find out more about his heritage throw up some shocking truths: is there a connection between the families? Meanwhile, Daniel's mother Harriet could never imagine that discoveries about her own family are also on the horizon . . .

Little Girl Lost

Margriet grew up as a lonely child in the old town of Hull. As she grows into adulthood she forms an unlikely friendship with some of the street children who roam the town. As Margriet acts upon her inspiration to help them, will the troubles of her past break her spirit, or will she be able to overcome them?

No Place for a Woman

Brought up by a kindly uncle after the death of her parents, Lucy grows up inspired to become a doctor, just like her father. But studying in London takes Lucy far from her home in Hull, and she has to battle to be accepted in a man's world. An even greater challenge comes with the onset of the First World War; will Lucy be able to follow her dreams – and find love – in a world shattered by war?

A Mother's Choice

Delia has always had to fend for herself and her son Jack, and as a young unmarried mother, life has never been easy. In particularly desperate times, a chance encounter presents a lifeline. Delia is faced with an impossible, heart-wrenching choice. Can she bear to leave her young son behind, hoping another family will care for him? What else can a mother do to give her son the life he deserves?

A Place to Call Home

When Ellen's husband Harry loses his farm job and the cottage that comes with it, they have to leave the countryside they love in order to survive. Harry sets out to find a job in the factories and mills of nearby Hull, and Ellen must build a new life for her family on the unfamiliar city streets. But when tragedy threatens Ellen's fragile happiness, how much more can she sacrifice before they find a place to call home?

Four Sisters

With their mother dead, four sisters and their father form a close bond. But when tragedy suddenly strikes and their father disappears on his way to London, the sisters have no way of knowing what has happened to him – only that he hasn't returned home. With little money left, they're now forced to battle life's misfortunes alone . . .

THE LONELY WIFE

Val Wood

CORGI BOOKS

TRANSWORLD PUBLISHERS
Penguin Random House, One Embassy Gardens,
8 Viaduct Gardens, London SW11 7BW

www.penguin.co.uk

Transworld is part of the Penguin Random House group of companies
whose addresses can be found at global.penguinrandomhouse.com

First published in Great Britain in 2020 by Bantam Press
an imprint of Transworld Publishers
Corgi edition published 2021

Copyright © Valerie Wood 2020

A CIP catalogue record for this book
is available from the British Library.

ISBN 9780552176705

Typeset in 11.25/13.75 pt ITC New Baskerville Std
by Integra Software Services Pvt. Ltd, Pondicherry

Printed and bound in Great Britain by Clays Ltd, Elcograf S.p.A.

The authorized representative in the EEA is Penguin Random House
Ireland, Morrison Chambers, 32 Nassau Street, Dublin D02 YH68.

Penguin Random House is committed to a sustainable
future for our business, our readers and our planet. This book
is made from Forest Stewardship Council® certified paper.

For my family with love and Peter as always

CHAPTER ONE

London 1850

Beatrix eased off her slippers and slid her feet beneath her petticoats on the small sofa in her bedroom, tucked a cushion behind her back, and with an idle, contented sigh picked up her book. There was something rather satisfying about a book held in one's hand and a whole afternoon of reading to look forward to. She glanced towards the window and saw that rain was still streaming down the glass, obliterating the London street scene and the gated garden in the square below.

Wednesday: she would have been meeting her friend and confidante, Sophia Hartley, for their fortnightly afternoon tea engagement today, but they had both cried off; Beatrix because of the vile weather and Sophia because she had said in the note that she'd sent with the boy that she had a dreadful summer cold and couldn't face coming out in the rain.

Beatrix reached for a box of bonbons on the small table beside her, one she was saving for such a day as this, and was about to pop a sweet in her mouth when

Dora's soft knock came on the door and the young maid opened it. 'Miss Beatrix,' she said quietly.

'Yes, Dora?' Beatrix glanced across at the carriage clock on her mantelpiece.

'Your mother . . . Mrs Fawcett has requested your presence . . .' Dora, who had only been in this first place of employment for three months, hadn't yet achieved the confidence to know how the mistress of the house, or her daughter either for that matter, should be referred to.

'She's what?' Beatrix gave a mischievous grin. 'Requested my presence! We're rather formal today, aren't we?'

'Yes, miss, we are. I told her that you were staying at home this afternoon because of the weather.'

'Yes, I'm sorry about that, Dora. You'll have missed the visit to your mother. We'll see if we can rearrange a day for another time.'

'Thank you kindly, Miss Beatrix,' Dora said gratefully. 'Ma wouldn't expect me in this downpour in any case.'

Beatrix nodded and picked up her book again. She had asked Dora to accompany her on the last two occasions when she had been out, and given her an hour off to visit her own mother whilst she and her friends took tea. If she didn't ask a maid to go with her, then her mother would insist on escorting her.

'But, miss!'

'What?' Beatrix looked up. 'Does my mother want something? I'm trying to read!'

'Your mother – that is, Mrs Fawcett – specially said—'

'I know my mother's name, Dora.' Beatrix sighed and tried to be patient. 'What is it that she wants?'

'Your *presence*, miss, or at least it's your father who wants it and he asked your mother to send up for you.'

'Oh, for heaven's sake,' Beatrix muttered, putting her feet down and back into her slippers before she stood up, the skirts of her morning gown swaying. 'Why didn't he come up himself? It's not as if we're living in a mansion!'

Dora's expression told her otherwise and she supposed that it would seem so to the young girl, considering the tiny terraced house she had come from, within thirty minutes' walk from this house in Russell Square.

'I don't suppose you know what he wants?' she asked, looking in the gilt-framed mirror and patting her tousled curls.

'No, miss.' Dora's own reflection, her straight hair and lopsided cap, made Beatrix reach up her hand to pull the cap straight. 'He went in to see Mrs Fawcett in the sitting room just after receiving the afternoon post, and they had a fresh pot o' tea.'

'Really?' Beatrix glanced at the clock again. Not yet three o'clock and they were having tea? Her parents were normally predictable and had tea at four; and why didn't they ask her if she'd like to join them?

Dora hadn't said there was any hurry, so she hunted for a bookmark to keep the place in the novel she was reading. Not that it was terribly interesting, she mused, a Gothic novel written in several parts as many were nowadays but not keeping her full attention; she might hunt out something else later. Perhaps Dickens; he never failed to hold her interest and it was alleged that he took the plots from his own life. She closed the door behind her and walked slowly down the stairs.

Her mother must have heard her for she came out of the study, much to Beatrix's astonishment as she rarely entered the sanctity of her husband's room, and stood waiting at the bottom of the stairs.

She began to whisper. 'Now you must . . . carefully . . . giving an answer.' Her voice dropped even lower as she leaned towards Beatrix's ear. 'Don't give your immediate—'

'I can't hear you, Mama! What did you say? Have you got a sore throat?'

Her mother shook her head and went on murmuring. 'Just listen, and don't . . . might be better than—'

'I don't know what you're saying, Mama. Is Father in his study? Yes? I'll go in.'

She knocked sharply on her father's door but didn't open it until she heard his tobacco-thickened voice instructing her to enter.

'Father,' she said. 'Is Mother all right? She seems rather agitated.'

'Oh, well,' he sighed, leaning back in his chair. 'That's your mother all over. Any little change and Mrs Fawcett thinks the world will fall apart.'

Beatrix frowned. 'And has something changed?'

'Sit down, Beatrix.' He indicated a chair with the stem of his pipe. 'We have a proposition to think on.'

'Have we?' She lowered herself into the battered leather chair. 'And does Mother not like it?'

Whether her mother liked it or not wasn't relevant in any case, she thought. Whatever the proposition was, if her father thought it suitable, applicable or valid then that is what it would be, no matter her opinion on the matter.

She interlocked her fingers and waited; waited whilst her father found his tinderbox and matches, filled his pipe and tamped down the tobacco before lighting it, then waited again for the hemp and tobacco to begin to smoulder. He drew on it carefully until a satisfactory curl of smoke rose from the bowl.

He could have done this whilst he was waiting for me to come downstairs, she contemplated, unless of course he thinks that I like to watch the theatre of it. Which I don't; nasty choking performance.

Her father gave a grunt which she supposed was the answer to the question she had asked, and then turned to her.

'Not every father of daughters would ask their opinion on an important matter,' he began. 'But it behoves me to do so as I have only one daughter. Had my son, your brother Thomas, been here I might have discussed it with him first, but as he is away in Ireland . . .' He rumbled on.

Why is it that my parents feel the need to explain relationships, Beatrix considered touchily? I know that Thomas is my brother and is presently abroad, just as I know that he's my father's son, *and* that my mother is also Thomas's mother. I also know that I am an only daughter. I really don't feel the need for further clarification of our happy family.

'And what subject is giving you concern, Father,' she asked passively, 'given the fact that you don't really need another opinion on it?'

'Well, it was this letter, which came today.' He reached across his desk to pick up an envelope. The bright red wax seal on the back was broken, but Beatrix could still

5

make out the imprint of a crest. Her father turned the envelope over several times before adding, 'This is the second letter following two face-to-face meetings and will shortly require an answer.'

'And is this important matter something I can help you with, Father, as your son is away in Ireland and I, your only daughter, happen to be at home today?' She couldn't resist the little cynical dig even though knowing that he wouldn't notice.

But he lifted his head and looked at her rather sharply and she wondered if perhaps she had gone a step too far; then, after observing her momentarily, he asked, 'Why, where would you normally be at this time of day?'

'Only out for tea with friends, Father, but today we cancelled because of the rain and Sophia Hartley's being rather unwell.'

'I see,' he murmured. 'Does your mother escort you?'

'N-no. I generally take Dora; our housemaid, Dora,' she clarified, in case he had forgotten, or hadn't noticed, they had a new maid.

'She's rather young to be your escort,' he mumbled. 'Not much more than a child. Even younger than you are.'

'I believe she's fourteen, Father, and I had my eight-eenth birthday in July if you recall.' She fingered her slender gold necklace. 'You and Mama gave me this.'

He grunted again. 'There's nothing wrong with my memory,' he answered. 'But there are many ruffi-ans in the London streets and a young maid such as Doris wouldn't be a match against them. So you must keep a scarf at your neck to cover the necklace when going out.'

To strangle me with, she thought, but she was relieved that he didn't insist that her mother should accompany her instead, for she would be much less of a match for a band of ruffians than Dora if by chance they should ever come across any.

'*Dora* and I always take great care, Father, and do not enter any disreputable areas.' She was aware that Dora did when visiting her family, but the girl insisted that many people living in the back streets of London were good hardworking people, and though others were unable to earn an honest living it didn't make them thieves. Beatrix believed her, though perhaps her father wouldn't.

'You were saying, Father.' She pointed to the letter in his hands. 'Something important?'

He gazed down at it, and she thought that for a few seconds he had a certain unease in his expression.

'Ah, yes. Yes, indeed.' He looked up at her and then down again and mumbled, 'Well, it does concern you, which is why I asked your mother to ask you to come down.'

'Concerns me?'

He nodded. 'Your mother isn't keen, but I think it *excellent* and I'm sure that you will too once you've given it some thought.'

She waited. This was the usual style of her father. Sometimes he took so long pondering over an issue that by the time he had made up his mind about it, the matter had passed him by and was no longer applicable or of his concern.

'And . . .' she prompted.

He looked at her again, as if he had only just remembered that she was included in this discussion. 'Erm, yes,' he said firmly, handing her the envelope.

'A proposal of marriage,' he announced. 'An excellent prospect. Exceptional credentials. Good family. You won't do better than that. Take it from me, you really won't.'

CHAPTER TWO

With parted lips she gazed at her father, who kept his eyes firmly lowered and puffed on his smouldering pipe. She swallowed and looked down at the envelope held lightly between her fingers. She might have thought it a joke except that her father never made any jest: never in her life had she heard him utter anything in the least humorous, a tease or a flippant quip. It was not in his nature so to do, so she knew he was deadly serious now.

She slid the letter from the envelope, glancing up at her father again as she did so. It was written on thick parchment, the kind one might receive from a bank or a lawyer's office; certainly not the sort of fine paper a young woman might expect to contain a proposal of marriage or terms of endearment; but here indeed, as she cast her eyes over the contents, is what it was: a proposal, but without blandishment. This was from someone who, she was inclined to think, had never even met her, but had received assurances of her suitability as a wife.

'Father,' she croaked, and then cleared her throat. 'Father,' she began again. 'I have never heard of this man. This . . . Charles Neville Dawley. *Who* – who is he and why does he . . . why would he offer me marriage?'

'There is no reason why you would have heard of him; you don't move in circles where you might meet young men.' Her father drew heavily on his pipe. 'But I can tell you his pedigree and how he came to hear of you . . . of us, your family.'

This is going to be very long-winded, Beatrix thought; there will be a long summary of Father's acquaintances. Not friends, for I don't believe my father has any, only people he knew when he worked at the bank. My mother has a few, from when she was young, and cousins too, though I'm not aware that they correspond very often; she has one or two connections through various ladies' circles, but to my knowledge there is no one close. Father wouldn't like that. They live very private lives. I sometimes feel that I was born into the wrong family.

She was on the whole a very positive, cheerful person; she and the friends she had met at boarding school in Surrey who lived in London often talked and laughed at the silliest things – things that would be beyond the understanding of their parents if they should ever happen to hear them.

'When I was at the bank . . .' her father began.

There, what did I tell you? Beatrix often had conversations with herself, asking questions and giving answers. I knew that would be where it began.

'More to the point,' he continued, 'it was when I was about to retire from the bank. I retired early, if you recall, after your grandfather died.'

Beatrix nodded. When her paternal grandfather died at the great age of ninety-one, he left his only son enough money and property to ensure that he could give up his position as manager at a London bank and live in comfort for the rest of his days, although not in luxury.

She had watched her mother deteriorate in manner and spirit once her husband began to spend his time at home, and she guessed that much of her pleasure in having the house to herself and being able to go out whenever she wished, without having to explain herself to anyone, had soon completely dissolved.

'I joined several gentlemen's clubs and philosophical societies.' Her father leaned back on his chair as if in contemplation. 'I didn't want my brain to disintegrate because of lack of use, you understand; I needed stimulation and motivation and I therefore chose from such establishments the ones I considered could offer those requirements.'

Beatrix swallowed a yawn; it was warm in the study. Her father rarely opened a window; he hated draughts, and with the warmth of the fire in the grate and the fug of tobacco smoke, which was making her eyes water, she felt she could quite easily nod off to sleep.

She roused herself. 'And so this was where you met Mr Dawley, was it?'

He looked at her, and, as she had thought when she saw his glazed expression, he had gone off on his own little trail of reminiscences, completely forgetting the starting point: the offer of marriage from an unknown suitor.

He sat up, flustered. 'No, no! At least, yes – his *father*! Not the son, although young Dawley was old enough to join the club, which he did eventually.'

Well, that's something to be thankful for, she considered. Although I was beginning to think that I might marry this unknown old man, for he would soon be in his grave and I would be my own mistress. She and her friends often had conversations about marriage, deciding that they would like to become old men's darlings and subsequently rich and merry young widows.

'Dawley is also in banking, but much higher up the ladder than I ever was or was likely to be,' her father continued. 'Private banking, you know. He told me that his son was looking for a suitable wife; not immediately, but a few years hence when he would come into an inheritance. I thought nothing of it at the time. This would have been about three years ago,' he added, 'when you were too young to consider.'

Is this how it works, Beatrix thought uneasily? Where does my mother come into this? Did she have an opportunity to meet a young man who might be suitable as a marriage partner for her daughter? Her *only* daughter, who would have been barely fifteen at that time. What was her mother trying to say as she'd whispered to her at the bottom of the stairs?

'And how old is Mr Dawley junior?' she asked. 'Several years older than I am, I'm deducing, if he was old enough to join your club when you first met his father.'

Her father pursed his lips. 'Oh, erm, he'll be in his early thirties now, I would think. A good age for marriage; got over that first flush of youthful exuberance, I imagine.'

Old, then! Past the flush of youthful exuberance? Is thirty the end-point? Did my father ever have that? Did his father? My grandfather obviously didn't spend much on excesses if he was able to leave so much to his son. Is that the whole point of life? Accruing money and property to pass on to the next in line?

She remembered her grandfather, although she hadn't met him more than half a dozen times. He had left her five pounds in his will. Her father said she couldn't draw it until she was twenty-one. She had been mildly disappointed, for she had planned that when she was a little older she would buy some new dresses and perhaps a bonnet or two, and would meet friends for coffee and cake at a grand hotel.

But now she reconsidered. If she married anyone, not just this Mr Dawley, would her money then become his? Perhaps she should wait until she had celebrated her coming of age and could spend her money, her five pounds, as she wished.

'I'm not sure if I'm ready for marriage yet, Father; and I would like a choice in the matter. I'd like to meet a young man and find that we each have some qualities that appeal.'

Her father's forehead creased a little as he considered what she had said. 'But isn't that exactly what I have been doing on your behalf? I surely must know best what my daughter requires in a marriage, and believe me, m'dear, you won't, as I said earlier, do better than young Dawley.'

'But you haven't told me of his attributes, Father! I don't know anything of his manner, his kindness to others. Of how he makes a living, for instance, or his hopes for the future; only that he is due an inheritance, and that tells me nothing about him.'

Her father leaned towards her and lowered his voice. 'It tells you, Beatrix, that he will become very rich; he is due to inherit a substantial country estate.'

'But what does he look like?' Her voice rose as she became even more uneasy. 'Is he tall, short? Portly or thin, dark-haired or fair? Have you actually met him? What does he know of me? He surely wouldn't wish to marry a stranger.'

'His father and I have exchanged views, and yes, I met young Dawley on one occasion, and he has seen you. It seems that you were both at a coming-of-age party last year; you were not introduced but he asked who you were.'

Susannah Cummings's party, she thought. There were so many people there it was impossible to be introduced to everyone; a total fiasco as far as I was concerned. I lost track of where any of my friends were and didn't meet one single interesting person to talk to. Mother came with me. I must ask her if she remembers Mr Dawley.

She stood up. 'I must ask you to excuse me, Father. I'm afraid I'm developing a headache.' She fanned herself with her hand. 'It's uncommonly warm in here. I'll leave the door open, shall I?'

'Erm . . . oh, yes, very well. We'll speak later. I realize it's a lot to take in immediately. Needs some thought. Yes, definitely needs thought. For the best, though, I'd say.'

She opened the door and felt the rush of cool air from the hall come in. She turned. 'Where did you say this country estate is?'

'I didn't say, did I? But it's in the north of England. In Yorkshire to be exact. Somewhere overlooking the Humber.'

Beatrix sat on the bottom step of the staircase, considering. The north of England! I don't even know where Yorkshire is! It's where the mills and coal mines are, surely, so how can it overlook the Humber? The Humber is an estuary. I don't want to live there; when would I see my friends? My mother? Would we have a carriage to come back to London or would we have to travel by train? Do they have trains in the north? Oh, I know! Miss Emily Brontë: she wrote about the area, as did her sisters. They lived somewhere on the moors. *Wuthering Heights*! That was it. Father said I shouldn't read it. I borrowed it . . . oh dear, did I give it back? It belonged to Marianne Foster, I think. It was very bleak, I recall. So sad that the author has died. I believe there's only Charlotte left.

The sitting room door opened and her mother peeped out; on seeing Beatrix sitting there a small smile touched her mouth and she beckoned her silently.

'You used to sit on the bottom step when you were a little girl,' she said softly. 'You used to say you were busy thinking.'

Beatrix nodded. 'Yes,' she murmured. 'I called it my thinking step, for when I talked things through with myself. Things I didn't always understand. Childhood can be very worrying.'

They sat opposite each other on either side of the fireplace. Neither spoke for a few minutes, and then her mother broke the silence. 'You don't have to agree to the . . . erm . . . suggestion, but there are reasons why you might wish to.'

Beatrix looked up from her contemplation of the gleaming fire irons. 'Don't I? What are the reasons? Am I allowed to know? It is my life in the balance, after all.' Am I being melodramatic, she wondered when she saw her mother's eyebrows rise and her eyes gleam?

'Since when have women been allowed to determine what should happen in their lives?' Mrs Fawcett asked between barely parted lips. 'I beg your pardon, Beatrix; has something passed me by without my noticing? How very remiss of me!'

'Mother?' She was alarmed. Her mother was quiet, placid, and rarely gave her opinion even if asked for it, not that anyone did, apart from Cook or the housekeeper. 'What is it? Do you know this man, Mr Dawley? Father must have told you about him and his proposal?'

Her mother stared into the smouldering coals of the low fire. 'He did,' she agreed. 'Just this afternoon, when the second post arrived.'

'You didn't know before today! Was the subject never mentioned?'

'Not to me. Your father and Mr Dawley senior have apparently discussed it at length for quite some time, and Mr Dawley's son has been told that you seem to be the most desirable prospect so far.'

Beatrix was almost speechless, but recovered enough to say: 'Father said that *young* Mr Dawley was at Susannah Cummings's party last year. Do you remember him?'

Her mother shook her head. 'There were far too many guests there for me to recall.' She shuddered.

16

'Such a dreadful occasion. We came home early, if you remember.'

'We did,' Beatrix agreed. 'I heard later that Susannah didn't enjoy it much either. Her parents had arranged it. It was held for her to meet people.'

'It was a search party for marriage prospects in the worst possible taste,' her mother exclaimed. 'Simply dreadful! However, what you must understand, Beatrix, is that your father is doing this with your best interests at heart. He is only doing what he is expected to do; it is how things are done. Like it or not, he is simply following a pattern laid down over decades – no, centuries – and there is really nothing that we can do about it.'

CHAPTER THREE

Beatrix began to weep. 'I don't understand,' she sniffed. 'I'm not ready for this. I thought that one day I'd be introduced to someone special and we'd fall in love.'

'You've been reading too many novels,' her mother remarked. 'This is real life for young women like you, as it was for me too.' She looked sad for a moment, before adding, 'On the whole I've been lucky. Your father hasn't been demanding; he has, I think, been satisfied with married life. He likes things to go well, doesn't like a fuss or any upsets, and I have managed to deflect most things that might irritate or bother him.' She hesitated for a second. 'He realizes that it behoves him to make sure that you also have a safe and secure marriage, and that is why he has taken it upon himself to find you a husband who will meet his own exacting standards.'

She sat still, gazing, it seemed to Beatrix, into another realm. Had her mother had romantic dreams, she wondered, or had the situation been explained to her by her mother so that she was aware of what was to come? Beatrix couldn't remember either of her grandmothers and so had no idea of what their standards might have been.

'Your father is also making plans of his own,' her mother went on. 'You know, of course, that Thomas will have this house if, or when, anything happens to your father.'

'You mean when he dies. Yes, of course.' Beatrix blew her nose on a handkerchief she had retrieved from her skirt pocket. 'It's to be expected.' She looked up. 'But he's not likely to die yet, is he? He's not that old!' Then she frowned. 'Where would you live if he did?'

'It will depend on what kind of legacy your father leaves me, and whether or not I can continue living here if Thomas should marry. That's the crux of the matter, Beatrix. Would you prefer to be dependent on your brother and possibly a sister-in-law whom you may or may not like? Or to have a husband and a house of your own to run?'

Are those the only choices, Beatrix pondered? And do I have to choose now? Why such a rush? Surely when I'm twenty-one would be soon enough. She drew a breath. Perhaps I'll think differently after I've met him.

'I think you should agree to meet Mr Dawley,' her mother added softly. 'He might be perfectly acceptable, and his credentials are excellent, but that doesn't mean he need be the only suitor you will have. If you don't find him agreeable then I will arrange a party for you, something rather more discreet than your friend Susannah Cummings's. We're not so desperate to lose you yet.'

19

It seemed, in spite of every positive word her mother uttered, the prospect remained inevitable, and she didn't want it. She wanted to enjoy her girlhood, meet her friends, go to balls; and once married, what then? If she married Mr Dawley she would be whisked away to a distant place and not know a single person. Would she be able to take Dora? She would need someone she knew. Would Dora want to go to the wilds of Yorkshire? Would there be household staff there already? Were there theatres, balls, art galleries or salons? She could not imagine for one moment that there would be. Heavens above! I have't even met him yet!

Her father wrote to young Mr Dawley inviting him to call the following week on Tuesday morning at eleven o'clock, when his wife and daughter would be pleased to receive him. He had been primed by his wife to suggest that day as it would give her time over the weekend to ensure that the drawing room, which was on the first floor, was given an airing by opening the windows for an hour each day but no more, for fear of soot and dust entering the room; that the cream carpet was brushed, the furniture shiny without any residual smell of wax polish, and the odour of vinegar inseparable from the cleaning of windows given time to disperse, so that it would appear that they had not made any extra effort for his visit.

Importantly, it would also mean that after Mr Dawley's departure Mr Fawcett would be able to have his dinner at the usual time of twelve thirty. Since retiring from the bank, he had requested that their mealtimes should change, as he preferred to eat at midday rather than at six o'clock as they used to when he kept office hours.

On the day before the visit, Beatrix had her hair washed, curled and parted down the centre with ringlets on either side of her face; at bedtime that night she wore a cotton cap over the curls pinned close to her head. The simple blue gown chosen for her to wear the next morning had been pressed and checked for any minor adjustments. Beneath it she wore a chemise and two wired petticoats but no corset, as she wanted to be comfortable during Mr Dawley's call.

At eleven o'clock exactly a chaise driven by Mr Dawley himself drew up outside the door. The boot boy was dispatched by Mrs Nicholls, the housekeeper, who had been keeping watch from the basement window, to take charge of the horse, whilst Dora waited at the bottom of the kitchen stairs to run up and open the front door to the visitor.

Beatrix, sitting nervously with Mrs Fawcett in the drawing room, heard the boom of his voice as he announced himself, and turned to face her mother in some trepidation. Her father was in his study off the hall with the door open so that he might be the first to receive their guest.

Mr Dawley removed his top hat, handed it to Dora without looking at her and turned to greet Mr Fawcett.

'Good day, sir. It's a pleasure to meet you again.'

'And you.' Ambrose Fawcett shook his hand. 'Shall we go up? The ladies are in the drawing room. Come this way.'

At the top of the stairs Dora appeared out of nowhere and opened the door for them, standing back as they entered and closing the door behind them.

Ambrose introduced their visitor to his wife and daughter, who had both risen from their chairs. Charles Dawley bowed as in turn they dipped their knees.

'It's a pleasure to meet you, Mr Dawley,' Mrs Fawcett said. 'Won't you take a seat?'

He waited until they were both seated again and then took one of the hard-backed Chippendale chairs that had belonged to Mrs Fawcett's parents. Beatrix's father stood with his back to the fire.

'The weather is much improved, is it not?' Dawley said. 'We have had considerable rain, but this morning my hopes for a fine day have been answered.'

Beatrix nodded. Why does everyone speak of the weather when first meeting someone, she wondered? Is it to break the ice? Then the absurdity of her unspoken comment, for they were in the middle of a wet summer, made her lips twitch. She turned it into a smile, and said, 'I believe we have a mutual acquaintance, Mr Dawley?'

He raised his eyebrows questioningly. 'We do?'

'I understand you were at Susannah Cummings's summer party last year.'

'Miss Cummings! Yes indeed. I had not met Miss Cummings until that evening. I was invited through a friend of a friend who had received an invitation.'

Beatrix nodded. 'I too,' she agreed, although it was untrue. 'So that is why there were so many guests; I found it impossible to speak to everyone.'

'Indeed,' he said. 'I am not fond of such assemblies, I'm afraid. I much prefer something more select.'

Beatrix could tell that her mother was pleased with the remark, for Mrs Fawcett commented, 'We are considering holding a small gathering in the autumn, Mr Dawley, no more than twenty invitations; perhaps you might like to join us if you are in London?'

He inclined his head. 'Most kind,' he answered. 'I should be delighted.' His glance took in both his hostess and Beatrix. 'I am spending some of the summer away from London, but will be home again at the beginning of September. That would be an event to look forward to on my return.'

Beatrix pondered. That means only two or three weeks away, as we're already halfway through August. Oh, dear. Is the die cast? He's rather handsome. I quite like fair-haired men, but I would guess that he is also arrogant, though perhaps I misjudge him. He must realize that he is being judged, just as I am, and we are all on our best behaviour. I at least can say yes or no if he should ask for my hand, I think, but once he asks he has to go through with it, and perhaps I do too unless I have a good reason to refuse him. I really would prefer to speak with him alone to find the real person, but of course that isn't possible. How very ridiculous.

They chatted about insignificant matters, until Ambrose Fawcett brought up the subject of the Crimea and the two men began to discuss politics. After fifteen minutes Mr Dawley got up to leave, and turned to address Beatrix's mother. 'I am free for most of next week before I go away. I would deem it a great pleasure if you and Miss Fawcett would join me for afternoon tea one day of your choosing. I am rather fond of Browns in Mayfair, if that would be convenient, and agreeable to you?'

Mrs Fawcett considered for a moment. 'Tuesday?' she said. 'Are you free on that day, Beatrix?'

Beatrix swallowed. 'Yes, I think so, Mama. Thank you, Mr Dawley.'

'My pleasure indeed.' He smiled, and Beatrix thought his smile seemed genuine. 'I will collect you at three o'clock.' He gave a courteous bow. 'Thank you for your hospitality.'

'Well!' Her mother, half hidden by the muslin drapes at the window, watched Mr Dawley drive away. 'He exceeded my expectations. Oh, goodness, I've got quite a headache with the tension. Will you ring for tea, Beatrix?'

Beatrix pushed the bell at the side of the fireplace. Her father hadn't yet come back upstairs after seeing their guest out. 'Shall we go down, Mama? We can be more comfortable in the sitting room, and Father is sure to have something to say.' The door opened and the other young maid came in and bobbed her knee. 'Would you bring a tray of tea to the downstairs sitting room, please, Annie? And tell Cook that we shall be ready for dinner at twelve thirty as usual.'

Downstairs, Mr Fawcett joined them and sat in his usual easy chair opposite his wife. The maid brought in the tea tray and put it on a small table next to Mrs Fawcett, and as she closed the door behind her he humphed a little, cleared his throat and said, 'I thought that went very well. No awkwardness or blank pauses, don't you agree?'

His question was to his wife, not to his daughter, and Beatrix looked from one to the other. Was she not going to be asked her opinion, or would it be her mother's responsibility to make a decision on her behalf?

Her mother repeated her view as she'd given it to Beatrix. 'Better than I anticipated,' she said. 'There was no strain, and he appeared to be a dignified gentleman with manners.'

So that is my mother's role, Beatrix thought. She must be sure that he is courteous, not at all boorish, and knows how to behave in company and therefore, she must hope, also towards his wife. It must be difficult to judge, although Mother will perhaps remember how it was when my father was chosen for her.

She suppressed a small sigh. It still doesn't seem quite right. He could be putting on a show, and yet why would he? Is he under pressure to seek a wife? He's over thirty, so why hasn't he married already? What if he wants to marry someone else, who isn't considered suitable?

'What opinion did you come to, Beatrix?' Her mother's words broke into her thoughts. 'A pleasant disposition, would you think?'

'Under the circumstances, yes,' Beatrix answered. 'It can't have been easy for him to be under scrutiny, any more than it was for me to meet a gentleman who might or might not ask me to marry him.'

'He asked you to meet him again,' her father broke in rather brusquely. 'That must surely have given you the confidence to realize he was serious.' He frowned, his shaggy eyebrows coming together like a fringe. 'I must tell you, Beatrix, that he is a very worthwhile figure, and after being made aware of you has singled you out. I have assessed him and his expectations and I can assure you that I do not know of any other with his credentials or prospects. Not only is he to come into an estate in Yorkshire,' he dropped his voice, 'but he is expecting an inheritance of five thousand pounds a year.'

Beatrix's mother drew in a gasping breath, and Beatrix licked lips which had quite suddenly become very dry. That was a very serious amount of money. She would definitely be expected to accept his proposal if he should ask.

CHAPTER FOUR

Beatrix and her mother had several discussions during that afternoon and the next day; her father had given them more details about Charles Dawley's inheritance, as far as he knew them at this stage. The Yorkshire estate had been left to him by an unmarried great-uncle, and was described as substantial, with land and farmsteads; it was situated in East Yorkshire with views over the Humber estuary and within an hour's carriage drive of the port and shipping town of Hull.

Her father had looked on a map and explained to them that the area wasn't as isolated as they had supposed. There were other country towns in the vicinity, such as Beverley and Brough, with villages nearby.

This news didn't give Beatrix much joy; she had been born in London and was used to stepping out of their front door into city streets, to take a walk around Russell Square gardens or hire a cab if she wanted to go shopping, although she had to agree with her mother when Mrs Fawcett pointed out that that was not always possible as of course she couldn't go alone.

'You might find that you have more freedom than at present,' she had said. 'If you have extensive grounds, for instance, you might perhaps enjoy creating a flower garden. Of course, there will probably be lawns and shrubberies already where you can walk without having to be escorted, and as a married woman you will be allowed to visit, with perhaps just a maid to accompany you.'

Beatrix knew her mother was guessing. She too had been born in London and now lived no more than a mile from her original home. She had known nothing else. Beatrix's spirits sank even further. I'm eighteen, she pondered miserably as she sat in her room; and I haven't yet had time to enjoy myself with parties and balls. I've only recently left school; it's only a month or so since my mother asked if I'd like to consider finishing school, and I said no. But I'm not ready for gardening! I don't know anything about plants, even though I love flowers. What is Mr Dawley going to do all day? Is he a city gentleman? Has he visited this estate in Yorkshire? Is that where he is going when he says he will be away from London? I must ask him when we meet. Am I supposed to know that he is going to inherit a fortune? Where does he live now?

She jumped up from her chair and hurried downstairs to knock on her father's study door. She opened it when he called out and reeled back as tobacco smoke covered her in a choking haze.

'Father,' she said, covering her nose and mouth. 'That can't be good for you!'

He coughed and spluttered. 'What?' he said. 'The smoke? Nonsense. I give a good cough and it clears my throat and chest. What can I do for you?'

'Father, where does Mr Dawley live now? Is he a London man?'

'His home is still with his parents in Hampstead, though I understand he has a town house of his own somewhere where he mostly stays during the week. Why do you ask?'

'I only wondered if he knows the country, and what he will do all day once he moves to the Yorkshire estate.'

'I have no idea,' he said bluffly. 'But with the kind of inheritance he will receive, there will be little he needs to do.' He stroked his beard and said thoughtfully, 'Although not having any employment is not necessarily a good thing for a youngish man; idle hands and all that. But I'm sure if it's a flourishing estate he will have to make sure that it continues to prosper.'

'What does he do now?' she asked cautiously. 'Does he have some kind of employment?'

'Banking.' Her father nodded. 'Like his father and the rest of their family.'

Beatrix walked slowly back upstairs to her room. I hope we get on, she considered, for it seems to me that we might be breathing the same air for most of the time. I hope he doesn't smoke a pipe.

The following Tuesday afternoon Beatrix and her mother waited in the sitting room for Mr Dawley to arrive. Her father didn't keep a carriage, for, he was fond of saying, what was the point? They had no stables, coach-house or mews for horse or vehicle, and then he would have to hire a groom which would be a waste, for he rarely went anywhere except to his club. That was within walking distance, and it was easy enough to send a boy to whistle for a cab if the weather wasn't conducive to walking. He never gave a thought to the fact that perhaps his wife or daughter might like the convenience of having one.

'What might we talk about?' Beatrix asked her mother. 'Please don't mention the weather.'

Her mother smiled. 'We could remark on Browns and the lovely cakes. Browns have been preparing afternoon tea for almost twenty years since it became fashionable. It has expanded greatly in that time.'

'Have you been, Mama? I haven't. If Sophia and I or other friends meet for tea we go to a little place just off the Strand, near Covent Garden. Such a heavenly smell of flowers, although sometimes rotting vegetables and other odours.' She laughed. 'I love the hustle and bustle of it.'

Her mother didn't answer the question of whether or not she had been to Browns, but only remarked that Beatrix was certainly a young woman of London. 'But you must be careful,' she added. 'And really, I'm not terribly happy about your being in that area. It's a working location, but there are also people without means there, so dress appropriately and don't flaunt your affluence.'

She didn't ban her from going, however, although the implication of vulnerability was clear. Instead, she changed the subject. 'We might get the opportunity of asking Mr Dawley about Yorkshire,' she said. 'There are most certainly many questions to be answered, but we must take it slowly and not rush into anything.'

'Really?' Beatrix asked. 'Meaning . . .?'

Whatever her mother meant would have to wait, for the doorbell rang and they both rose to their feet to greet their escort, who guided them to a smart brougham and took the reins himself. When he handed them down outside Browns, Mrs Fawcett thanked him and asked, 'You prefer to drive yourself, Mr Dawley?'

'Oh, every time,' he said, and lifted a finger to summon the boy to stable the horse. 'I prefer my own carriage, but I realize it is not quite as comfortable as this one, which belongs to my father.'

'I hope we're not depriving him?' Beatrix chipped in.

'No, not at all,' he said as he escorted them through the door. Beatrix was surprised to see that Browns was only a small hotel. 'He rarely uses it in the summer, as he prefers to walk. Good afternoon, Mary.' He greeted the woman who came towards them to take the ladies' coats and gloves and his grey top hat. 'I have reserved a table.'

'Yes, we have it ready for you, Mr Dawley.' She smiled at Mrs Fawcett and dropped her knee. 'If you would follow me, ma'am – miss.'

She led them through into another room where there were only two tables, one of them not set for tea. At the other, which was laid with fine china, she pulled out a chair for Mrs Fawcett whilst Mr Dawley performed the same office for Beatrix, leaving the facing chair for himself. He handed his gloves to Mary, and then, turning to Mrs Fawcett, asked, 'Would you like me to order, Mrs Fawcett? How do you like your tea?'

'Light, please, with lemon.'

'I will have the same, thank you.' Beatrix looked around. There was a fresh floral centrepiece on the other table. Too large to leave in place should anyone

31

else wish to come for afternoon tea. I think Mr Dawley has booked the room, she thought, and not just our table. It's lovely and very private. A perfect place for a *tête-a-tête*. Just as well I'm with my mother.

'You're obviously a regular here, Mr Dawley,' Mrs Fawcett said. 'I used to come, but I confess I haven't been for a while. It is as nice as ever it was, though I suspect much busier.'

'Indeed, it is rare to get a table without booking, and I have heard rumours that they might be expanding. I hope that if they do it won't lose its special atmosphere.'

How polite we are; Beatrix gave a small sigh. It must be the English way, or perhaps this is a prelude to speaking of something more serious. A run-up, or an overture or a prologue. Whilst her mother and Mr Dawley mused over various cafés and coffee shops they had known, she contemplated the various descriptions that could be used for the situation they were currently in.

Then something struck her, and without thinking clearly enough she leaned forward, saying in a whisper, 'I hope I'm not being very forward, Mr Dawley, but you and my mother seem to know some of the same places.' She dropped her voice even lower to ask, 'Would it be very rude if I asked your age?'

'Beatrix!' her mother gasped in a shocked undertone. 'Whatever are you thinking of!'

Charles Dawley blinked and then laughed heartily. 'I would say that your mother is years younger than I. That is the good fortune of ladies who are perennially young.' He put his hand over Mrs Fawcett's on the table. 'Don't be cross with Beatrix, Mrs Fawcett – I may call you Beatrix, mayn't I?' he asked, looking directly at her. 'I am thirty-one, having had my birthday in June.'

'Ah, so you are thirteen years older than me,' Beatrix told him. 'My birthday was in July, and Mama is – I'd better not say or she'll be very cross with me.'

'Indeed I will, and rightly so.' Mrs Fawcett was interrupted by two maids who came in with trays laden with teapots, sugar bowls, and cake-stands displaying tiers of finger sandwiches, cream cakes, bonbons and various other confections. 'Shall I pour?' she asked, picking up a teapot. 'And now that the ice has been broken, so to speak, I am given to understand that you will shortly be moving north, Mr Dawley. How do you feel about that, being a gentleman of London birth?'

She passed a cup and saucer across to him, and then a small jug of milk, before pouring another for Beatrix and passing her a plate of lemon slices. Beatrix looked at her in awe. So that is how it is done when serving tea for guests or strangers, she thought. She too served tea when at home but only for the family, and now she saw that a certain flair was needed: the skill required to be sure that no tea dripped on to the saucer, and the ability to make small talk at the same time. It was an art she had yet to learn, and she wondered if her lessons were about to start.

She caught up with the conversation when Mr Dawley said, '. . . and so I will travel to Yorkshire at the end of the week. I visited when I was a boy, and quite often since, and I remember having the freedom to roam over the meadows quite high above the Humber, and being able to see ships, coal barges, schooners and other types of shipping travelling in both directions, and the county of Lincolnshire on the other side of the estuary. The Humber is not at all like the Thames, at least not the London end, as it runs through countryside rather than a town.'

'And do you like it?' Beatrix asked. 'Will it feel like home?'

She thought that he hesitated for a second before answering. 'I love it, although it might take a while before it feels like home. Anywhere would, don't you think?' He turned to Mrs Fawcett for her opinion, and she nodded. 'For a short while,' he went on, 'I will need to return to London quite frequently as I have business interests here, and will therefore keep on my own London town house, so as not to intrude on my parents.'

Oh, Beatrix thought, that's a good idea. It will be a convenient sort of toe-hold for coming back to town; it must be quite boring in the country. That could influence my decision if he should make me an offer.

'You might like to come and visit,' he suggested, looking first at Mrs Fawcett and then at Beatrix. 'Beatrix? Not yet, as I must see how habitable the house is. A housekeeper is looking after it; she's been there for many years in my great-uncle's employ. If it is in good order we could perhaps make up a house party, if Mr Fawcett is willing?'

'Perhaps so,' Mrs Fawcett answered, though Beatrix thought that she wasn't showing very much enthusiasm. 'After our end of summer gathering, perhaps? Plans are under way for that.'

Are they really, Beatrix reflected? No one has told me! Are my mother and Mr Dawley playing some kind of game that I know nothing about?

'Of course, of course,' Mr Dawley replied. 'Early September, I believe you said?' He smiled. 'That should work out admirably.'

Mrs Fawcett smiled back. 'Indeed! Excellent,' she remarked. 'May I pour you more tea? And what about another of these delicious cakes? Beatrix?'

CHAPTER FIVE

Mrs Fawcett had decided that they would book rooms at an exclusive hotel for the small party. All Beatrix's friends were invited, along with their brothers and parents, and canapés and wine, champagne and non-alcoholic drinks were served. Not all the fathers came, giving their excuses as was expected, but some of Beatrix's friends' brothers brought along their friends, so that there were more young men than young women. All eyes turned when Charles Dawley, who was one of the last to arrive, came through the door, every-one realizing that here was a guest who didn't fit into any slot, being younger than any of the parents but older than the other young men.

Beatrix, who was nearest the door, moved gracefully towards him, knowing she was looking her best in the new evening gown her mother had insisted she should wear. The white embroidered muslin with its low neck-line, puff sleeves and deep pointed bodice waist on a full skirt showed off her petite figure, and her hair was coiled at her neck and tied with white lace. At her throat she wore her gold necklace.

She dipped her knee to Charles Dawley and he in turn bowed and took her hand, and pressed it to his lips. 'How lovely you are, Beatrix,' he murmured. 'What colour is your hair? Not quite blonde, not quite red? Gold, I think, would be a worthy description?'

She blushed slightly and thought that it didn't matter; the blush would enhance her appearance. She kept hold of his hand and led him over to her mother and father, who were speaking to Sophia's parents, and saw the look of approval on their faces.

So this is what it's about, she contemplated. We all put on a show to give the right impression. She saw Sophia standing to the right of her mother with her eyes opened wide, her lips apart and a look of astonishment mixed with envy on her face, and had to admit to herself that Charles Dawley cut a fine figure of a man, being a head taller than most of the other men and wearing a fine wool black frock coat and narrow striped grey trousers with a dark red waistcoat. He had visited his barber since their last meeting and his fair hair just brushed the back of his collar.

'We're so pleased that you could come.' Her mother gave him her hand and lowered her head but didn't dip her knee on this occasion, whilst Beatrix's father shook his hand and introduced him to the people who were standing near them. Then Mrs Fawcett and Beatrix took him round the other guests, and as most of them knew each other they were soon all merrily chatting and laughing. Charles Dawley, Beatrix noted, was obviously quite used to socializing and didn't find it difficult in the least to talk to people he didn't know.

After they had done the rounds of introductions he drew Beatrix discreetly to one side under the pretext of getting her a glass of lemonade from the tray being held by a hired manservant, and murmured, 'You have a very merry group of friends, Miss Fawcett. Have you known them long?'

'The young ladies, yes. I was at school with some of them, but I didn't know all of the gentlemen until this evening, except for the brothers of my friends.'

'And are some of them suitors?' he asked teasingly. 'Are they vying for your hand?'

She cast a glance towards the young men. They were mainly her age, only one or two past the age of twenty-one. 'I hope not,' she said candidly. 'They're rather young for marriage, I think.'

His face creased into a smile and he leaned towards her. 'That's what I was hoping you would say.'

She looked at him, wondering whether or not she should flirt, except she didn't really know how to, or whether to ask outright if he were a suitor, when disappointingly her mother appeared at her shoulder.

Food was offered on trays; finger sandwiches and little cakes and then more trays of champagne and lemonade; Beatrix held her glass of lemonade and gazed longingly at the champagne and thought that if her mother hadn't been there she would have liked to have tried it.

Charles Dawley obviously saw her, for he took one glass from the tray and handed it to her mother, and with a quick sleight of hand took another and exchanged it for the lemonade Beatrix was holding, which he put on a side table. She gave him a covert glance and smiled, and took a sip.

When her mother excused herself and moved away to speak to someone else Charles Dawley led Beatrix towards the chairs set against the wall where they could sit and watch the other guests.

'There's a possible fellow for you.' Charles nodded in the direction of a red-haired young man who was listening seriously to one of the young ladies.

'That's Arthur Tennyson,' Beatrix answered. 'He's the brother of a friend. I think he's quite keen on Maria Lowe; she's the dark-haired one over there with her parents and my mother. My friends Sophia and Eleanor are standing next to them.' She paused. 'Do you do much of this?' she asked suddenly. 'Partying to meet young ladies?'

He glanced at her, then laughed and took her hand and shook his head. 'No,' he said. 'I don't. But we men are expected to find a suitable wife who is able to adapt to our position in society.' He looked into the distance. 'It's ridiculous,' he murmured, barely opening his mouth, and turned back to Beatrix. 'Shall we run away together; away from this charade?'

'What?' She stared at him, then licked her lips and tasted the lingering fizz of champagne. 'I'm under age,' she whispered. 'I can't marry without my father's consent.'

He gazed at her for a second, and then said softly, 'Shall I then go to him and ask for his permission?'

She swallowed. Was she ready for this? It would mean a change of her whole lifestyle, and he had said nothing of love. 'You must be quite sure,' she said quietly. 'For I can tell you now that he will give his approval.'

'And what about you?' he asked. 'What would your answer be?'

She hesitated, and then murmured. 'I know nothing of marriage. This – *arrangement* . . . has come as a great shock to me; I wasn't expecting it to happen yet. I was looking forward to attending balls and dances first. But . . .' She looked up at him, and thought she saw some emotion in his eyes. She was drawn to him in concern. He hadn't been ready either, she thought, even though he was a grown man. Why was that? Why should there be such a great hurry for him to marry?

'I can give you balls and dances, if that is what you want,' he said quietly. 'If that would make you happy.'

'Will you be kind to me, and loving?'

Again she saw the flicker of something: sadness or emptiness, she couldn't tell, but he nodded and said, 'I will do my best, my dear Beatrix.' He stood up and held out his hand as if he had made a decision. 'Then if you will allow me, I will speak to your father now and he may announce it tonight if he chooses.'

Beatrix drew in a startled breath. Would there be no courtship, no walks together so that they might get to know one another? She had always understood that was the usual way of things. He would only know of her from what had been described by her father, and did her father really know her? Had her mother told him how to define her?

They would only discover each other's foibles and habits after marriage, and she supposed it was the same for anyone contemplating matrimony. And it would be too late then. She hesitated over her decision for a brief moment. It would be a risk whoever I accepted, but my parents think that Charles Dawley is a good candidate for marriage and they must know better than I do. She stood up and held out her hand, which he took and gently stroked with his thumb.

'If you change your mind in the cold light of day,' he said softly, 'I will release you.'

She swallowed again. 'I won't change my mind,' she said, as together they walked across to where her father was standing and looking in their direction. 'A promise is a promise.'

After consulting her mother, her father did choose to make the announcement. He tapped on a wine glass and told the throng that he had some splendid news and would like to announce that Mr Charles Dawley had asked for the hand of his daughter Beatrix in marriage; he and his wife had agreed to the betrothal and Beatrix had accepted.

'We are delighted, of course,' he harrumphed. 'It has been an unusually short courtship and Beatrix is still young, but we feel she will be in very capable, and – erm,' he turned to his wife, who was murmuring something, 'and, erm, yes, indeed, very capable and caring hands.'

There were whispers, mainly from the older guests, some critical that this was not the way things were normally done, and then the tinkle of glassware as others tapped their wine glasses and the young ladies waved their fans or clapped their hands.

The happy couple were separated then as various people claimed their attention. The gentlemen tried to ascertain Charles's business or professional status, but he gave nothing away, bar that he was in banking as his father was. He revealed nothing about his inheritance. When asked how long he had known Beatrix, he said smoothly, 'I have known *of* Beatrix for a very long time and admired her from afar, but have only recently had the pleasure of meeting her, which had been my dearest wish.'

Beatrix turned round when she heard the breathy whisper of Sophia in her ear. 'You secretive monkey,' her friend murmured. 'Why didn't you say?' And then some of Beatrix's other friends gathered around her, wanting to know how they had met and when the wedding would be.

'It's all happened so quickly,' she told them, 'that we haven't made any arrangements yet. We shall simply enjoy our engagement.' She gave a huge sigh and clasped her hands together, suddenly feeling the most tremendous flurry of excitement.

'How very exciting,' Maria Lowe exclaimed. 'And he's so handsome and elegant.' She glanced across at Arthur Tennyson and unconsciously made a pouting *moue* before lowering her voice. 'He looks incredibly rich, Beatrix. Have you discovered his worth?'

I will not invite *you* to the wedding, Beatrix considered scathingly as she gazed at her without answering. I will cut you from now on, for I have discovered *your* worth by your question and I hope that Arthur doesn't ask for your hand. He is too nice a man to be saddled with someone like you.

Sophia, intuitively knowing Beatrix's feelings, grasped her hand. 'We are so happy for you, Beatrix; Mr Dawley seems utterly charming.' She kissed Beatrix on the cheek, thus sealing their friendship. 'We are so thrilled for you, and absolutely green-eyed with jealousy!'

CHAPTER SIX

The first thing to be arranged was a supper engagement when Charles's parents and sister would meet Beatrix. Mrs Fawcett discussed the date and the menu with Beatrix, and then told her husband they would need temporary extra kitchen help for Cook, and a hired butler and manservant to wait on table. She then asked the housekeeper, who did not live in but came in daily, whether two temporary parlour maids would be sufficient.

'Mama,' Beatrix said, blinking away a tear, 'if you don't mind, I'd like to ask Dora if she will come with me after I'm married. I must have someone who knows me.' Tears had come frequently since the betrothal had been announced in some London newspapers. The sight of the announcement in print had made her realize the magnitude of the change to come, and wonder whether she had made the right decision.

'She's not really a lady's maid type of person,' her mother said, from where she was writing at her escritoire. 'She was taken on as a general housemaid.'

'I know,' Beatrix said. 'But I like her and I can trust her, and if she's willing we could offer her some training in arranging my hair and my clothes and so on, and she's a good seamstress so she can help me with other types of sewing. I'm sure she'd rather do that than cleaning and dusting or serving tea.'

'She might not want to go,' her mother said. 'She's a London girl, after all. There's no point in taking someone who will weep to come home the moment she steps over the threshold.'

But might not that be me too, Beatrix wondered? I have no idea what is in front of me and I haven't seen Mr— erm, Charles, since the night of our betrothal. I suppose that he's working at the bank.

It had been five days since the end of summer party, and she hadn't even received a note from him, but perhaps on Saturday he might call. When she asked her mother what she thought, Mrs Fawcett was preoccupied with the details of Wednesday's dinner and said impatiently that he was probably busy with other things.

'Life goes on as usual, Beatrix,' she said irritably. 'It doesn't stop just because someone has become betrothed.' Then she lifted her head and smiled at her daughter. 'I'm sorry,' she murmured. 'I realize it is all new to you and everything is happening too fast, but I'm sure it will work out all right.' She paused for a second as if to say something else, but then sighed. 'This is all new to me too. I didn't think you would be marrying yet, either.'

'But it won't be just yet, will it?' Beatrix asked anxiously. 'I thought maybe next year, in the spring or summer, perhaps?'

'Your father suggested just before Christmas, but I said no. We don't want anyone saying you are marrying in a rush.'

'Why would anyone say that?' Beatrix said naively, putting down the glove that she was stitching to strengthen the seam. 'Not that I want to marry in the winter. I'd far rather marry on a sunny day in summer; and besides, I'd like to get to know him first.' She looked pensive for a second, and then applied herself to her sewing again. 'And he – Mr Dawley – did say if I changed my mind in the cold light of day he would release me.'

Her mother pushed her chair back from the desk. 'When? When did he say that?' She didn't wait for an answer. 'He was joking, Beatrix! Don't even think of it! Plans – arrangements are being made now! Discussions about the church, the reception; the Yorkshire house is being put in order for you.'

'But I haven't even seen it yet! I might hate what they're doing. How does anyone know what I like, or what I might prefer?' She raised a flushed face towards her mother. 'Surely I should be asked my opinion? Do I not have any say in this?'

Mrs Fawcett bent over, her hands covering her face, and didn't answer.

'Mama?' Beatrix said tearfully.

Her mother lifted her head and gave a deep sigh, then moistened her lips and cleared her throat. 'No, my dear,' she said softly. 'I'm afraid you don't. Not unless you want to see us all lose face: your father, me, and most of all you. Don't think that anyone else will ask for your hand if you reject this offer now, for they won't.'

*

Mrs Fawcett wrote and asked Mr Dawley to call. 'Our daughter would like to ask you about the Yorkshire estate, so that she is prepared for what she will find. She is young, Mr Dawley, and quite naturally is anxious about what to expect there once you are married.'

She addressed the letter to his parents' home in Hampstead; she had no address for his London town house and was quite surprised when a reply came the next day, saying he would call on Saturday unless he heard from her that the time was inconvenient.

On Friday Beatrix was in her room when the door-bell rang, engaged in the task of emptying a trunk of some of her childhood toys, and books that she hadn't read and was unlikely to look at now. She lifted her head, wondering if it might be Mr Dawley calling on the off chance that she might be at home. But then, she thought cynically, that might not be considered *proper*.

Dora tapped on her door. 'Miss Beatrix, Mr Dawley has called. He's with your mother in the sitting room and she has requested that you go down. Let me tidy your hair, miss,' she added. 'You're all tousled.'

'I've had my head in the trunk,' Beatrix said. 'Do I look all right?'

Dora patted the top of her head and ran her fingers through her hair. 'Lovely, miss.' She smiled. 'Mr Dawley should see you like this,' she said. 'Just natural, without any fol-de-rols and suchlike.'

'He might change his mind,' Beatrix said blithely, slipping her feet back into her shoes, and she wasn't sure if she would care or not if he did.

'You could sue him for breach of promise if he did, miss,' Dora told her, 'and then you could keep his money all for yourself.'

Beatrix laughed. She would definitely ask Dora to come with her, she considered. With her plain speaking and common sense she would keep her own spirits up. As she ran downstairs she thought what a sensible head Dora had on her young shoulders; perhaps they'd do their growing up together. But how did she know about breach of promise?

'Miss Fawcett. Beatrix!' Charles rose from his chair and put out both hands to greet her. 'How are you? You look lovely,' he said. 'Have you done something with your hair?'

Beatrix patted her head. 'I'm afraid not. If I'd known you might call I would have done something with it!'

She saw his brows rise and the quick glance at her mother, and then he said, 'I do apologize for coming without warning, but I was nearby and couldn't pass without taking the chance of finding you at home.'

'You must always call if you are in the vicinity,' her mother said. 'We are not so formal that we would always expect a card.'

'Of course not,' Beatrix said happily as they all sat down, her fears allayed. 'I was wondering how you were. Mother has written to your parents, haven't you, Mama, and we'll expect you all for supper next week. I didn't realize you had a sister.'

'Anne, yes. She's a little younger than me. She's twenty-eight, and still single as yet. She hasn't found anyone she wishes to marry.'

'Nothing wrong with that,' Beatrix's mother said. 'Better no one than someone unsuitable.'

Charles shifted in his seat. 'Yes indeed. It can be an emotive subject for you ladies.'

Mrs Fawcett inclined her head. 'Indeed,' she murmured. 'Will you excuse me for a moment?' She rose from her chair. Charles half stood and then sat down again as she left the room, leaving the door open. He smiled at Beatrix.

'I'm sorry I haven't been able to call,' he said. 'I hope you haven't thought that I've neglected you?'

Beatrix began to murmur reassuringly, but he went on, 'I've been on a quick journey to Yorkshire. There were some projects I needed to put in hand, but was unable to until my great-uncle's will was declared.'

'Oh,' Beatrix said. 'Has there been some difficulty?'

'No, not really, just boring legal details, but it's in place now.' He leaned towards her and put out his hands, and she gave him hers. He gently squeezed them. 'You haven't changed your mind?' he said softly.

She shook her head. 'No,' she murmured. 'I haven't, but I admit I've had a few moments of indecision. Only,' she added swiftly, 'because I have so little knowledge of what will happen next, and when. My mother said that my father has suggested we might marry around Christmastime.' She saw a little frown appear on his forehead. 'I think it's too soon. We hardly know each other.'

'I think you are exactly right,' he said, giving her fingers another little squeeze. 'There's no rush whatsoever. Perhaps the spring would be rather nice? Springtime and a young bride.' He smiled. 'What could be lovelier? And we need time to think about where we should go for a honeymoon, or whether we should go directly to Yorkshire. Would you like to visit the house first? We could ask your parents if they would like to see where their daughter will be living after our marriage.'

'That would be lovely,' Beatrix said, quite excited by the prospect. 'Perhaps your family would like to come too?'

'Heavens no! My father would hate it. When he used to go to visit his uncle he could never get back to London fast enough. I used to love it, though. Great-uncle Neville had never married and wasn't used to children, so he didn't discipline me in the slightest. I could do whatever I liked.'

'Are you pleased to be going back to live there?' she asked. 'It must be quite different from London.'

She thought she saw a shadow of concern cross his face, just as she had once before.

'Ah, well,' he said. 'That was then, when I was young and carefree. Things are different now. I did say, I think, that I will have to come back to London from time to time.' He looked up as Beatrix's mother came back into the room, and dropped his hands from hers.

'That's all right,' Beatrix said cheerfully. 'I could probably come with you and visit my parents too.'

'Of course,' he said smoothly, and then wagged a finger. 'But I venture to say that you'll love the place so much you'll hardly ever want to come back.'

Beatrix felt much more settled and reassured after his visit, and on the Monday morning she and her mother went shopping for a dress suitable for her to wear for the supper with Charles's family. She chose a deep blue that suited her eyes and bought a pale blue shawl sprinkled with embroidered forget-me-nots. She would wear her hair in a chignon, threaded with blue ribbon.

On Wednesday evening Dora helped her climb into the stiffened petticoats and fasten the back buttons of her dress, and it was then that Beatrix asked her whether she would accompany her to Yorkshire after she was married.

'Do you mean for the journey, Miss Beatrix, or . . .' She hesitated. 'To stay?'

'To stay,' Beatrix said, and wondered what she would do if Dora refused. To go alone amongst strangers was unthinkable. 'As my personal maid,' she added. 'I wouldn't expect you to do other housework.' Although, she thought, I have no idea if there will be other help there. No one has thought to tell me yet. I'm only assuming there will be staff already in the house. Perhaps I'll find out this evening.

'We could offer you training, Dora,' she coaxed. 'There are agencies, I understand, who can teach you what is expected of a lady's maid.'

Dora fastened up the top button and smoothed her small hands across Beatrix's shoulders to straighten the fabric. 'Oh, I expect I'd manage, miss,' she said. 'I'm quite adaptable.' She tweaked a curl on Beatrix's forehead. 'I'm fifteen tomorrow,' she added casually. 'So I'm quite grown up. But I'll still have to ax my ma and da first.'

'But you'll come if they allow it?'

Dora beamed. 'Yes, please, miss. I did tell my ma that you were getting married and going to live out of London and that I'd like to go with you if you axed me.'

'And what did she say?' Beatrix wondered how Dora had gleaned that information.

'She said as she hoped that you'd come and ax her yourself.'

'And so I will.' Beatrix took one more look in the cheval glass. 'We'll go tomorrow.'

'Not tomorrow, miss.' Dora shook her head. 'Tomorrow's ironing day; Ma will be fair wore out. The day after will be all right.'

The doorbell rang and Beatrix jumped. 'I'll go, miss,' Dora said. 'I'll go and welcome your about to be in-laws!'

CHAPTER SEVEN

Charles Dawley's parents seemed overwhelmingly grand; they were also overbearingly pompous. Mrs Dawley was a tall, stately woman, taller than her husband, who was stout with good living and bore a florid complexion probably due to over-indulgence of the grape. He was the chairman of the family bank, where Charles had begun his career with a ready-made directorship.

Their daughter Anne was slim and thin-faced, with narrow lips and a long nose over which she peered short-sightedly through a lorgnette. She gazed at Beatrix long and hard through it at introduction, before turning away and sitting down, and Beatrix immediately determined that they would not become friends.

Oddly, it seemed to Beatrix, Charles arrived separately from his parents and sister, driving himself in his own vehicle and arriving before they did. I can perhaps understand why he doesn't live with them, she thought as they sat at the supper table, for they are so very proper and have no humour whatsoever.

She did, however, discover more about the Yorkshire estate as the senior Mr Dawley described the house, the farms and the land. He had often visited the place with his own father when he was young, as well as when he was older; and he hated it. 'Don't like the countryside at all,' he boomed. 'Never did. Give me city streets any day.'

His uncle had lived to a great age, and only died at the end of the previous year at almost a hundred. 'I thought he was going to outlive us all,' Mr Dawley said brusquely and without sentiment, 'and that Charles would never get his inheritance. It was always meant for the eldest son in the family, you see. My father had been the younger brother, just as I was, so even though my older brother died at two I wasn't saddled with it, thank the Lord, though I might have gone to law about it if the old duffer had died sooner. But I couldn't be bothered any more, and he'd willed it to Charles by then. So you'd better get cracking, the two of you.' He helped himself to more wine from the carafe. 'No time to lose. Just don't go giving birth to girls.'

'Father!' Charles said warningly. 'There are young ladies present.'

'Hmm! What? Oh, yes! Well they'll have to learn what's what sooner rather than later.'

'But not from you, sir.' Charles leaned across and took the carafe from him. He turned, murmuring his apologies to his hostess. 'I do beg your pardon, Mrs Fawcett. I believe my father imbibed too well before leaving home.'

Mrs Fawcett nodded but did not excuse the manners of Charles's father; and Beatrix put her hand to her face to hide a smile, knowing that her mother had seen that the Dawleys were not so very grand after all. Good manners registered high in her mother's belief.

She and her mother retired to the sitting room when the guests had left and her father sought refuge in his study with his pipe and slippers, muttering that he hoped that would be the last he saw of them. 'Not young Dawley,' he was swift to say. 'I don't mean him, not in the least. He's obviously cut from a finer cloth than his father; not that I remember old Dawley being as disagreeable as he was tonight. Retirement doesn't suit him. Maybe his wife is too demanding; that'll be it, I'd say. Some wives are.'

He'd shut the door behind him, and his wife had stared meaningfully at it before turning away, mumbling beneath her breath, 'And so are some men!'

'What did Mr Dawley mean when he said there was no time to lose?' Beatrix asked her mother.

'I don't know,' Mrs Fawcett answered. 'Perhaps because Charles is over thirty. That isn't old for a man to marry, but he will need an heir to carry on the name.' She sighed. 'You could indeed give birth to daughters first.'

'Oh,' Beatrix murmured. 'Is that why I was chosen, to provide an heir? Not because he caught sight of me at Susannah Cummings's party?'

'There must have been lots of suitable young ladies present that evening, but you obviously stood out,' her mother said consolingly. 'He asked who you were, didn't he? He wouldn't have done so had he not been impressed.'

Was he, though, Beatrix wondered? Or did I just look suitable? An innocent young woman. Not frivolous, not flirty like some, and never having known any young men apart from the brothers of friends. My father and Mr Dawley must have discussed me at some length. I'm not sure how I feel about that. I always thought that I would have a say in my marriage, that I would meet someone and fall in love; but am I being foolish and romantic? Is this why parents take control, to be sure that their sons and daughters make a 'good match'?

She sighed. Am I a lamb to the slaughter? Charles seems nice, though; a gentleman, unlike his father, but old enough to choose his own bride. She pondered on this as she recalled the night when he'd said he could give her parties and balls if that was what she wanted. I would quite like some excitement in my life. Will I find that in Yorkshire?

'Could we go to visit the Yorkshire estate, Mama? Charles did say we could if we wished. We're almost into September, and now that the Dawleys have been to supper and we've met them . . .'

Her mother nodded. 'We'd have to make sure that Charles's parents don't say they'll come with us and spoil it for you. I'll drop a note to him and say it is your request; that you'd like to see the house where he is proposing you might live. I'll tell him that it would be just the two of us. I'm fairly sure that your father won't wish to accompany us.'

What my mother means is that she won't tell him, Beatrix realized. She'll tell him the day before departure and say she had been sure he wouldn't want to come. He always says he doesn't like rail travel in any case. He doesn't even like going to Brighton, and that isn't far compared with travelling to Yorkshire.

'Your Mr Dawley is most accommodating,' her mother said three days later. 'He has suggested we travel next Wednesday, spend the day at the house on Thursday and return home on Friday. If we agree, he'll notify the housekeeper to make things ready for us!'

'Oh, how lovely.' Beatrix was immediately uplifted. This journey will decide me, although my mother said it's already too late to change my mind. 'Yes,' she said positively. 'Let's do that, Mama.'

She felt it was imperative to speak to Dora's mother to ask permission for Dora to come with her to Yorkshire. She told her mother where she was going, but not her father, as she was sure he'd say that her mother should go with her to find out what kind of family they were, and Beatrix already knew. Dora's mother was a cleaner and did ironing in her own time at home, and her father worked on the London docks, getting work whenever he could.

I have to make a stand, she thought. I am soon to be a married woman, after all, and I will need to be able to make decisions.

'I've put out your plain grey dress, miss,' Dora said on the day they were to visit her mother.

'This grey?' She looked at the plain gown hanging on the wardrobe door. 'But this is my everyday dress. It's not very elegant.'

'I know, miss. That's why I chose it. Don't forget where you're going. There're a lot of poor people down where Ma and Pa live; and don't wear your gold chain either, miss,' Dora warned. 'We don't want any-body snatching it. You could wear a white collar with the frock, if you like?'

'No, it's all right,' Beatrix said, and wondered when she would actually get the chance to make a decision of her own. 'I expect you know best.'

Dora nodded. 'Yes, I do, miss. But it's all right for me to look neat and tidy cos then everybody will know I'm in work and be pleased for me.'

'I see.' Beatrix undid the chain round her neck. 'So what will your mother be doing today, Dora, if she's not working in someone else's house?'

Dora picked up the grey dress and slipped it over Beatrix's head. 'Oh, today's her day off. She'll just be cleaning her own 'ouse.'

On Dora's advice Beatrix wore a plain navy hat borrowed from her mother and a navy shawl draped across her shoulders. They crossed the Russell Square gardens and headed towards the site of the new King's Cross railway station.

'You seem to know your way about, Dora,' she puffed. 'Could we slow down, please?'

'Beg pardon, miss,' Dora said. 'I'm used to rushing, you see. If I've got ten minutes to spare when I'm out on an errand, then I sometimes run home and make sure everybody's all right.'

'Why, who else is there? I thought you were the only one!'

Dora laughed. 'How could that be, miss? My ma and da have been married for eighteen years. I'm second eldest and there's six more after me.'

They had approached streets behind the station, not anywhere that Beatrix knew, and she saw that there were empty spaces where once there had been houses, now demolished for the building of the new railway and station. The streets were packed with vehicles, horses and wagons and men pushing wheelbarrows and handcarts, shouting out their wares or calling to one another and creating such a ruckus that Beatrix felt dizzy.

'Are we nearly there? We should have got a hansom. We've passed several waiting for fares.'

'Oh, my ma wouldn't have liked that, miss! The neighbours would've had sumfink to say and my ma's very private. Anyway, we're nearly there; round this corner – and here we are, number twenty-four. We've got the whole of the ground floor,' she said proudly.

Beatrix looked at the shabby paintwork on the door and windows but saw that the net curtains were clean and the doorstep was well scrubbed; her eyes lifted to the window of the upper floor and she saw that although the pane of glass was grubby with soot the curtain up there was also clean.

It must be difficult to keep a house fresh and unsoiled in an area like this, she thought, and as she stepped inside at Dora's invitation and into the parlour, as Dora called it, she swiftly looked around and saw that the copper kettle and saucepans shone brightly and the rag rug in front of the hearth was well shaken.

Has this been done especially for my visit? she wondered, but as soon as Mrs Murray came through another door she knew it hadn't, for Mrs Murray, as round as a ball, wore a brown pleated bonnet and a spotless white apron over her skirt, and was wiping her red hands on a clean rag whilst a small child was tucked under one arm.

'Morning, miss.' Mrs Murray didn't dip her knee and somehow Beatrix was glad of it; she felt that she was on equal terms with the keeper of this house which smelt of soap and polish, and something else; she wrinkled her nose. Soup! Onions and – what else? Fresh market aromas!

'Good morning, Mrs Murray.' She smiled. 'There's a good smell. Am I interrupting your midday meal?'

'Not a bit, miss. I've always got a pan of soup simmering.' Dora's mother indicated the pan on the low fire. 'With all my brood what might come in at any time of day, there's always sumfink ready and waiting.' She pointed to an easy chair. 'Won't you sit down, miss? Do you fancy a cuppa tea – a Rosy Lee as we say round here?' She handed the baby to Dora, who tickled its tummy.

Beatrix laughed. 'I'll certainly sit down, Mrs Murray, but we won't stop for tea, thank you, for we must be getting back, but I wanted to be sure that it was all right to take Dora with me to Yorkshire. Not yet of course; my wedding isn't until the spring.'

She blushed as she explained. Saying it aloud made it seem real and imminent, even though it was still some months away.

'I've talked it over with her pa, and he says it's all right for her to go, even though it's so far up north. I'll knit her some scarves and mittens and woolly jumpers, cos I expect the winters'll be bad up there.'

Beatrix's mouth rounded into an O. She hadn't really considered the weather, and perhaps even the spring wouldn't be as warm as London. 'Yes,' she murmured. 'That's a very good idea.'

When they left, Beatrix was reassured that Dora's parents were pleased for Dora to travel with her. In fact her mother seemed more than pleased that her daughter was going up a step, as she called it, by going to live and work in a mansion. Beatrix heaved out a breath. She wished that she was so positive. It seemed very exciting, but she was also very nervous.

They crossed the road to head back in the direction of Russell Square and as they looked carefully both ways to avoid the hansom cabs and cabriolets that were hurtling in both directions, she caught sight of a fair-haired man in a top hat waiting to cross from the opposite side. As she and Dora arrived on the pavement he was just hurrying off it, and for a minute she thought it was Charles; she turned to look back, but he was lost in the milling crowd.

CHAPTER EIGHT

Charles Dawley hurried across to the temporary booking office and paid for three first-class tickets to Hull for the following week. He put them in his inside coat pocket and went back outside into the hectic bustle. A woman was selling flowers and he bought a bouquet of lilies and roses, paid over the price she asked for and hurried back across the busy road, dodging the traffic as he headed towards Judd Street.

Fifteen minutes later, for he knew all the shortcuts, he was hurrying down a narrow terrace of houses built in the previous century, taking a key from the briefcase he was carrying and inserting it into the front door of one of them. The door was unlocked. Surely . . .! He pushed it cautiously; although this end of the street was in a respectable area, from time to time there would be a burglary if a careless neighbour had left a door or a window unlocked.

She was home; there was always something different about the atmosphere of the house – her perfume, a scent of the exotic, a charge of energy – but he entered the small hall guardedly. He had wanted to be there first.

A slipper came sailing across at him, catching him on his shoulder, and he made ready for its twin. She had a terrible aim, but he smiled as he entered the sitting room and saw her standing there with it in her hand.

'You are pig!!' she screeched. 'Eenglish pig!'

'Hello, darling.' He laid the flowers carefully on the chenille-covered table. 'I didn't think you'd be home yet. I was hoping to surprise you.' She hurled herself at him and he caught hold of her arms before she hit him. 'What in heaven's name have I done to deserve this welcome?' He held her fast and kissed her cheek.

'You are Eenglish pig,' she shrieked again. 'I hear about you. What you have done.'

'What? How have you heard? Who told you?' He knew exactly what she was talking about but was surprised she had heard the news; he had wanted to tell her himself.

'On the train, from the ship. I saw your friend Pearson. He tell me. He saw it in the newspaper.'

Typical of Roger Pearson, he thought. Roger would have taken great delight in imparting the news; he had designs on Maria himself. But Charles blamed his mother, for she it was who had placed the announcement of the betrothal in *The Times* when he had said specifically that she was not to; he wanted to do it himself when the time was right and Maria had returned from her visit to Spain.

'I told you that it would happen soon.' He kissed her cheek tenderly and then her lips. 'I warned you before you went away.'

She shook back her dark hair, then reached to kiss his mouth and nipped his bottom lip with her teeth.

'*Ow*, you Spanish bitch,' he hissed at her. 'Now you're for it.'

She tossed her head. 'You get nothing from me' – she stopped his hand from lifting her skirts – 'until you tell me.'

He unfastened the buttons on his coat and shrugged out of it, then sat down on the small sofa and patted the seat next to him. She sat down and put her head on his shoulder.

'It was not good to hear this news from your friend,' she said petulantly. 'He spoil coming home for me.'

'He is not my friend, Maria. Only someone I know.' Pearson had done it deliberately, he knew that. The coincidence of meeting her, travelling alone: he would have hoped that Maria wouldn't come home. He would have been ready with an offer himself. But he didn't know Maria, or understand their relationship, which was long and strong.

'Then tell me,' she said, her anger fading. 'You say you love me, yet you marry this Eenglish woman.'

'I have to; I've explained it to you several times. I will lose my inheritance if I don't marry, and I can't marry you.' He turned and kissed her cheek again. 'Not when you are married already.'

He had met her ten years before, when he and his friend Paul Constable had taken time after university to spread their wings and have a roistering time before settling down to a normal life of business, finding a wife and bringing up a family in time-honoured fashion as was expected of them. They were both well-to-do young men with great expectations; Charles especially with the prospect of a vast inheritance and another on his father's demise.

It was unfortunate that the young men had chosen Spain to do their roistering, for they found that desirable young women there were as firmly attached to their mothers' sides as English women were, apart from those who made their living in bars and hotels.

It was in a Madrid hotel that he had met Maria, married to a man her father had chosen for her. She was working as a chambermaid and had been red-eyed with weeping one morning when she arrived in his room to change his bedding, in which he was still sleeping. He'd sat up and asked her what was wrong and she'd poured out a sorry tale and showed him the bruises that she'd received from her brute of a husband the night before.

Once he arrived back home he couldn't stop thinking about her, and at the earliest opportunity he went back to Madrid, travelling long hours by ship, train and local transport, and found her still working in the same hotel. It was there that they became lovers. She was five years older than him, and totally obsessed by her he hatched the craziest of plans, went back to London and rented a house which he subsequently bought, returned to Spain, and brought her over to England to live with him as his mistress.

Whether his parents were aware that he had a mistress he neither knew nor cared, but eventually over the years he thought that his father had probably guessed, and if his mother did know she would emphatically deny it and would never accept her. Otherwise he took care who knew about Maria, for she couldn't live in isolation and she needed friends when he was working at the bank. She had accepted that there were certain places where he couldn't take her, and those who didn't know him well considered him to be a confirmed bachelor, which didn't deter some mothers of eligible daughters from inviting him to their balls and parties.

He had told Maria of his need to marry to claim his inheritance, for his great-uncle, a bachelor himself, had deemed that the beneficiary of his will must be married before he was thirty-five and the father of a son who in turn would inherit the estate. If he did not comply with these conditions, then the bulk of the legacy would go to the next in line, some second cousin Charles had never met who was married with two sons already.

'It's not as if it will make any difference to us,' he told Maria now. 'It will be a marriage in name only, except,' he said with some reserve in his manner, 'that she will have to give me a son.'

'*Pfft*,' she exclaimed, pushing him away from her. 'And then you will stay in this Yorkshire place and leave me alone here in London.'

'You know that I won't; haven't I already set up a bank account for you? It is true that I will have to stay there for a while to settle – erm – Beatrix in the house and discuss the new arrangements with the estate manager and the farmers.'

Before he had met Beatrix, he had taken Maria on a visit to the area, staying in an inn near the market town of Beverley where no one would know him. He had shown her the old house above the estuary from the top of a hill and she had admitted that it was very pleasant, but she had not expressed any wish to live there.

'I am a London woman,' she had said haughtily. 'I live near gardens. I know Kensington and Russell Square.' She had shrugged. 'I like these places, and they have lots of people in them. Here' – she had cast her hand to describe the view – 'it is very green, yes, and big sky and rushing river, but not like London.'

'So you'll be happy to stay in our little house whilst I come to Yorkshire from time to time,' he had asked, and was gratified when she said yes.

He had increased her allowance and booked her on a course to improve her English but was never sure if she attended; her accent didn't change one jot and she never came up with any new words except sometimes unsavoury ones that she had heard out in the street. She had found her own friends, women like her who had come to London with a man; once a year she went back to Spain and stayed in a good hotel where her mother came to visit her, but never her father, for when he discovered that she had gone to England he had called her a whore and said she was dead to him.

Charles adored her. She was full of life and merriment; she could cook, and she cleaned the house herself, saying that no English maid or cook could do it better than she could. He was pleased, for it meant that their cosy love nest was never invaded by anyone they didn't know, but only by people they allowed in. The house was full of colourful cushions and exotic shawls draped over the furniture, and there was always a tantalizing aroma of food when he came home.

'So when you marry this Eenglish woman,' she asked now, 'will you tell her about me?'

'No,' he spluttered. 'I will not! You are my secret. She is very young, only a girl; she wouldn't understand. If she found out she would call off the wedding, and then . . .' He assumed a very serious expression. 'If the news got out I would lose the entire inheritance.' He lifted his hands in mock despair. 'Everything! We would have nothing, not even this house, and you would leave me and look for a rich old man to keep you!'

She clasped her hands to her chest. 'Ah! Yes, it would have to be an old man, for no young man would want me now I am getting older. Thirty-three I am now. I have passed the first hotness of my youth.'

He gave her a startled look and then smiled. It wasn't only her English that hadn't improved; her ability with figures was failing too. He was fairly sure she would be thirty-six or seven on her next birthday.

'So,' she went on. 'You may marry this Eenglish girl and we won't tell her. You will buy her a ring, yes?' She scowled at him.

'Yes. It is the usual thing to do. Would you like one?'

She nodded. 'Yes, of course, but I will choose it. I will have ruby, I think.'

He sighed. Whatever was he getting into? But if it would pacify her, so be it. He had yet to tell her that he would be travelling up to Yorkshire the following week. He would do it later today and get it over with.

She put out her hand to him. 'Come,' she said, and shook back her mane of dark hair. 'I have present for you too.'

He rose from the sofa and picked up the flowers from the table. 'Better put these in water first.'

She smiled and took them from him and placed them back on the table. 'Later,' she said softly. 'First you must come with me.'

He felt his pulse quicken. How could any young English woman compare with Maria who was leading him by the hand up the narrow stairs to their room on the first floor? The room was filled with light that could be shrouded in seconds by the muslin curtains that hung at the window and fell in graceful folds around their huge double bed, veiling them in secrecy and mystique.

CHAPTER NINE

Charles collected Beatrix and her mother in a hired cabriolet to take them to the railway station. He had reserved a compartment for them for the first part of the journey, but there would be several changes before they arrived in Hull. He bought newspapers at the news stand and made sure the women were comfortable, for he said, sighing, that it was a very long journey and he hoped they wouldn't be bored. 'But there are several stops on the way that will give us enough time to stretch our legs and buy refreshments.'

'You really needn't worry about us, Mr Dawley,' Mrs Fawcett told him. 'Beatrix and I are quite used to travel, unlike my husband who doesn't like it at all. That is why I didn't invite him to come with us this time even though I knew he would grumble about being left behind.'

'Which he did,' Beatrix interjected, laughing. 'He was not well pleased that we were coming to Yorkshire without him.'

Charles nodded. 'Well, another time. There will be plenty of opportunities for him to visit once you have settled in and made the house as you like it.'

Beatrix looked at him and then at her mother and back at him again. The train whistle shrieked and a head of steam blew just as she began to speak, and her voice was drowned out by the clamour.

'Sorry, you were about to say?' Charles said politely as the noise died down and the wheels began to turn as they got under way.

'I was expressing surprise that I am to be given complete freedom to design the house, when the only thing I have ever designed is my own bedroom!'

'*Carte blanche*,' her mother murmured. 'How wonderful.'

For a fleeting moment, Charles thought of Maria and the style she had imposed on their home. He suspected that the young woman he was about to marry would have the same sense of design as her parents, or her mother at least, which from what he had seen on his visits was without any originality or flair whatsoever.

'We will bring someone in to decorate. My great-uncle hadn't touched it in years, in fact he shut up some of the rooms that he never used. If you would prefer it, we could bring in a designer. The house needs some loving care.'

It will be a challenge, Beatrix thought. Am I up to it? The thought of designing her own style using colour, fabric and furniture excited her, yet also made her fearful. It is to be my home – *our* home, she reminded herself, looking across at Charles, who was opening a newspaper; it should reflect both our personalities. But I know nothing about him; we know nothing about each other, not our likes or dislikes, our foibles or dispositions. We're total strangers.

She glanced at her mother. She wore the faraway expression that sometimes appeared when she was sitting in silence, when any previous conversation was over, considerations and opinions were concluded, and Beatrix's father had determined the outcome. Beatrix had noticed this often when she was a child and thought that her mother had withdrawn from the present and gone off on a journey of her own, leaving everyone behind. This, she considered, was what she was doing now, but wherever she had gone she appeared to be happy.

At one point on the journey, when Charles had left the train at a station halt to take a walk, Beatrix murmured to her mother that she hoped she would be able to help her in choosing materials and furniture. 'You will know the best places to buy such things,' she said, and was gratified to see her mother's expression come alive.

'I would love to, Beatrix, and I would expect that you will be able to obtain the best quality fabrics in the north, which is renowned for its textile industries.'

'I don't know what to expect,' Beatrix confided. 'I've been looking out of the window as we've travelled and we've passed lots of green fields and little villages when I was expecting mills and tall chimneys.'

'There will probably be plenty of factories in Yorkshire, and rightly so if the area is to thrive, but in Hull there'll be fishing as well as heavy industry; your father said it was a major fishing port and famous for shipbuilding too.'

'Oh,' Beatrix said, and spied Charles striding back towards the carriage. 'I didn't know that.' She privately thought that it wouldn't be the quiet little backwater she had expected after all.

It was late when they arrived in Hull, and Charles asked whether they would prefer to stay at the Station Hotel or travel on for another hour up to the house. 'We can hire a carriage easily enough,' he said. 'But only if you're not too tired.'

'I'd love to go on,' Beatrix said eagerly. 'Mama, what about you? Are you tired?'

'Not in the least,' her mother said. 'We must make the most of the time we have.'

'Very well.' Charles signalled to a porter to take their luggage. 'You can have a pot of tea and perhaps a slice of bread and beef in the hotel whilst I see to the hire of a vehicle. I will try to find the driver that I've used before.'

He took them in through the door leading from the station, saw that they were comfortable, and ordered a pot of tea. When a young maid came to take their order for food he slipped away.

'It's rather nice to be looked after, isn't it?' Beatrix said, gazing up at the domed ceiling in the entrance salon, where chairs and small tables were available for the convenience of guests.

'It is.' Her mother followed her gaze. 'It's not something I'm used to.' She gave a little smile. 'Perhaps you are going to be lucky in your father's choice of husband after all.'

Beatrix turned to look at her. 'Did you have doubts?'

'Some, at first. I thought it was all being finalized too quickly. But my reservations are gone now, Beatrix. I'm sure everything will be splendid.'

I hope my mother is right, thought Beatrix, sitting alone with their luggage whilst her mother went to the washroom. We are all being very polite with each other, and even after this long journey I am no nearer knowing anything about Charles or his ideas for our future. She let her mind wander free. Or is he waiting for me to be alone, without a chaperone who can hear everything he says?

Charles came back to tell them there would be a carriage waiting outside the hotel in half an hour. He leaned his head against the back of his chair and gave a deep sigh, closing his eyes briefly. When he opened them he saw her observing him.

'How are you feeling?' he asked. 'Nervous? Excited?'

'Both of those, in truth,' she said candidly. 'I'm going into the unknown. I've never been to Yorkshire. I've never had a friendship with a man, let alone an engagement to be married.'

'I said to you that I wouldn't hold you to the engagement if you changed your mind,' he said softly. 'You haven't yet received a ring, although I have seen one that I think you might like. A diamond, classic cut, set in gold.'

She pressed her lips together. 'What would you do if I changed my mind?'

He laughed. 'Die of a broken heart, of course.' They both saw her mother returning. 'See the house first,' he said quickly. 'And then decide.'

'I have decided,' she said in a low voice. 'It was a promise. I don't break promises. I'm just nervous.'

He nodded, as if he were satisfied, and then suggested that as soon as they had eaten they should depart. Beatrix rushed away to the ladies' washroom before they left, and Charles turned to Mrs Fawcett. 'Beatrix is nervous,' he said. 'I don't know what I can do to allay her fears.'

'She's young, Mr Dawley – Charles. Besides, every bride is nervous. They are told what to expect from a marriage and yet not all marriages are the same; some bring joy, but many bring dissatisfaction.' She gazed at him quite frankly. 'I'm sure it's the same for men, except that they are usually more aware of the truth.'

Her voice had a steely edge to it as she went on. 'For people like us, the odds are stacked against women being equal partners in a marriage. People from the lower orders of society might find love and equality, but if they are living hand to mouth and every day is a struggle, there will be little enjoyment of it.'

'You sound bitter, Mrs Fawcett,' he said mildly.

'I am not,' she answered. 'Only disappointed.'

'For your daughter?'

'No, not at all.' She gave a mocking half smile. 'For myself.'

Charles told them that they would travel west from Hull, first along Hessle Road, where the fishing boats and trawlers were docked, into the village of Hessle, and then making an uphill climb from the flat lands of the estuary through the lower reaches of the Wolds to their destination above the village of North Ferriby.

His description meant nothing as the area was unknown to them, and darkness had fallen when they arrived at the house, though there was half-light from a three-quarter moon hidden behind thin cloud. They dropped down from the summit of a high hill, and as the carriage turned up a private track Beatrix saw the gleam of water far below. At the top of the track, which had the driver swearing as the carriage rocked in the deep, uneven ruts, she saw the outline of a large house with other buildings she took to be barns nearby.

She turned to her mother, who smiled and murmured, 'Nearly there.'

Beatrix nodded and said quietly, 'It's a long way from home, isn't it? No neighbours, no shops.'

'It's a different life.' Her mother took her hand and said hesitatingly, 'If you really don't like it—'

'I've promised,' Beatrix broke in. 'I will like it.'

A short, stout woman, wearing a long woollen coat and a bonnet, opened the door to them and they stepped into a large hall. The walls were lined with dark wood, deep alcoves set in them holding some kind of statuary; they couldn't make out what as the only light was from a low fire at the end of the hall and a floor-standing ironwork candle holder with spluttering candles burned almost to extinction set against the wall halfway down the hall near a heavy door.

'Welcome, ma'am, miss,' the woman said. 'How de do, Master Charles? You're a bit late. Thought mebbe you'd stopped over in Hull for tonight.'

'No, we decided we'd come all the way here. The ladies will be glad of refreshment; it's been a long journey.' He turned to Beatrix and her mother. 'Mrs Fawcett, Beatrix, may I introduce my great-uncle's houseskeeper, Mrs Luke Newby? Mags, this is Mrs Ambrose Fawcett and her daughter, Miss Fawcett.'

The woman gave a nod of her head to them both, and Charles disappeared to see to the luggage.

'It's most kind of you to wait up for us, Mrs Newby,' Mrs Fawcett said. 'Do you live in?'

'Oh no, ma'am. Never have done. We onny live next door. I was allus here afore Mr Neville Dawley was up of a morning, preparing his porridge and mekking the fire in his study. He was an easy man to please.'

She paused a second, and then, looking straight at Mrs Fawcett, asked, 'Would you mind tekking a bite to eat in 'kitchen, ma'am? It's 'warmest place to offer you right now. Chimneys have been swept and I've been lighting fires in each room in turn to keep them aired over 'last few weeks; no sense in lighting them all with nobody to enjoy them, but 'beds are all aired now and made up ready for you.'

Beatrix spoke up when Mrs Fawcett showed no sign of doing so. 'That will be fine, thank you, Mrs Newby,' she said, taking her cue from her mother. 'There's nothing more inviting than a cosy kitchen, is there?'

'Well, I wouldn't call it cosy, miss,' Mrs Newby responded. 'Kitchen has been little used since Mr Dawley's funeral, God bless his soul.'

Mm, Beatrix thought. A different view from that of Charles's father, who seemed to regard his uncle as a nuisance for living so long.

'Aye, he'll be sorely missed in these parts,' Mrs Newby went on. 'Would you come this way, ma'am, miss?' She led them to the door at the side of the candle holder and they entered an enormous kitchen, with every kind of cooking accoutrement hanging over a heavy iron range. 'I've made soup and cooked a ham, so perhaps you'd like that with bread and mustard? I'm not a cook, but I know Mr Charles likes that for his supper when he visits.'

'Indeed, that will be very nice.' Mrs Fawcett softened. 'It's difficult to know what to offer strangers, is it not?'

'Aye, it is, but I understand you won't be strangers for long?' She lifted an enquiring eyebrow towards Beatrix, who blushed.

'That's right,' she said shyly. 'Charles and I are betrothed.'

'Aye, so I hear.' Holding a thick cloth, the housekeeper lifted a huge black pot from the kitchen range where the fire burned low and placed it on a mat on the large wooden table, then turned to reach into one of the many cupboards and bring out three bowls.

'Shall I serve you now, ma'am, or wait for Master Charles? Ah, I hear him coming now. I'll dish up and it'll be cooling.'

Beatrix had heard nothing, but Mrs Newby was obviously attuned to every squeak or footfall in the house, for a minute later Charles pushed open the door.

'Do start,' he said. 'You must be famished.' He sat on a stool at the head of the table. 'The famous soup of Mags Newby! What is it today?' He bent to sniff the bowl's contents. 'Ham, celery? What else?'

'Oh, onion, potato, anything to hand, Master Charles. You know me, nothing gets wasted.'

She sliced the ham into thick and succulent slices and placed three large plates, a small bowl of mustard and another of horseradish on the table, with slices of bread and a pot of butter to the side.

'If you'll excuse me now,' she said, 'I'll pop upstairs and check the fires, for I'd guess you won't want to be late out of bed. Master Charles, I've put you in owd Uncle's room. I hope as you'll be happy with that? It's well aired and 'linen's fresh.'

They ate their soup in near silence, Beatrix and her mother almost too tired to talk, but both managed to say how good it was, and how tender the ham.

'Mrs Newby said she wasn't a cook,' Mrs Fawcett remarked, 'and yet that was delicious. Was she your great-uncle's housekeeper for very long?'

'Yes, I believe so,' Charles answered. 'Certainly I remember her from many years ago. The Newbys are a local farming family.' He hesitated. 'They were good friends of my great-uncle. They took great care of him as he became older and more infirm. Much more than his own family did.'

CHAPTER TEN

Beatrix and her mother were in adjoining bedrooms; a fire was flickering in each room and thick curtains hung at the tall windows, whilst soft sheets and blankets covered the beds, topped by feather quilts.

Mrs Fawcett was asleep in minutes, but Beatrix, having thrown back the quilt and pulled one of the curtains aside a few inches, lay in semi-darkness listening to the silence.

In London there was always some sound after dark: the clip-clop of hooves or rumble of a cart, or drunken voices singing or shouting; and then, as dawn broke, the clank of milk pails over a dairy maid's shoulders, or a whistle from a baker's boy as he passed with a basket of freshly made bread, and always the reverberation of cabs and delivery carts, the hammering and crashing as old buildings were demolished to make way for new, and the constant hum and throb from the nearby streets of the world's largest city.

Here, she couldn't hear anything but the buzz of her own ears; she lay still, listening: surely there was something? She drew up the quilt and closed her eyes; when she opened them she saw that it wasn't completely dark after all, for the pale light of the moon she had seen earlier was filtering through the gap in the curtains.

She lifted her head when she heard a rustling and twittering below the window. There must be creeper on the walls, and birds nesting within it, perhaps shuffling in their nests to get comfy, she thought. Then a bark of a dog, or perhaps a fox, she couldn't distinguish which; a few minutes later she heard the hoot of an owl, a sound she rarely heard from her bed at home. He's on the hunt. Gone out to look for supper. The thought pleased her and she turned over on her pillow, tucked her hand beneath her cheek and was instantly asleep.

When she awoke, daylight was streaming through the gap in the curtains and she turned on to her back to take in the size of the room, which was large, and its contents: the wide wardrobe with a drawer beneath it, much like her own at home, a chest of drawers, a marble washstand bearing a bar of soap in a saucer, a jug and a bowl, with a towel hanging from the rail beneath.

She slipped out of bed and put on her dressing robe, then dipped a finger into the jug, which contained cold water for washing. If Mrs Newby lives next door, which wherever it is must be quite a way, she mused, I suppose we can't expect her here early enough to bring up hot water. She poured water into the bowl and soaped her hands, then splashed her face and picked up the towel. Drying her face and hands, she went to the window and looked out.

'Oh,' she breathed. 'How lovely!'

Below her was a green meadow fringed on either side by thickets of bushes and trees and leading down to a wood below; beyond, between gaps in the trees, she caught glimpses of the long estuary with ships and barges plying in each direction. On the southern bank was a low rise of tree-lined hills and tall chimneys issuing thick smoke.

It looks as if the estuary has cut through the land at some time in the long ago past, she contemplated. I wonder if from the other side, Lincolnshire I think it is, the people looking across the water at us will see a mirror image.

Seabirds were wheeling and dipping in flight over the meadowland, some with black heads and wing tips; others, noisier than the black-headed ones, were grey-feathered with white underbelly and black wing tips, and these she thought were herring gulls like the ones she had seen on Brighton beach.

She was eager to explore and dressed quickly, taking from her travelling bag the stout walking shoes that she used for wet weather when at home. She had packed them at the last minute as she was sure she had read or heard that the weather in the north was much colder and wetter than in the south. She wrapped a shawl across her shoulders, quietly opened her door, and listened to hear if anyone was about.

There was no sound from her mother's room and she didn't know where Charles was sleeping; she guessed that it was still very early. As she crept down the stairs, a grandfather clock at the bottom showed her it wasn't yet six o'clock, so she tiptoed to the front door. In the daylight she could see it was made from a massive slab of oak that she hadn't noticed last night as they came in. She stood on tiptoe to slide back the bolt and then turned a heavy iron key, which she thought would screech but didn't, and pulled open the door. Feeling the rush of air, she breathed in the scent of grass and greenery and bonfires and stepped outside, closing the door quietly behind her.

There were half a dozen wide steps leading to the drive and she walked down them and on to the damp grass, then turned to gaze up at the big, square, stone-built house with its tall chimneys. Georgian, maybe, she thought; older than our London house. Her eyes tracked from left to right, from the windows above and those below on either side of the door, and came to rest on an attached lower-roofed stone building set slightly back from the main façade, with its own front door.

The sun, risen now in the wide sky, shed a rosy golden glow over the stone and the autumn hues of wisteria, and she heaved a breath. Oh! It's huge and old and lovely! Am I really going to live here? To be mistress of all this? How will I manage such a house? I have no experience, so who will help me? Charles? I haven't heard him express any enthusiasm.

He told me that he would have to go back to London from time to time, to attend to bank matters. Does that mean he needs to earn a salary, and if so, will there be money to spend on the house? But he will receive the inheritance, so surely there will? I must ask him. I need to know.

She turned again to look down the long meadow. Though the grass was long, there were imprints of circles as if there had once been flower beds or even ponds. 'There has been a lawn, I think,' she murmured, and wondered if it had all been put to grass for ease of labour and whether sheep or cattle had grazed here.

It would be nice to have flower beds, and maybe a pond with water trickling over a statue. I don't know how that could be achieved; could water be pumped from the house, or from a water tank?

She sensed a movement behind her and turned her head.

'Ma'am – erm, sorry; miss? I didn't mean to startle you.' Removing a floppy hat to reveal thick and curly reddish hair, a tall broad-shouldered man dressed in grass-stained trousers and a dark brown shirt, with a short beard and blue smiling eyes, stood before her.

'You – you didn't,' she answered. 'I was lost in thought. Do you work here?'

He laughed. 'No. At least, yes, sometimes, if there's a job that needs doing. We keep an eye on the place now that Uncle Nev has gone.'

'Uncle Nev? Do you mean—'

'Sorry,' he said again. 'It's what we called Mr Dawley, or sometimes Squire. He wasn't really our uncle, though it felt as if he were. We miss him,' he said softly. 'I'd known him all my life.'

She felt the scrutiny of his deep blue eyes and said, 'I'm Beatrix Fawcett, and you are . . . ?'

'Edward Newby. You met my mother last night.'

'Ah, yes!' She smiled, feeling more comfortable now that she knew the connection. 'She fed my mother and me with delicious soup.'

He nodded. 'She's famous for her soups. Did you have a good journey, Miss Fawcett? It's a long trail from London.'

She agreed that it was, and then said, 'Your mother told us last night that she lived next door, but I don't see any other houses. There are the barns behind, but—' She shrugged, and glancing at the attached building nodded towards it. 'Or perhaps that's where she meant?'

'No!' He grinned. 'There's a door inside there that leads into the main house. Owd uncle used to put his relatives there on the rare occasions they came to visit. We live a mile up the lane; it was part of Dawley land at one time, until . . .' there was a mere fraction of hesitancy, 'until my father bought it from Uncle Nev.'

'Next door is a mile away!' She smiled. 'I can't imagine what my friends will say when I tell them.'

'Are you a city g— Erm, young lady?' he asked.

'London born and bred,' she said shyly, and then glanced up as the front door opened and Charles stepped out, saw them and ran down the steps.

'Good morning, Beatrix. Forgive my mode of dress.' He had come out without his jacket. 'Morning, Eddie.' He nodded to Edward Newby.

'How do, Charles. Brought Miss Fawcett to view the house? You've chosen a good time, weatherwise.' Edward raised his eyebrows. 'We've finished harvesting; we could have done with an extra pair of hands!'

'Another time, perhaps. It's only a brief visit to show Miss Fawcett and her mother the house.'

'Am I led to understand that congratulations are in order? My mother said there were.'

'Oh, yes, certainly.' Charles affected surprise at the question. He took hold of Beatrix's hand. 'Miss Fawcett has agreed to be my wife after only a short courtship.'

He lifted her hand to his lips. 'And why should a man wait when there is the delightful prospect of marriage to such beauty and poise before him?'

'Why indeed.' Edward Newby's eyes were veiled as he answered. 'A Christmas wedding?'

'No, no!' Charles gazed tenderly at Beatrix and put a hand on her shoulder. 'We decided on a spring wedding. A bride needs time to prepare, so I'm told; although,' he gazed at Beatrix as if he couldn't tear his eyes away, 'next week wouldn't be soon enough for me.'

There's something happening here that I don't understand, Beatrix considered. They have had some confrontation, I would guess, but they are not likely to tell me.

'Have you known each other long?' she asked, looking from one to the other. 'You seem to know each other quite well.'

'I used to come when I was a boy, as I've mentioned,' Charles said. 'Eddie's father taught me to shoot.'

'To shoot?' Beatrix's eyebrows rose in alarm.

'Rabbits,' Edward Newby broke in. 'My father was a good shot. Still is. He's never maimed any animal.'

'Poor rabbits,' she murmured.

'You wouldn't say that if you were a famer, Miss Fawcett,' he commented, 'and I'd reckon you wouldn't say no to a slice of rabbit pie either.'

She conceded that she probably wouldn't, and on the topic of food Charles said that there was breakfast waiting in the range so they had better go inside.

Edward Newby put on his hat again and tapped his finger to it as he said, 'It's nice to meet you, Miss

Fawcett. I expect we'll meet again in the spring when you come to live here. I hope you'll like the area; it'll be a lot different from what you're used to, but you'll find folk welcoming, especially when they hear you've come to live in Neville Dawley's old house.'

'Charles Dawley's house now, Eddie.' Charles looked at him pointedly. 'The deeds are signed and sealed.'

'Aye, I'm sure they are,' Edward held his gaze, 'but it'll be a generation before folk round here will call it yours: as I said to Miss Fawcett, owd uncle is sadly missed.'

CHAPTER ELEVEN

'If you're prepared to walk I'll show you the estate,' Charles said after they'd finished breakfast. There was a fire burning in the large black range in the kitchen; Mrs Newby had come early and cooked bacon, sausage and eggs and placed them in the bottom oven to keep hot. She'd left a note to say she was sorry she couldn't stop but she had to prepare food for the workers who would be arriving at the home farm.

Beatrix thought that she would have liked to see what the men were doing now that harvest was over, and where it was stacked, but as they were only here for a short stay she wanted to explore the house and gardens. Remembering the barns she had seen, she asked Charles if there was farmland with the estate as well as the long meadow.

'Oh, yes,' he told her, 'but much of it is rented out. There were three other farms, until Neville Dawley saw fit to sell one of them to the Newbys some years ago.' His mouth pinched as he spoke. 'The Newbys were always cosy with him, even back as far as Eddie's grandparents. Or maybe he thought that we, the city Dawleys, might break it up or sell it off after his death.'

He shrugged. 'Which we might. He also renewed the rental terms for the other farms just six months before he died, so their rents can't be increased for another twelve months.'

'That was a very nice thing to do, wasn't it?' Beatrix responded. 'His tenants must have been grateful, especially the Newbys, who had helped him out over a very long period of time.'

Charles threw a quick glance at her, a small frown above his nose, and murmured, 'I'm sure they were.'

Was that a touch of resentment she heard? Was there some animosity between the families? Mrs Newby didn't seem aware of it; she was at ease in the house at any rate, almost as if it were her own judging by her comings and goings. More likely there might be antipathy between Charles and Edward Newby. Charles would be the elder by five or six years, she thought, so it was doubtful that they'd played together as boys. Oh, I don't know. Perhaps I'll find out once we're married and maybe I'm totally wrong.

Beatrix asked her mother whether she would like to join them, but she decided she would have a wander around on her own. She said she'd like to explore the house and the attached cottage if Charles didn't object, which he didn't.

'Perhaps you'd look at some of the old curtains, Mrs Fawcett?' he said. 'Some seem quite threadbare in places, as do the carpets. They will perhaps only be fit for burning. The whole place has been neglected and needs a lot of work.'

'Of course. I'll have a look at them,' she said. 'But if the curtains and carpets have some wear left in them, then a cottager might be glad of them? They will no doubt have been of good quality.'

'Originally, yes, though I doubt if my great-uncle would have bought new even though he lived here all his life. I gather that he wasn't a great spender. Typical Yorkshireman,' he added.

Beatrix kept on her sturdy shoes, realizing how useful they were, and took her shawl out with her. There was a cool breeze, even though the sun was warm. A beautiful day, she thought, except for the small black insects that tickled her forehead and tangled in her hair.

'They're what the locals call thrips,' Charles told her as they stood outside the door. 'Harvesting has disturbed them. You might be more comfortable wearing a bonnet.'

'Yes,' she said. 'I'll get one from my room. I won't be a moment,' and she turned and went inside. 'I don't know what I was thinking of,' she told her mother, who was in the hall, about to start her tour of the house. 'I never go out in London without a hat.' She ran upstairs towards her bedroom.

'You've tasted freedom,' her mother called out.

It's true, I have, she thought as she went outside again with her bonnet shielding her face. I feel quite excited at the thought of living here and having the liberty to do whatever I want without having to consider convention, or constantly having someone with me, except of course if I should be calling on acquaintances.

She asked Charles about their neighbours as they headed down the meadow towards the wood. 'Will anyone call on us, do you think? I do hope they do, as I

– *we* – will know no one at all.' She looked up at him. 'Unless you already do, of course?'

He took hold of her hand and tucked it under his arm. 'People will call,' he said. 'Everyone in the neighbourhood will want to know the new owner and his bride, so that they can be first to boast that they have met Mr and Mrs Charles Dawley.'

They were approaching the woodland and Beatrix was delighted to hear the sound of birdsong and rustling in the trees which she felt sure would be squirrels. She saw too that some of the trees were shedding rusty gold leaves.

'Be careful you don't trip and fall,' Charles urged as they found a path into the wood. 'There are broken branches and brambles underfoot. There's a lot of thinning out to do. I'll get someone in to do it over winter. There'll be plenty of available labour once all the harvest is brought in.' He turned towards her and pulled her close. 'May I have a real kiss now?' he asked. 'Not just a chaste kiss on the cheek?'

She lifted her face to his. She had never been kissed before and wondered how it would feel; she moistened her lips with the tip of her tongue but flinched as he put his hands about her waist and then slid them up and ran his thumbs across her breasts, over her nipples, before putting his lips to hers.

'You are an innocent, aren't you?' he murmured, and she nodded.

'Yes,' she whispered, and couldn't have said how she felt, except rather afraid, but in an excited way. She hoped that he didn't want anything but a kiss. She wasn't ready; she wasn't prepared.

He drew away from her. 'I won't hurt you!' he murmured.

She dropped her gaze. 'I know,' she said quietly. 'It's just that I know nothing about love. How could I? But I will trust you and I'll try to make you happy in our marriage.'

He nodded. 'I'm sure that you will,' he said, and smiled down at her, but she felt that the smile didn't quite reach his eyes and hoped that she hadn't disappointed him with her lack of passion.

'I think we must come on another day to look at the wood,' he said, turning to go back. 'After it has had a clearing out of dead wood. We don't want you falling and injuring yourself. Shall we walk back and you can perhaps tell me how you envisage the garden; there used to be flower beds when I was a boy, and rose trees.'

'Roses would be lovely,' she enthused. 'And the perfume would drift towards the house. Is there an orchard? It would be nice to see apple or pear blossom in the spring.'

'At the back of the house,' he told her. 'There's an apple orchard, or there used to be. When Uncle Neville inherited the estate as a young man he planted an orchard and brought pigs in to graze on the windfalls.' He gave a huff of breath. 'He became a proper farmer, didn't just play the role. Luckily for him there was enough inheritance to bring the place up to scratch; his own father had neglected it, being always busy with business matters and never having time to look after the estate.'

'And will you do the same?' she asked. 'Will you continue his good work?'

He turned a slightly startled gaze towards her. 'I can't actually see myself getting my hands dirty, but it has to be worked at a profit or it will fail, so I'm hoping to find a manager to oversee it. I know nothing about livestock, or looking after land for that matter.'

'But you were pleased to have inherited it?'

'It's worth a good deal of money.' He gave a short derisory laugh. 'Of course I'm pleased.'

That wasn't what I meant, she thought. I was thinking of the production of crops and what will be made from them, and keeping dairy cows for the milk or sheep for their fleeces. Am I just a city person with romantic ideas of country life? I realize it will be hard work and not always successful, but surely there would be more satisfaction in bringing in the harvest than counting up numbers in the banking world.

She sighed. But I know nothing, except – she breathed in the aroma of corn, of long grass, of wood smoke and scents of the coming autumn – I feel that I could be happy here.

Rather oddly, Charles seemed to be bored with looking over the estate. He only glanced at the long meadow grass and didn't go in the barns and stable block at the rear, and when they glimpsed Beatrix's mother through the windows of the annexe he suggested that she should join her and have a look at it together.

'Charles, what will we do with the cottage?' she asked. 'And we must speak of carpets and hangings and furniture for the main house – and how much should be spent.' She pressed her lips together, frowning anxiously. 'I have never had to ask for money; Papa always took care of our finances.'

He put his hands on her shoulders. 'What a dear little thing you are,' he said. 'I have never in my life known a young woman who considered money to be of the slightest importance except for spending on gewgaws.' He laughed, this time with genuine amusement. 'I can quite see that you will never overspend your allowance!'

'Oh, I won't,' she said, open-eyed in astonishment that he might even consider that she might. 'Once I know what it is I will be exceedingly careful.'

'We'll discuss that after we are married, my dearest Beatrix. Don't you worry your sweet little head about it.' Gently he pinched her cheek between his finger and thumb. 'Off you go with your mother. I'm going to see if I can find some coffee beans in that vault of a kitchen. Come back when you're ready.'

She watched him as he walked towards the main house, wondering exactly what it was about what he had said and the manner in which he had said it that made her think he was treating her like a child.

She stood outside the front door of the annexe and looked down towards the wood. There was a dust cloud hanging in the air and she could hear occasional shouts and laughter coming from neighbouring fields, and she thought how perfect the weather must have been for harvesting. Next year, she thought. Next year perhaps we might bring in our own harvest. I don't know how long it takes to till the land and sow the seed and gather in the crops, but I would like to find out.

As she turned to go inside, a fluttering thought struck her that she might be growing something within herself in another year; perhaps she would be carrying a young farmer or landowner to continue tradition. She took a deep, trembling breath. For I think I might have been chosen for that very purpose.

CHAPTER TWELVE

Beatrix and her mother discussed carpets, curtains and furniture on the train journey back to London. They'd made notes of what was needed for both houses, and Charles had been right: the carpets had been in a deplorable state and some of the curtains were threadbare and would need replacing.

'Did you see the piano, Mama?' Beatrix asked. 'Pushed up into a corner of the hall? I missed it when we arrived.'

'So did I,' her mother said. 'Though I don't know how. I tried out a few keys; it definitely needs a good tuning!'

Charles was listening with half an ear and an amused smile on his lips. Finally he broke in and said, 'Have you thought of which church you will choose for our wedding, Beatrix?'

'Well, yes, I have,' she said shyly. 'I'd thought at first that I would choose St Giles . . .'

Charles took in a whistling breath and began to shake his head.

'I know what you're going to say,' Beatrix said, 'and my father felt the same. St Giles is too close to the

Rookeries, and we don't want any trouble from anyone living down there.'

'Quite right, we don't; nor do we want our guests to be fearful of losing their pocketbooks. And then of course there are the new sewers that are being built in the vicinity. Most of the nearby roads are being dug up!'

Her eyes opened wide at his comment; she hadn't known about the sewers. 'So I thought St George's in Bloomsbury; it's a beautiful church, and not far from Russell Square.' She bent her head as she was speaking, suddenly shy of what lay ahead.

'A good choice, Beatrix. I quite agree,' Charles said, glancing at her mother, who gave an understanding smile and a nod. 'Shall we say April?' He slipped his hand inside his coat pocket, withdrew a slim leather diary and flipped through it. 'The first week in April? Would that be a suitable time for a wedding? Can you dear ladies be ready by then? The banns will need to be read and we'll also need an appropriate location for the wedding breakfast; would you like me to arrange that or would Mr Fawcett prefer to organize it himself?'

'He won't object if you should suggest somewhere, Charles,' Mrs Fawcett told him. 'In fact I rather think he would be relieved. You will know of somewhere suitable. Mr Fawcett is not someone who is used to socializing,' she added.

Beatrix was relieved too. Her father wouldn't know of a fitting venue for the wedding breakfast of a wealthy man and his young bride whereas Charles would, even though her father would pay the expense of it.

Oh, my goodness, she thought. Is it happening? I'm going to be married! Am I ready for this? I love the old house and the countryside where we will make our home, but my friends and parents will still be in London and I'll be alone in another county, away from everyone and everything I know, with a husband who is very rich and rather handsome, with whom I have agreed to spend my whole life without knowing if he is in the least kind or loving.

Once they were home again events proceeded at speed. She and Charles, with Dora accompanying them, visited St George's church together to arrange the reading of the banns and confirm the wedding date. Afterwards they went for coffee in a café and he asked Beatrix where she would like to spend her honeymoon.

'What about Paris?' he asked. 'Have you ever been?'

She confessed that she hadn't and that she would like to. 'But is it safe?' she asked. 'It has had some trouble, I understand.'

He shrugged dismissively. 'Where is safe?' he said. 'There is turmoil in any country. But it seems to be. We could of course go to the Lake District in the north of England. It's peaceful there and the scenery is beautiful.'

I have never been there either, she mused. In fact I am not widely travelled. Papa would never go further than Brighton and Mama and I knew every inch of it and got terribly bored.

'I'd like that,' she said eagerly. 'I'm sure it will be lovely; and then afterwards we can go straight on to Old Stone Hall instead of coming back to London.'

'Old Stone Hall!' He laughed. 'Is that what you call the house?'

She blushed. 'It seems like a good name for it. It's built mainly of stone with some brick at the back, and maybe if we give it a name the locals will stop thinking of it as Neville Dawley's old house.'

He lifted his chin and gazed at her under lowered eyelids. 'Mm,' he murmured. 'You're quite right. What a clever little thing you are; not only beautiful, but astute too.' He took hold of her hand, beneath the table for Dora was sitting nearby tucking into cake, and said quietly, 'I think you will make a good mistress of Old Stone Hall. You are discerning and probably imaginative and will put your touch on what is at the moment a crumbling, decaying old mansion. In a few years' time in the right hands it will probably be worth a lot more than it is now.' He gave a meaningful nod. 'And if we hire a manager to bring the estate up to date, that too will increase in value.'

She became a little alarmed. Was he only thinking of the place as an investment? She hoped not; she was thinking of it as a home, somewhere to enjoy living in and bringing up a large family, not only the one son Charles required to secure his inheritance.

'I'm really excited now,' she said, 'and looking forward to making the house into a home, Charles. I do hope that you don't have to spend too much time in London, because—'

He interrupted briskly. 'I'm not a farmer, Beatrix. Not even a gentleman farmer with a team of labourers or a farm manager to do my bidding; I'm a banker.'

'But surely you could be, with the right man in charge.'

He laughed. 'Absolutely not! I'm a city man. Oh, yes, of course I'll spend time in the country, make sure my little wife is safe and well and that everything is running smoothly, but I must continue with my business interests. You surely must understand that?' He paused, almost, she thought, as if he were taking stock of what he had said.

'And,' his thumb stroked the palm of her hand and around her wrist, making her feel fluttery, 'you'll probably want to come to London too, to see your friends and your parents?'

'Oh yes, of course I will. Your town house will be so convenient, won't it?'

He paused momentarily. 'Yes, yes indeed, if in fact I keep it. I have given thought to the idea that I might sell it and get something smaller. I won't entertain there once my base is in Yorkshire. We'll see.' He closed the conversation. 'If your girl over there has finished her second slice of cake, shall we leave? Much to do; April comes ever closer.' He smiled, and she was reassured.

Beatrix and her mother decided that Dora would benefit from some tuition in the art of becoming a lady's maid. To brush off her rough edges, as Mrs Fawcett said, and polish up her rather harsh London accent; she would also be taught how to look after Beatrix's wardrobe and how to dress her hair for visiting or receiving guests.

Beatrix wondered about the last suggestion, as she didn't think there would be much in the way of social visiting, in spite of what Charles had said about neighbours wanting to meet them. The house needed attention before they could think of entertaining. If anyone invited them to call, they would have to make clear that the invitation couldn't be reciprocated immediately.

She was keen to begin the renovation of the house and wondered if Charles knew of anyone who could start the work, or even whether she might suggest that they ask Edward Newby to recommend someone. She was unsure if that proposal might be treated with scorn.

Charles sent a note to her father a few days before Christmas to ask if he might call on Beatrix, and on being told she was filled with a mixture of trepidation and elation until her mother said, 'Don't worry, my dear. He is probably bringing you a special gift before your marriage.'

'What?' Beatrix whispered. 'What might it be?'

Her mother shook her head and sighed. Beatrix was becoming a bag of nerves and tension. She ran her fingers around the third finger of her own hand where she wore a simple gold band. Mr Fawcett had never thought of giving her a ring to mark their engagement; they were not fashionable when she and her husband married, although she would have liked to possess one, but no amount of hinting had penetrated her betrothed's understanding.

'An engagement ring?' Beatrix breathed. 'He did say he had seen one that he thought I might like, but has never mentioned it since.'

'Well, I might be wrong,' her mother teased. 'Perhaps it is only a box of bonbons.'

But it wasn't. It was as her mother had suggested. A very pretty ring with a single diamond surrounded by a cluster of others to make the shape of a flower. They were alone in the drawing room when Charles slipped it on to her finger.

'It's taken quite a long time,' he said. 'And I dare say you might have thought I'd forgotten, but I hadn't. It was the jeweller who was delayed. He is extremely busy at this time of year.'

'It's beautiful,' she said, feeling very emotional and weepy, and wondered how she could ever have doubted him.

That's got that over with, he thought with a breath of relief as he left Beatrix's home and drove back to the house he shared with Maria. Beatrix was happy with the ring he had given her, and now he was about to give Maria the one she had chosen from another jeweller, which had cost him twice as much as the one he had given Beatrix. Tempestuous Maria had to be pacified. When he married Beatrix he would be forced to keep Maria sweet. There was no knowing what she might say or do, and she knew her worth; she wouldn't be kept silent with mere baubles.

And who could blame her? He pulled into the inn yard where he stabled his mount and kept the chaise. She had already suffered under a brutal husband; she was vulnerable, and kept everything of value that Charles had ever given her locked away against any eventuality for fear of being abandoned, even by him, which was impossible, he assured her time and time again.

But she simply nodded and smiled seductively and didn't trust any man, not even one who had pledged his undying love.

CHAPTER THIRTEEN

Christmas was spent quietly at home, with Charles making a brief visit on Boxing Day. Beatrix had written to Charles's sister Anne, inviting her to be an attendant at her wedding; she had also written to her friends Sophia and Eleanor, commonly known as Nell, whom she had known for many years. Both had replied immediately, expressing their great pleasure, and Sophia in particular saying she was thrilled to be asked as she was sure it would be the wedding of the year and she hoped to meet a beau there. Anne, however, took over a week to send a formal reply indicating that the date in her diary was free and she would be able to attend.

'Please yourself,' Beatrix muttered and put the acceptance card on the drawing room mantelpiece, whereas she took Sophia's and Nell's upstairs to her room.

There had been no letter from her brother Thomas, who was serving in Ireland with his regiment; Beatrix's father had written to tell him of his sister's forthcoming marriage, and then her mother had written too, but still there was no reply. Beatrix shrugged; she would be disappointed if he didn't come, but he was a lazy letter writer in any case and rarely penned more than a few lines. She suggested to her parents that perhaps he had been moved on now that Ireland seemed to be quieter, and maybe was on the high seas or travelling through the deepest of jungles, for she was fairly sure that the last time they received a letter, about six months ago, he was expecting to be posted abroad again. Maybe he'd gone to India or Burma where there always seemed to be an uprising or trouble of some kind.

It won't make any difference, she thought. Charles's friend Paul Constable is to be his best man and the ushers will be their friends. But she worried slightly that there would be more people on Charles's side than on her own, and she would have liked to have her brother there.

'It doesn't matter,' her mother said calmly when she mentioned the guest list. 'It's not about quantity, it's about quality, and I'm sure that everyone on our side will be more than equal with those on the Dawleys'.'

Final fittings were being made on Beatrix's wedding gown as March drew to a close. She had decided on white satin, following the example of the queen who had chosen white on her marriage to Prince Albert, and white was now the height of fashion. With it she would wear an overskirt of Nottingham lace, and a headdress of orange blossom with a trailing chiffon and lace veil.

She saw tears in her mother's eyes when the seamstress came to do the final fitting and carefully pinned Beatrix into the dress. 'You look – you *are* – beautiful, my dearest Beatrix,' she said softly. 'You will make a lovely bride. I hope the sun will shine on your happiness.'

Someone knocked on the door. The seamstress, with pins between her lips, looked up in alarm at Beatrix who was standing on a stool.

'Yes?' her mother queried.

'A letter has come from Thomas,' her husband boomed from the other side of the door.

'You can't come in,' Mrs Fawcett called back. 'It's unlucky.'

'Thought you'd like to know,' he said. 'He's hoping to be here in time.'

'Oh, hurray! Thank you, Papa. We'll be down shortly; we're a little tied up at the moment.' Beatrix giggled. They had just over a week before the wedding day.

'Do you think Thomas will wear his uniform,' she asked her mother, 'or will he wear a tailcoat?'

Her mother smiled. 'He'll want to show off,' she said, 'so he'll wear his uniform if I know my son. But I'm glad he'll be here and safe home.'

The three bride's attendants were making their own arrangements regarding their gowns for the day. Beatrix knew that her two friends had good taste in clothes, and Sophia had written to say she would wear blue tiered silk and ask if Beatrix would like to see her gown. Eleanor was going to wear pale rose muslin with white sprigs and both would wear a circlet of flowers in their hair.

Beatrix had written back to say she would wait to see them in their finery on the day. She had no idea what Charles's sister would be wearing, or even if she would travel with them to the church as she had been invited to do.

Her two friends arrived together at eight o'clock on the wedding morning, each with a maid to help them into their gowns. Beatrix and Dora helped Mrs Fawcett dress in her wedding outfit, a deep blue tastefully fitted gown with a slight train and bustle, which she preferred to the more fashionable hooped crinoline; a pale blue extravagant hat completed the ensemble.

As Mr Fawcett was struggling to fasten his cravat the doorbell rang, and Dora hurried downstairs as Beatrix whispered, 'It will be Charles's sister.' But it wasn't, it was Thomas, tired and travel-stained, but smiling because of arriving in time.

Beatrix's father had hired two carriages, which drove up with the horses' tails neatly braided and gaily bound by ribbons. Beatrix and her father were to travel together, with Dora in a new dress and jacket sitting in front with the driver. Unusually for Mr Fawcett, who rarely noticed what his wife or daughter wore, he complimented them both on looking *splendid*.

As his mother had predicted, after a quick wash, a blade over his chin, and a brush through his hair, Thomas was ready in his uniform to escort his mother and Beatrix's attendants in the other carriage. He gazed at his sister as she came slowly downstairs into the hall where everyone was waiting, and for a moment didn't say anything, but then he took her hand and kissed it. 'You look beautiful, Beatrix,' he murmured. 'Your husband-in-waiting is a lucky lucky man.'

Some of their neighbours came out to watch and wave and call Good luck and Happy day, which surprised and pleased Beatrix as she barely knew them.

What I need, she thought as she and her father followed the other carriage, is good luck and a happy future, not just the one day. Does every bride feel as nervous as I do? Unsure of what is in front of me as I marry a man I don't really know? Is Charles feeling the same? He doesn't know my temperament, but perhaps I am easier to understand, being young and, I suppose, inexperienced.

But no, he won't be nervous. He probably knows lots of females and had his choice of possible brides; I suppose I should feel elated that he chose me. But I'm still anxious.

Charles looked in the mirror, fastened his grey frock coat, adjusted his cravat and reached for his top hat from the hall stand. He'd had a few anxious days. To keep her out of the way, he had promised Maria a week in Paris, and only two nights earlier had arrived home from the bank and announced that he had been called to an important meeting in Scotland. Maria was furious; she had her portmanteau packed and ready.

'Darling Maria, I'm so sorry. I'll have to cancel the tickets, but we can go next month.' He'd put his arms round her and kissed her cheek, but she'd pushed him away.

'Where is this Scotoland place? Are there shops and places to eat? I will come with you.'

He'd laughed heartily. 'It will take us days to get there by train and coach and then when we arrive there are mountains and lakes and – and goats. Lots of goats and sheep.'

'No!' She yelled at him. 'Not goats—'

'Listen,' he said. 'Why don't you take your friend Bianca? She can have my ticket and share your room; you'll have fun with her, won't you? You can shop, and the food is good in Paris, and you and I can go at another time.'

He had seen that the plan was appealing. She'd made a petulant *moue*, but soon brightened and shrugged her shoulders and he knew he was on safe ground.

'Come on, let's go and ask her right now, and then you'll be able to look forward to it again.'

'All right,' she'd conceded. 'But what do they eat in this Scotoland?'

'Oh, erm – something called haggis,' he said. 'It's a kind of meat pudding; sheep's liver and brains, I think, and wrapped in the sheep's stomach. I don't think you'd like it. I think it's a sheep's stomach,' he'd added thoughtfully. 'Or it might be a pig's!'

'Disgusting!' she shrieked. 'Agh! You will be sick!'

And so the day before the wedding she had gone off with her friend Bianca, who was thrilled to be given such a treat. They'll enjoy it, he convinced himself. They will spend money, eat and drink and flirt with handsome Parisians and teach them a thing or two. He had seen them off on the ship and hurried to his parents' house to attend to last-minute things, including pacifying his sister who didn't like anything in her vast wardrobe of expensive gowns but had refused to buy anything new.

That evening he met Paul and gave him the ring to look after. Paul wanted to know what he had done with Maria and laughed when he told him; then the two of them went out to a restaurant where there was sure to be good food and entertainment with desirable young women for company. Yet oddly enough, he couldn't drum up any enthusiasm for the delights on offer. 'I'm marrying someone in the morning,' he told Paul as they sat drinking brandy after their meal. 'I'd better save myself.'

'Fine,' Paul said. 'I'm feeling greedy. Can I have your girl too?'

Charles had nodded moodily. 'Help yourself. Just save enough energy to get to the church in the morning.'

'What is so special about your bride-to-be . . . about Beatrix?' Paul asked. 'How does she stand out above all the others you considered?'

Charles shrugged. 'I'm sick of the whole thing,' he said. 'I never wanted to get married in any case; I have a perfectly happy relationship with Maria, but I'll lose the inheritance if I don't marry and it's worth a lot of money!' He drained his glass and signalled for another. 'I'm tired of flirty girls with no brains, but Beatrix . . .' He paused. 'Well, she's different. She has sense, she's incredibly beautiful but not aware of it, and I don't think she'll be afraid of money. But she's not a spendthrift, she'll be able to handle it; her father is a banker, after all. And,' he smiled and tossed back the brandy, 'she's quite innocent, which is very appealing, and although she's as slender as a wand she probably doesn't realize that she has good childbearing hips.'

Grinning, he finished his brandy and ordered another, then paid the bill and headed home to his own house and empty bed where he slept until six.

He bathed and dressed, made and drank coffee, then slipped on his frock coat. 'Right then,' he muttered as he brushed his hair, taking a final glance in the mirror. 'Best get on with it. I'm not sure what I'm getting into, but she's a malleable young woman; it's got to be worth the risk for the end prize. Master of my own estate and not reliant on my father, damn him! We just have to be sure of producing a son to make the inheritance secure.'

The bride's carriage arrived at St George's church just as the bells of the city began pealing as if all the churches in London were telling of Beatrix's arrival; she felt that her legs would give out beneath her and she had to wait a few seconds before taking her father's outstretched hand to assist her down.

Through the haze of her veil she saw her mother and brother and her bridesmaids, including Charles's sister Anne, waiting at the door. She was pleased that she had chosen to hide her face beneath the veil, for she felt that her skin must be pale with nerves despite the slight blush of rouge that she had brushed over her cheekbones.

She shivered as she put her cold hand into her father's warm one; she hadn't held his hand since she was a little girl and was slightly comforted by the contact, despite knowing that he had brought her to this situation before she was ready. But it is too late now to change my mind.

'Are you cold, Beatrix?' he asked, looking down at her as they reached the door.

She nodded. 'Nervous,' she whispered, and he gently squeezed her fingers.

'Half an hour and it will be done and you'll be wed.'

She looked up at him and thought that the comment brought her little consolation. She lifted her head and straightened her shoulders, then watched her mother and Thomas disappear inside the church as her bridesmaids clustered around her. With Dora's help they spread out the train of her skirts before Dora then went inside and waited behind the door and the bridesmaids moved down the aisle to the front where the groom and his best man were waiting, leaving Beatrix alone with her father.

'All right, Papa,' she murmured. 'Let's get on with it. For better or worse.'

CHAPTER FOURTEEN

The church was full of flowers and Beatrix sensed her mother's touch as the perfume of roses and lilies in huge vases suffused the church; the pews had dainty posies of violets tied to them with yellow and white ribbons. The organ music soared as she began her journey down the aisle, holding firmly to her father's arm, and she heard choral music coming from somewhere hidden within the church.

Definitely my mother's influence, putting her own good taste into the occasion, she thought, and wondered when she had had the time to arrange it without herself knowing. She slid her gaze towards her, giving her a loving smile as she passed, before lifting her head to see Charles half turned towards her.

He seemed taller as she stood beside him; taller than her father yet not quite the height of Thomas. She'd forgotten too how fair his hair was, and saw he had grown his sideburns thicker and longer, to the level of his cheekbones.

She saw him swallow and moisten his lips with the tip of his tongue. Strangely, he gazed at her as if she wasn't the one he was expecting; a blink of his eyelids, as if he was startled, and then suddenly he smiled and held out his hand.

She gave her bouquet to Sophia, who beamed at her, and then, lifting her veil, she turned to him and put her hand in his.

You're beautiful, he mouthed. *Adorable,* and she lowered her lashes.

She couldn't have said whether the time was long or short; it seemed dreamlike and illusory as they exchanged their vows, said prayers, sang hymns, signed the register and she became Beatrix Emily Louisa Dawley, no longer Miss Fawcett.

They turned to walk together up the aisle, past people on either side who nodded or smiled, and some who seemed to view her with curious interest; and then they were outside and congratulations were given and she touched hands with people she didn't know and dipped her knee to those who were older.

And then they were off, the congregation throwing rose petals and laughing and chatting as she and Charles were climbing into a carriage and pulling away towards the hotel where they would have their wedding breakfast. They waved and smiled and Beatrix saw her mother watching with an expression that she couldn't quite comprehend; then, as if she had suddenly come awake, Mrs Fawcett lifted her head and turned to meet the earnest gaze of a tall man with thick silver hair standing close by, who was watching her and not the bride.

She saw her father next to Charles's father; both were nodding and talking and she wondered if they were congratulating each other on a transaction well done, or discussing financial matters, or commenting on the weather.

Beatrix turned to look at Charles. He was leaning his head against the plush cushions with his eyes closed. He opened them, sensing that she had turned, and sighed. 'Well, that went very well, didn't it?' he said. A remark that wasn't exactly complimentary she thought; nor did it bring her joy.

'Did it?' she murmured. 'Was it as you expected it to be . . . or not?'

He sat up, as if detecting some misgiving. 'It was wonderful. *You* were wonderful.' He took her hand. 'You are very beautiful; so serene.'

'I didn't feel serene,' she admitted. 'I was very nervous.'

He reached to kiss her cheek. 'So was I,' he confessed. 'But that's over and done with. Now we can enjoy ourselves.' He paused for a second, soothingly stroking her hand. 'You might not guess it, Beatrix,' he said, 'but I am a very private person, and there will be people at our wedding breakfast who might question you on how we first met, and where, and – and so on. I would prefer it if you didn't give them chapter and verse. Our circumstances have nothing to do with anyone else, and I don't want anyone to think that our marriage was arranged. Can I rely on you not to disclose that? I'd much rather they were told that I fell in love with you the very first time I saw you.' He leaned in and kissed her again. 'Which of course is perfectly true. I wouldn't have asked you to marry me otherwise.'

'Of course you wouldn't,' she murmured. 'You would hardly commit yourself to a lifetime with someone if you didn't care for them, would you?'

She gazed at him and he looked back with a question in his eyes, as if he was not quite sure if his new wife was being ironic. Yet both knew that this was an agreement, a commitment entered into for a reason other than love; and Beatrix had yet to discover what that reason really was.

The hotel was close to Richmond Park, within sight of stately homes and beautiful countryside. Painted white, with a double oak door, it had clearly once been a very grand house. The windows were thrown open as it was such a lovely day, and a concierge was waiting to greet them.

Several other carriages arrived shortly after they did. Anne had decided to travel with her parents. The two other bridesmaids, the best man, one usher and Thomas travelled squashed together, disregarding the convention that young ladies shouldn't travel unchaperoned with young men, and they laughed and chatted amiably.

Close behind them came Beatrix's parents and two cousins on her mother's side; following them were Charles's parents, his sister and an aunt. Various other friends and relatives came along, but overall they numbered just under forty, which everyone agreed made a select party. Some guests had elected to stay until the next day, but Charles and Beatrix were travelling to another hotel for the night before moving on the following morning to a destination that Charles refused to reveal.

At the table after the meal there followed various toasts to the newly married pair with Paul, the best man, making jokes about Charles waiting until he was an old man before snatching up his beautiful young bride. Beatrix's father didn't seem to understand the humour and kept turning to his wife for explanations.

Beatrix glanced about her. Her friends Sophia and Nell looked lovely and flirted with all the young men, including her brother. Sophia remembered Thomas from when they were very young, but Nell didn't, and Beatrix thought that her brother looked more handsome than any of the other men present. Then it occurred to her that the other male guests were all older than Thomas, more Charles's age, and, since they were unaccompanied, were probably unmarried too.

None of them has snatched up Anne, she considered thoughtfully, but she doesn't seem in the least interested in them; perhaps she prefers not to marry, for she is probably worth a fortune and will lose it all if she marries.

She observed everyone in turn as she drank her champagne and became more introspective as her glass was refilled. She knew only her own relatives and the few friends here, and although she had been introduced to everyone else she couldn't remember their names or who they were. She looked across the tables, searching for the elegant man with the silver hair who had stood behind her mother outside the church, but she didn't see him. He had been the smartest, most elegant male guest of all. I wonder who he was? A friend of Charles's father? Or of my father? I didn't see him greet anyone. He must have been in one of the back pews, for I didn't notice him on the way in or out of church. A relative of my mother's perhaps, but then why isn't he here? I didn't see the final guest list.

A pianist came in to play and the guests moved to comfier chairs in another room where Beatrix and Charles circulated between them all. He murmured to her, his hand resting on her shoulder, that they should change and depart in about an hour. She was pleased that they were going on elsewhere, for she didn't want to spend her first night as a married woman beneath the same roof as her parents, Charles's parents or their friends, as that would be embarrassing both that evening and the following morning.

'Will you help me change, Mother?' she asked quietly at the appropriate time. 'And take my gown home?'

Her mother gave a sad smile. 'And take it to *my* home, Beatrix?' she murmured. 'And keep it there until you come back to London? Yes, of course I will.'

Of course, Beatrix considered, the only home I've ever had in my life is now my parents' home and not mine. Old Stone Hall, which I must make into my home, is hundreds of miles away. She felt anxious, rather uneasy and yet excited too.

'That's what I meant.' Her voice cracked. 'The gown will get dusty at Old Stone Hall. The workmen are already there clearing out and getting ready for our . . . occupation.'

They went up the stairs to her parents' room, where Beatrix's luggage was waiting. She took a deep breath as she took off her veil and headdress, and then as her mother unfastened the buttons she slipped out of her gown, which billowed like a cloud at her feet. Her mouth trembled, and as her mother picked it up and laid it on the bed, ready for packing later, she whispered, 'Oh, Mama, what am I going to do, so far away from you?'

They waved goodbye as everyone came outside to see them drive off. Both had changed into comfortable yet smart and fashionable travelling clothes, and their luggage was packed on top. Dora was up with the driver. She was being dropped off once they were back in London and would make her own way to Russell Square, where she was to stay until it was time to travel to Yorkshire.

They had been blessed with fine weather all day and Beatrix half wished they could have stayed in Richmond a little longer so that they could have walked in the park, but the driver was going very steadily so that they could enjoy the view of rolling countryside, stately trees, acres of green meadowland and an occasional glimpse of London's tall buildings on the skyline.

'Where are we going?' she asked. 'Am I allowed to know, or is it to be a surprise?'

He gave a merry grin. 'You'll be surprised to hear that we are not travelling far; only a few miles, in fact. Tomorrow we have a very long journey north. Our destination is Windermere, in the Lake District, where we shall be spending our honeymoon.'

'Oh, how lovely.' Beatrix was delighted. Then she exclaimed as she saw a herd of grazing deer. 'Look!' Not more than a few yards away maybe fifty or more red and fallow deer were cropping the grass. The driver had slowed right down so as not to startle them, and his passengers had a good view.

'So I hope you don't mind,' Charles went on, 'that I've booked a rather splendid hotel within a short distance of Euston as our train leaves at six fifteen in the morning. You'll see lots of deer whilst in the Lake District, and mountains too, and waterfalls,' he added, as if to make up for the foreshortened stay near Richmond Park. 'We shall have to buy you some sturdy boots and then we can go fell walking.'

'That sounds lovely,' she said, her eyes still on the deer. Then she turned to look at him and wondered why he hadn't thought of having the reception in the splendid London hotel instead of travelling to Richmond for just a few short hours. Was it meant to impress her, or their guests? He must have had a reason, but she couldn't think what it might have been.

The London hotel was very grand and they were given an en-suite dining and sitting room adjacent to the bedroom, where she saw with a fluttering inside her there was a very large bed. Charles had ordered afternoon tea to be served on their arrival and a light supper with champagne at eight o'clock.

'Ah!' Beatrix sighed and sat on the sofa. 'It was a lovely day, wasn't it? Do you think your sister enjoyed herself? She seemed rather quiet, but perhaps she always is?'

He shrugged, unfastened and took off his coat, and sat down beside her, putting his arm around her shoulder. 'There's no knowing with Anne,' he said. 'She isn't interested in people, and particularly not in men. Father has tried to marry her off several times, but she's not having it. She'll be an old maid, she says, and please herself, not a husband.'

'Your father will make sure she's comfortably off, won't he?' Beatrix asked. 'Otherwise, how will she manage?'

'There's money in the family, Beatrix,' he said idly. 'She won't be without, and besides, she's very smart and is aware that London is full of gold.'

'What!' She was astonished. 'Real gold? Really?'

He put his head back and laughed. 'London's bank vaults are brimming with gold bars.'

She turned to stare at him. 'But there's so much poverty! So many people with nothing!'

He shrugged. 'That's their hard luck; it's a matter of being born in the right place at the right time.'

As she was about to protest, there was a knock on the door and Charles called, 'Come in.' As Beatrix expected, it was a maid pushing a trolley piled high with dainty sandwiches and luscious cakes; she placed them on a low table, dipped her knee and backed out again. Beatrix smiled and thanked her, but Charles simply stretched his arms as if he hadn't noticed her.

After the comment he'd made she felt quite guilty at eating in such luxury, but she was hungry, having been too nervous to eat during the wedding breakfast, and thought that it was a long time until supper. She poured tea for them both, remembering that Charles took milk with his, and handed him the cup and saucer, a small jug of milk and a plate for the food.

He seemed quite relaxed, eating and drinking and commenting on the hotel and on various aspects of the day, then he got up from the sofa and wandered over to the window. 'It's a lovely afternoon,' he murmured.

Beatrix swallowed. It was hours from supper time – and afterwards; what would they do now? 'Shall we take a stroll?' she suggested.

He turned his head and smiled quizzically. 'No, I don't think so. An afternoon nap sounds more appealing, don't you think, Beatrix?'

She took a nervous, shortened breath. During the day, she speculated. Is that when . . .? I suppose it doesn't matter, yet I always thought that bedtime was . . .

In truth she hadn't given the matter much thought until recently, as she had never had any reason to, but now she found herself blurting out, 'I must tell you, Charles, that I know nothing.' She swallowed hard again. 'I don't . . . know what to expect of you . . . or know what you expect of me.'

Leisurely he came towards her and put out his hands to pull her up towards him. He put his arms around her waist and drew her close, nuzzling into her neck. 'Knowing nothing sounds perfect to me, Beatrix.'

He gave her gentle kisses on her cheeks, her eyelids and her lips, and she drew in small, warm, shallow breaths as he aroused her.

'It will give me the greatest of pleasure to teach you, Beatrix,' he said softly. 'Trust me,' and he turned her face up towards him with his hands and ran them, firm and strong, from her chin down her throat and round her neck, and she had a slight feeling of panic as she thought how easy it would be for a man to choke a woman with a slender neck such as hers.

'Trust me,' he repeated softly. 'I will do my best not to hurt you.' His hands ran down to her breasts and on around her waist and found the buttons on her gown, which one by one he unfastened.

He's done this before. The thought came with certainty as her gown slipped to the floor; she had no doubt that he was an expert as she stepped out of her gown and he took her hand and dizzily she followed him as he led her to the room next door with the bed.

CHAPTER FIFTEEN

It was early; dawn's pale light was filtering through the curtains when she awoke after a fitful night's sleep. Beatrix couldn't at first recall why she was naked and wondered what had happened to her nightgown. Was she wearing it when she came to bed? Her body ached and she felt bruised and sore. She had a blinding headache; she was alone, and remembering the previous night thought briefly that Charles might have left. Had she been so useless as a wife that he had walked out?

It had been wonderful to begin with as he pulled her on to his knee and explored her body with his fingertips. He had placed two glasses on a side table and a bottle of champagne in an ice bucket at the side of the bed and insisted that they both drank; but then quickly and silently he had aroused her to a pitch that ended in pain, and didn't seem to realize that he was hurting her and wouldn't hold back no matter how she gripped his arms with her fingernails or gasped for him to stop.

But where was he? She would have to explain that she was – had been – a virgin and that she hadn't been ready. She lay back on the pillows. I suppose that no one thought to tell me that it might hurt. She listened. Who was whistling? And then she heard the splashing of water and humming. She sat up, listening to the sounds coming from the bathroom. Charles? He was in the bath!

'Beatrix! Are you awake?' His voice sounded thick and slightly slurred. 'Come on. Bath time; we have a train to catch.'

She climbed out of the high bed and pulled the sheet after her to cover herself. Where was her nightgown? She frowned as she saw that her trunk hadn't been opened. Then she began to remember, though she had difficulty in bringing to mind which had been day and which was night. They had had tea and gone to bed where they drank champagne; her mind closed over what happened next, before she fell asleep. Then they had got up and Charles had insisted that they ate dinner in their dressing robes and drank wine with the meal, even though she had little appetite as she felt so uncomfortable. And then Charles had opened a brandy bottle and poured a small glass for her and a large one for himself.

'I can't,' she had said when he put it in front of her. 'I haven't ever drunk brandy.'

'This is a very special occasion, my dearest little wife,' he'd said firmly. 'We have just married and must drink a toast to us and our son.'

'But,' she'd protested, 'we can't have made a child yet, surely?'

He'd patted his nose. 'I think you are probably right. What a clever girl you are.' He'd drunk his brandy straight down and got up, topped up Beatrix's glass and held it to her lips. 'Come on! Open wide.' He'd stroked her neck so she had to open her mouth and had gently poured in the brandy, which had burned as it trickled down her throat.

'That's better,' he'd said, and carefully licked up the spillage from her chin. 'Don't want to waste it; it's the best money can buy. Come on, just a drop more.' And he'd held the glass against her mouth, even though she protested, and poured in the rest of the brandy so it spilled down her neck and on to her breasts.

I can't recall what happened next, she thought as she stood outside the bathroom door. I only know that I wasn't in control of my head or my body and neither am I now. How am I going to get through the day?

Charles came out of the bathroom wrapped in a towel and smiled at her. 'Aphrodite standing before me,' he murmured and reached out to pull the sheet from her, but she snatched it back and held it against her to hide her nudity.

'Beatrix!' he said patiently. 'Dearest Beatrix, you're my wife! You mustn't be shy of me. Come here.' He held out his hand. 'I've run a bath for you.'

She took his hand. 'I'm sorry,' she whispered. 'I didn't – I don't know—'

'Shh,' he said and led her into the bathroom. He slipped the sheet from her, and with a hand on her waist carefully helped her into the bath, then turned his back and closed the door behind him.

She lay, almost comatose, with the water easing her aches and wished she could stay longer, but was aware of pressing time if they were to catch the early train. I suppose I will learn, she thought. I wonder if all men are the same in their desires?

The hotel brought a carriage to the door to transport them to nearby Euston Station for the train to Manchester. Two porters hurried with their luggage and they caught the train with minutes to spare before it departed with a great huff of smoke and steam.

The hotel had packed them a hamper for lunch as they had had only a snatched breakfast of buttered toast and a slice of ham. They had the carriage to themselves on this first leg of the journey, and at Charles's suggestion they ate something from the hamper to sustain them.

Beatrix began to relax now that they were on their way. After eating they watched the scenery as it rushed past and soon began to doze a little. Charles came and sat next to her, and putting his arm around her tucked her under his shoulder so that she might lean on him and sleep. Perhaps, she thought sleepily, it will be all right after all.

It was almost dark by the time they reached Oxenholme station, after changing trains at Manchester. 'Nearly there,' Charles murmured. 'Next stop Windermere, and a good night's rest.'

Beatrix peered out of the window. They had been lucky once again to have the carriage to themselves. 'You have been before, Charles, haven't you?'

'Only once,' he said. 'When I was a boy. I loved it; beautiful scenery, mountains to climb if you have enough breath, deep lakes to sail on. Yes, it will be a nice break for a few days.'

'Only a few days?' she asked, having hoped for more.

'Afraid so. Then we shall cross into Yorkshire and see how things are at the house. I'm sure you're looking forward to being there?'

'Oh, I am,' she said eagerly. 'We can decide on which of the bedrooms to paint. Although perhaps the morning room and sitting room should come first, or maybe the kitchen. And then we'll need furniture—'

He interrupted her. 'I'll only be able to stay a day or two before going back to London. I'll see you settled in first and ask Mrs Newby to find you a permanent housekeeper. You'll be able to sort out housemaids and so on yourself, won't you? And what about your London girl?' He went on without pausing for breath. 'Shall I ask your mother to send her on to you with an address label pinned to her coat?' He laughed as he spoke, and she knew he didn't have a good opinion of Dora.

'No,' she said, drawing in a breath at the magnitude of the challenges in front of her. 'I'll write to Mama and arrange that. I'll need her to bring a few things with her.' He hadn't said anything about money, and she hesitated before saying bravely, 'What shall I do about paying tradespeople and ordering furniture and suchlike, Charles? Will you give me the details for setting up accounts and ordering?'

'Ah, of course! Sorry.' It seemed by his expression that he hadn't given it a thought. 'We'll discuss all that when we arrive at the house and I'll set up a bank account when I'm in London.' He smiled and nodded and seemed relieved. 'You seem to be very organized already, Beatrix. Well done!'

*

128

She had never seen such beautiful countryside; never in her life had she seen such high craggy mountains or such a huge lake as Windermere, where white sails and white swans floated serenely in harmony. They stayed in Bowness, a village of old cottages and cafés where they had tea and cake, and being blessed with sunny skies took a sail on the mere.

To her delight they followed in the footsteps of her favourite poets, Wordsworth, Coleridge and Shelley. They walked the fells, higher than she had ever been, and came down in the evenings to their hotel to eat suppers of freshly caught fish and tender venison, and delicious desserts made from local eggs, butter and honey.

They stayed two whole days and on the third day caught a train to take them into Yorkshire. Beatrix was disappointed to leave such a beautiful place, but was nevertheless looking forward to seeing Old Stone Hall again, although with some trepidation at the thought of being there alone until Dora arrived.

I'll ask my mother if she will come with her, she decided as the train chugged along. And I'll ask Thomas to come too if he hasn't already gone back to his soldiering duties.

She thought of enquiring if her father would visit too, but she doubted if he would, and felt a little sad, despite his being a funny old stick, fixed in his odd ways. She would miss him precisely because of that.

This is being grown up, she contemplated, gazing unseeingly out of the train window. It's a wholly different world that I've entered, one in which I have to make decisions for myself without my parents to advise me or suggest what I might do.

'You're very quiet, Beatrix.' Charles interrupted her thoughts.

'Oh, just contemplating,' she said brightly. 'I've loved the Lakes, Charles. Perhaps we'll go again some time?'

'Yes,' he said steadily. 'Of course we will.'

CHAPTER SIXTEEN

Builders and carpenters had been in the house under Mrs Newby's supervision; they'd checked the roof to make sure that it was watertight, fixed drainpipes back to the walls and replaced some of the rotten window frames.

Mrs Newby was in the house when they arrived, having lit a fire in the kitchen and another in the main bedroom, and Charles asked her if she knew someone who could come in and give the inside walls a fresh coat of paint throughout.

'Mr Newby can do that, Master Charles,' she said. 'No need to pay some expensive painter when he can do it for half 'price they'll charge. He used to do it for Uncle Nev.'

Beatrix saw Charles's cheek muscles tense when Mags voiced the name of Uncle Nev, but he must have thought her idea a good one for he agreed. He nodded. 'Very good,' he said. 'Ask him to speak to Mrs Dawley and she can decide what she wants.'

For a second Beatrix thought Charles was talking about his mother and wondered why she should be consulted, then was struck by the realization that he meant *her*. She put her hand to her mouth to hide a smile; how very bizarre.

Carte blanche, her mother had murmured, *how wonderful.* Beatrix had wondered at the time what she meant and always intended to ask her. Had her mother never had the freedom to do whatever she wanted or buy whatever she required without asking? Perhaps I'm lucky that Charles is so generous, but I must be careful not to exploit his liberality. Then reasoning entered her mind. Perhaps he had never before had an abundance of wealth, and now he had and was willing to share it.

'Charles,' she said, on the evening before his departure. They were sitting in the kitchen as there was no fire in the sitting room, nor any comfortable chairs, but only a very battered one that had been Neville Dawley's and Charles was sitting in now. Beatrix was perched on a stool. 'I've been thinking.' She put her head on one side, considering how to put the question. 'Whilst you're away I won't be able to get about. There are no hackneys, no omnibus, and everywhere,' she lifted her shoulders, 'is too far to walk, although I can get to Mrs Newby's as she's only a mile away. But there's no one to send on an errand until Dora arrives, and so . . .'

He glanced at her as if wondering what her query would be.

'Well, I don't ride, but could I possibly have a pony and trap to get about in? To go down to the village, for instance?'

'Have you ever driven a pony and trap?'

'N-no,' she admitted. 'But it can't be all that difficult, can it?'

He crossed his arms and gazed at her. 'Mm,' he said. 'I see your point, although I can't think that you'll want to go anywhere in particular; but yes, I realize that you'll be alone until your maid arrives.' He rubbed his hand across his chin. 'Of course you must have some kind of conveyance. Ask Mags if she'll ask Eddie to find something for you. Tell him not to spend the earth on a pony, and I'll look around for something suitable when I get back.'

'Thank you,' she said. 'That will be splendid.'

He continued to gaze at her. 'I'll expect more than just thank you,' he said softly. 'Don't think that I won't.'

She lowered her eyes and gave a small smile so that he would think she was still shy but pleased. But she wasn't; she was just exhausted by their night-time activities. She had also felt on tenterhooks since they came back and had plied him with questions on what improvements he would like to see when he came home.

'Home?' he'd queried. 'Does it feel like home to you already?'

She'd looked at him questioningly. 'Why yes, or at least almost. I love the house, and when we've bought furniture and curtains and such it will be just perfect. I'll ask my mother to order catalogues. Are you sure that you don't want to discuss the improvements with me? You'll need to feel comfortable, won't you, and I thought that perhaps you'd like the little room off the hall as your snug, or your office?' She was thinking of her father and the room that was his very own, a hallowed place only used by him unless he invited someone in.

'Mm,' he muttered. 'Yes, possibly. Leave that for now. Just have a coat of paint put on the walls, and I might bring a desk and chair from the London house.'

'Perhaps your parents might have a spare chair? It's rather comforting to have something familiar, isn't it?'

'I don't find it so,' he said coldly. 'I want nothing from my parents' house.'

And that bald statement gave her no feeling of well-being at all. She didn't know what answer to give, or even if he required one.

Early the next morning a hackney carriage came to take him to the railway station. He'd told her that there was a branch line in North Ferriby where he could catch the train instead of driving into Brough or Hull, which she was surprised to hear. Charles gave her a brief kiss on her cheek before climbing into the hackney and she stood on the steps and waved good-bye. She was not sure whether she felt relief at his departure, liberation at having the house to herself, or dismay that she would see no one until Dora arrived.

It was a bright morning, promising a good day of sunshine. The sky was clear and blue with only one or two drifting fluffy cumulus clouds, and she thought it was too nice to stay indoors. She picked up a note-book and stepped down on to the drive to begin a walk round the outside of the house. She stopped and looked through the windows of each room, assessing how they would look to strangers; dark, some of them, she thought, and in need of brightening up.

White paint was needed, or cream possibly, she decided, and she put her hand to her forehead to peer further in. A dark wall at the far side, perhaps;

teal, or a dark red, and the other walls lighter, or even papered. That would be nice, she mused. Our walls at home – my parents' home, I should say, she mumbled to herself – have only paint, but I have seen samples of lovely wallpaper, though I believe it is very expensive.

A big comfy sofa in the sitting room, she thought, the covers to coordinate with the colour on the walls. Sofa tables, one in the alcove with shelves above it for books; another side table, or possibly a cabinet against the wall to display precious china. Not that we have any yet. The piano – where should we put that? Not the hall where it is now. It looks as if it's just been put there to be out of the way. In the drawing room, I think, or possibly the sitting room, and then if— I mean *when* we have children they can learn to play.

She began to feel excited; she had never designed anything before, except for rearranging her own bedroom at home: having her bed moved so that she could see the shifting clouds in the sky above the rooftops when she woke up in the morning, and asking if a comfy chair might be put by her fire so that she could curl up and read.

She moved on towards what she thought of as the Little House and wondered why it had been built when the main house was so large. Not for servants, surely, when there were roomy attics on the top floor?

Perhaps one day I might live in it, she thought, when the son that Charles so longs for takes over the main house. Again she looked through the windows and thought how substantial it was, certainly not a little house. It was much larger than the terraced house her parents had; it looks very cosy, she thought, and I could feel very comfortable in there. Then she berated herself, for she was planning without Charles, when he might be the one to outlive her.

She continued on to the back of the Little House, which here was built mostly of brick. A boot scraper was attached to the wall by the kitchen door, and she looked through the glass in the top of the door to see a narrow passageway that still had rubber boots standing on tiered shelves and a mackintosh and cap hanging from a hook.

Uncle Nev's? she thought, and then dismissed the idea; the master of such a grand house would surely not use the back door.

She turned her attention to the courtyard with its brick-built sheds containing wheelbarrows, spades, axes, ropes and mechanical instruments for purposes that she couldn't even begin to guess at. At the back of one of the sheds was a battered trap or jaunting cart with wooden wheels. Behind these buildings was another courtyard with stabling, with two loose boxes and wet and mouldy straw heaped on the paving slabs; hanging on the walls were saddles, halters and bridles.

Beatrix went inside. Here, she thought, was a former lifetime; and feeling extremely nostalgic for someone she didn't know, and had never met, she lifted down from a shelf a battered top hat that must once have belonged to the famed Uncle Neville, blew the dust off it and placed it on her head.

'Hello, anybody there?'

A man's voice was calling and she went back outside, still wearing the top hat.

'Hello?' she called back and Edward Newby appeared round the corner. 'I'm here – exploring,' she added.

'Morning, miss. Begging your pardon – ma'am?'

She flushed. 'Yes,' she said. 'Charles and I were married last week.'

'My compliments,' he said, and touching his hand to his chest, gave a short bow of his head. 'I'm looking for '*maister*.' He grinned and tapped his forehead as if he were wearing a cap or tugging his forelock.

She tried to hide a smile, but didn't succeed. 'You won't find him, I'm afraid. He returned to London early this morning.'

'Oh!' He seemed surprised. 'Ma said you'd just arrived. I knocked on the front door but no one answered.'

'That's because there's no one in,' she said, and her voice cracked a little. 'There's no one here but me. Can I do anything for you?'

He stood looking at her, his forehead creased, and his grin disappeared. 'You're here on your own? No maid, no mother with you?'

'No,' she said bravely, and took off the hat and ran her fingers round the brim and put her chin in the air. 'Charles had to get back to London – to his office.' She blinked several times and went on tremulously, 'That's why I'm exploring.' She looked behind her towards the stable block and the sheds, the Little House and the main one, and suddenly realized the extent of it all.

'I hadn't realized there was so much.' Her voice trembled. 'I didn't see it all when I came last time. It's huge!'

137

He nodded and kept his gaze on her. 'It is. Would you like me to make you a pot of tea? I know where everything is.'

She blinked again, and this time her eyes were moist with tears and beginning to overflow. 'I can at least do that,' she said in a strangled voice. 'But won't you come in and have one with me? I have a few questions the *maister* told me to ask you.'

He nodded again. 'Yes, of course I will. I'll be glad to.'

CHAPTER SEVENTEEN

Edward filled the kettle and placed it on the range whilst Beatrix searched in the cupboard for crockery and then in the pantry for milk.

'Your mother has been very kind for thinking of us,' she said hesitantly. 'I'm not sure – well, I mean, I don't know what arrangements have been made, about expenditure for tea and milk, and – and coal and things,' she said in a rush. 'And her time, too, in looking after the house. Has Charles seen to that, do you know? He hasn't told me.'

He gave a shrug. 'Shouldn't think he's even thought of it,' he said candidly. 'But Ma won't mind. She'll consider it neighbourly. She was always in here looking after Uncle Nev. I expect he recompensed her.'

She nodded and gazed at the kettle, which was just starting to steam. 'She must tell me,' she said, and then confessed, 'I've never done anything like this before.'

'Been married, you mean?' He grinned.

She blushed scarlet, and he flinched, as if realizing that he had embarrassed her.

'I haven't been married before, no,' she murmured, 'but I meant I've never had a house to look after. My mother took care of household things and there seemed to be no time to prepare me. Everything happened so quickly.'

He got up, took a teapot out of the cupboard as Beatrix had forgotten, and began to make the tea. 'How long have you known Charles?'

'Since last August,' she said, and thought how time had sped by since then.

He stirred the tea and put the pot on the table and she watched entranced. She had never thought that a man would know how to do such a thing; certainly her father and her brother wouldn't.

'Love at first sight, was it?' he asked ironically, as if he knew that it wasn't.

Mindful of Charles's words on their wedding day, she nodded; but as she watched him stir and then pour the tea, a rich golden brown colour, much stronger than she would normally drink, she suddenly decided to tell him the truth. 'Arranged,' she murmured.

He looked up. 'I beg your pardon?'

She swallowed. 'It was an arranged marriage,' she confessed. 'My father knew Charles's father and they arranged it between them. I was persuaded to meet Charles, and did a couple of times, and – and we seemed to be – to be . . . compatible.'

He gazed at her, his lips parted, and then he pushed a cup and saucer towards her and remained silent.

'It seemed,' she went on, 'well, almost as if it were an ultimatum. And yet,' she frowned as she thought about it, 'it can't have been, because he was old enough to make up his own mind.'

'Not under any pressure from his father, as you were,' he muttered darkly.

'My father didn't force me to accept him,' she said in his defence, 'but . . . he said I'd never get a better offer.'

He picked up his cup, leaving the saucer on the table, and walked across to the window, where he stared out at the yard and shook his head. Then he turned and looked at her.

'There'll be a lot of money involved,' he said, his voice like flint. 'Property. Land. Investments. You'll be a very rich young wife.'

She gazed back at him and wondered why he seemed angry. She licked her lips. 'I don't know. My father said there was an estate.' She lifted her hands to encompass the house and gardens. 'This is it, I suppose?'

He gave a muffled, strangled grunt and came to sit down again.

'I asked Charles if I could have a pony and trap so that I could get about,' she said quietly, adding, 'I'll be here on my own until Dora – my maid – comes, and he said that I should ask you if you would arrange it, but not to pay a lot for the pony as he'd look around for a suitable one when he comes back. I noticed there was an old trap in one of the barns and wondered if I might use that, but if, as you intimate, there will be a lot of money, perhaps I could have a . . .' her voice trailed away, 'a better one.'

'Charles's got a good eye for horseflesh, has he?' Edward said cuttingly. 'Knows about horses and ponies? Probably seen them at the race track and knows the difference between those and the ones sent to the knacker's yard.'

She took a sip of tea; it was hot and strong and she rather liked it. 'Are you angry with Charles?' She looked at him over the top of her cup.

'Yes, I am!' he said frankly. 'He shouldn't have left you here on your own. He should at least have stayed another few days until you felt comfortable here. Surely there was nothing so urgent that he had to dash back to London?'

'I don't know; work, he said; at the bank.'

They finished their tea in silence. Then he spoke again. 'Right; I have an idea. My Aunt Hilda Parkin, my mother's sister, has a son. Aaron has just turned thirteen and is a very handy lad. They live in Hessle, which isn't far from here, not as the crow flies. He's left school and is looking for work. I could fetch him today and ask him to stay overnight and you could test him out; he can fetch coal in, chop wood and do anything you ask him to, even drive a pony and trap. If he suits you maybe you could offer him a job?'

There was a pause as Beatrix considered the suggestion. 'Where would he sleep?' she asked at last. 'I haven't thought through the question of staff. We had a boot boy at home – my parents' home, I mean; he came every Monday, Wednesday and Saturday, but went home to his mother's each night.'

He shook his head. 'No, that won't do. He'd have to live in.' He glanced round the kitchen. 'For now we'll make up a bed in here, and if you decide he'll do, we'll make him a room above one of the stables.'

'That's very kind of you,' she said gratefully, her tension easing. 'May I call you Eddie, as Charles does?'

He lifted his shoulders. 'If you like, but my name is Edward.'

'I'd like to call you Edward.' She smiled. It was a gentlemanly name, she thought, and I believe that is what he is.

'And what shall I call you?' He gave her a lopsided grin and raised his eyebrows, and she knew he was teasing, for she could only answer to Mrs Dawley.

He asked if she'd like to come with him to pick up Aaron and she said she would. She ran upstairs to collect a warm shawl and wondered if she was doing the right thing by travelling with a single man. She decided to take the risk of gaining a reputation so early in married life, and looked for the key to lock the front door.

'You don't need to bother with that round here,' he assured her. 'Nobody will come, though we could get you a dog if you like. Dogs make a racket when strangers turn up.'

'You said no one would come.' She turned to him as they pulled away.

'They won't. The house has been empty since Nev died. There's nothing worth taking in any case.'

She thought of the worn carpets and curtains that she and her mother had decided to give away, and realized that if anyone did break in and steal them they must be desperate, in which case they were welcome to them. Then she thought of her own belongings in her trunk upstairs and gave a deep sigh.

'What's up?' he asked as they turned off the long drive and headed down the hill in the direction of the estuary.

'Nothing.' She shook her head. 'I'm just coming to terms with having to adjust to a different life. For instance, at home in London I wouldn't be driving out with a man who wasn't a relation; not without a companion.'

His mouth turned up in a grin. 'Oh dear, oh dear! You mean that someone might see us, assume the worst and tell your husband?'

She glanced at him. 'Yes. And what will your aunt think when we turn up at her house?'

He laughed. 'When I tell her why we've come she'll be overjoyed to get Aaron from under her feet and earning a living. That's what she'll think; and what's more, she'll be thrilled that she's the first in the district to meet you, apart from my mother.'

She nodded, mollified, and added, 'And another thing: in London we would never go out leaving the door unlocked. That would just be asking to be burgled.'

He turned and looked at her and she saw how his blue eyes shone with merriment.

'Just as well you left, then.' He shook his head in mock horror. 'Who'd want to live like that?'

'I'm serious,' she said. 'I think that perhaps I might like to have a dog to protect me, and for company too.'

She exclaimed at seeing the river so close by, the tide high and lashing the banks. 'Do people fish here?' she asked.

'Yes,' he said. 'Dover sole, flat fish, some cod, eels.' They continued on towards Hessle and drew into the square. 'There are good shops here, too: butcher, grocer and so on. It would please them if you gave them your custom.'

'Oh, yes, I will. Perhaps I might visit the butcher now? Do you have time? I could buy some lamb chops for my supper. I'll have to open an account.'

'He'll be delighted.' His grin returned. 'Shall I take you in and introduce you?'

'Please,' she said. 'My mother always told Cook what she wanted, and Cook gave the butcher or grocer the order.'

'I expect you'll do that too,' he said kindly, 'once you have some staff. But the butcher will be most impressed if he thinks you've come in especially to meet him.'

He drew up outside the shop, where there were rabbits and chickens hanging on a rail above the window, still dressed in their fur and feathers. Beatrix carefully avoided looking at them as she followed Edward inside.

He was right. The butcher was very pleased to meet her; he gave her the lamb chops she asked for, telling her they were local, then insisted on wrapping up a parcel of pork sausages and a quantity of minced beef, telling her that they would all keep for a week in her cold larder, and finally saying that it was good to know that there would be a lady living in Mr Dawley's old house after so many years.

'Well now,' Edward remarked as they left the shop, 'we'd better visit the grocer and greengrocer now or we'll be accused of favouritism, as Mr Bull will certainly spread the word that he's been honoured by a visit. And you must be sure to share your custom with the Ferriby community too, and some of the other villages, Swanland and Brough; it will be expected of you. Most of the villages are self-sufficient, with their own butchers, bakers, dressmakers, shoemakers, carpenters – and undertakers,' he added with a grin. 'I might suggest you visit church as soon as possible, too.'

'I will,' she said nervously. 'But I'll wait until Dora can come with me.'

CHAPTER EIGHTEEN

Edward's young cousin Aaron was overjoyed at the prospect of working at 'Uncle Nev's house' and rushed to get his things together so that he could travel back with them. Beatrix decided that as everyone was still calling the house Uncle Nev's, she must do something about it before Charles returned; she was quite sure that he wouldn't like it.

As she sat waiting for Aaron with her hands folded in her lap, she told Mrs Parkin that the house that now belonged to her husband Charles Dawley would be known in future as Old Stone Hall.

'Old Stone Hall!' Mrs Parkin exclaimed. 'Is that because it's built of old stone?'

'Erm, yes! Indeed,' Beatrix said. 'Exactly.'

'Well, my word.' Mrs Parkin put her fists on her ample hips. 'I wonder what folks'll mek of that? It's allus been known as Nev Dawley's house!'

Edward rescued Beatrix from the need to answer. 'Neville died, Aunt Hilda,' he said. 'You knew that his next o' kin would be coming, and if the name of the house changes it has nothing to do with anyone else.'

'Oh, of course,' she flustered. 'I didn't mean owt, miss, erm, Mrs Dawley, 'course not, and I'm very grateful for 'opportunity for Aaron. He's a good lad, not a slacker, not by any means.'

Beatrix rose to her feet as Aaron came back into the room with his possessions in a canvas sack he had flung over his shoulder. 'Cheerio then, Ma. I'll mebbe see you at Martinmas, if not sooner; if I'm tekken on, that is.' He gave his mother a kiss.

'Aye, be a good lad,' she told him. 'And behave well in front o' your betters as you've allus been taught.'

It could have been a moving scene, Beatrix thought as she said goodbye to Mrs Parkin, but for the fact that Aaron was only going to the next village a couple of miles away; just a nice walk on a fine day. But on the other hand, she considered, as Edward handed her into the cart, it was probably a huge step for a schoolboy starting his very first job and hoping he would do well.

'Sorry,' Edward mouthed and gave her a grin as he tapped the pony gently on the back with his whip to move her on. Beatrix lowered her head and smiled.

'We sometimes say not quite all there in 'top attic,' he murmured so that Aaron didn't hear. 'Though we'd fight anybody outside the family who said it. She's kind-hearted, thinks the sun shines out of her family, and . . .'

'Doesn't like change,' she finished for him. 'I understand that.'

'And trustworthy,' he said. 'And that's worth a lot. She's also a widow, and has had a struggle to keep her head above water.'

Edward left them at Old Stone Hall with the promise that he would come back later to see if there was anything he could do. Aaron found a corner near the kitchen range where he dropped his sack and immediately went out to fill coal hods and buckets and chop wood. When he came back, he stood cap in hand and asked if he could take a look round the yard and the stables and have a tidy up.

'There's quite a lot o' mess out at 'back, dirty straw an' that, and it's best to be burnt so's not to attract vermin. Oh, and there's not much coal left; you'd be as well ordering another load from Jim Dring.'

Beatrix wrinkled her brow. 'Jim Dring? Is he . . .?'

'Aye, coalman,' he answered. 'He lives down in 'village. I can slip out later and ask him to deliver if you like. It's cheaper if you can afford a load.'

She didn't understand all he was saying, not yet tuned in to the local accent and missing words. 'Where is it?' she asked. 'The coal cellar? I haven't been through the whole house yet.'

'Oh, not a cellar, miss – missus, beggin' your pardon. It's a shed. Brick built so nice an' dry. It's out at 'back. There's still a bucket or two left and quite a lot o' sleck, so no hurry.' He pressed his lips together. 'Mebbe I'll go tomorrow and finish tidying up today.'

'That's a good idea,' she said. 'Probably best to make a plan for what needs doing, and then when you've decided on that come and discuss it with me.'

She saw how he straightened his shoulders and put his head up, full of pride that he had been given the opportunity to organize his own tasks and work on his own initiative rather than be given orders; and she too was pleased with herself for behaving like the mistress of the house.

Mags Newby came in at noon, driving the cart that Edward had used earlier and bearing a large pan of vegetables peeled and scraped and ready to cook. She tipped a hod of coal into the range to heat it up.

'I've tekken 'liberty of ordering a load o' coal, Mrs Dawley,' she told Beatrix. 'It'll come tomorrow morning, first thing.'

'Oh, thank you,' Beatrix said. 'I've been discussing it with your nephew Aaron; he said we'd need more. That will save him a journey.'

'I heard he'd come over. My sister'll be right pleased; he's a grand lad is Aaron. Allus willing.'

'Mrs Newby,' Beatrix said, 'could I ask you something? What is sleck?'

'Sleck?' Mags looked puzzled. 'Do you mean like in coal sleck?'

'Yes, I think so.'

'It's coal dust. It can put a fire out if you put too much on, but it can also keep a fire in all night. Why do you ask, miss?'

Beatrix gave an inward sigh. She obviously looked too young to be called *Mrs.* 'Aaron said there was quite a lot in the coal shed, and I didn't understand what he meant.'

Mags Newby suddenly smiled and Beatrix saw her son Edward in her. 'You'll soon pick up on local sayings, miss – Mrs Dawley,' she corrected herself. 'You'll have to forgive me – you look such a slip of a girl to be running a place like this, but I'm sure you'll manage. And do you think you could call me Mags, like everyone else does? And mebbe it would come easier if I called you ma'am, rather than Mrs Dawley? Your husband is still Master Charles to me as I've known him since he were a lad; except in company, o' course. I know my place.' She grinned.

Beatrix found herself choked up with emotion; everyone she had met had been friendly and welcoming, easing her into her position of mistress of this great house. Even Aaron was eager to please and she was sure that it wasn't only because she would be paying him a wage, which hadn't even been discussed yet. I might have to ask Edward about the appropriate amount, she thought, for I have no idea.

Mags put the kettle on the hob and when it had boiled she made tea, telling Beatrix that if she would make a list of her immediate needs she would help her out with them if she could. Paint for decorating the walls was the first thing Beatrix thought of, followed by old sheets for covering the floor. Mags said they should first take up the carpets and get rid of those that were past redemption, for she was sure that Master Charles would want new.

An hour later, Beatrix felt positive that Mags and her husband Luke would be able to organize everything that was needed, including asking Mrs Parkin to come in and scrub through the whole house, starting the next day.

'She'll be glad of 'work, ma'am,' Mags said. 'She's also 'best washerwoman *and* cook in 'district, though she's backward in coming forward, if you get my meaning.' Then, seeing Beatrix's look of bewilderment, added, 'Too fearful to ask.'

'I do understand,' Beatrix said. 'I feel that she might be useful, though, and I need all the help I can get, so perhaps you could tell her that I'd be very grateful if she could help out.'

Edward came back later, as he'd promised, and had a word with Aaron about clearing out one of the lofts above the stables. 'Choose the one you prefer,' he told him, 'bearing in mind there might be hosses coming, and we'll make it comfortable for you if Mrs Dawley finds you satisfactory. You could make a nice den up there,' he added, and the boy's eyes gleamed.

By the evening Beatrix was exhausted with planning and decision-making, and when she had eaten the lamb chops and a dish of vegetables, and Aaron had finished the sausages and mashed potatoes that his Aunt Mags cooked for him, he curled up in his corner by the range and fell asleep immediately, cheered by the thought that he would see his mother in the morning. Beatrix went upstairs to her bedroom, where there was a bright fire burning and the bedsheets had been turned back. She changed into her nightgown, but before getting into bed she looked out of the window and saw a full moon riding high in the sky.

She saw the stars, too, and was suddenly filled with a longing to see them, not through glass as she always had done in London, but from outside. Impulsively, she put on her dressing robe and then, thinking the night air might be cold, picked up a shawl from a chair and wrapped it about her shoulders.

The bedroom door creaked slightly as she opened it, and she paused, mindful of Aaron in the kitchen. But the kitchen was a long way down and she felt that he probably had a child's ability to fall asleep easily. She crept down the stairs and across the hall, turned the key in the door, and stepped outside.

She gazed up and was delighted that she had come. The sky was filled with stars, more than she had ever seen in her whole life, and the moon was shining above her. She was as thrilled as if she had captured the night, and sensing that it was a good omen for a new life she walked down the steps on to the drive and then the grass, and felt the dampness seeping through her slippers.

She lifted both arms and held the shawl above her head, swaying as if she was dancing; she swirled, her head tipped back to see the vault of never-ending sky in all its glory, and felt a dizzying freedom that surprised and enchanted her. She kicked off the slippers and danced barefoot across the grass, running and leaping, and turned to see the old house with its long windows reflecting the moonlight and lighting up the meadow down to the deep pool of darkness which was the wood that bordered the edge.

She was content after a day well spent, and feeling secure because she wasn't alone; there was someone else in the house, and even though Aaron was only a boy he was broad-shouldered and strong and would protect her. Not that she was afraid, even out here alone under the stars, and she knew now with complete surety and confidence what changes she would put in hand to make this house her own.

She thought of Edward saying that Charles shouldn't have left her alone, and wondered, not for the first time, why he had gone back to London so quickly. What was so urgent that he couldn't wait a day or two longer and share this experience with her? But if I'm truthful, she thought, as she made her way inside, locked the door and climbed the stairs, I'm quite pleased that he's not here. She gave a soft chuckle. I am at least assured of a good night's sleep.

She snuggled down between the sheets and felt the warmth of the stone hot water bottle against her cold toes. She could relax now, undisturbed, whilst she thought of her wedding day and the short time she had spent in the Lake District. She hadn't known how lovely it would be; and neither, she thought as she drifted into sleep, did I ever imagine that I would one day become mistress of such a lovely house as Old Stone Hall.

Nor did it cross her mind that her barefoot dancing had been watched by another. Edward Newby, reviving the nightly patrol he had begun during his frail old friend Uncle Nev's final illness to check that the old man and his nurse were safe, had come to be sure the young mistress and his cousin were locked up for the night, and instead saw a slender and graceful young woman dancing on the grass beneath the silver moonlight.

He stood, mesmerized and unseen in the shadow of trees and bushes, his arms folded across his chest, his lips parted, hardly daring to breathe but his heart beating fast, as this loveliest of young women, like an ethereal will-o-the-wisp, performed her moonlit dance.

CHAPTER NINETEEN

Charles stepped off the London train and hurried towards the entrance, hoping to beat the other passengers out of the station and catch a hackney. He paused momentarily to pick up some flowers from the usual seller and thrust coins into her hand, and then ran to the cab stand.

He gave the driver instructions and leaned back against the seat, blowing out a breath. How long can I last in this charade, he wondered? In some aspects, the double life he was leading was stimulating and exciting, but it was also tiring. Fortunately Beatrix wasn't demanding, unlike Maria.

Would she be home? He hadn't written to say when he would be back, but had sent her a picture postcard of the Lake District and the mountains, knowing that she wouldn't know it wasn't Scotland and writing on it *Missing you!*

The driver dropped him two streets away, as instructed. It didn't do to advertise that you could afford to hire a carriage and let everyone see where you lived, even though it was at the better end of the narrow street. When he walked briskly towards his house with his small amount of luggage and the flowers clutched in his other hand, he saw lamplight shining through the curtains of the front window.

Ah, he breathed. Let's hope she has had a good time and spent plenty of money, and doesn't ask too many questions. To save searching for his key, he rapped firmly on the door.

'Who is it?' he heard her shout, and he smiled. She had strict instructions never to open the door.

'Buy a bunch o' flowers, lady,' he called back in what he hoped would pass for a woman's high-pitched voice. 'I ain't had nuffing to eat today!'

'Go away, villain. I ain't got anyfing you'd want.'

He put his mouth near the door. 'You'd be surprised, lady,' he said gruffly. 'Just open the door and let me show you.'

He heard the rattle of the bolt and chain and the door opened a crack, enough to show one dark eye shining back at him.

'Pity a poor old woman,' he went on. 'Got one last bunch o' flowers, kept especially for you, missus.'

'Don't call me missus,' she screamed.

'Open the damned door then,' he said in his normal voice, tiring of the game. 'I'm ready for a decent glass of wine.' He sniffed. 'And you're cooking; what is it?'

The smell of something fishy – prawns, salmon, maybe mussels, something hot, paprika – ah, *paella*, came drifting from the door. 'You're cooking paella! Let me in before I break the door down.'

'All right, all right! I open it.'

He heard her removing the chain and turning the doorknob and there she stood with a knife in her hand.

'For God's sake, Maria, put that down!'

'It might not be you,' she said, holding the knife in the air. 'Might be someone sound like you.'

He gave a deep, exasperated sigh. 'Who would know what lengths I go to to persuade you it's me!' He took hold of the wrist which held the knife and squeezed; she gave a yelp and opened her hand. 'I've told you before, you lift your knee or foot and aim where it hurts the most. Now come here.'

He dropped his bag, threw the flowers on the table and hugged her, nuzzling into her neck.

She put her nose to his face, sniffing him as a dog might. 'Hmm, you smell nice. You pig, you 'ave been with a woman.'

He nibbled her ear. 'Those Scottish women, they wouldn't leave me alone, dozens of them. It's the whisky you can smell. They made me bathe in it.'

She widened her eyes, unsure whether to believe him or not.

'How was Paris?' he asked, sitting down on a small sofa and pulling her on to his knee. 'Did you meet any handsome Frenchmen?'

'No!' she pouted. 'They not interested in Spanish girls. Only in fair *Eenglish* ones. But, I tell Bianca, Charles will kill me if I have affair with these foreigners, so I restrain myself. *Restrain*, that is a good word, yes?'

He nodded. 'Yes, a very good word.' He put his head back, tiredness suddenly enveloping him. 'Come on. I'll wash and change out of these travelling clothes and we can eat and then go to bed. I'm really tired. Heavens, Maria,' he said as she raised herself off his knee. 'You've eaten well.' He smiled. 'Lots of curves.'

157

She gave a twirl and rolled her hips. 'I say to Bianca, my man Charles he likes me like this. He don't like skinny women.'

He squeezed the ample flesh around her waist. 'I do like skinny women,' he said. 'I like most women.' He ran his hands up her blouse to her breasts. 'But I like plump ones best.' He picked up the bag that he'd dropped on the floor. 'I'll just take this up. Will dinner be long?'

'Five minutes only.' She waved a spoon at him. 'I know when you come, you see, so that dinner is ready.'

'How did you know?' He frowned. 'I didn't know myself until this morning.'

'I go to Euston railway station and ask what time the Scotoland train come and so I cook every night at the same time.' She patted her stomach. 'That is why I get fat.'

He was touched that she would go to such lengths, but drew in a breath and said, 'No point in doing that, Maria; there are so many changes at difference places and on different days.'

'But I get it right, yes?'

'Indeed you did, clever girl,' he agreed, deciding to leave the news that he would be going again for some other time.

He was worried, though, that she might find out about the wedding from someone else, particularly if she should meet such a person as the odious Roger Pearson, who, although he hadn't been invited to the ceremony, would have heard about it and would relish telling Maria. Pearson would enjoy her humiliation and Charles didn't want that.

'I have something to tell you,' he said on the second evening.

'Something good?'

'I don't think you will like it, but it had to be.'

'What?' Her eyes creased and he saw the deepening lines on her cheeks. 'You going to leave me?'

'*No!* Never.' He put his arms round her. 'Never ever! But do you remember that I told you that I had to get married to claim my inheritance?'

She nodded and whispered, '*Sì.*'

'Well, before I went to Scotland,' he lied, 'I married a young woman and took her to the other house.'

Her mouth dropped open. 'She is young? Younger than me?'

'Yes. She has to be young to be able to have children.'

Her eyes widened. 'You sleep with her already?'

'Of course. How else will she give birth?' He smiled and shrugged. 'It means nothing, Maria. You know how it is.'

She nodded. 'I know. Poor girl,' she murmured. 'It is not nice to know she isn't loved by her 'usband, but only that her body is useful to him. I know this.'

He took in a breath. Put so bluntly by his mistress, who herself had escaped from a brutal husband, it unnerved him. 'I'm not unkind to her,' he explained in mitigation. 'She knows it was arranged. She has a nice house to live in; she will have money to spend.'

'There are no shops near that 'ouse,' she frowned. 'No people. What will she spend money on? Does she 'ave friends there?'

He hadn't really thought about that. He had only wanted to escape as fast as he could and get back to

159

London. He had behaved impeccably towards Beatrix, he thought. He had treated her well, told her she could arrange the house as she wanted it; how many husbands would do that? All she had to do was produce a son to make them even richer than they were now. Surely, any wife would be happy with that.

CHAPTER TWENTY

The following morning Beatrix heard the heavy rumble of the coal cart and through the kitchen window saw Aaron and the coal man leading the horses to the coal house at the back. She went out and asked the man to set up an account and bring a regular order.

Half an hour later, she heard the crunch of boots on the gravel and saw the postman with a rucksack on his back emptying the contents of it into Aaron's hands. When he came in with them she saw that as well as letters the post had brought the catalogues that her mother had ordered for her. Oh, goodie, she thought excitedly. I can look at them after breakfast, which it seems that I shall have to cook for myself as Mrs Newby hasn't yet appeared.

'Aaron,' she said, 'have you had breakfast?'

'Aye, I have, ma'am,' he said. 'I took 'liberty of cooking 'rest of 'sausages and had bubble an' squeak wi 'taties and 'leftovers.'

'Sorry? You had what?'

'Bubble an' squeak, ma'am. And a couple o' eggs as well. And bread,' he added.

Still unsure what he'd eaten, she just nodded and said, 'Good, that's all right then. Don't want you going hungry. Do you have any idea what time your mother will get here?'

'About eight, I expect. She'll want to get 'other bairns off to school first,' he said.

'Other bairns? Do you mean children? Have you got sisters and brothers?'

'Onny three now,' he told her. 'Five, seven and nine they are. Two lads and Alice, she's the one who's five. My da died a year after Alice was born so there won't be any more now. We had our Albert but he died when he was eight. I expect Ma will be pleased there won't be any more,' he said disarmingly. 'I don't mean about me da,' he added quickly. 'I mean that there are too many mouths to feed already.'

'I know what you mean, Aaron,' she said, wondering how on earth his mother had managed to feed and clothe four children without a husband to provide for them.

At that moment the woman herself opened the door and came in huffing and puffing and apologizing for being late. It was ten minutes past eight.

'I like to be sure 'bairns have a good breakfast afore they leave for school, ma'am. It's a long day otherwise.'

'Of course,' Beatrix said. 'At the moment it doesn't matter too much what time you start; we can make a timetable to suit us both once we're organized.' She smiled. 'Aaron has cooked his own breakfast; you've brought him up to be useful, Mrs Parkin.'

Mrs Parkin nodded. 'Oh aye, he's a good lad.' She turned to him. 'But don't hang about. I expect you've plenty to do.'

'Oh, I have,' he answered and touched his forehead to Beatrix before putting on his cap. 'I'm on 'second part of 'plan.'

Beatrix went into the long cool larder and brought out eggs, as she didn't really know what else to cook for her breakfast. She looked about for a frying pan. Mrs Parkin saw her dilemma and asked whether she would like her to cook an omelette for her.

'I would, please,' Beatrix said. 'I'm afraid I'm not very useful at cooking.'

Mrs Parkin washed and dried her hands and put on an apron that she'd brought with her. 'I don't suppose you've had much practice, have you, ma'am? If you'd like to set yourself a place, cos I don't know where anything's kept in this house, I'll cook you an omelette if there's owt to put in it, or scrambled eggs if there isn't.'

There wasn't anything to put in it, not even a crumb of cheese, but there was milk, come from Beatrix knew not where, and Mrs Parkin produced the best scrambled eggs that she had ever tasted.

Mags came in as she washed up her own and Aaron's crockery, and when she had finished she followed the two women upstairs. She found them in one of the topmost bedrooms discussing what to do first.

They both turned when she came into the room. 'We were just saying, ma'am, that we'll tek 'curtains down on these windows. They won't wash; they're so old that they'll fall apart if they meet water.' Beatrix agreed with them, and within minutes a choking dust cloud filled the air.

'I was allus on at Uncle Nev to fetch them down,' Mags croaked. 'But he never would. Allus said somebody else could do it one day.' She sneezed. 'I just knew it would be me.'

'I'm going to get Aaron,' Beatrix said. 'He's young enough to climb up and take the rest down and he can make a bonfire with them.' She turned to go out of the door. 'He can take the carpets up too. They're filthy.'

By mid-afternoon, two of the top floor rooms were emptied, the windows and floors washed and fires burning in both grates. Beatrix was highly pleased and stood by each door in turn with her arms folded, admiring the effort that had been made.

'I'll make some tea,' she said. 'You deserve it.' She could smell the bonfire out at the back. Aaron had got quite a blaze going.

Hilda wiped a hand across her nose, leaving a dusty smear across her face. 'Just a minute, miss – ma'am.' She had glanced out of the window. 'Looks as if you've got company.'

Beatrix crossed to the window and looked down to the drive. A carriage had pulled up and as she watched the driver jumped down to open the door. To her amazement her father stepped out and put his hand inside to help her mother down.

'Papa!' she shrieked. 'Mama – oh, how wonderful! And Dora!' She dashed out of the door and flew down the stairs.

The two women looked at each other. 'Well, it was a nice thought,' Mags said, 'but I reckon we'd better mek our own tea. And for everybody else as well.' Then they took in each other's dirty faces and hands and both began to laugh.

*

164

Her father caught Beatrix as she ran down the front steps. 'Steady there,' he said. 'Where's the fire?'

'Out at the back,' Beatrix said, misunderstanding his attempt at humour. She gave him a hug that startled him. 'It's so good to see you. And Mama,' she said, kissing her mother on the cheek. 'How did you know we'd be here?' She didn't wait for an answer, but added, 'And, Dora, I'm so glad to have you back.'

'We took a chance and came uninvited,' her mother said. 'Your father was eager to come and look at the house. But whatever have you been doing? You've got a dirty face!'

Beatrix rubbed her cheek with her fingers. 'We've been taking curtains down and lifting carpets up! Well, I haven't,' she laughed. 'But Aaron and his mother and Mags have. I was just going to make them some tea, so come along in, and we'll all have some. Papa, what do you think?' She saw her father's eyes travelling across the house's façade, and Dora too was staring as if she couldn't believe what she was seeing.

'Very nice,' her father said steadily. 'It's much larger than I expected.'

She led them into the house. 'We'll have to go into the kitchen,' she told them. 'There's nowhere else ready yet. Mags – that is, Mrs Newby – and Mrs Parkin will be making tea now, I expect.'

'I remember Mrs Newby from my previous visit,' Mrs Fawcett told her husband. 'She made us a pan of delicious soup.'

'She did,' Beatrix agreed. 'Mrs Parkin is her sister, and Aaron is Mrs Parkin's son. He's very useful. He's living in with me whilst Charles is away.'

Her mother's eyes opened wide and her father exclaimed, 'What! Why, where is Charles?'

'In London,' Beatrix told them awkwardly, not wanting them to be annoyed or find fault with him. 'He had warned me that he would have to go back from time to time.'

'But surely not yet!' her mother murmured. 'You've barely been married a week!'

'I know,' Beatrix said, embarrassed. 'We only had a few days in the Lake District before we came back here, and – and then Charles had to leave almost immediately. I didn't mind,' she added hurriedly, opening the door to the kitchen. 'I have great plans for the house and I've been able to think about it and start now that Mrs Parkin and Mags have come, but it was decided that Aaron should stay with me, rather than go home every night. He's only a boy,' she added, in case they were imagining a grown man.

She introduced Dora to Mags and Mrs Parkin, who had scrubbed their hands and faces and were presiding over kettle and teapot. 'Dora is staying on,' she explained to them, 'so you'll be seeing a lot more of her. She'll be my right hand,' she said happily. 'You've no idea how pleased I am to see you here, Dora.'

Dora dipped her knee. 'Thank you, ma'am,' she said. 'I'm pleased to be here.'

They drank tea, and Beatrix wondered how she was going to give her parents and Dora a meal when there was no food in the house. She hadn't expected visitors, least of all her parents; it was so unlike them. She knew that Mags had come in the cart and drew her to one side. 'Mags,' she whispered, 'could I ask you a favour?

Could you drive to Hessle and buy some provisions so that I can make my parents something to eat?'

'You're going to cook, are you, ma'am?' Mags gazed at her quizzically.

'Well, I need to learn sooner or later.' Beatrix sighed ruefully. 'I have never felt so useless.'

'Not your fault, I suppose,' Mags nodded, 'but I suggest that now isn't a good time to begin. I'll nip down 'hill and see if anybody's caught owt off 'riverbank; and then *I'll* cook it. We can't go wasting good food.' She took off her apron. 'I'll go and tidy meself up and get off.'

Dora had overheard some of the conversation. 'Could I come with you, Mrs Newby?' she whispered. 'I need to know where the shops are, and I know how to cook a simple meal, ma'am,' she added to Beatrix.

Beatrix felt the burden lift from her; of course, Dora would have been taught by her mother. Then she gave a silent chuckle. If the girl thought she was going to find a street full of food shops, she was going to be disappointed. She was not in London now.

CHAPTER TWENTY-ONE

Mags and Dora had a useful conversation as they drove down to the riverbank, where Mags found someone she knew who was packing up after a good day's fishing and bought some of the flounders he had caught.

She showed Dora the village, the small railway station where sometimes the main line trains stopped, and told her that there was another station in Brough not far away where the trains did stop, but that it was a good walk from there to North Ferriby village.

She also told her that Mrs Dawley would need a housekeeper, as Mags herself couldn't come full time.

'I haven't minded helping out,' she confided in Dora, 'and I'll stop till she finds someone. I couldn't think of leaving her to manage on her own when she didn't know anybody or anything about running a house. But I reckon she'll manage very well once she's found some domestics. She's got some grand ideas about renovations, or so my son Edward says.'

She clicked her tongue to urge the pony onwards and dropped her voice, even though they were the only ones on the road. 'I can't understand why Master Charles shot off to London so quick, and them onny just married. Not right,' she said disapprovingly. 'Not right at all.'

Dora made appropriate muted sounds but didn't comment; she never would have done, but during her recent training she had learned how quickly just a word or two of inappropriate agreement or disagreement could easily grow into something bigger amongst loose tongues.

In any case, she thought, as they trotted on, she had her own views on Charles Dawley. She hadn't liked him from the start, finding him arrogant and haughty. He rarely noticed her, and she conjectured that he would never perceive anyone below stairs as being worthy of his consideration.

Mags Newby was still on the same subject. 'I remember him when he was onny a lad,' she said. 'If he'd been my boy he'd have had 'sharp end of my tongue many a time. He thought he knew more about everything than anyone else, but our Edward allus put him right, even though he was younger than Charles.' She laughed. 'He never would be put upon, and many was the time he would tell him he was wrong and prove it. He was nivver scared of him.'

'What does he do?' Dora asked, changing the subject. 'Your son Edward?'

'He's a farmer. Looks after our home farm. It was part of Uncle Nev's estate originally – Mr Neville Dawley, I mean to say. Edward has been to farming college; aye, he's right clever is our Edward,' she said proudly. 'Uncle Nev saw that when he was young and encouraged him to get a better education than he might have done.'

'That was thoughtful of him,' Dora said. 'There aren't many gentlemen who would do that.'

'Aye, well, he'd known us all a long time. He was good friends with my in-laws, like family they were, and then when my husband Luke had his . . .' she paused, as if she were saying too much, then went on, 'his accident and couldn't work, Nev couldn't do enough for us. Some estate owners might have turned us off 'farm but Uncle Nev said that he'd see that 'family were all right. Edward was onny a lad at 'time and wanted to be a farmer, but he was far too young, so Nev brought in a foreman and he stayed on for years! Stopped on even when Edward went to college, until he came back and was able to tek over.'

She took a breath and finished her long story. 'Luke was trampled on by a herd of cattle, you see. Lost 'use of his legs. He can walk, but not well, and he still helps out on 'farm when he can and looks after account books an' that. He's not a shirker, oh dear no.'

They turned on to the long drive leading to the house. The sun was dipping and making long shadows across the track; flocks of birds made patterns in the sky as they headed for their nesting sites. Dora heard the squawks of gulls and thought how they got everywhere; she often saw them by the Thames, but now she also heard the honking cry of geese as a wedge flew over in V formation, heading downriver; clouds of bats were swooping near the house.

Mags pointed above her head. 'Greylags, look,' she said. 'And some mallard.'

'And bats. I don't care for them much,' Dora said. 'Scary.'

170

'Won't hurt you. They all have a place in 'scheme of things.' Mags pulled up close to the back door, and as Dora jumped down from the cart she thought that tomorrow she would have a good look round the outside of the house. There was such a lot of it, far more than she had envisaged, and she wondered how Mrs Dawley would manage it all.

She wouldn't have much help from her husband, that was for sure. Dora couldn't envisage that he would be a man who would like getting his hands dirty; but then, he didn't need to. He obviously had plenty of money to pay someone else to do so. Besides which, she speculated, he has other fish to fry. She had seen that for herself. She had known that he wouldn't be here and was glad of it, coming as she did for the first time with Mrs Dawley's parents. So why had he married Beatrix Fawcett, one of the sweetest young women she had ever met and deserving of someone far better than him? What had been the advantage?

I expect I'll find out at some time, but I won't like it. Whatever the reason.

She asked to be excused whilst she took her trunk upstairs to the room she had been allotted, but Beatrix insisted that Aaron would carry it and to Dora's surprise Mr Fawcett offered to help him and carried some of the lighter things. Dora had brought all of her belongings, knowing that she would be staying a long time with only the occasional journey home.

Her room was on an upper floor but not in the attic as she had imagined; not that she would have minded, she thought, as the view over the meadowland and down to the estuary was superb. But perhaps she had

171

been given this one as it had already been cleaned and there was a fire burning, though it can't have been prepared for me, she supposed, as I wasn't expected yet.

Beatrix's father was prowling about, opening and closing doors to look into various rooms, and when he came down from the attic he saw Dora through her doorway.

'Well, this is a how-de-do, don't you think, miss?' he commented, obviously forgetting what her role was. 'However will Beatrix manage all of this?'

She came to the door. 'It is very large,' she agreed. 'Mrs Dawley will need a great deal of help to manage it all; a housekeeper and maids for a start.'

He seemed to puzzle over the name *Mrs Dawley*, but then his face cleared. 'Ah, yes, yes indeed. And are you here to help her? What will you be doing – or are you a friend?'

Dora hesitated, and then answered, 'I'll be Mrs Dawley's personal maid, sir. I will do whatever she wants me to do.'

'Good,' he exclaimed. 'I'm very pleased to hear it. She's going to need someone.' He turned towards the stairs. 'Can't imagine why her husband had to dash away to London. Bank directors were never so busy in my day that they couldn't take time off whenever they wanted to.'

Dora's eyes followed him as he went down. Had he forgotten that she had been a maid in his house? When they journeyed here he hadn't questioned his wife as to why she was travelling with them. She smiled. He had always been absent-minded, often calling her by different names, and she had answered to them all.

She sat on the bed and looked about her and thought of his comment about Charles Dawley. Charles certainly hadn't had bank business on his mind when she had last seen him.

Mid-afternoon on the day before they were due to catch the train from London to Yorkshire and after she had finished her chores and her packing, she had asked Mrs Fawcett if she could visit her mother to say goodbye as she didn't know when she might see her again. Beatrix's mother said that she was sure that she would be given time off at least once a year, but of course she must go whilst she could.

'Wear something nice and appropriate so that your mother might see how you will look in your new role,' she suggested. 'She will be pleased.'

'Thank you, ma'am,' Dora had said, but had had reservations about visiting her family's district in her new finery. But Mrs Fawcett didn't know that and so she dressed in her navy dress and coat, with a rose-coloured scarf at her neck and a navy hat trimmed with grosgrain, and carried downstairs a grey cloak which she put over the banister rail whilst she went to show Mrs Fawcett how she looked in her new attire.

Mrs Fawcett murmured her approval – well, she would, as she had been with Dora to choose it – and then off Dora went to call on her mother.

She had taken a different route from her usual one to avoid the Rookeries, which could be safely walked through during the light of day, providing you knew where you were going and didn't lose your way and find yourself in a court from which there was no exit;

but never ever, without fear for your life, during the hours of darkness.

Dora's family had lived all her life within walking distance of the Rookeries, an area packed with sooty courts in undrained narrow streets where the poorest, meanest of houses, many without doors that had been burnt for firewood, or with broken windows patched with cardboard or rags to keep out the cold and rain, were rented to those who could afford nothing else. Barefoot children sat unclad on the coldest of days in grimy doorways that gave little shelter; and criminals, drunkards, prostitutes, thieves and murderers shared this place with innocents and called it home.

The area had seen much in centuries past, first the plague and then the Great Fire which had partially destroyed it; every schoolchild, including Dora, had known of its history. Now it was promised that clearance would begin, and it had, but slowly, for first a place must be found to house the vagrants and those without hope.

Ten minutes' walk away and still within sight of St Giles church, which Beatrix had considered for her marriage vows, were houses of working people who were comfortably off, though not rich: senior clerks and grocers, managers of businesses not necessarily their own, dressmakers and chemists, who kept their doors and windows locked and often kept a dog.

It was on the corner of one of these streets that Dora had paused by a grocer's shop window and, whilst seemingly viewing items on display, buttoned up her cape to hide her coat and dress and pulled her hat down over her eyes. Several people passed as she did so, and when they were in front of her she stepped out to turn the corner.

Several individuals had sloped off into adjoining streets but she kept walking straight on and almost caught up with a couple she had noticed previously. She slowed her footsteps rather than overtake them and kept her head lowered. They turned a corner and so did she.

Most of the houses along here were rather nice, she thought; very respectable, with clean lace curtains covering the whole of the windows, shiny front doors and locks on the gates of the minuscule front gardens. The kind of house she wouldn't mind living in herself, if ever her ship came in.

Her attention was caught by the couple in front. Both slightly the worse for drink, she mused as she watched them swaying from side to side, the woman giggling and pushing the man away as he leaned towards her to kiss her and grab her skirts.

'No. No, you must wait,' she heard her say. 'It is not far. Wait until we get 'ome.'

She was foreign by the sound of her protests, but he appeared to be English, with fair hair beneath his lopsided top hat.

'Come on, come on.' His words were slurred and his hands reached for his companion. 'Can't wait.'

Dora was about to cross the street to avoid them when the woman grabbed the man and pulled him across to the other side. She was a big woman, with a mass of dark hair which was pinned with some kind of exotic flower.

''Ere we are,' she said. 'Now we are 'ome; you see I tell you that it is not far.' She opened the small gate, which apparently wasn't locked, and pushed him towards the door, where he staggered and made another grab for her. It was then that Dora had seen his face, as he'd turned towards the woman, and she was wholly convinced that it was Charles Dawley.

CHAPTER TWENTY-TWO

Before her parents went home, Beatrix and her mother went through the catalogues of furnishings: curtains, carpets, furniture, and another catalogue which was advertising the latest accoutrements in kitchenware. In this was a column headed *Situations Wanted and Required*, and Beatrix eagerly scanned the pages before passing it to Dora.

'Here's an interesting one, ma'am.' Dora began to read: 'Yorkshire-born housekeeper with many years' experience of working in London, wants to come home!'

'Oh!' Dora looked up and saw Beatrix's bright expression. 'Does she give more detail?'

'Yes. Very well experienced, I'd say, ma'am. She's forty and has worked in only two situations in twenty years, and she says her present employers who are retiring abroad will give her an excellent reference.'

'Why don't you write to her, Beatrix?' her mother suggested, looking up from another catalogue, 'and I could give her an initial interview in London.'

'Yes!' Beatrix agreed. 'Please. You could tell her what I require, and I expect she'll have to give notice first in any case.'

'Not if her employers are moving abroad,' her mother said. 'They will probably release her as soon as she gets another position, so let's hope she's suitable. Good. Things are moving on.'

And indeed they were, for the day after her parents left a wagon pulled by two Shires arrived with two men on board and a load of Yorkshire stone which they stacked neatly at the side of the drive. They asked if they could tether the Shires on the grass and then took out their spades and picks and began to dig up the drive in front of the house steps.

'How are they getting on?' Edward asked when he came by mid-morning and saw Beatrix issuing instructions to the men. An area of grass as well as the stony drive had been dug up and piled next to the mountain of stone slabs.

'Very well,' she told him, 'but this isn't going to be big enough. It needs to be twice the size to make a decent terrace.'

'Ah! A terrace, is it?' His lips lifted into a grin.

'Yes. It has to be large enough to take a small fountain in the centre and to have tables and chairs to sit at when the weather is warm.'

His grin widened. 'This is Yorkshire, ma'am,' he said. 'And we're near the Humber. Can't say it's ever warm enough to sit out.'

'Oh, it will be,' she responded gaily. 'You've probably been too busy to notice.'

'I notice at harvest time,' he laughed. 'That's when we want it to be hot!'

'Well, there you are then! What did I say?'

'And where's the water coming from for your fountain?' he asked.

She was stumped by that. 'Ah! Mm! I don't know.' She paused to think. 'I'll have to find someone who knows about these things. I should have asked my father; he might have known.'

Edward had briefly met her father whilst her parents were staying and was quite convinced that Mr Fawcett wouldn't have the slightest idea of how water might be brought into a garden except by turning on a tap. He couldn't help a big smile crossing his face and then he laughed out loud as she pressed her lips together and scowled at him.

'You know, don't you?' she demanded.

'Yes,' he spluttered. 'Yes, I do. Or at least I know someone who does.'

He couldn't explain it; couldn't possibly articulate why he had the absurd manic desire to pick her up as she scowled at him and swing her round and round until he made her laugh. He felt it in his chest, in his throat, in his very breath. But he only gazed at her, his heart pounding, until at last she said, 'What!'

He swallowed. 'What?'

'I asked first! The water! How do we get it to the fountain?'

He relaxed. 'Oh, that! I'll ask *my* father. He'll know. There are deep wells sunk throughout the grounds that store water in case of drought. I'll ask him if there's one here at the front.'

A superior smile slid across her face. 'You see! I knew there'd be a solution.'

He nodded. 'You were perfectly right.' He gave a sweeping bow. 'I bow to your superior intellect, ma'am.'

Beatrix narrowed her eyes. She was enjoying this game. 'Quite right!' she said haughtily. Then she laughed too. 'One to me then. Will you come in and have a cup of tea? I need to ask you something.'

Anything, he thought as he bent over the kitchen table and looked at a sketch she had made, her head next to his. Ask me anything and it will be done. I'm on dangerous ground here; if Charles should come in right now I'd be banned from the house and her presence. But where on earth is he? Why isn't he here discussing the things she wants? Or perhaps I can guess.

They'd debated the fountain and how big the terrace would be and now they were discussing the woodland at the bottom of the meadow.

'This morning when I woke – which was quite early, about six o'clock. I never woke at that time in London, but I'm sleeping so well here – I looked out of the window and saw that the sun was shining on the tree tops and making a golden trail across the middle of the wood. Does that sound silly?'

He gazed at her and shook his head. He hadn't really been giving his full attention to what she was saying, only watching the way her lips moved and how her eyebrows rose when she was expressing something which pleased her, and how her eyes sparkled with enthusiasm, and committing all these images to his memory.

'And I wondered,' she continued, 'if – well,' she put her head to one side, 'how would it look if we thinned out the trees down the middle and made a walkway through so that we could see the estuary properly from the house?'

He nodded. 'You could do that; but then you wouldn't see the golden trail of the sun in the morning if the trees were cut down.'

'That's true,' she said thoughtfully.

'But some of the trees could be thinned out to make a woodland path to walk down, and other tree branches trained to meet and make a canopy. And you could plant climbers, like wisteria or honeysuckle, or even roses if there's enough light. The woodland does need some work,' he added. 'It's been neglected for a number of years. But you'll need a landscape gardener for that, or someone who understands trees and their habitat. They'd give advice on what will work in this location. There's ash growing in there, and beech, and an understorey of hazel and holly and probably wild cherry too, so you need someone who knows what they're doing.'

'Yes, of course. I'm trying to run before I can walk, I suppose,' she said wistfully. 'It's so lovely just as it is, but it needs something more to make it perfect.' She sighed. 'Perhaps I should concentrate on the house first. The woodland can wait.'

He picked up his battered old hat. 'No, I don't think so. We'll find somebody for your woodland and they can get on with the plans and the pruning whilst you're organizing the house. You'll want it looking its best when folks start sending out their calling cards.'

She stared at him. 'Do you think that people will start to call?'

'Sure to,' he answered. 'I get asked all the time if I've met the new owners.'

'Really? But I can't invite anyone back until we have furniture to sit on.'

'But there's nothing to stop you visiting, is there? You have your maid now. She can go with you, can't she? Is that the done thing?' He grinned teasingly, but he saw that she was perfectly serious.

'Dora,' she said softly. 'Yes, that will be acceptable, I think, as I haven't a husband at home.'

Charles arrived early evening two days later and she greeted him enthusiastically, even though she had seen him frown as he stepped down from the carriage and saw that the grass and some of the drive had been dug up.

'What's going on here?' he demanded as Beatrix ran down the steps to greet him.

'This is to be our new terrace,' she enthused. 'These young men are doing such a good job of work.'

The men, who were working late, touched their foreheads to him.

'Whose idea was this?' he asked tersely.

She clasped her hands together. 'Why – mine, Charles! Who else? I thought – I thought it would enhance the front of the house and in the summer we could sit out and – and take tea.' She bit her bottom lip. 'Don't you like the idea?'

He took a moment as he gazed at the area that had been staked out on the grass and some of the stone that had already been laid, then turned to her and taking her by the elbow led her up the steps.

'Yes,' he said. 'It's a good idea.' He looked down at her, and patted her arm. 'But another time, if you want to start a big project you must discuss it with me first.'

'I would have done,' she said, almost tearful with relief, 'and I would have written, but I didn't know where to find you. They only started two days ago, and have worked so well. It should be finished in a week.'

'Where did you find these men?' He frowned. 'Are they local?'

She swallowed and told a partial lie. 'I think so. Luke Newby came to see me to ask if there was anything he could help with and I mentioned this; I'd been thinking about it for a few days. I'd seen a picture in a magazine that I'd been looking through with my mother.' She led him through into the kitchen, where most activities still continued. 'But of course you don't know – my parents came, and brought Dora. You remember Dora, don't you?' she prattled on, not sure why she was nervous. 'My father was most impressed by the house. Such a pity that you missed them. But I'm so glad you're here, Charles. There's so much we have to discuss.'

She moved across the kitchen to fill the kettle and put it on the bars of the range; he looked at her curiously. 'What are you doing?'

'I'm going to make you some tea; or coffee if you'd prefer? Mrs Newby's sister has agreed to come in part-time to help out, but she's not here at the moment.'

He took hold of her wrist. 'I will not have my wife doing menial work,' he said cuttingly. 'Call your maid and tell her to make the tea.'

'You're hurting me, Charles.' She tried to pull away. 'Let go and I'll call her.'

He dropped her wrist. 'Are there no bells in here?'

'Bells? What bells? I don't understand. Oh! No,' she gasped, rubbing her wrist, and registering his meaning. 'Only on the board.' She pointed up on the wall where the bell board via which the servants could be summoned to every room in the house was fixed. 'I don't even know if those work.'

'Then call her,' he said abruptly.

'Charles,' she said tearfully. 'I don't think you realize how difficult it has been for me. I've been alone here since you left for London until my parents came with Dora. There's a limit to what I've been able to do myself.'

He put his arms around her. 'Poor little wifey,' he whispered into her ear. 'You've done so well.' He kissed her cheek and then the tears that had gathered on her eyelashes. 'This wasn't your expected role, was it? Your role was to be my wife and mother to my sons.' He held her away from him and gazed at her. 'No sign of that yet?'

'Hardly.' She gave a hiccuping mumble. 'It takes two people to make a baby, you know, and as you haven't been—'

She reeled, staggering into the table, as the slap across her face shocked her completely.

CHAPTER TWENTY-THREE

She eased herself down on to a chair and took several deep breaths. She had caught the side of her hip on the corner of the kitchen table as she tumbled, and felt the throbbing there as well as on her face.

Charles was leaning towards her. 'I'm so sorry, my darling,' he said softly. 'You took a nasty fall. It wasn't my fault, was it? I didn't mean to hurt you.'

Her mouth trembled. Did he mean that? Was it accidental?

'I – what happened?' she said shakily, and with trembling fingers touched her burning cheek. 'I need some water. Will you call Dora, please?'

'Of course. Just stay still.' He walked swiftly to the stairs door and opened it, calling loudly. 'Dora! Dora! Come quickly.' He went up a few steps and called again until Dora appeared at the top.

'Sir,' she said, hurrying down. 'I didn't realize you were here.'

'Be quick,' he said sharply. 'Do you have sal volatile? Or know where it is kept? Mrs Dawley fainted and fell against the table, injuring herself. Hurry. Have you any brandy?'

'I don't know, sir. I'll look in the kitchen cupboards. We'll give her some water, sir.' Dora rushed past him and saw Beatrix leaning against the back of the chair with her eyes closed.

'Whatever has happened, ma'am?' She took a cup from the cupboard and poured water into it from the kettle, but Beatrix didn't answer. Dora put her hands round the cup; it wasn't too hot. She put a small amount of sugar in it and swished it round, then knelt by the side of the chair and put her hand at the back of Beatrix's neck to lift her head and help her drink.

Charles unearthed a half-bottle of brandy from a cupboard. 'Here we are, this will help.' He took the cup from Dora and poured a generous amount into the warm water. 'A hot toddy is just the thing.' He took over the giving of the pick-me-up and Beatrix sipped though her teeth chattered against the china.

'Thank you, Dora,' he said. 'I'll help her upstairs to bed. You'll be all right now, my love,' he said to Beatrix. 'Just rest for a while and you'll be fine.'

'Madam is going to have quite a bruise on her cheek, sir,' Dora said. 'She must have hit the table as she fell.'

'She did,' he agreed. 'I tried to catch her but she slipped out of my grasp.'

He helped Beatrix upstairs, unbuttoned her gown and gently sat her on the bed before stepping towards the window and drawing the curtains, even though it was still light. Beatrix watched him. Had she really fainted? She gently touched her cheekbone. It was tender, but the skin wasn't broken. She closed her eyes as she saw Charles begin to turn towards the bed and drew her legs beneath the sheets, lying back on her pillow. She began to shake, and tried to control the tremor.

She hadn't fallen and she hadn't fainted, no matter what Charles had said to her and Dora. He had hit her across her face, causing her to fall, but she wasn't going to confront him. If she had to do a little playacting so that he believed his own lies, then that was what she would do. She could only hope that it was just a misunderstanding and wouldn't happen again.

She drank the rest of the brandy and water and decided to stay in bed; she didn't want to speak to him, not yet. Charles, urging her to rest, said he would ask Dora to bring her a light supper later and went downstairs.

She heard him open the front door and she slipped out of bed and from behind a gap in the curtains watched him as he inspected the work the men had been doing. She saw him walk across the grass and drew back as he turned and scrutinized the front of the house. As he strolled towards the steps she climbed back into bed, sliding between sheets, blanket and eiderdown and closing her eyes.

She heard him come up the stairs and move in and out of the bedrooms, and was pleased that she had asked Mags and Mrs Parkin to take down all the old curtains and wash the windows and woodwork prior to the decorating that would start the next day when Mr Newby was able to come.

A light knock fell on the door and she didn't answer, but the door was slowly opened and from beneath her eyelashes she saw Dora coming over to the bed. She opened her eyes as Dora whispered, 'Can I bring you some hot milk, ma'am?'

'Later, thank you, Dora,' she said softly. 'I'll just rest for now, if you'll help me into my nightgown. Is there anything we can give Mr Dawley for his supper?'

Dora beamed. 'There is now. Mrs Parkin has just this minute come to the kitchen door and brought a meat pie. She said she'd made two and thought you'd like the second one. I'll scrub some potatoes and put them in the oven to bake. She also brought a bag of peas, so I'll shell them to serve with it.'

Tears came to Beatrix's eyes. 'How kind everyone is,' she murmured. 'Did she ask where I was?'

'I forestalled her and told her you'd gone to lie down as you had a bad headache; but not that you'd fallen, ma'am. She said she'd be here tomorrow morning.'

Beatrix closed her eyes again and from the effect of the brandy must have fallen asleep. She woke some time later when she heard a knock, and again didn't answer; the door was quietly opened and she heard Dora whisper at her side that she had brought her hot milk and now was going to bed and hoped that she would have a good night.

She sat up to drink the milk and wondered if Charles had also gone to bed, in the bedroom that he had used on their visit with her mother before their marriage. She thought perhaps he would continue to use that room once the decorating was finished and new furniture installed; he would surely expect his own bedroom and not assume he would share hers. She hoped that that would be the case. She put the glass down on the bedside table and drawing up the sheets slid down and closed her eyes.

But he hadn't gone to bed. She heard him pause on the landing outside her door, and then she heard his knock and the doorknob turned.

Charles had finished off the brandy and sat staring into the fire before going up to his room. He'd mishandled the situation, he realized that. He hadn't meant to hurt Beatrix, but he had taken offence at her words and the slap was spontaneous.

Of course he knew that she couldn't conceive if he wasn't there, but she shouldn't have made it so obvious. He sighed. It was not going to be easy to deal with two women of entirely different temperaments; Beatrix clearly wasn't used to confrontation, unlike Maria. He and Maria often had fights; he had had many a scratch to show for them. But always, always, the issues were discarded and forgotten as they tumbled into bed.

But it wouldn't be the same with Beatrix. She had led a sheltered existence and he would lay money that she had never received more than a mild rebuke from her parents, and that her brother had never felt the strap from his father's hands as he had from his when he'd been a boy.

Yet he didn't feel that Beatrix was made of china; she hadn't cracked at that first blow and gone into hysterics, but she would question the impulse behind it. She would ask why and he would make up a plausible reason, but he must also establish that he was master here.

He undressed and put on his dressing robe, crossed the landing to Beatrix's bedroom, and knocked softly. Receiving no reply, he turned the doorknob and opened the door. If she were asleep, all well and good: she would be more malleable than if she were awake and ruminating on the events of early evening.

He bent over her. She appeared to be sleeping, and he whispered her name. She made a small response in her throat, and crossing to the other side of the bed he slipped in beside her.

'Beatrix, my darling.' His voice was muted and gentle. 'Are you awake? Do say that you are.' He stroked her neck and shoulders, which were bare except for the thin silk straps on her nightgown, and he felt a yearning desire as he ran his hands down to her small waist and over the curve of her hips. He heard her breathy gasp and smiled. 'How are you feeling?'

'All right,' she murmured. 'A little achy. I'll be all right.'

'Of course you will, my brave girl.' He continued to stroke her and he heard her breath quicken and her body move against his hand. That was better, he thought. A little hesitancy or reluctance was tantalizing and seductive; he wouldn't rush, they had all night. He had been in too much of a hurry on their honeymoon, used as he was to the fiery temperament of his mistress.

'How lovely you are,' he whispered. 'And how lucky I am to have you as my wife.'

She turned to him. 'Do you mean that, Charles?' she murmured sleepily.

He lifted her hand and gently kissed the inside of her wrist. 'Of course I do. I am so fortunate.'

And at that moment he did believe it. She was not only desirable and lovely, she was capable too: he had seen the forethought that had gone into the design of the terrace when he'd observed how the men had set out her plan with sticks and string where the terrace and fountain would be, and he had no doubt whatsoever that she would create the house interior with the same passion, elegance and flair.

He had originally thought that she would follow the style of her parents' home, taking her inspiration from them, but she hadn't; she was definitely a woman with her own ideas, foresight and creativity. A cut above many women he had known.

He gathered her into his arms and she didn't resist. Yes, he thought as he kissed her, forgetting that his introduction to Beatrix had come from his father and hers. I have done very well in choosing such a wife.

CHAPTER TWENTY-FOUR

Charles stayed four days, overlapping the weekend, and discussing her various suggestions; he really couldn't find fault with any of them, yet he questioned most before giving his approval, including hiring a landscape gardener to thin out the woodland and make the path that Beatrix longed for.

He talked to Luke Newby about the decorating of the main house and suggested he brought in a team of men to help him; Luke couldn't climb a ladder or even a pair of steps, and the rooms were large, the hall big enough to use as a ballroom. The stairs and banister and upstairs landing were oak, and they were badly in need of cleaning up and waxing to bring them back to their original beauty.

There appeared to be no tension now between him and Beatrix, and although she had a slight mark on her fair skin and a bruise on her hip where she had hit the table, she was not suffering any other ill effects from her fall. He kissed her gently every morning and came to her bed every night, and as she responded to his touch he no longer compared her to his mistress, for they were, he decided, as unlike as it was possible to be, one innocently seductive and the other earthy and shameless.

Going back to his own bed each night, spent and exhausted, he couldn't help but muse that as soon as Beatrix produced a son and he could claim his final inheritance, his life would be perfect.

Although Beatrix reluctantly admitted to herself that she was easier in her mind now she and Charles knew each other better than they had previously, she was still cautious and considered carefully what she said or suggested, and tried not to do anything that might cause him any annoyance. He appeared to be repentant about the blow he had given her, though he never admitted that he was at fault. She admitted to herself that she was naive in the ways of men whilst he was obviously experienced in his love-making and knew how to tantalize and tempt her; and yet there was something missing in their relationship. She couldn't determine what it was; perhaps because they hadn't known each other for very long before their engagement and didn't yet have that ease of friendship and understanding that came with time? But that didn't explain the sudden anger that had erupted. Was that in his nature? Do I have to tread on eggshells to keep him calm?

Perhaps it takes every couple years to embrace each other's foibles, behaviours and idiosyncrasies before they can ease themselves into a happily married state, she pondered; she thought of her father and his habits: the way he tapped his pipe, for instance, and how he made that whooshing sound in his throat as he sat down. Her mother's little cough, too, which always indicated that she was about to say something she felt was important. But she had never been aware of any tension between them and surely she would have seen the signs.

But now I can get on, she thought, feeling reprieved as she stood on the steps and waved Charles good-bye. The terrace was almost finished and Charles had expressed his approval; they were waiting for the fountain and statuary to come and be put in place and then the water to be piped in from the under-ground well.

Aaron had asked his Uncle Luke if he could borrow his pony and cart to take Mr Dawley to the local station to catch the train. Luke only ever used old and patient ponies since his accident and the one he had now was very elderly and needed great encouragement to move on.

Beatrix reminded herself to ask Edward if he had found her a pony and trap. She thought that she would learn how to handle one before Charles came home again. Coincidentally, Edward called at the end of that day and found her in the annexe discussing paint with his father.

'Maister gone, has he, missus?' he asked with a wry grin. 'Everything in order for him?'

She frowned and looked sternly at him, covering her smile with her hand. Luke didn't see the smile and scowled at his son.

'Now then,' he said sharply. 'You mind your man-ners in front o' Mrs Dawley.'

Edward pulled his hat off and clutched it between his hands with his head down. 'Beggin' your pardon, ma'am,' he muttered. 'Meant no offence.' Then he laughed. 'My father can't shake off his serfdom,' he said. 'It's ingrained in him.'

His father grumbled at him. 'Nev Dawley allus treated us well and don't you forget it.'

Edward nodded at him. 'He did. He was a gentleman, not like some.' Then he turned to Beatrix, losing his smile. 'Only joking, Mrs Dawley.'

She didn't answer. There was obviously an old feud still festering between Edward and Charles and she had no intention of becoming involved in it.

To change the subject, she asked what he thought of the colours she had chosen.

'What are you going to do in here?' he asked her.

'I thought plain cream walls to brighten it up. The floors have been cleaned and are waiting to be polished when we've finished painting, and if anyone should come to stay, say my parents, or . . .' she paused, 'Charles's, they could stay here. It's going to take a long time to do the main house.'

'Charles's parents won't come,' he assured her. 'Not unless you invite them to something grand, a ball or a dinner where you invite notable guests. Then they'll come, prepared to lord it over everyone, not knowing that some of your neighbours are people of breeding who don't care about money or those who are involved in it.'

Beatrix pressed her lips together. 'My father was involved in banking,' she said in a low voice.

'He didn't own the bank though, did he?' Edward looked at her. 'That's a different matter entirely.'

A letter came from her mother a week later saying she had interviewed the Yorkshire-born housekeeper and was very impressed. She gave such a glowing report of Lily Gordon that Beatrix was inclined to say send her at once, but instead wrote a list of questions and asked her mother to arrange another interview, and if the responses were all positive to suggest to Mrs Gordon that she come on a six-month trial contract as soon as she was able.

There! she thought as she screwed the lid back on the ink bottle and put away her pen. That's another thing done; and Mrs Gordon can advise me on what staff we'll require, for I'm convinced that eventually we'll settle into this community and when the house is decorated and furnished we'll be able to invite guests to stay.

I love the openness and fresh air of the countryside, she thought, but I admit that I would like to have a little company. I miss the chatter of my friends when we used to walk along the city streets to look in the shop windows.

The first calling card arrived the next day, with an invitation to her and Charles to visit a Mrs Stokes, who lived in nearby Hessle. She had brought the card herself, but Dora, who answered the door, told her that Mrs Dawley was not at home. She had learned such things at her training class, though this particular task would not usually be her role, but that of the housekeeper or a housemaid.

'How lovely,' Beatrix exclaimed when Dora handed her the invitation card. 'I will return the compliment. I must ask Ed— erm, Mr Newby about a pony and trap and then I will be able to drive myself on such occasions. But this is for *tomorrow*; it says she is holding a charity event. What can I wear, Dora? Most of my clothes are still in boxes. The lemon silk, perhaps; will you search it out and tidy it up, please? Oh, how exciting! Such a pity that Mr Dawley isn't here.'

But she was quite pleased that he wasn't when she arrived at Mrs Stokes's house the following day in Luke Newby's old trap, driven by Aaron wearing his best tweed jacket, who said he would wait if it was to be only half an hour, which, Beatrix knew, was more than the maximum time visits were expected to last in London. However, it turned out to be far too short a visit for Mrs Stokes, who expected her guests to stay all afternoon, helping themselves to savoury and sweet fancies and buying the objects on sale.

Charles wouldn't have liked it at all, she thought, and I am overdressed; it was an informal gathering held in a very grand but untidy drawing room. Mrs Stokes told Beatrix that the house was hers and that it was so tightly tied up with legalities that her husband couldn't get his hands on it.

'Not that he would want it, poor dear,' she laughed. 'He says he'd be bankrupt if it were his as he'd feel compelled to repair the roof, the windows and the brickwork, whereas I,' she fluttered her fingers in the air, 'couldn't care a jot as long as it doesn't fall about my ears. It is mine and I love it just as it is.'

Her husband briefly looked in and was casually introduced, and then disappeared along with some of the other husbands.

Mrs Stokes had a daughter, Rosetta, of about Beatrix's age, a little quieter than her mother but as positive as her father that when the house eventually came to her she would have it repaired, providing there was enough money left in the family pot, and adapted into separate apartments for letting to people with little or no money so that they could have the benefit of the country air and the possibility of work in the district.

'I'll have to marry a man with money,' she said. 'I'm looking now. Then he can pay for it. There's fishing and shipping in Hull, Mrs Dawley – may I call you Beatrix? You can call me Rosie – and there's a lot of industry nearby where people can find work. You're very beautiful, aren't you?' she went on unexpectedly. 'Is that why your husband asked you to marry him, or are you very rich?'

Fortunately she didn't wait for a reply but dashed away to greet someone else. Beatrix was grateful to see her go as she couldn't for the life of her think of an answer to give.

So much for living near the local gentry, she pondered as Aaron urged the old pony home an hour later. They don't give a fig, in Mrs Stokes's parlance, about doing the right thing. If they want to hold a party or call on friends they do just that; they don't stand on ceremony at all, or do what's expected of them. But then, she considered, maybe they expect others lower down in the pecking order to follow the rules.

She glanced about her. They'd come down to the estuary and were passing a shipbuilding yard; a ferry boat was making its way to the landing stage. The gulls were following it, cawing and screeching, and Beatrix gave a deep sigh of pleasure. I really like it here.

CHAPTER TWENTY-FIVE

When Charles next arrived he was in a high state of excitement; he was not in the money business for nothing, he told Beatrix. Being the man he was, always keeping a sharp eye on stocks, shares and business in general, he had seen how cereal crops and other agricultural products were rising in value and that many farmers were in profit, some for the first time in years. The population of Britain was growing rapidly and needed to be fed, and it had dawned on him that he had land that was lying barren and unused.

'What we must do,' he enthused during supper on the evening he arrived, 'is employ a farm manager, someone who is college trained, one who will watch the markets at home and abroad, and know what to plant and grow to make a profit whilst feeding the people of this country.'

Beatrix gazed at him in astonishment. Well, isn't that what I suggested previously and he said that he wasn't a farmer but a city man! He was totally disinterested, and now he's discovered that farming is unparalleled. I don't believe for one minute that he is interested in feeding the population, but only in the profit he'll make. But he'll have to risk a significant amount of money before that happens. I'm not a banker's daughter for nothing either, she fumed: I do, or *did*, read the newspapers too.

'I agree, totally,' she responded mildly. 'Would Luke Newby know of anyone?'

There was no point in suggesting Edward, who would have been the most obvious person to ask, for Charles would have pooh-poohed the very idea, but Luke, if he were approached by Charles, would ask him anyway.

'Exactly the man I was thinking of.' They had adjourned to the sitting room, which was now in use, decorated and furnished in a comfortable manner, some new pieces and some left by Neville Dawley which had only needed refurbishing; the drawing room was still in disorder, cluttered with pots of paint and ladders and trestles, and boxes containing rolls of wallpaper.

'Being a local man, Luke will be bound to know of someone suitable, or at least know someone who does. But' – Charles raised a finger – 'I must have a modern man, with experience, who knows what is happening at home and abroad.'

'We'll also need a team of men,' Beatrix suggested. 'They should live nearby; and there'll be expenditure on horses, wagons, machinery . . .'

Does he realize what an undertaking it will be, she pondered? Has he even looked in the barns and sheds at the back of the house, or even at the outbuildings further up the hill? She was developing a proprietorial feeling for all of the property. It wasn't a huge acreage, but a substantial one, Edward had told her when, at her request, he had taken her to look over the Dawley land and pointed out which areas were rented out to tenant farmers; he'd also shown her the acreage which he and his family farmed.

'Oh, yes, my dear,' Charles said condescendingly. 'Of course! But you mustn't worry your head about it.' Then he smiled, but his eyes narrowed. 'Once we have our son we won't have any money worries at all. Not that we have any now,' he added. 'But I look forward to receiving the full inheritance.'

She hadn't felt her usual energetic self lately, but she wasn't going to say anything to him about that in case he jumped to conclusions and then was disappointed. It might be nothing; there was so much to do that she had probably just tired herself out. She was really hoping that Mrs Gordon would soon accept her offer of the housekeeping post and could take over some of the duties that really, she considered, I shouldn't be doing as mistress of the household.

'Why was the proviso made?' she asked. 'Why did Neville Dawley make the stipulation that you must have a son before you could claim the full inheritance?'

'I've no idea,' he said idly, even though he did. 'Just an old man's whim, I suppose.'

Luke Newby's team of decorators had finished the annexe, which Beatrix had named the Little Stone House; the furniture she had ordered from local Hull suppliers, comfy sofas and side tables, dining table and chairs, lamps and cushions, beds and bedding, was beginning to arrive. Mags knew a seamstress who had cut and sewn the richly coloured heavyweight curtain material that Beatrix had ordered, and Mags and Mrs Parkin hung the results from the rails over muslin drapes, instantly transforming the rooms.

'Very nice,' Charles said approvingly when he saw it, and meant it; again, he was totally surprised at Beatrix's flair. It was quite different from Maria's extravagant town style, and was just right for a country house. 'We could live in here until the main house is ready.'

'We could,' Beatrix enthused. 'That would be lovely. It's such a dear little house.' Although, she considered, it wasn't little by any means. 'Does that mean that you'll be able to spend more time here?' She was going to say *at home*, but she felt he still hadn't the feeling of belonging in the property that she had, which she had felt on the first occasion she had visited.

'Sadly, no,' he sighed. 'I am so very busy, and under constant pressure. You do understand, dearest, that I must be seen to be doing my bit, as one day when my father retires I will be in sole charge.'

This wasn't strictly true. His father had said that he must show more aptitude towards banking matters if he wished eventually to take over from him; that there were others who were more efficient who had the bank's interests just as much at heart.

Charles had sniffed, but hadn't argued back. Those others his father mentioned were employees, not the son of the family business as he was.

'So will – you speak to Luke whilst you're here?' Beatrix asked now. 'About finding a farm manager?' She had almost made the error of saying shall *we* speak to Luke, but had instinctively realized it would be the wrong thing to say; she was sure that her role was seen as that of the little wife at home, whereas, in fact, she already knew more about the farmland and the estate through talking and listening to Edward and Luke, and even young Aaron, than Charles did.

'Yes. Tomorrow, if he calls, and if not we'll take a walk to see him. It's not far.'

The next morning Dora cooked another excellent breakfast, and Beatrix was just thinking that she must pay her extra for all the additional work she was doing when they heard the jingle of harness and the clip-clop of hooves on the gravel. She went to the window and saw Edward climbing from the seat of a very smart governess cart, painted in black with gold trim and drawn by a shiny black pony with a long tail and a star on his nose.

She gave a little gasp. 'Oh! I asked Mr Newby to look for a pony and trap. I do hope this is it! Look, Charles, isn't it lovely?'

Charles stood behind her, following her gaze. When he saw who it was who had brought it, he rested his chin on the top of Beatrix's head and put his hands on her waist in a possessive manner, running his thumbs over her hip bones, which, she thought, was ridiculous and embarrassing even though Edward wouldn't see as he wasn't looking their way.

'Very trim,' Charles agreed. 'You'll be able to take me to Brough railway station when I go to catch my train.'

'I don't know how to drive it yet,' she laughed. 'The pony is sweet, isn't it?' She turned to look up at him. 'Shall we go and look at him? It is a him, isn't it?'

Charles gave a snigger and patted her bottom. 'Looks rather like it. Yes, let's go and see what Eddie considers to be good horseflesh.'

Surprisingly, the two men chatted quite amiably as they discussed the merits of the pony, and the trap which, Edward said, wasn't new, but he and his father had done it up, repaired and painted it so that it looked brand new. Beatrix was reminded of something when she examined it, and with a little rush of pleasure realized that it was the one she had discovered in one of the barns when she had first explored. She caught Edward's eye and gave a nod of approval.

'Excellent,' Charles said agreeably. 'Now someone has to teach my lovely wife how to drive.'

'Aaron could do that,' Edward said. 'He's a good driver. You'll need just a day or two, Mrs Dawley, and you'll manage fine.'

Beatrix smiled. She was making herself known to the pony, who nuzzled into her hand looking for a tit-bit; she was glad that Edward hadn't offered. Aaron was a good compromise, especially as he was now in full-time employment with them; he'd proved himself very useful and would do anything he was asked to do.

'I was thinking, Eddie,' Charles said, stroking his beard, 'of bringing the land back into production. It seems a pity to have it lying idle.'

Edward put his head on one side and stared at Charles. 'Really? To grow what?'

'Ah! Well, there's the rub. I'll need to take advice.' Charles pursed his lips. 'I thought I'd bring in a manager. Someone youngish, up to date with modern farming practice.'

Edward crossed his arms. 'Are you serious? The land hasn't been farmed for quite some time. Nev's father was one of the first to enclose in this area. He planted

205

hedges and trees and the cattle were sheltered; he grew varied crops, but the population kept on growing and from what I understand they couldn't keep up with the demand, especially after the old man died and Nev had to manage on his own.'

'I know,' Charles said. 'It was neglected.'

'Not when we were young,' Edward said in defence. 'Nev managed back then and brought in more workers, and rented out land, but it became too much for him; we forget how old he was. My da offered to help him out but there was little he could do. We suggested that he put cattle or sheep in the bottom field or rent it out to some other farmer, but he was having none of it.'

'Awkward old cuss,' Charles muttered. 'Will it take much to bring it back to giving a good yield?'

'Patience is the most important part of farming,' Edward told him, 'and it's a crying shame not to use valuable land. You could start with cattle or sheep to nourish the fields, and maybe in another year you can plant potatoes and turnips, and the following year feed the cattle with the produce and then plant winter corn. You can't rush.' Charles seemed to be losing interest, but Beatrix was listening and was enthusiastic. 'Shall I ask around?' Edward went on. 'There might be someone from my year at agricultural college. I was lucky enough to have a job to come straight into, but there might be some who were not so fortunate.'

Charles exhaled a deep breath and glanced at Beatrix, who raised her eyebrows and gave him an encouraging nod. 'What do you think, Beatrix? Shall we take a chance at farming? Can you keep accounts?'

'I'd love it, and yes I can,' she said ardently. 'The land was surely meant to be productive, not lie idle. It wasn't meant only to be admired for its beauty, although we'll do that too.'

Edward agreed, gazing at her. 'There's no finer sight than a field of golden corn, or cattle or sheep grazing in a meadow.'

'All right,' Charles decided, feeling amiable. 'Let's do it.'

CHAPTER TWENTY-SIX

Beatrix's plans for becoming a farmer's wife, keeping chickens and digging a pond for ducks at the back of the house in a grassy area that had once been the orchard, but now had tired and decayed old trees that needed digging out and replacing, had begun. A gang of local men had been recruited by Edward Newby and were already hard at work.

Then one morning she had a sudden violent bout of sickness which knocked her completely off her feet, sending her post-haste back to her bed, and unfortunately coinciding with the arrival of Lily Gordon, who came to the house late that afternoon wearing stout shoes and a raincoat and carrying a rucksack on her back and a suitcase in her hand. She had walked the three miles from the station in Brough without any effort at all.

'I wasn't aware that the train would stop at North Ferriby,' she said, 'but I can't tell you how much I enjoyed the walk, Mrs Dawley.' Dora had made her a cup of tea and brought it to the sitting room, where Beatrix was resting on the sofa. The housekeeper looked about her. 'This is a *lovely* house,' she enthused, 'and beautifully situated. I do hope I'll be suitable for you. I'm longing to come back to my home county, even though I have thoroughly enjoyed my time in the south.'

'I hope so too, Mrs Gordon,' Beatrix told her. 'There's quite a lot to do, as my husband and I are new to the house and the area. I'm London born so it's a whole new experience for me, but I love it here.' She paused. 'Unfortunately, my husband can't be here as often as we would wish as he's tied to business matters in London, but household affairs are my world and not his, and I would value your advice on what and who will be needed. The former owner, a relative of my husband's, was a bachelor and did little with the house, which as you will see we are presently renovating into a family home.'

Mrs Gordon nodded. 'I understand from your mother that you are newly married? You must miss her and her advice,' she said softly. 'It can't be easy to be so far from family and all things familiar just now.'

'It isn't.' Beatrix felt her eyes well up and hoped that she wasn't going to weep in front of this newcomer. 'Especially as I'm feeling rather unwell just now. There has been such a lot of organizing to do that I think I've tired myself out.' She heaved a breath. 'However, I'm not often ill so I don't suppose it will last.'

'Well, I will do what I can to help, ma'am.' Mrs Gordon rose from her chair. 'If I might start as soon as I have unpacked, I will ask your maid . . . ?'

'Dora Murray. She's a Londoner too and had come to be my personal maid, but she has found herself doing just about everything in the house since she arrived. I really don't know what I would have done without her. She's very capable, and she's only a girl.' She smiled, feeling a huge sense of relief. 'She will show you to your room. You must say if there is anything you require, or need to know, and perhaps tomorrow we can discuss matters in more detail.'

'Thank you, ma'am. If I might have a wander round the house on my own to familiarize myself? I'll try not to disturb you.' Mrs Gordon gave a discreet dip of her knee and left the room, smiling at Dora who was waiting to show her upstairs.

After a good night's sleep, Beatrix woke refreshed the following morning. I feel so much better now that Mrs Gordon is here and seems so very capable. I do hope she'll stay. She put her feet to the floor and immediately felt bile in her throat. 'Oh, no.' She reached under the bed for the chamber pot just in time, and then, after ringing the bell for Dora, climbed back into bed again.

But it was Mrs Gordon, not Dora, who knocked and entered a few minutes later, wishing her good morning in a very cheerful voice.

'I think I'm going to need a doctor,' Beatrix said tearfully. 'I've been dreadfully sick again, and I felt so much better last night. Would you ask Dora to ask Mrs Newby if she can tell us the name of a doctor and ask him to call?'

Mrs Gordon plumped up her pillows, straightened the bedspread and stood with her hands folded in front of her before answering. 'I most certainly will, Mrs Dawley, but I wonder if you have considered that it could be a natural occurrence that's making you sick?' She raised her eyebrows questioningly.

Beatrix gazed back at her, a query on her lips. 'Erm . . .'

'Forgive me, ma'am,' Mrs Gordon said evenly. 'I have only general medical knowledge, but could it be possible that you are with child? I've known others with similar symptoms, and pregnancy has been the cause.'

'Oh!' Beatrix gazed at her wide-eyed. 'I didn't think . . . I don't really know what to expect. I . . . I don't know the signs.'

'Sickness is one of the earliest ones,' Mrs Gordon answered kindly, 'and it doesn't usually last more than a couple of months. Allow me to bring you a glass of hot water with a squeeze of lemon if there is any. That will ease it and you'll be able to get up and feel fine; until it happens again tomorrow morning,' she added with a crooked grin.

'Well, ma'am, I could have told you that,' Dora proclaimed when Beatrix mentioned to her that she could possibly be pregnant, hence the sickness. 'My ma was just the same.' She gazed over Beatrix's shoulder into mid-air as she buttoned up her gown and said, 'Should we call the doctor to confirm, ma'am, before you give Mr Dawley the news?'

How much has she guessed or discerned about my marriage, Beatrix wondered? She has been very protective of me since that so-called fall, and I trust her completely; she's very discreet, and I know she won't discuss my condition with anyone until Charles has been told.

'I think so,' she answered. 'If I write a note, will you slip out and ask Mags where he lives? You can take the trap if you like, and if it's nearby perhaps you could call? That would be a nice little outing for you, wouldn't it?'

'Oh, yes, it would. Do you trust me with the pony, ma'am? I've only ever had a go on the milk cart when I was young. I'll ask Aaron to get him ready, shall I?'

Beatrix laughed. 'You're only young now, Dora,' she said.

'Yes, I know, miss – ma'am, I mean – but my ma always said I had an old head on young shoulders.'

Beatrix laughed again. She felt much better already. 'I think your mother was right, Dora. Mothers usually are.' She looked pensive for a second or two. 'I wonder if I will be when I'm a mother.'

'I expect so,' Dora answered wryly. 'Shall I ask Mrs Gordon to make a list for the grocer so I can give it to him whilst I'm out?'

'Yes,' Beatrix said vaguely. 'But that isn't her role. I need a cook and a housemaid – two, probably. Mrs Gordon has come as housekeeper. I wonder if Mrs Parkin would come as cook. She's a very good cook and I'd so much prefer someone I know. Will you ask Mrs Gordon to come and speak to me when she has a minute? We must sort things out soon.'

Within the week, Mrs Parkin had agreed to try out as cook. It was the first time she had been offered a full-time position and she seemed to have grown at least two inches taller because of it. Mrs Gordon advertised for two housemaids and took on one of them. The local doctor, Dr Brewer, came to introduce himself and confirmed that Beatrix was expecting a child, and gave the approximate date of birth some time in April, or possibly May.

Beatrix wrote to Charles asking if he could come home fairly soon as she had something important to tell him, and addressed the letter to him at the bank, marking it personal and confidential. She wrote a much longer one to her mother, giving her the news and telling her that Charles didn't know yet.

Charles arrived at Old Stone Hall three days later and greeted the news that she was expecting a child enthusiastically. 'Riches!' he declared, making her own joy sink like a stone as she realized that his delight was quite different from hers. The anticipation of a son to bring him the full inheritance was the pleasure he was waiting for, not the child itself.

'And if the child is a girl,' she said softly. 'Will you still be pleased, even though you will have to wait longer for your son?'

He gazed at her and frowned. 'If it's a girl I shall be hugely disappointed in you, Beatrix. A son is what I need, *and,*' he said, wagging his finger at her, 'I need him soon. The years are moving swiftly on; the damned stupid rules laid down regarding the inheritance mean that we haven't got long, so watch out, because otherwise you'll be in a constant state of pregnancy.'

He took himself off to introduce himself to the housekeeper, as Dora had opened the front door to him on his arrival, and to ask Mrs Gordon for a jug of coffee to revive him after his journey, leaving Beatrix stunned. She wondered how she could possibly have been manipulated into such a position. I can't give him a son to order. We don't have a choice about whether it's a boy or girl; doesn't he understand that? I dare not tell him. He's so very touchy about his manhood.

He gave no indication of this kind of behaviour when I first met him, she thought; in fact he seems very like his father when he and Mrs Dawley came to dine and Charles chastised him for his language and conduct. Now he is behaving in the very same manner. Is this what wealth does? Does it mean that you can run roughshod over anyone, including your own wife?

She was shaken and dazed and yet knew that she mustn't let him see it; one small chink in the armour which she must wrap around herself for protection, or one hint of vulnerability, would without doubt make him feel stronger. She didn't know how she had come to this conclusion, but it was what she now believed. Physically, she couldn't protect herself, but whilst she was carrying his child he wouldn't risk any harm's coming to her.

But I believe I am his match intellectually and logically, she mused, and I must use that without his realizing. She sighed, feeling downhearted. I was excited by the thought of a good marriage. Foolishly, I thought that love would grow. How gullible I was, and how misled. Of course a miracle could happen, and if I produce a son Charles might become tender and loving, but I'm not sure I believe in miracles, and we simply do not have a choice when it comes to the biological gender of a child. I could almost wish for a girl just to spite him, but I would fear the consequences.

She got up from her chair and wandered to the window. The grass was long and at the bottom of the meadow, near the wood, someone was cutting it – who was it? Aaron! Aaron was scything the grass with long, smooth strokes; he'd done it before, she guessed from his surety in using the scythe. What a useful young fellow he is, and how lucky we are to have him.

Suddenly she felt brighter, though a lump came to her throat. The sky was blue with only a few wisps of cloud; she could smell the newly cut grass and could hear and see birds in flight as they swooped and caught the insects thrown up from the scythe.

I belong here, she thought. This is my home now. Here is where I will bring up my family. Male or female, I'll teach my children to be kind and loving to others and not to think that money is the answer to misfortune, but often the cause of it. She sighed. As for Charles, I can do nothing about him; he is steeped in avarice, there is no other description. Perhaps he was once caring and compassionate, I have seen glimpses of it, but that person is not here. He has gone and I don't know where.

CHAPTER TWENTY-SEVEN

The weather had been sunny, with occasional light showers of rain in the evening which refreshed the earth and the plants and shrubs that Beatrix had bought or begged from neighbours and Aaron had planted wherever she indicated. She had never cultivated a single plant in her life, but she asked questions or looked up information in various catalogues and went with her instinct, crossing her fingers that what she selected would grow strong for the following year.

Many invitations to attend luncheons and summer garden parties had been received, and once the sickness had abated Beatrix had attended many of them alone, with Dora driving her in the trap, and excusing Charles's absence due to pressure of business; when he was at home, he accepted the invitations and was charming to their hosts and attentive to Beatrix, insisting on her taking his arm and finding her a chair on every occasion.

In fact she didn't need any mollycoddling, feeling fit and healthy and enjoying the excellent cooking of Mrs Parkin, who was in her element, particularly as she was able to choose new kitchen utensils, pots and pans and serving dishes, and was given a girl just out of school as a scullery maid to clean up after her and tend the fire in the range.

As late summer drew on, Beatrix thought fit to invite just a few select guests that she had particularly taken to; Rosie Stokes was one, whose eccentric mother had been the first to send an invitation to Beatrix. Two other young ladies from Brough arrived accompanied by a lady's maid who was carried off by Dora to help with the tea things, for they were to sit on the chairs on the terrace at the front of the house, near to the new fountain, which was much admired.

'How lovely. Very reminiscent of Italy,' Rosie said in her loud, clear voice. 'Such a clever idea bringing something so artistic into the heart of Yorkshire. But your husband isn't a Yorkshireman, is he, Beatrix? Is he well travelled?'

'Charles is indeed well travelled,' Beatrix replied, 'but it was my idea to have the fountain and the statue. I admire sculptures for their grace and artistry; this is a copy of the Roman Apollo.'

Margaret, one of the young women from Brough, giggled behind her hand. 'He is very well endowed, is he not? I'm sure it can't be taken from life!'

Beatrix was silenced by her immodesty, the other young woman gasped and hid her face, but Rosie simply looked at them and then at Beatrix and raised her eyebrows in ridicule.

'Silly girls,' she murmured aside to Beatrix so the others didn't hear. 'What did they expect? I made sure I knew all I needed to know about the male anatomy in case I was asked to marry any of them,' and then she casually added, as if the remark had been of no consequence, 'I must tell Mama of your taste and style. She might want to ask your advice on decorating the drawing room. Papa says she must have it done soon and get rid of the grubby wallpaper and shredded carpets for fear no one will ever visit us again.'

By October the Little Stone House was fully decorated and everyone moved in there until the main house was finished. Workmen with scaffolding and ladders had been brought in to reach the very high ceilings, clean the oak panels in the hall and polish the staircase and banisters, and all that was left was to finish and furnish the bedrooms on the top floor which were not yet needed, though Beatrix had earmarked one sunny room at the front of the house for a nursery, and the smaller room off it for a nursery maid.

She dared not think of the expense that had been entailed, but she had noted the cost of every single thing that had been bought and shown it to Charles whenever he came home and he hadn't turned a hair, but simply remarked that it was a pity she couldn't have worked in banking.

Not that I would have wanted to, she had mused after the remark, but why couldn't I? Because I'm a woman?

At the beginning of December, when they had moved back into the main house, she said to Charles she would like to invite her parents to stay at Christmas. 'They'll be lonely at home, especially as Thomas won't be there either; he's abroad again, but even if he were not it's doubtful that he would be given leave.'

'Ask them by all means,' he agreed. 'But I won't ask mine. I put up with them during the year' – implying that he saw them often – 'and I certainly don't want to entertain them over Christmas.'

He was wondering what he should do about Maria. His place should be with Beatrix, especially their first Christmas together, for people would talk if he were absent, but previously he had always spent Christmas Day and Boxing Day with Maria. A dilemma, he thought. Dare I suggest she should go home to Spain and see her mother?

When he returned to London, he put the proposal to her. He hadn't yet told her that Beatrix was expecting his child, but now he took the opportunity to do so and anxiously awaited her reaction.

She was silent and looked sad, and he gathered her into his arms, nuzzling into her neck. She didn't respond, and turned away from him. 'No!' she said. 'I will stay here. My mother will have to be at home. My father will expect it. It is his only 'oliday. I will stay here and go to Mass. I will ask Bianca if she will come and stay with me. She too will be abandoned and alone, just like me.'

He flinched, but realized that it was true.

'You will come home for Three Kings Day in January,' she told him firmly. 'That is when we will celebrate.'

What else could he do? Three Kings Day was a traditional festival for Spaniards, who gave out presents then to celebrate the coming of the three wise men with their gifts for the Christ child; in England the occasion was celebrated as Epiphany. He would have to tell Beatrix that there was a crisis at the bank.

'All right,' he said, kissing the top of her head. 'We'll have a special day of our own and I will bring you a gift. What would you like?'

Maria thought for a moment. 'A gold bracelet set with diamonds.'

He took a breath. Maria knew her worth; that was for certain. She had a stack of jewellery that he had given her over the years yet she hardly ever wore any of it. He nodded. 'If the child is a son you will have a necklace to match.'

She pursed her lips. 'If it is a girl it can be gold only. I am not a greedy person.'

My first Christmas in my own home! Beatrix's spirits rose as the holiday came nearer and she felt more and more joyful. Neville Dawley's boudoir piano had been cleaned and tuned and stood in splendour in the drawing room, and she couldn't help but run her fingers across the keys each time she came into the room and wonder if he had ever played it. New furniture, beds and bedding had arrived and were in situ in the main house, and Beatrix had looked for but not yet gathered holly, mistletoe and other greenery and had asked Edward if he would dig up a fir tree from the wood.

She had seen one the right size and he'd said he would dig it up with the roots intact so that they could replant it after Christmas and keep it growing healthily for the following year. Her parents were arriving on the twenty-third and she wanted to decorate the house so that it would be filled with Christmas candles and the scent of fir when they entered, though she wouldn't dress the tree until Christmas Eve. To increase her delight, her mother had written to say that Thomas might be with them, as they had received a letter from him to say he was coming home.

The Newbys were giving them a home-reared goose and Mrs Parkin, on Beatrix's instructions, had ordered a leg of pork from the butcher, for Mr Fawcett was particularly fond of pork with apple sauce. She had made a Christmas pudding earlier in the autumn and had constantly fed it with brandy since. Beatrix had worried that Cook, as she was now known, would miss out on her own family Christmas dinner and had suggested that all the staff, including Dora and Mrs Gordon, should eat together at the large table in the kitchen, and that Aaron and Mrs Parkin's other children might like to come too. They had all gladly agreed and a turkey was ordered for their table.

'I hope we've ordered enough food,' Beatrix confessed to her mother on her arrival. Mrs Fawcett had bravely travelled alone on an earlier train, as her husband had decided to wait at home for Thomas, who didn't know that they were to spend Christmas in Yorkshire and wouldn't be in London until the evening.

'I'm sure you'll have enough food for an army,' Mrs Fawcett murmured when she had explored the larder and the cold room where a large chicken, a brace of pheasant which someone had left hanging outside the kitchen door, the goose and a turkey were all now hanging from hooks in the ceiling. Jellies were setting in their moulds on the top shelf of the food safe, whilst on the lower shelves were pork pies and French-style pâtés that Mrs Parkin called potted meat, which she had made by her own hand. 'I have never seen so much food for one family.'

'It won't be wasted,' Beatrix told her. 'We'll share it with those who have very little; Edward – Newby,' she added, so as not to appear too familiar, 'has told me of several such families.'

Her mother lifted her head in interest. 'That's Mags's son, is it not?'

'Yes,' Beatrix answered casually. 'You've met him. The Newby family have been very helpful. Perfect neighbours,' she said, and then added, 'Come along, Mother. We're not supposed to be in here. The kitchen is Mrs Parkin's domain.'

It was lovely to be in the sitting room with just her mother for company, and they sat companionably by the fire after supper and chatted about other Christmas-times until her mother asked when Charles would arrive.

'I – erm, I'm not sure,' Beatrix faltered. 'You know how it is with banks; having to be sure everything is finished before closing for the holidays.'

And that was the rub, because of course her mother did know, having lived with her father for so many years. She had always known to a minute when he would be home from the bank, and now Beatrix felt her questioning gaze on her.

'He will be here in time for Christmas,' she murmured with a certainty she didn't feel; how would she excuse him to her parents if he should be late? 'It will depend on the trains, perhaps; you know how they don't always run to time.'

Her mother, without conveying any sign that she was perturbed by Beatrix's anxiety, suddenly smiled and nodded and said brightly, 'Wouldn't it be amusing if Charles and your father and Thomas all travelled together?'

Which was exactly what did happen, and having gone through to Hull they arrived in a hired carriage close on midnight at the same time as a company of carollers, who had begun to sing 'Good King Wenceslas' to rouse the occupants.

'Have we food and drink for them?' Beatrix was asking anxiously. She rang the bell for Dora, who reassured her at once.

'It's all right, ma'am. Cook was expecting them. She's heating up the Wassail bowl and we're to let them in at the end of the first carol. I've brought your shawl. Would you like to open the door, ma'am?'

Beatrix was overcome by emotion as she stood by the door to welcome them. The Newby family were there, all singing with great gusto, Luke Newby in a deep bass, leaning on a stick, his wife Mags slightly behind in time, and Edward standing at the back with the other villagers, men, women and children.

'How lovely,' her mother was whispering behind her. 'And look who's here,' she added as the carriage drew up and first Charles, then Beatrix's father and brother stepped down. 'How perfect.'

'Oh, yes,' Beatrix said softly; 'it is.' She smiled to see her brother, so tall and handsome in his uniform, and her gaze moved on to her father and Charles, who seemed surprised to see so many gathered there; but then her attention strayed to the group of carollers and she saw Edward Newby amongst them, his eyes on hers and holding them until she looked away.

CHAPTER TWENTY-EIGHT

'Such a splendid start to Christmas,' Emily Fawcett enthused. 'The very best I've ever experienced.'

Beatrix agreed. The company of carollers had been invited inside to sing more carols and Christmas hymns, before shaking hands with everyone and trooping off to the kitchen to partake of the food and spiced wine that, unbeknown to Beatrix, Cook had prepared for their refreshment.

When the carollers had gone, the family sat by the fire talking. The men drank brandy, Beatrix's mother took a small glass with a splash of hot water and a sprinkling of sugar, and Beatrix sipped at a cup of chocolate.

Charles tossed back his second brandy. 'I must apologize,' he said, standing up, 'but I'm exhausted – such a busy week – and I must go to bed.' He bent to kiss Beatrix's cheek. 'Don't get overtired, Beatrix,' he murmured, and turned to the Fawcetts. 'I'll see you all in the morning. Please make yourselves at home.' He looked round the sitting room at the Christmas greenery. 'It looks splendid, Beatrix.'

She smiled, delighted that he had noticed. 'Tomorrow we'll dress the tree. I waited especially for you to help with it.'

He blinked as if he hadn't expected this, but nodded.

'Thomas, do you remember how excited we used to be when we were children?' Beatrix smiled at her brother. 'I couldn't reach to put the angel on the topmost branch so you always had the task and I was so envious.'

Thomas laughed. 'I remember trying to lift you once and we almost knocked the tree over.' He gazed at her critically. 'I wouldn't like to try it now!'

Charles looked from one to the other, a fleeting expression of envy crossing his face, which he was quick to conceal. Clearly, Beatrix thought, he hadn't experienced a Christmas such as ours with his sister Anne. Ours were never extravagant, but simple and full of contentment and fun until Thomas left home at sixteen to become a soldier. Christmas was never the same afterwards.

Her father and then her mother went upstairs after Charles; her father too was ready for bed after the journey, but Thomas sat on. 'I'm dog-tired,' he said, 'but I know I won't sleep yet. I've been travelling for several days. I might sleep late in the morning, though. Will that be all right, not anti-social?'

'Of course it will,' she said. 'Just make yourself at home, as Charles said.'

'I've forgotten how to do that, Bea,' he murmured. 'It's been so long since I've been anywhere that I could call home.'

He pondered for a moment or so, and then asked, 'Does Charles spend much time here?'

'Very little. He did warn me,' she said softly. 'He said he would be going to London a lot, because of his work at the bank, you know, but he spends more time in London than he does here.'

He picked up on the regret in her voice. 'I don't recall Pa working long hours at the bank, not once he'd reached senior level; and isn't it a private bank that the Dawleys run?'

She nodded and sighed, but didn't say more.

'Perhaps when you have the baby he'll spend more time here,' he suggested. 'What man wouldn't want to!'

She didn't answer him, but said, 'Never mind about us; what about you? Where have you been?'

'Lately, back in Ireland,' he told her. 'I did write, several times, but I have no idea what happened to my letters. It's been chaos for so long. But I'm done with that now,' he added heartily, which sounded false to her ears. 'Thank God,' he added. 'There are many Irish who'll never recover from the effects of the famine.' He leaned forward towards the fire, and clasping his hands together he dropped his voice. 'I've something to tell you, Bea, that I haven't yet told our parents.'

'You're not in trouble?' She was alarmed; he had had a worthy career in the army.

'No!' He shook his head. 'No,' he repeated emphatically, 'but I've handed in my commission. I've served ten years and have had enough of the army; I want a different life. A home of my own, with a wife and children.'

She sat back and looked at him. He'd always proclaimed that a life in the army was the best occupation for any man. 'And – have you found someone whom you wish to marry?' she asked teasingly, not thinking for a moment that he would have had the opportunity. But he nodded.

'Yes,' he murmured. 'I have; and here is where the story begins.' He rubbed his hands together as if striking a spark to light a flame. 'I have spent so much time away,' he said softly. 'Burma; then British India, where I learned most about army life, and I'm not saying I didn't enjoy it, I did. I learned about the culture of another country, but I always felt that we didn't belong there. It was not *our* country; we had effectively bought it and moved in.

'Then on to Ireland, where there was so much strife and bitterness, and every day could have been our last. Yet the country people, those who tolerated us – who realized that soldiers are under orders – were warmhearted. Most of them, though, wanted rid of us; we were killing them – or at least the landholders were.' His voice was harsh. 'Killing them by starvation, which was terrible to see or tolerate or even imagine.'

Then he raised his head and smiled. 'And that was where I met Maeve. You'd love her, Bea. I've known her for two years, though we've had to meet secretly. Her father would have killed us both had he discovered that she was walking out with a British soldier.' His face set. 'But that's not all, Bea. We haven't told anyone else and don't intend to; but I wanted to tell you, as this will be the only opportunity, and to ask you, when the time is right, to explain it to our parents. As soon as Christmas is over, Maeve is taking some leave from the hospital where she works – she's a nurse, and volunteered to work over Christmas and Boxing Day instead – and then she'll catch the ferry to Liverpool and wait for me there.'

Beatrix put her hand to her chest, feeling not a physical pain but an emotional one, as if she knew what he was going to say next.

'Where are you going?' she whispered.

'I've booked passages to America. The Irish are going in their thousands looking for a new life. We'll travel separately, but on the same ship, and will be gone before her father realizes. She'll write to tell him as soon as we land. I'll travel as a civilian, as a commercial traveller looking for a new opportunity.

'I don't need money,' he went on. 'I've saved from my pay over the years – and that's another thing. You must tell Pa not to include me in his will; Mother will be glad of the house if Father predeceases her.'

Something clicked in Beatrix's head; something her mother had once said about the house, sons, and daughters-in-law, but she couldn't quite grasp the essence of it.

'He'll be upset,' she whispered. 'Mother will be too – and not knowing; not able to say goodbye.'

Her throat felt as if it were closing up and she could hardly get her words out. 'I'll miss you,' she croaked, and felt an incredible sadness, for she sensed that her brother would be gone from her life for ever, and even though he had served away so often in his army life, there was always the thought that he would turn up at some point when they least expected it.

'I'll keep in touch,' he assured her. 'But not imme-diately. I've thought we might eventually move north, over the border into British territory. I might not stick out like a sore thumb if we do that, because many British emigrants go there in the hope of buying land, and that's what I have in mind.'

'I don't know what to say.' Her mouth trembled. 'I'll have no one in the family to rely on once – once . . .' She meant to say after their parents had died, but that seemed like treachery, as if she were hastening them away, which was ridiculous as they were not yet old.

He stretched his long arms towards her and grasped her hands. 'Of course you will, you goose,' he exclaimed. 'You'll have your own flesh and blood; you're carrying the first of the next generation already, and no doubt there will be more.'

It's not the same, she wanted to say; she and Thomas had a shared history and that could never be re-created, not even with her own children. But she didn't say so, for he had chosen his own life and his life partner, just as she had; but he had chosen for himself, and she had chosen to comply with her father's wishes. Had she done the right thing? It had seemed so at the time, although she had had some doubts; now, it seemed, only time would tell.

CHAPTER TWENTY-NINE

Christmas had gone far better than Beatrix had expected, though at the back of her mind the whole time was the thought that this might be her last one with Thomas.

He had risen early, not having overslept as he'd thought he would and not wanting to waste precious time in bed. He and Charles decorated the topmost branches of the Christmas tree and Beatrix and her mother placed the candles and decorations lower down, whilst her father sat in an easy chair and directed operations, something he had always done, even though no one ever listened to him.

The three men travelled back to London together on the day after Boxing Day, Aaron driving them to the station squashed into the governess cart, which Thomas described as a tub. Beatrix's mother had decided to stay on for a further few days. 'It was quite easy to travel alone, and I was in a ladies only carriage,' she explained. 'I felt that for the first time in my life I had a degree of independence.'

Beatrix pondered for a moment. 'Do you think there will ever come a time when women will take it for granted that they can travel on their own wherever they want to?'

'Some can already; didn't Mrs Gordon come alone? Dora could too, if she was brave enough, and I don't suppose either of them would travel in a ladies only carriage.'

'It's only the pampered ones who feel restricted then, Mama? People like you and me who have been taught to obey society's rules.' She lifted her head, stretching her neck and putting her shoulders back. 'I've made a new friend,' she went on defiantly. 'Her name is Rosetta Stokes and she lives with her parents in Hessle. She and her mother are quite eccentric, her mother particularly so; she collects old jewellery and ornaments and suchlike and then invites her friends and neighbours to come to tea and cajoles them into buying something so that she can give the money to charitable causes. I think that some of their friends probably buy back what they've given in the first place. They both have complete independence in what they think or do and Mrs Stokes's husband, who is a most amiable man, just goes along with whatever his wife says. Rosie says that it's her mother's house.'

Mrs Fawcett looked sceptical. 'Well, I can't possibly imagine how the legalities of that have been worked out. Unless . . .' she hesitated, and lowered her voice, 'unless, of course, she's not married to the man she calls her husband!'

Charles's visits became more frequent once they were into the New Year; sometimes he would turn up unannounced on a Friday night and return to London on the Sunday or early Monday. Other times he would arrive midweek and leave on the Friday, and Beatrix decided that there was no pattern to it that she could follow, so she asked Mrs Gordon to tell the house-maid to light a fire twice a week in his bedroom and on other days to have it laid ready in case he came unexpectedly.

Is he concerned about me, she wondered; is that why he comes so irregularly? There is really no need; the baby isn't due for ages yet, at least I don't think it is. She had become used to his not being there; unconsciously she had made a role for herself, arranging the house as she wanted it, and now most things were in place. She was looking forward to designing the garden, for they were employing a full-time gardener and an apprentice who were now clearing out dead branches and spindly decaying trees from the woodland and had nodded seriously when she had asked about making a path through the middle of it.

Edward Newby had found her down there one bitterly cold February morning, watching the gardener at work, and told her that he had thought of someone who might be suitable as a farm manager. He'd offered to walk her back to the house to discuss it, and she was glad to take his arm as they went because a brisk wind had got up and was chilling her to the bone.

'You shouldn't be out on your own, Beatrix,' he chided her. He called her by her given name only when they were alone; when Charles was there she was always Mrs Dawley.

'I'm all right,' she said a little breathlessly. 'It's just the cold wind that takes my breath away.'

'Do you take a rest in an afternoon?' he asked.

'You're such an old woman,' she said crossly. 'What do you know about pregnancy?'

'More than you, obviously! I am a farmer, in case you hadn't noticed.'

'It's different with sheep and pigs and – and other animals,' she grumbled.

'Is it?' He grinned. 'And how would you know, Mrs Dawley?' he answered mockingly. 'How many kittens and pups have you helped into the world?'

'Well, none as it happens,' she said, pausing to take a breath. 'I was never allowed a dog, though we had a kitchen cat. It wasn't ours; it just lived in all of the houses nearby. I wanted to keep it but it wouldn't stay. It used to wander about going to whichever house had the best food, I think.'

He put his hand beneath her elbow to help her up the front steps. 'I'm going to get you a dog,' he said softly. 'I said before that I would, but I wasn't sure if you were ready to have one; now I think that you probably are, and it's as well to get it now and settle it in before the baby comes. I'll come and collect you tomorrow morning, and you can choose whichever one you want.'

She huffed but thanked him, and wondered how she could look after a dog when she would have a child to care for too.

'The intention is that the dog will look after you, Beatrix,' he said softly, and she thought he must be reading her mind. 'Not the other way round.'

He came as promised the next morning in his trap and she told Dora that she was going to pick up a puppy.

'Shall I come with you, ma'am, or will you be all right?' Dora paused with an armful of Beatrix's silk camisoles that she was going to wash.

'I'll be all right; I'm only going to the Newbys'. I won't be long.'

She was no longer worried about other people's opinions if they saw her driving in Edward Newby's trap. For one thing there was rarely anyone about, and should anyone happen to pass by she would give them a cheery wave if she knew them, or dip her head graciously if she didn't.

'What kind of dog is it?' she asked as they set off. 'The one you are giving me.'

He shrugged. 'I don't know yet. Depends on who Nellie has been meeting.'

She glanced at him. 'Who's Nellie?'

He looked back at her and she saw the corners of his mouth quiver. 'Nellie is the mother of the pups.'

She blinked. 'Oh! How many has she got?'

He shook his head. 'Mm, possibly four!'

'What do you mean – possibly four? Haven't you counted them?'

'She hasn't had them yet; but I'm guessing she'll have them today.'

She was silenced for a moment. 'How – how can you tell?' she asked in a small voice.

'Well, she's had pups before and I've always kept dogs around the farm and you get used to their habits. Nellie for instance starts nesting when she's near her time; she goes to the same corner of the barn, where I've set up clean straw and a bowl of water, turns round and round to get comfortable and then makes her bed.' He laughed. 'Then she rests and I have a chat with her, and when she's ready she just gets on with it, and I keep looking in on her to make sure she's all right.'

'I see,' she said in a low voice as they pulled through the Newbys' gate. 'Doesn't sound too difficult,' she said, clearing her throat.

He came round to her side to help her down and took her hand. 'It isn't,' he said softly. 'It's the most remarkable and natural occurrence in the world.'

She swallowed. 'I believe you,' she whispered. 'But still daunting, nevertheless.'

He nodded. 'I suppose it is, the first time.' Then he smiled and handed her down. 'But Nellie's had several litters. She'll be fine.'

Edward brought her a wooden chair to sit on in a corner of the barn where he said Nellie wouldn't notice her. He said she was almost ready. 'She'll be all right with us here as long as we're quiet,' he whispered, and Beatrix just nodded and watched transfixed as Nellie gave birth to one glistening pup, and then another; then rested for half an hour or so and had two more.

Edward walked softly towards the straw nest and crouched down on his haunches next to Nellie. He offered her his hand and she licked it and then drank some water from the bowl whilst Edward moved backwards to watch her licking and cleaning the pups.

'One more, I think,' he murmured, and Beatrix turned her glance to him and thought that she had never seen a man and might never see another with such an expression of tenderness as he was wearing now. She felt a sudden raw surge of yearning. I could, I believe, in another life or time, have loved such a man as this.

CHAPTER THIRTY

It was perhaps not quite as easy as Nellie had made it seem giving birth to her puppies, Beatrix considered candidly, but then Edward had said that she had already had several litters.

She put her head on her pillow, feeling content, and watched the nurse attending to the babe before putting him into her arms. She couldn't quite believe it. She looked down on his closed eyes fluttering beneath the lids, his fine blond hair still sticky on his head. He's mine! My son. How quickly the sensation of love and protectiveness flushed through her mind and body.

'Ma'am.' The midwife came to her side, and spoke quietly. 'Is it your intention to put him to the breast, or shall I give him a drop of sweetened water? It is only a preliminary; you don't have to . . .'

'No. I will.' He's mine, she thought again, but he doesn't know that yet. She unfastened the strings at the neck of her plain cotton nightgown, bought purely for the purpose of childbirth, and placed his cheek against her breast. Almost immediately he turned his head, his mouth opening and moving instinctively towards her.

This is our special time together; in a few minutes the midwife will open the door, go downstairs and announce to Charles and my mother that Mrs Dawley has been delivered of a healthy boy.

Mother will hold back, I know she will, allowing Charles the privilege of being the first to see his son. He'll be pleased. This has been his great desire and I have fulfilled it. How would I have felt if the child had been a girl? A little afraid of his reaction, no matter how sweet and lovely she might have been. He doesn't want a child to play with, to be proud of, or to love for itself.

Ouch! How strong his jaws were! The midwife looked up as Beatrix drew in her breath and came to her side. 'We'll put him to the other side now, ma'am. We don't want him to make a meal of it, only to show him where lunch will be available.'

Beatrix smiled, and wondered how often the midwife had spouted the jest to other new mothers.

'For a brief while only, ma'am. Then cover yourself and let Nurse put him in his cot whilst I fetch your husband to take a look at him. It's a proud day for any father.'

Cover myself! Does she not realize how babies are conceived? Beatrix took a deep breath. Should I simply tell him that it has been very difficult and that I am very tired, and not mention that in fact I couldn't help but think about Edward's dog Nellie giving birth to her pups and barely making a sound but just getting on with it, as Edward would have said?

The midwife told me I had been very good in not making a fuss, and I felt as if she were praising me for my achievement. I'm becoming cynical; I wonder why.

Charles came in quietly, almost reluctantly. He's scared, she thought; he's expecting – what? A dishevelled wife, a squalling babe, whereas everything has been tidied away. Soiled sheets rolled up in a corner, the baby with his clean sponged face to show to the world, and here I am waiting for a cup of sweet tea to revive me.

'Hello, darling wife.' Charles bent to kiss her cheek. 'How are you feeling?'

She quashed the desire to say *I'm deliriously happy and very well*, and said softly, 'A little tired if I'm honest, Charles. But it will pass.' She raised a limp hand towards the crib. 'Take a look at our fine son.'

He walked round her bed to look into the crib. 'I can't see him,' he complained. 'He's covered up so closely.'

'Mrs Beddows, will you lift the baby out so that my husband might hold him?'

'Oh, no, I don't want to hold him!' Charles stammered. 'He's too small. I might drop him. I just want to see his face.'

The midwife lifted the child from the crib and removed the shawl from his face and head so that Charles might see him.

'Ah!' he murmured. 'Hmm. Not much hair. Does he have a look of either of us, do you think?' He directed the question to Beatrix.

'Why yes!' she exclaimed. 'He definitely has a look of you, quite clearly, but perhaps it's not possible to see oneself. But it's most certainly there; do you see the likeness, Mrs Beddows?'

'Irrefutably.' The midwife raised her eyebrows as if she was quite used to pandering to bewildered husbands. 'The absolute image.'

Mrs Beddows and the nurse went out of the room after Charles, who was going downstairs to open a bottle of champagne, and Beatrix's mother came in to take their place. She had different ideas about likenesses.

'He looks just the same as you did, Beatrix,' she murmured as she leaned over the crib. 'Your nose, your colouring,' she continued, ignoring the fact that Charles was fair-haired too, even fairer than Beatrix whose hair was a shade of reddish-gold. 'He's so sweet,' she went on. 'I must telegraph your father; he will be thrilled.' She paused. 'And Thomas too. He will be pleased to hear the news, but—'

'We can't tell him yet, Mama; not until he writes.'

She had told her parents only a month before of Thomas's departure and his plans to be married, when she knew he and his wife-to-be would be safely on the high seas heading for America. She didn't tell them that the couple might then travel north. That they were gone, she thought, would be enough for them to bear for the time being. Now she knew that the blow would be softened by the arrival of a new baby to indulge.

'Ask Aaron to go to the Brough telegraph office,' Beatrix said. 'Unless Charles is going to send news to his parents.' Though I doubt if he will be in a hurry to do that, she thought. He'll make them wait. 'Tell Papa his name, won't you? Laurence Charles Thomas.

I think it has a nice ring to it, don't you, Mama? Laurence Charles Thomas Dawley.'

'Yes, I do. Did you choose the names?'

'Two of them,' she said. 'Laurence was my choice and Thomas of course, but Charles insisted his name should be included.' She shrugged. 'Proof that he is his son.' She gazed at her mother. 'As if proof should be needed.'

'What is happening to you, Beatrix?' her mother asked softly. 'Are you becoming a sceptic?'

'I don't think so, Mama. But I'm growing up and seeing things differently.'

Her mother frowned. 'Charles is not doubting his son, surely?'

'No, and there is no need for him to do so. He knows I was a virgin when we married,' she said frankly, knowing that she could now speak openly to her mother if she wished. 'But he still questions me, asks me who I see, where I have been. As if I could have gone anywhere during the last few weeks.' I wonder, though, she thought, if it is the kettle calling the pot black.

They heard footsteps outside the door and changed the subject as Charles came into the room with a bottle of opened champagne, followed by Dora with a tray of glasses which she placed on a side table. Mrs Beddows and the nurse slipped back in behind them.

'Congratulations, ma'am,' Dora said, 'and sir. May I take a look at the baby?'

'Of course you can, Dora.' Beatrix smiled at the girl, who was clearly thrilled to see the infant. 'Move his shawl a little to see him properly. Don't you think he's wonderful?'

'He is, ma'am, and has a look of both of you.' She turned to Charles. 'Don't you think so, sir?'

'Mm?' Charles was handing Mrs Fawcett a glass of champagne. 'Well, yes, I should hope so. A small glass for you, my dear?' he asked Beatrix, who nodded, and then turned to offer one to Mrs Beddows, although he ignored the nurse and Dora. The latter dipped her knee and departed, but turned at the door and asked Beatrix by a hand sign behind Charles's back if she would like a pot of tea, and Beatrix gave an imperceptible nod.

Charles raised his glass. 'Well, shall we drink good health and wealth to my son, Charles Laurence Dawley? May he thrive!'

'Indeed,' Beatrix murmured and took a small sip. But he is to be *Laurence* Charles Thomas Dawley, she amended silently, not the other way round, and he is my son too.

After a while everyone went downstairs to let Beatrix rest, with the nurse in the room next door in case she needed anything. The following day, a newly engaged nursemaid would arrive. Dora knocked quietly and came in with a tray of tea and biscuits.

'Are you feeling all right, ma'am?' she asked.

'I am, Dora,' Beatrix said honestly. 'It wasn't quite as difficult as I'd expected, just tiring. How would your mother have been after childbirth?'

'Oh, she'd have been up and scrubbing potatoes for the next meal, I suppose.' Dora laughed. 'But maybe not with the first one, but then I wouldn't know about that. I reckon she'd have been proud of you though; most ladies like you would've made a fuss, I reckon.'

Beatrix closed her eyes and rested against the pillow once she'd drunk her tea and nibbled on a biscuit still warm from the oven. Mother asked if I were becoming a sceptic. I don't think I am, but I'm not a naive, gullible young girl either, which I probably was a year ago.

It was early May, just over a month after their first wedding anniversary, and she thought that Charles would be pleased that she had so swiftly fulfilled her obligation to provide him with a son and heir. Incredible that I was caught so quickly, she considered, seeing that he has spent so little time here. But now I think I know why, and I must accept it.

She had often wondered where Charles's London house was situated and he had vaguely explained it, but had never given the address as she had asked, saying always that she should contact the bank if ever she needed to send him an urgent message.

'I'm always at the bank,' he'd said. 'I spend very little time at the town house; I bed down there and eat breakfast, and have supper at a local restaurant. I don't need a housekeeper; I employ a woman once a week to clean up after me and use the Chinese laundry for my personal linen.'

She had accepted this. Why would she not? It was how he had always lived since leaving his parents' house, or so he said, until one morning in early February, after he had left to catch the London train, when she had wandered into his room to find the housemaid gathering up his laundry: the bedsheets and towels, his undergarments, and the shirts he had worn during the two days he had been at Old Stone Hall.

Beatrix had looked out from his window; a rime of frost covered the front lawn and she'd thought that it looked like a skating rink. She'd turned and decided that she would go back to bed for an hour; it was not quite seven o'clock.

Something white had dropped out of the laundry bundle and she bent to pick it up. A handkerchief, but not one belonging to Charles. This was fine lawn, smaller than the kind a gentleman would use, but not one of hers either. It was richly embroidered with a red flower in one corner.

Instinctively she put it to her nose. A faint but exotic perfume sprang from it, making her catch her breath. She looked at it again. It had been beautifully ironed, each corner neat and straight and making a perfect square. It hadn't been used.

She heard the girl coming back upstairs and slipped it into her dressing gown pocket.

'Beg pardon, ma'am.' The girl dipped her knee. 'I was going to pull 'blankets back to air. Shall I leave them for now?'

'No,' she'd said. 'Carry on with what you were doing. I'm going back to bed for an hour. Tell Cook I'll have breakfast upstairs this morning so you can clear the breakfast room.'

She'd pulled out the handkerchief from her pocket and climbed back into bed. Again she put it to her nose. She tried to imagine the kind of woman who might wear perfume such as this; not anyone like her. Someone sure of herself, unafraid of turned heads; exotic, like the perfume that was drifting towards her.

Not a woman of the streets, she'd thought; not that she knew what they were like, but she imagined they wouldn't be able to afford such a fragrance as this; this was expensive.

How did the handkerchief come to be tangled up with Charles's shirts and pillowcases? It must have fallen out of his trouser pocket, but what was it doing there? Had it been slipped in deliberately so that it could be found? To torment me?

The answer had come swiftly into her head leaving no room for doubt. Charles has a mistress. *She* was the reason he spent so little time with his wife and wouldn't give her his London address. Did she live with him? Was she feeling neglected, as Beatrix herself did? Did she feel jealous? Did she even know he was married? Or had she slipped the handkerchief into his pocket to remind him of her?

Now, three months later, she lay perfectly still on her pillow, yet inwardly she was shaking. I have fulfilled my obligation; my role was always to be a wife and bearer of sons. I can accept that now. The other woman must be very special to him but, for some reason, not suitable for the role that I accepted.

If this woman cares for Charles, then I'm truly sorry for her. She turned her head to look at her newborn son, who lay in such sweet repose that tears of joy slipped from her eyes. I, she thought, am the favoured one. My role cannot be taken from me. Can it? Can I be sure?

CHAPTER THIRTY-ONE

Beatrix had never confronted Charles over the question of the handkerchief or how it had come to be in his room, for what was the use? He would be angry if she asked him; he would probably deny it, too, and he would, she had no doubt, make her pay for the accusation of unfaithfulness.

When Laurence was baptized Beatrix made sure that the vicar had the names written down in the right sequence. Her father stood in for her brother Thomas as one of the godfathers and Charles's best man Paul was the other; for a godmother she asked Sophia Hartley, who travelled down with Beatrix's parents. She had toyed with the thought of asking Charles's sister Anne, but Charles had pooh-poohed the idea, saying she wouldn't want to be involved in the least, and indeed she did not accompany her parents on the occasion even though she had been invited.

'What we will have,' Charles announced the next day, when he came across Beatrix alone and bent over the sleeping Laurence in his cot, 'is a party to celebrate. Not immediately, but soon.'

Beatrix's heart sank. 'What kind of party?' she asked. 'We had a celebratory lunch yesterday. Could we wait until I'm fully recovered?'

'Of course,' he said smoothly. 'I was thinking of midsummer when we can eat and drink outside. Perhaps use Little Stone House as a place for the guests to stay?'

Beatrix felt protective of the little house; she had taken great care in choosing the right colours for the walls, comfy squashy sofas, beautiful curtains and a long mahogany table and chairs in the dining room. She was especially pleased with the excellent paintings of Yorkshire landscapes and local shipping scenes she had managed to find for the walls.

Before she had given birth to Laurence she had travelled into Hull by train with Dora and had discovered that the town had galleries with wonderful pieces of local art, and good shops where furniture could be made to her own specification and she could see patterns of the very best Axminster carpets for her approval.

'We'd have to move the good furniture,' Charles went on. 'Some of the people I know don't have your restraint or good taste, Beatrix.' He ran his hands around her waist and down to her hips. 'How long will it be – before . . .?' He whispered into her ear. 'You are looking particularly seductive.'

She gave a breathy sound. 'Not just yet, Charles,' she murmured. 'Perhaps a month?'

'A month!' he muttered, drawing away from her. 'As long as that? Are you afraid of getting caught again?'

'Oh!' she said, trying not to show alarm. 'That wouldn't be good for me or the child, would it? I'm sure the doctor would say it isn't advisable, but I will ask him when I next see him, so that we can be ready. Now what about this party?' She changed the subject. 'Who would we invite?'

But he had become annoyed at his perceived dismissal and left the room to join the family downstairs; she sat on the edge of the bed looking down at the sleeping Laurence. Perhaps it would be good to have people to stay, she considered. Perhaps I'm becoming a stick-in-the-mud because I'm alone so often.

I could ask Sophia if she would come, and perhaps she might find a husband from the gentlemen Charles knows. I will invite Rosie and Mrs Stokes, she giggled to herself: they would liven up the stiff London shirts with their eccentricities. Yes, I'll tell Charles that I'm quite agreeable, and once we have a date we'll take the good paintings down and replace them with reproductions, and do the same with the Axminster carpets and Aubusson rugs; I'd hate to have wine spilled over them. But perhaps I'm being unkind. Most of our guests will be used to quality furnishings, and in any case I'm being fussy over objects that don't really matter. Besides, it will be rather nice to show how lovely the house is.

We could have it in July, on my birthday; that would remind Charles of the date, for he completely forgot last year. It was inevitable, I suppose, for we still barely knew each other. This year I will still only be twenty, not even of age yet. But does it matter, I wonder, once a woman is married and under her husband's dominance?

But when, later, she suggested July, Charles said that the weather in July was unpredictable and he would prefer August. Beatrix said nothing, but she knew that she would be thinking more about bringing in the harvest by then. It would be their first, and their farm manager, Simon Hallam, had said it was promising to be a good one.

Simon Hallam had come to them at the recommendation of Edward Newby. He was twenty-five, and although he and Edward hadn't been particular friends at farming college they had known each other well: after finishing his education he had gone abroad to discover what other countries did to improve their farming culture.

He was very knowledgeable, and Beatrix blessed the day when he arrived for an interview and didn't appear to be at all perturbed to discover that his prospective employer, though willing and eager to learn, was a young woman brought up in the city of London.

'Let's start small, Mrs Dawley,' he'd advised. 'Farming can be a tricky and expensive business, and we are also at the mercy of the weather. I propose we take on a foreman and two horse lads to begin with, and hire local labourers for the rest.'

Once the position had been offered and accepted, he'd gone with her and Edward to look over the land and earmarked the buildings where the foreman and horse lads would live once they began hiring, the fields to be planted with wheat as their first crop and the ones they would use for livestock. On Edward's suggestion she also asked him to choose a pair of Shire horses for working the land and to look at the old equipment in the barns to assess what was workable and what would be required. She'd breathed a huge sigh of relief, for although she could look after the accounts she wouldn't have known where to start on any kind of farming schedule.

'Well done, Beatrix,' Edward had murmured as they walked back to the house, and Simon Hallam had gone off to draw up a programme so that she would know what to expect and could give her approval or voice her queries.

'I haven't done anything yet,' she'd said. 'It's you I've to thank for bringing Mr Hallam here.'

He'd seized her hand and swung it as if they were children, and grinned. 'You took the bull by the horns, didn't you?' he said. 'Do you know what that means?'

'Ye-es, I suppose,' she'd replied, rather taken aback by the fact that she was holding hands with a man who wasn't her husband.

'You seized the situation and dealt with it yourself and without anyone else's say-so or permission,' he'd said. 'I notice that Charles isn't here to put in his pennyworth.'

She'd laughed and loosened her hand. 'You do talk in riddles, Edward. But Charles agreed to go ahead with the plan and I didn't in the least expect him to become involved. I'll write to him and explain what is happening.'

He'd given her a significant glance. 'So you'll be to blame if it doesn't work?'

She'd raised her eyebrows and given a slight nod, and he'd taken her hand again, swinging it until they were in view of Old Stone Hall, when he released it. 'So we'll have to make sure it doesn't fail, won't we!'

Now, as she looked over the lawn from the sitting room window and thought of that day, she thought how incredible it was that so much had happened in so little time. The two residences were all but finished and she was the mother of a fine boy and running an estate. And for the simple things in life, there were daisies in the lawn. She had asked the gardener's lad to leave some patches of them when he cut the grass, for she loved to see them during the day and especially in the evening when they looked like stars in the dusk.

Charles, his parents and Paul had returned to London soon after the baptism, and her parents and Sophia had left the following day. She was alone again but for the servants. This won't do, she thought. I am fed up with my own company so I will go calling. I feel fit and well, I've been churched and Laurence is baptized so no one will refuse us, and I will take my lovely boy out on his first visit. She rang the bell for Dora.

'Ask Aaron to bring up the pony and trap,' she told her. 'You're happy to drive, aren't you?'

'Yes, ma'am. I love it,' Dora said eagerly. 'Where are we going?'

'We're going calling.' Beatrix laughed. 'I'm taking Laurence out visiting. First we'll call on Mrs Stokes and Rosie. They won't mind about the time, but if they are not at home I'll leave my card; and then we'll go to see Mags, because she hasn't seen the baby yet. So best bib and tucker, Dora, and a warm blanket for Laurie.'

'Laurie! I like that, ma'am. Laurence will fit him better when he's older. Are you taking the nursemaid?'

'No, I'm not. She can have an hour off whilst I take my son out.'

'Is it the done thing, ma'am?' Dora asked. 'It's all right for such as my mother, but for ladies like you . . .?'

'I'm visiting friends, Dora; they'll be pleased to see me. It's a lovely day and we'll take extra blankets so that Laurie doesn't catch cold. He won't, will he?' she asked, a little anxious now that Dora had queried the outing.

'I wasn't thinking of him catching cold, ma'am, I was thinking of what people might say.'

'I don't care what people might say,' Beatrix said petulantly. 'I'm going to do what I think is right. I don't want my child to be mollycoddled. I want him to grow up hardy and strong and able to make his own decisions without reference to society's rule book.'

'Very well, ma'am, and I'll bring a warm shawl for you too whilst we're driving.'

'Thank you, Dora.' Beatrix smiled. 'Whatever would I do without you?'

As they drove off in the pony and trap, another thought came to her. I think we should have a carriage, and then I could travel during wet weather and bring the nursery maid if I wanted to, though at the moment I'm very happy to hold Laurie on my knee. Charles can afford one; he's always telling me about the wealth he will have now that he's produced a son. Nothing to do with me, of course!

Rosetta Stokes and her mother were very pleased to see her and not in the least taken aback by her travelling alone with only a maid, and were delighted to greet the infant Laurie.

'His colouring is very like yours,' Rosie remarked. 'Which of course is a good thing. Fond relatives will comment that the child favours your side!'

'They will, of course, though Charles's colouring is very similar,' Beatrix said, and considered that her mother had already mentioned that Laurie looked just like her as a child and Charles had asked if he favoured him. He will be a blending of the two of us, she thought.

'I have been reading in the newspapers about Mrs Caroline Norton, the socialite,' Mrs Stokes commented, referring to nothing they had been discussing but obviously eager to impart news. 'She's in the public eye again. You'll have heard of her, I expect? No?' she uttered in a surprised tone when Beatrix shook her head and murmured that she hadn't. 'I would have thought you'd have been sure to have heard of her, being a London gel. But perhaps you're too young?'

'Of course Beatrix is too young, Mama,' Rosie broke in with a great sigh. 'We both are! I only know of her because you've spoken of her so often.'

'She's one of my heroines,' Mrs Stokes asserted. 'Such a brave woman. Fighting her corner against all those influential powerful men.'

'Mother's favourite hobby horse,' Rosie remarked laconically. 'Poor Papa. He always goes out of the room when Mama begins one of her tirades, in case anyone thinks she's talking about him!'

'I *never* need to discuss your father,' Mrs Stokes commented. 'He is the most amiable of men.'

'Always does what Mama wants, she means,' Rosie added in a low voice, and Beatrix smiled.

'So who is Caroline Norton?' she asked. 'Why should I have heard of her?'

'Every woman should mark her words even if they live in a perfect marriage.' Mrs Stokes got into her stride. 'She embodies a warning to all women and has already influenced an Act of Parliament. She and her husband live quite separately, and she is about to bring another case against him.' She laughed. 'A most dreadful man,' she went on. 'Every woman will agree, and her case against him this time is that she has referred her creditors to him, for as I expect you will know, my dear, a husband is liable for his wife's debts!'

CHAPTER THIRTY-TWO

Beatrix left Rosetta and her mother with her thoughts in a whirl. She had stayed for only fifteen minutes but Mrs Stokes had regaled her with every detail of the apparently infamous society rebel and reformer Caroline Norton, who had taken her husband to court on several occasions; he had done the same to her and had even levelled the accusation that she and the Prime Minister, Lord Melbourne, who was a friend of hers, had engaged in an adulterous affair.

Seemingly she had written a book based on her own experience of living with a brutal husband, who had refused to give her access to her children and banned her from seeing them.

Why would Mrs Stokes tell me such a tale, she thought as Dora steered the pony in the direction of the Newby farmhouse. I feel quite unsettled. I'm a new mother, after all, and don't wish to hear such things; but then she reconsidered. I suppose that every woman should know of Caroline Norton and the struggle she had to try to gain custody of her children. The law was changed as a result, and yet in spite of it all she didn't win that conflict, for her husband took the children off to Scotland where the new English laws didn't apply.

Mags Newby greeted her enthusiastically, took Laurie from her as she bade her sit down, and put the infant on her own knee. 'We'd heard you'd had a son,' she said. 'And you're a right bonny bairn, aren't you?' she cooed at him. 'I do love young babbies. They're so helpless and dependent on us, aren't they? I wish I'd had half a dozen more.' She looked up at Beatrix and her voice dropped. 'Edward and his sisters had a brother once, but we lost 'little lad even afore he'd started to walk. Got pneumonia he did, so nothing could be done.'

'I didn't know,' Beatrix said softly. 'I'm so sorry. It must have been very difficult for you.'

She couldn't imagine the sorrow that she would feel if Laurie was taken from her, and with a sudden flash of pity she thought of the society woman championed by Mrs Stokes, who had had her children taken from her but had made it possible for other women to gain custody of theirs.

Edward, followed by his father, came in just as she was leaving, and she saw him take a sudden breath when he saw her with Laurie in her arms.

'Good day, Mrs Dawley,' he murmured formally. 'You look . . . very well. Might we take a look at your son?'

'And put a silver coin in his palm,' Luke Newby said over his shoulder. 'Ma,' he called to Mags, who had gone into the kitchen to fetch something, 'have you got a silver sixpence?' and followed her out of the room.

'He's a handsome lad,' Edward said softly. 'Has the look of his mother, no question about it.' Without touching the baby's face, with the tips of his finger and thumb he gently pulled back the shawl to take a better look, and nodded. 'Her tender skin and golden hair.'

Beatrix flushed and swallowed. 'We – er, we couldn't decide whose side he favoured,' she murmured. 'We'll perhaps have to wait awhile.'

Luke came back in holding a coin in his hand and Edward with a crooked grin stood back. 'Da's a believer in these old superstitions,' he jested. 'It's supposed to mean he'll always have money in his hand, or some such make-believe.'

'Ah, well.' Luke Newby touched the baby's open palm with the coin and his tiny fingers closed around it. 'There, you see, it's as well not to take owt for granted.' He looked at Beatrix. 'It's a clean coin,' he said. 'We washed it under 'tap just to be sure.'

'Thank you,' Beatrix said gratefully. 'You're all very kind.'

Mags came back carrying a basket of apples. 'That's because we're relieved that Charles didn't bring some toffee-nosed young woman to live in Uncle Nev's owd house,' she commented. 'We wouldn't have been happy about that.' She handed the basket to Dora, who was waiting by the door. 'P'raps Cook can mek use of these,' she said. 'They're early June drop, but good enough for baking. Thank you for bringing your new bairn to see us,' she said, smiling, and peeking at the child once more. 'Tek him home now. Keep him clear of any chills or draughts and he'll thrive.'

Edward went before them to open the door, letting Dora with the basket of apples out first and taking Beatrix's elbow to make sure she didn't trip over the step.

'Thank you, Edward,' she said softly, and glancing at him was confused by the expression on his face as he led her to the trap. It wasn't so much a look of sadness as an indication of loss or hurt, and she knew instinctively that it was to do with her.

Charles's summer party was held in August. There had been a spell of long hot days so fortunately the harvesting hadn't yet begun; it was being held back a week to take advantage of the weather. Beatrix had invited Mr and Mrs Stokes and Rosetta, who had become a particular friend, but they had already accepted another invitation, but her friends Sophia and Eleanor had accepted. Most of the guests were accommodated in Little Stone House, but apart from Paul, Beatrix didn't know any of Charles's friends, and as she wasn't sure who were married and who were not she didn't want to risk her own friends' welfare and gave Sophia and Nell a room in the main house close to her own.

She was introduced to the men who had brought their wives – or fiancées, as they described them; it was a word Beatrix had not heard before – and she vaguely hoped that Mrs Gordon had arranged enough beds. But it appeared that it didn't matter too much, and, rather uncomfortably, she came to the conclusion that not all of them were married, or at least not to the young women they had brought with them.

Charles's friend Paul had come alone but knew most of the other men, and he was the one who was most courteous towards Sophia and Eleanor, bringing them glasses of champagne and serving them from plates of sweet and savoury pastries, little pastry cups filled with freshly cooked shrimps or cheese and local dishes of syllabub, flummery and sorbets.

For those with a heartier appetite, Cook, assisted by Mags, had made a pork pie, boiled a ham, roasted a leg of pork and made rabbit stew to be eaten with a batch of freshly made bread; to follow was apple pie or steamed pudding with cream or custard.

Beatrix, wandering amongst the guests, came to the conclusion that very few of them would have savoured any better food than they were eating now, and as the evening drew on and the guests pulled on warm jackets and shawls and placed blankets over their knees to sit sipping their drinks until late, the men dug deep into their pockets and put money in an empty dish to give to Cook.

Charles came and put his arm about Beatrix's waist, kissed her cheek and murmured, 'Well done, Beatrix. A perfect occasion.' He lit a cigar and said casually, 'If you're feeling tired don't feel you must stay up late to act as hostess. This crowd,' he lifted his hand to indicate their guests, 'will be here until midnight at least.'

'Oh, will they?' she said. 'Well, in that case I might take my leave. It's past ten o'clock and I was awake very early this morning. Mrs Gordon and a maid will stay up to clear away.'

He kissed her cheek again. 'Off you go then. They'll understand.'

'I'll say goodnight,' she said, and he nodded.

'I'll be in later,' he murmured as she moved away to take her leave of the guests. As she walked towards them she saw Sophia and Eleanor rise from their chairs and Sophia shake her head at Paul and move his hand from her arm. She greeted them and said she was going inside and saw a look of relief on Sophia's face.

'We're going in too,' Eleanor told her. 'It's been lovely, Beatrix.'

Beatrix said goodnight to everyone, the men kissed her hand and thanked her for her hospitality, the women smiled sweetly and she turned to go in. She found herself facing Paul, who took hold of both her hands and kissed her cheek, which she found rather strange considering she hardly knew him.

'Thank you, beautiful lady,' he slurred, and she realized he was inebriated. 'Charles is a very lucky fellow. I must remind him that he has a lovely little wife here. Never mind gallivanting in London,' he waved a hand around, 'this is where he should be.'

'Yes, thank you,' she murmured. 'Goodnight. I'll see you in the morning.'

'That you will.' He touched the side of his nose. 'If not before.'

She walked away towards the house, Sophia and Eleanor by her side. 'Odious man,' she muttered, pleased that he was staying in the annexe and not the main house. 'I hope he didn't upset either of you? He seemed so charming to begin with.'

'He was,' Eleanor said. 'But he's had too much wine. He'll be sorry in the morning.'

Dora must have been watching from the window, for the door was opened as soon as they reached the top of the steps. 'Cook's making hot drinks, ma'am,' she told Beatrix, and looked at Sophia and Eleanor. 'Would you like them upstairs, miss?'

Sophia and Nell looked at Beatrix, who smiled and said, 'Let's all have them in your room, shall we? Then we can have a gossip about everyone.'

Her friends giggled and Dora smiled. 'I'll bring a tray up, ma'am,' she told Beatrix. 'Cheese and bis- cuits? A slice of fruit cake?'

'Some sliced ham and mustard and bread,' Beatrix said. 'I've hardly eaten anything. I was too nervous before and now I'm starving. Let's have our own party upstairs. Come on, before anyone else comes in and catches us.'

And feeling like schoolgirls again, they all ran upstairs.

CHAPTER THIRTY-THREE

Had Charles had his way, that year's summer party might have set a precedent for an annual revelry, but the following summer Beatrix was pregnant again and suffering badly from morning sickness which kept her in bed most mornings for months. She told Charles she couldn't cope with so many guests and Charles, annoyed, said he would halve the number of invitations. Beatrix reluctantly agreed.

When Charles arrived with Paul he was driving a brand-new black-and-red-trimmed brougham which he had ordered from a York carriage maker; he told Beatrix that he had also put in an order for a second-hand clarence in good repair with a waterproof hood, large enough to carry her and one other person plus two children.

'You'll need something sturdy for the roads around here,' he had told her, and she had shrugged and said, 'Yes, of course.'

He hadn't been to Yorkshire for two weeks and she saw that he'd caught the sun: his forehead was a fading red and the skin on his nose was peeling, his hair bleached almost white. 'It must have been very hot in

London,' she remarked. 'I'll search out some calamine to take away the soreness.'

'I've been in Rome,' he disclosed, as she was gently smoothing on the lotion, and added that he had attended an international banking meeting, which she didn't believe for one moment. 'I wore a hat but it didn't protect sufficiently. A crazy idea to hold a conference there in the summer. I won't go again.'

And he wouldn't; he had vehemently told Maria, whose idea it had been that they should take a holiday in Rome, never to ask him to go abroad in the summer again. Reluctantly she ministered to him when he suffered heatstroke that kept him in a darkened room; then she had closed the curtains and left him there whilst she went off to explore the city.

Beatrix, on the other hand, had kept on her sun bonnet whenever she went out during the hot weather, and at the end of June and beginning of July, when haymaking was under way and she had gone out in the fields to help with refreshments, she put up her parasol, with the result that her face and neck were only lightly tanned and the fine hairs on her arms were golden.

Now, in mid-August, the harvesting of the winter corn began and the local community, as traditionally it always did, helped out in everyone's fields. Whole families came to work, men, women and children moving from farm to farm to ensure a rich harvest for all. The calls and shouts and laughter could be heard over the fields and hedges as everyone began work, and some of the party guests wandered up the lanes to watch the corn being cut and stacked, but when it was the time for the Dawley fields to begin they beat a hasty retreat as swarms of thrips and flies descended on them. The party was not considered a great success as the guests scurried indoors to escape.

At the beginning of December Beatrix gave birth to a girl who was as blonde as her brother and named her Alicia Emily, choosing the names herself as Charles suggested she should. She gathered he wasn't as interested in his latest child as he might have been had the baby been another boy.

But Beatrix was delighted with her dainty daughter, and when Dora brought Laurie to see her in her cot the toddler put out his arms to embrace her, smacking his lips in an attempt to kiss her.

'They'll be good friends, ma'am,' Dora said, lifting Laurie on to Beatrix's bed so that she could give him a cuddle.

'I hope so, Dora,' she said. 'My brother and I were. It's so important.' She thought of Charles and his sister Anne and wondered if he ever saw her, for he had never invited her here for any function or a family visit, and although Anne wasn't a woman she particularly cared for she felt that she was missing out on family life, just as Charles was.

Charles's parents didn't come for the christening. She wondered if they too considered that a granddaughter wasn't as important as a grandson who would carry on the family name, but she was upset and a little annoyed by what she considered a slight. Her own parents had come and her mother was delighted that her granddaughter had been given her own name as a middle one.

A year on she suffered an early miscarriage and the doctor warned her to wait a little longer before becoming pregnant again. It was fortunate, she thought, that Charles spent so little time at home, having lost the limited interest he had had in the fortunes of the farm or the estate, except for looking at the balance sheets. He came mostly by train, leaving his smart carriage at home for use on the London streets rather than the rural roads of East Yorkshire. The clarence when it came was easily big enough for her and a maid and the children, surprisingly comfortable and well sprung in spite of being old, and could be pulled by one horse.

A youngster just out of school was taken on as general lad and Aaron was given the role of full-time carriage driver. He wore a heavier cape and a top hat set at a jaunty angle as he drove the spry young horse; the pony was put out to grass until the children should be big enough to be put on his back and amble gently round the paddock.

Wheat prices had risen steadily and the farm was in profit; throughout the country, oats and barley continued to be grown for the English market and there was always work for the agricultural labourer. Beatrix paid their regular local workers well above the average received by the itinerants who appeared for every haymaking or harvesting.

The Crimean War had begun and she was pleased to think that her brother Thomas was well out of that situation. Her parents had received a letter from him to say that he and his wife Maeve had arrived in Canada; they had bought a plot of land where they were raising buffalo or *bison* as they called them, which out in the wild were rapidly disappearing.

Beatrix felt fit and healthy and fulfilled. Her children were thriving, the estate was prospering and she had a good and easy friendship with Rosetta Stokes. Sophia and Eleanor came to visit regularly and both young women had become engaged to be married.

She caught the train to London on a few occasions to visit her parents, leaving the two children in the care of the nursery maid, Dora and Mrs Gordon, and met Sophia and Eleanor for tea and shopping just as they had when they were young and carefree.

She always told Charles when she was coming to the city and he called for her at her parents' home and took her out to lunch or dinner. Never did he ask her to his London house, and her suspicions that he had a mistress increased, for he was a lustful man who would not have endured a monastic life for long, and it seemed to her that they were living entirely separate lives.

As she travelled home in the ladies only carriage she mused that she had more lively conversations with Edward and even with Hallam than she ever did with Charles, who on his infrequent visits to Yorkshire would bed her and depart the next morning, leaving her feeling rather soiled, for there were no words of love or affection.

On one of these occasions she became pregnant again; she wrote to tell him, but it seemed he felt no urgency to come and it was two weeks before he arrived. Laurie and Alicia hardly knew who he was and were shy of him; he looked over the estate and remarked that it seemed to be running satisfactorily, and left again for London on urgent business.

It was a month after Laurie's fourth birthday when Beatrix gave birth to another son. Will Charles be pleased that it's a boy, she wondered, or won't he care? Charles arrived to see them two days later, telling her he had been tied up with business deals. He inspected his second son, who was as blond as his brother Laurie and his sister Alicia, and when she suggested the names Ambrose Neville after her father and Charles's great uncle, and as Neville was Charles's middle name, he said, 'Yes, if you wish. Have you enough children now?' as if that were her main role in life.

I would like to have another child, she thought, a girl as sweet as Alicia, but I would like the conception to be consummated in love and affection rather than carnal lust.

Charles sat on the end of her bed and gazed into the cot where the babe lay sleeping. 'How old is Laurence now?' he asked. 'Five, is it?'

'Four,' she murmured, her face set, wondering how he could forget the date of such an important event and his main reason for marriage. He had achieved his goal and ensured his inheritance, but hadn't in the least longed for any other children. He never played with them or appeared to take any interest in their welfare; she had sometimes caught Laurie's questioning expression when Charles arrived, as if he were wondering who he was and why he had come.

'Mm,' Charles murmured. 'Another year then before I put his name down for my old school.'

She pulled herself up on her pillow. 'What? No! He's far too young to think of school. I'll arrange a tutor when he's ready. He knows his numbers up to twenty already, and some of the alphabet . . .' She was horrified.

He seemed amused. 'I don't mean to *send* him to school! I meant only to put his name down. The places get filled up very quickly. Of course it will help that I was there—'

'But you hated it,' she said. 'You have told me so several times.'

'I did, but it didn't do me any harm, did it? He'll start when he's seven.'

'He will not!' she exploded. 'He can have a tutor first and then go to Pocklington or York as a weekly boarder. I will *not* have him going to London where I'll never see him except in the holidays.'

He leaned across to her and with his finger and thumb pinched her chin, none too gently. 'Take care, Beatrix. You have just had a child; don't get into a state.'

But she was already in a state; she felt her heart racing and her head throbbing.

'We'll talk of it at some other time,' he said soothingly as the door opened and the nurse looked in, alerted by her raised voice. Assuming that a family quarrel was taking place, she left quickly as Charles stood up to leave.

'Take care, Beatrix,' he murmured. 'Don't forget that the children of a marriage belong to the father, not the mother. It is the father who makes the rules.'

CHAPTER THIRTY-FOUR

'Which isn't true, of course,' she said to Rosetta when she called to see her. 'At least, according to your mother,' she added anxiously. 'It's only after the children turn seven.'

'I don't know much about it, to be candid,' Rosie said. 'Mother rants on about many issues, but I understand it's called the Custody of Infants Act or something, which was brought in after Caroline Norton's case. Permission to petition the courts for custody of the children by the mother. But why are you worrying? It surely isn't likely to happen. Why would your husband do that? He couldn't bring the children up himself, and he wouldn't want to.'

But he might do out of spite, Beatrix thought after Rosie had left. He doesn't like resistance. If I don't agree about schooling when Laurie reaches seven, then he might just take him, no matter what I think. He won't be bothered about Alicia, but maybe Ambrose when he reaches the same age.

She looked down at the sleeping infant. Am I becoming obsessed? It's a long time before then and I know I'm being unreasonable, but even the thought of it is making me anxious and I feel ill with the worry. What if he asks his mistress to take care of them? Men can have mistresses and nothing is thought of it, yet if a woman takes a lover her husband can divorce her, leaving her destitute.

Dora spoke to Mrs Gordon and suggested that Mrs Dawley needed to see the doctor. 'She's not eating,' she whispered, 'and she's spending too much time in bed, which is not like her; she's generally full of energy. Do you think we should ask him to call?'

'I do,' the housekeeper agreed. 'Although her parents are coming soon and she might perk up then; it's always a happy time.'

'Yes, it is,' Dora said, 'but we want her well before then. I'd like to ask him – he will at least be able to reassure us that she isn't ill.'

The doctor came as if on a routine visit, listened to Beatrix's heartbeat and checked her pulse. 'You're a very fit young woman, Mrs Dawley, but you seem a little lethargic. Nothing bothering you, is there? You're not worrying over the baby?'

'No, not at all,' she murmured. 'But I have felt very tired since the birth.'

'That is to be expected, so you must eat well and build up your strength,' he said kindly, having been told by Dora that her mistress seemed to have lost her appetite. 'Giving birth is a natural process but you must take care of your own health as well as the infant's. Sometimes,' he added thoughtfully, 'mothers can feel rather weepy after childbirth, which is not unusual. It is an emotional time.'

He gathered up his instruments and put them in his leather bag. 'A tot of brandy in warm milk wouldn't go amiss to help you sleep at night and won't hurt the child in the least. It is most unusual for a woman of your background to feed the baby herself, and it can take the strength from you. So if the child is to thrive you must look after your own health, and if it proves too much for you then perhaps you might hire a wet nurse.'

He stood up to leave. 'Now, I suggest you get up and dressed, have a light lunch and take a short walk in your garden. It is a bright sunny day, but wrap up so you don't take a chill; and perhaps take your other children with you. I'm sure they are missing their mother's company.' He gave a short bow. 'Good day to you, Mrs Dawley. I will call to see you again in a week or two.'

She felt that she had been given a kindly and well-intentioned reprimand, which made her rather cross, but she rang the bell for Dora to bring her a skirt and jacket, grumbling beneath her breath that she hardly ever indulged herself and after all she had just given birth and why shouldn't she stay in bed sometimes.

'Of course you must rest, ma'am,' Dora agreed with her when she voiced her complaint. 'But your parents are coming and Cook needs to know your plans and Mrs Gordon will want to know—'

'I know, I know!' Beatrix interrupted, pulling on her skirt, and Dora stepped forward to fasten the buttons. 'And don't think I don't know who sent for Dr Brewer, because I do! He wouldn't have come round just on the off chance that I needed him.'

'He might have done, ma'am,' Dora said, 'but we had noticed that you were not as well as you were with Miss Alicia, so we were only taking precautions.'

Beatrix put her head down and took a deep breath, and then patted Dora's hand. 'I'm sorry, Dora. You did perfectly right. I'm just feeling a little weepy, that's all. It will pass.' Or I hope it will, she pondered. I must keep strong for the sake of my children. Perhaps I am wrong about Charles. I must make a fuss of him next time he comes, interest him in family affairs and the events that are taking place on the estate. Perhaps we should invite neighbours here for supper. Yes, that's what we'll do, as soon as I'm feeling well again. I'll ask Mr and Mrs Stokes and Rosetta, and those nice people from Hessle who invited me to their house.

She had been meeting more and more people and invitations had come regularly until it had become known that she was expecting another child; no doubt they would begin again once autumn was over, for most of the people she knew were either farmers or estate owners and they were coming up to a busy time of year.

But there again, she thought, the last time they were invited to supper with neighbours and Charles agreed to attend, it was mainly these same farmers and estate owners and their wives who were present. Some of the men, much older than her or Charles, had congratulated Charles on marrying a young woman who, they had heard, had a natural talent for understanding farming practices; incredible, said one who had quaffed a great deal of port, in a woman not born to it as their wives were.

Charles had been annoyed; he was at a loss to talk to these countrymen until the conversation turned to American methods and the prices the farmers there were commanding for their grain. As commercial prices and financial markets, if not livestock ones, were within his understanding he had turned the discussion to figures, stocks and shares until they were listening to his every word.

Mrs Gordon tapped on the door and Dora opened it.

'Begging your pardon, Mrs Dawley,' the housekeeper said, 'but Mr Newby and Mr Hallam are here, enquiring when you might be available for a discussion.'

'I'm coming down now, Mrs Gordon. Is it warm enough to have a cup of tea outside?'

'It is, ma'am, but I'll ask the maid to put a blanket on a chair for you. Shall I offer the men a sandwich or a warm scone? Cook has just taken some from the oven.'

Beatrix smiled at the thought, a small rush of happiness spreading through her. 'Please,' she said. 'That would be lovely.'

Through her window she saw the two men going down the steps on to the terrace and pulling three chairs away from the tables, and then a maid coming out with a blanket which she laid over the back of one of them. I don't know what's the matter with me, she pondered. I am so very lucky.

She walked slowly downstairs, holding on to the banister. I shall feel better for being up and about; I've stayed far too long in my room. What was it Thomas used to call it – *cabin fever*! She took another deep breath. She missed her brother. He had often been out of touch when he was in the army, but now he seemed to have disappeared from her life entirely.

A young maid appeared from the kitchen stairs to open the front door for her; she was carrying a cushion. She dipped her knee. 'Afternoon, ma'am. I'm Kitty. I onny started a week ago.' She was dressed very neatly in a white apron and cap over a navy dress with dark stockings. Mrs Gordon was very particular about choosing the right staff and had permission to select and employ as she thought fit.

'I hope you'll enjoy working here, Kitty,' Beatrix said. The girl thanked her and dipped her knee again as Beatrix passed her and went slowly down the steps, then darted past her as she reached the terrace and placed the cushion on the blanketed chair before turning and going back to the house. The two men both came forward and Edward took Beatrix's hand to lead her to the chair, removing the blanket from the back of it and carefully covering her knees as she sat.

'Mrs Dawley,' he said. 'We didn't realize this was your first outing or we wouldn't have disturbed you.'

'It's quite all right, Mr Newby,' she said, and nodded towards Hallam. 'There had to be a first time. I'm perfectly well, just a little unsteady on my feet because of being so lazy in bed when I should have been up and about.'

'It's good to see you again, ma'am,' Hallam said, 'and congratulations on the arrival of your new son.'

'Charles will be very pleased,' Edward said quietly. 'To have two sons.'

'Yes. Yes. He's delighted, naturally.'

Kitty brought out a tray bearing a teapot and a milk jug, a cup and saucer for Beatrix and two larger mugs for the men, and another maid followed with sandwiches, scones and a dish of butter.

'We didn't expect this, ma'am,' Hallam said, as if embarrassed.

Beatrix laughed. 'I rather think that it might be to ensure that I stay outside in the fresh air for a short time. My housekeeper sometimes forgets that *I* am mistress here.' She poured the tea. 'Please help yourselves to food; I realize you must get back to work, and I don't want to hold you up, but tell me what I can help you with.'

It was nothing very much and she wondered why they had come at all when the matter in question, that of sharing the work of the upcoming harvest between the Newby land and hers, had always been done that way without the need for any discussion.

Hallam ate a sandwich and drank his mug of tea, confirmed what they were to do during harvest, and then took his leave. It wouldn't do, Beatrix understood, to linger in front of his employer when there was work to be done. But Edward sat on opposite her and they discussed various matters; would the good weather hold, would Charles be here for the harvest, and would they be having a summer party again, to which she said a firm no.

'I doubt that anyone would come if Charles asked the same people as last time,' she said. 'It would have been quite funny if Charles hadn't been so annoyed.' She smiled. 'Seeing everyone fleeing from a cloud of thrips! Do they bite?'

'Mmm! Possibly. I don't know. I've never been bitten. Been stung by wasps and bees and once by a hornet, which I wouldn't want to repeat, neither the sting itself, nor the words I came out with. But never by thrips.'

She leaned back in her chair and took another sip of tea and a short silence enveloped them. 'So what was the real reason for you and Hallam coming today?' she asked. 'Not to discuss the coming harvest.'

He gazed at her for a second and then replied quietly, 'It was my proposition, not Hallam's; he simply followed my suggestion in good faith.'

She put her cup on the table and waited. It wasn't an uncomfortable silence, just a pause in conversation between friends; but he kept his gaze on her as he leaned forward, his elbows on his knees, his legs clad in rough working cords, his hands clasped loosely together.

'Have I got a smut on my face?'

He shook his head. 'If you had, I'd be tempted to do the unforgivable act of touching your skin to brush it away, but no,' he shook his head again, 'you haven't.' His voice dropped to a whisper. 'But I still have the utmost desire to feel the touch of your skin beneath my fingers. I've missed you, Beatrix.'

CHAPTER THIRTY-FIVE

It wasn't the first time she had sensed his intense gaze upon her but she had always tried to convince herself that the reason for it was the subject matter they were discussing. She hadn't seen him for several weeks; she had kept herself from public gaze as her confinement came nearer, and he never came when Charles was here. It seemed as if he had learned to work out when Charles would visit and deliberately stayed away.

Visit, she thought vaguely. Like someone who only stayed a short time and didn't make himself at home here; that was Charles exactly. She was fairly sure that some of the younger maids were unsure of what role he played.

Edward dropped his gaze and she took the opportunity to stand; she had her back to the house, and no one looking through the windows would have seen anything amiss, just two people who knew each other engaged in conversation. She was unnerved but not disturbed, though she felt a pulse in her throat gently throbbing. He too stood up.

'I'm sorry,' he began, but she lifted a hand and with a slight movement of her fingers indicated that there was no need for apology.

'Would you allow me to escort you?'

'Yes, please, Edward.' Her calm answer suggested that there wasn't any concern over his previous words. 'If you would accompany me up the steps to the door. I'm still a little unsteady on my feet.'

'Of course; you must take care!'

She saw the movement of his Adam's apple as he swallowed, aware, she thought, that he had spoken of things he shouldn't. 'Yes,' she said, crossing the terrace and lifting her skirts over the bottom step with one hand, conscious that she was holding one of his with the other.

The door was opened by Dora. 'I was just coming for you, ma'am,' she said primly. 'The doctor said you must have only a short stay outside.'

'How everyone looks after me,' she remarked lightly. 'Thank you, Mr Newby. Perhaps we can discuss the matter again, although I'm sure that you and Mr Hallam will manage perfectly well without me for a little longer.'

Edward gave a slight bow, his hand on his chest. 'You brighten our dull talk of everyday matters, Mrs Dawley. We'll try not to disturb you too much.'

He backed away and Dora closed the door behind him. 'You'd better take a rest, ma'am,' she said censoriously. 'You're a little flushed.'

'It was the talking, I expect,' Beatrix said, but in truth she felt animated and alive. 'I'll sit downstairs in the sitting room, Dora, and then I'll feel part of household life again rather than being cut off upstairs. And will you ask someone to bring the children down? Laurie and Alicia I mean, not the baby. I must give them lots of attention, and not let them think that their noses have been pushed out of joint by Ambrose.'

Dora smiled. 'It's good to see you looking better, ma'am,' she said. 'The fresh air has done you good. I wonder what pet name you'll use for Master Ambrose?' she added.

How odd, Beatrix considered, that such a tiny baby is already *Master* Ambrose. 'I don't know,' she said. 'Amby? Brosy? I expect the children will decide.'

I don't suppose it will be Nev, she thought. I don't think Charles would allow that, even though it's his name too.

The children came downstairs to be with her. I will not have them confined to the nursery; they will have the run of the house. It's their home after all. They had chosen books to bring down with them and Beatrix took them from the nursery maid, telling her that if Ambrose was asleep she should go to the kitchen and have a cup of tea. As the young maid dipped her knee and thanked her, Beatrix tucked a child under each arm and began to read them a story.

Charles alighted from the train at King's Cross and crossed the concourse. Outside he saw a horse tram coming towards him and put out his hand for it to stop. The journey would save him some walking time and he was tired. Tired of the repeat journeys he had to make between London and Yorkshire.

He didn't take a seat but stood on the platform and put his hand in his trouser pocket for a coin to give the conductor. Waving away the change, he felt a little swell of conceit that he could do so with impunity because he was rich.

He pondered that if he had a bigger house in London he could keep the carriage there, rather than in the mews stables a ten-minute walk away. He didn't allow his driver to collect him from or drop him at the house and was adhering to his rule that his address was only known to close friends such as Paul; even his parents didn't know it.

If I had another house in a better district, I could rent an apartment in one of the hotels for Maria, except that she would never agree. She likes her *leetle 'ouse* as she calls it, thinking that it belongs to her. The tram slowed and he jumped off at a corner, and gave a satisfied huff of breath. Women, he thought. They have such an exalted sense of themselves, Maria with the London house and Beatrix with the children, when in fact they have nothing except on their husbands', fathers' or lovers' say-so.

There was no way round it, he considered as he walked on. A better house in a better district would attract attention and soon neighbours would find out who he was and be even more interested in Maria. She was a woman who was noticed and word would get around that she was his mistress and not his wife, and then . . . He sighed. People were so nosy, groping about to find some juicy titbit that they could gossip about. Not that it would matter if Beatrix did find out about Maria, for she could do nothing about it, but it would reduce her standing in the local community if whispers were heard, and she would be diminished, like that London society woman from a few years ago, Caroline something. She had an affair with Melbourne, so it was said. Many of her former friends deserted her, but she fought back, went to law, and wrote a book. You had to admire her spirit. But Beatrix wouldn't retaliate against what she might consider injustice. She's a true gentle-woman, he thought, and yet it's quite incredible how she's looking after the estate. I can't fault her on that.

He gave a wry smirk as he approached his front door. Beautiful, gentle, she brought out the worst in a man. He put his key in the lock but it wouldn't turn. Damn Maria, she's left the key in the lock again. He hammered on the door.

Yes, he thought. I'll take my boys if Beatrix makes any objection about their schooling, and she can keep the girl. Alicia. Sweet as she is, I couldn't look after a little girl. Unless of course I asked Maria to take care of her if Beatrix made any trouble; I could hold it against her as a threat. But no, he thought as he heard Maria fumbling at the other side of the door. Not Maria. She wouldn't bring her up to be a lady, not as the lovely Beatrix would.

'Come on, come on,' he snapped as she eventually opened the door.

'I didn't think you were coming,' she said. 'You are late.'

'The train was late.' He threw his top hat on to a chair. 'I wasn't. I told you I was coming back tonight.'

'Huh,' she mumbled, picking up the hat and brush-ing the pile with her fingers. 'You have been to York-shire again; you are always late when you have been there. You have been to see your new son. Yes? What is he like?'

He shrugged. 'Just like the others. Small, pink, not much hair.'

'But a boy; you are pleased, I expect?'

She was peeved, he could tell. Probably a little jealous, but she wouldn't say so. He breathed heavily. 'Is there anything to eat?' he said. 'I'm hungry.'

'Of course.'

He saw the change in her as she relaxed; happy not to speak of things she knew nothing about.

'I have coffee ready for you and I have made chicken and chorizo stew with rice. Good, yes? And from the market today I buy shrimp to start.' She kissed the tips of her fingers in an extravagant gesture to show how delicious they were. 'Nothing better, eh?'

He smiled and patted the sofa for her to sit. He kissed her plump cheek. '*Perfecto*,' he said.

CHAPTER THIRTY-SIX

Beatrix quickly recovered her health and gave much thought to the few minutes of being alone with Edward. She must, she decided, steer clear of any private conversation with him, and always be sure that someone else was in the room or nearby in the garden so that nothing questionable could occur.

It was a pity, she reflected, for she enjoyed his company, and there was no one else, apart from Rosie, with whom she could be so completely at ease.

Edward's demeanour towards her that day had revealed that he was more than fond of her, and it wasn't appropriate behaviour for an unmarried man to display towards a married woman. She had been kept awake on many a night since as she reflected on the issue, and had come to the conclusion that it was not only a dilemma for him. How could she be sure that he wasn't merely playing games, for wasn't that what men did? But her main worry, the one that caused her to toss and turn, was that she was also attracted to him, yet she dare not show it. She could not possibly give Charles any reason to even think she had taken a lover.

It seemed that he had come to the same decision for his visits dropped to occasional calls; his reasons to see her were few, as Hallam was running the estate very efficiently and Edward considered that he was, in fact, superfluous, which didn't suit him at all. From childhood he had been used to calling at Neville's home, but it no longer belonged to Neville. Those days were gone, and as he was a thinking man, and knowing Charles as he did, he realized that any slip or impropriety regarding Beatrix could mean a ban on his ever seeing her again; and as for her, he wouldn't take the risk of her being in peril of Charles's anger. He had seen it in action when they had both been young, although Charles should have been old enough to control it.

Once a month, Beatrix and Hallam had a meeting in the downstairs study to discuss various plans for the future; originally she had assigned the room to Charles, but he clearly didn't want it, and had never brought a chair of his own as she'd suggested.

So she made it her own. The walls were lined with bookshelves, and she bought a mahogany desk with deep file drawers which were kept locked and the key hidden. There were two comfortable leather chairs, one for her and one for Hallam, or Charles if he deigned to sit upon it, and two leather-covered stools. Whenever Hallam came she kept the door open on to the hall, or if it were a sunny day they sat outside in full view of the house.

I must be cautious, she considered, for I feel as if I should be on my best behaviour at all times.

When her parents came to visit her mother often played with the children whilst Beatrix discussed monetary matters with her father. When she had lived in London with her parents she had thought her father exceedingly measured and often slow; she realized now that he was simply careful, and never in any calculations did he make mistakes or errors of judgement.

She never told Charles that she discussed business with her father or asked his advice as he sat opposite her at her desk, for intuitively she thought that he would object. She knew that her father was an honest and honourable man; she couldn't be completely sure that she could put Charles in that category. Once, he had asked her if Hallam helped her with the books, for, he said, they were as perfect as any bank clerk's.

'Hallam! Certainly not!' She had been upset. 'It is his business to run the estate efficiently and to give me the prices we are paying for grain and livestock. It is mine to add up the figures and make sure we are in profit.'

They had bought a small herd of prize cattle to see how they would thrive. They would need at least another twelve months, Hallam said, to find out if it was a worthwhile venture. The manager had also suggested they bought Berkshire pigs, which proved to be a good idea. 'It's an old pedigree pig, ma'am,' he told her as they stood watching them grunting and snuffling happily in the orchard, chasing the hens and eating up the windfalls. 'Docile and easily managed.' Someone had told her that Neville Dawley had brought pigs into the old orchard to do the same but she couldn't recall who. Probably Edward, she considered, for he knew as much about the old man as anyone.

When the sows farrowed, Laurie and Alicia were taken to see the tiny black piglets. They squealed in delight when they saw them wearing what they called their white socks, and wanted to play with them. She decided not to make the children aware of the pigs' ultimate fate as she considered that they were as yet too young to know.

Again on Hallam's advice she bought a pair of goats to clear up some of the overgrown pasture land. When the nanny gave birth to a pair of kids she took the children to see them being born and it reminded her of when Edward had taken her to watch Nellie whelp her pups, to give her an inkling into birthing: a lesson, she thought, especially for her.

She had never forgotten that day; his kindness and tenderness towards the dog as she delivered her pups and, too, his strong arm as he helped her back to the house. The pup she had chosen had become a good yard dog, always on the prowl, and she had chosen another when Nellie had her next litter.

On the eve of the start of harvest, she drove alone in the governess cart to the top of the hill that ran alongside the house, to the very edge of their land. Coming to a narrow track she had stopped, tied the reins to a tree branch and trod carefully down the steep bank to lean on a fence and look out at the distant view.

Never did I think, when I was a young city girl, that I would one day be scratching at pigs' ears or rubbing ears of corn through my fingertips to discover if it was ready; or standing, as I'm doing now, at the top of a hill contemplating a perfect golden landscape with

286

woodland below me and a walk running through it where a glimpse of the Humber can be seen.

Never in a million years could I have imagined this. I'm *almost* completely happy. I have three beautiful children, a lovely home that *I* have made; what more could any woman want? She heaved a deep regretful sigh that had been gathering inside her for a long time. Just a husband who loved me. That would have been *my* dream. Someone who cared for me above all others and all things, with a love that we shared.

Not a man who had married me so that he could achieve *his* dream of immeasurable wealth. He could have chosen anyone to attain that, but I just happened to be there, and suitable. My poor papa. A sob caught in her throat. He thought he was doing the right thing, and I think he realizes now just what he really acquired for me. A loveless marriage.

Did I expect too much? Was I just a foolish romantic girl? Is this what happens when women and girls are under the control of their fathers and husbands? Would I have made the same choice if I had had the freedom to do so? Many would think I'm lucky, and so I am. I know that I am. But I'm also afraid. Afraid that my life isn't under my control; and afraid most of all of losing my children, as Charles once said that I could.

And then, all of this – her eyes swept the landscape, the golden corn ready for harvesting, the deep estuary sweeping on towards its destination, the songbirds high in the blue sky, and she lifted her arms as if to reach it – without my children, it would all be worthless.

She turned away to climb the bank and go back to the pony and cart, her eyes blurred by tears. Someone was standing there beside it: a figure dark against the bright sky. She wiped her eyes and cheeks with her fingertips but couldn't stop the flow. Edward! The one person who might have given her comfort; the one with whom she had taken the decision never to be alone.

He stepped down the bank to reach her.

'You followed me,' she said accusingly.

'Yes,' he admitted, 'I did. I saw you pass by and wanted to be sure that you were safe.' The reason he gave wasn't strictly true. His true instinct had been to see her alone again just one more time.

'Why should I not be?' she asked defiantly. 'One day women will rise up and be able to choose what they want to do with their lives; some do, even now.'

'Not women like you,' he said softly. 'Women like my mother and sisters.'

'Yes,' she insisted, her emotions high and therefore blaming him for all inequalities. 'Cosseted women just like me.'

He gazed at her with the same look of tenderness she had seen before, which took her breath and anger away.

'I hope you're right,' he murmured and reached for her hand, 'but my intention was only to ensure that you came to no harm on this unstable track – it was not to interfere in your life.'

'I'm sorry.' She began to sob, all her fears tumbling in a torrent of uncertainty. 'I do know that – that you have my interests at heart . . .'

'You don't know everything.' He gently stroked her fingers, the forbidden skin that he so wanted to touch. 'You don't know that I want to take care of you and I can't; all I can offer you is the promise that if ever you need me, if you are ever afraid, then run to me and I'll be waiting.'

CHAPTER THIRTY-SEVEN

When Laurie reached five, Beatrix arranged for him to have a female tutor. He now knew the whole alphabet and all his numbers and she didn't tell Charles that she had taught him herself up to now. She had also begun to teach the children to play the piano as she had done when she was young; now she played it with Ambrose on her knee and allowed him to bang on the keys with his tiny fists. The *plink plonk* sound made him chortle with glee.

Charles didn't mention school again, but Beatrix sent for prospectuses from various private local day schools and from boarding schools in Pocklington and York, so that if he should bring up the subject she could show him them to prove that she wasn't against Laurie going away to school, as long as he remained within easy reach.

It seemed that Laurie was keen to learn; he was a lively child and absorbed whatever his tutor, Miss Andrews, taught him, but it was apparent to everyone but Charles that his heart was in the countryside, and with the animals that grazed in the fields, and he gladly went in the cart with Aaron to deliver the *lowance*, as the labourers called their midday meal of bread and cheese or slices of ham or beef and bottles of cold tea.

'I'll not have him mixing with the navvies,' Charles said when he arrived one day, quite unexpectedly, to discover that Laurie had gone with Hallam to the fields where the horse lads were ploughing.

'I don't understand,' Beatrix stammered. 'They're not navvies; we have regular full-time farm workers, for haymaking and harvesting and right through to winter ploughing with the oxen; and then there are the horse lads who look after the Shires . . .' Surely, she thought, he must have looked at the wages book to see how many they employed, both in the house and on the land.

He caught hold of her wrist. 'I don't care what you call them or what they do, I'll not have my son mixing with them and picking up their bad habits and language.'

'He'll be so disappointed,' Beatrix pointed out. 'He loves being outside. I was going to ask—' She stopped. Perhaps this wasn't the right time, and his grip was tight on her slim wrist.

'What!' he said. 'What were you going to ask for now?'

Have I asked for much recently, she thought? I don't recall. Nothing for myself, of that I'm sure. 'He likes the horses,' she stammered. 'The dray horses and the Shires. I wondered, could – could he have a pony of his own and be taught to ride, do you think? He rides the pony, but he's very old now.'

She could see that he was considering, his narrowed eyes flickering over her face, and she could tell that his sharp mind was calculating whether or not it would be to his advantage.

'Some of his young friends have ponies,' she dared to continue; Laurie had been on visits with her and had met the children of local farmers and gentry, some with vast acreages of land and some with only few; most of the children around his age were able to ride or were about to learn. 'They have tuition,' she went on; 'they are not allowed out on their own.' Which she knew wasn't strictly true. Many of them were as competent on horseback as they were on their own two feet.

He let go of her wrist and she rubbed it gently. 'I'll think about it,' he said abruptly. 'He can't have everything he wants. There's a limit. And besides,' he added, 'what will we do with a pony when he's away at school?'

She swallowed. 'Alicia could ride it,' she offered, 'and if he were a weekly boarder he'd—'

'Alicia! Don't be so *ridiculous*! She's still an infant, and I've told you that Laurence is going to my old school. I've put his name down already so there's nothing more to be said on the subject.'

She felt faint. He could change his mind before Laurie reached school age, but would he? Charles had said Laurie would start when he was seven, but some children were sent away to boarding school much earlier; dare she cross him further and risk his doing that?

'Please, Charles,' she begged. 'Give him longer at home. He's only a little boy.'

He laughed. 'Two years,' he said. 'Two more years for you to make him into a namby-pamby mother's boy. Don't spoil him too much or he'll never live it down when he gets there. They don't like weaklings.'

He drew a breath, and for a second Beatrix thought she saw contrition and that he was going to change his mind and say he was only joking. But he turned away from her and left the room.

Charles ran up the stairs and into his room and stood for a minute trying to still his pounding heartbeat. What was it that had brought back that vivid memory so sharply: a small boy backed into a corner with other boys nipping and pinching, standing on his toes and making him cry? He hadn't known who to reach out for in his mind: not his mother, for she had never shown much interest in small boys, not even her own son, and certainly not his father, who would have told him to stand up for himself and be a man.

Was this what he wanted for *his* son? He drew himself up, lifted his chin. It hadn't done him any harm, had it? A teacher had come along just in time; he hadn't had to sprag on any of them, and they very soon found others to torment. He had joined in, finding satisfaction in getting his own back as he pummelled some unfortunate younger boy.

He'll be all right, he thought. It will make a man of him, just as it did for me. His mother spoils him, giving him everything he wants. A pony! Some part of him wanted to say yes, that he was rich enough to buy his son a pony; well, he thought, we'll see. I'll decide later. We all have to wait for the things we want most. Look how long I had to wait before old Neville popped his clogs and left me the estate. Years. We all thought the old beggar was going to live for ever.

For Beatrix the following year flew by; she had told Laurie on his sixth birthday that when he was a big boy of seven he would go away to school and come home in the holidays. At first he was excited at the thought of being with other boys, and then he said that perhaps he'd like to stay at home after all and learn with Miss Andrews, because he'd miss bringing in the harvest and seeing the calves and the lambs and even the little pigs; he'd turned his blue eyes towards his mother and his lips had trembled.

'I'd miss you, Mama, and I don't think Alicia would like me being away, and Amby will cry cos really he's still only a baby.'

She nodded and felt like crying herself, but they still had a year, she said, trying to comfort herself as well as Laurie, and explained that he would be almost a big boy when he was seven.

But Charles, for reasons best known to himself, arrived one day in late October, all smiles, and told Beatrix that the next day he was taking Laurence to Beverley as he had an early Christmas present to collect.

She couldn't think what it might be and was full of tension as the next morning Charles told Aaron to bring the clarence to the front of the house and ushered Laurie into it. He climbed in after him and called, 'We'll be home for supper,' and Laurie waved an anxious goodbye.

He never considered asking me along, she thought. I would have quite liked a day out in Beverley. She had been on a few occasions but never seemed to have the time to visit the minster or St Mary's church, both of which she was told were worth a special visit.

'Where has Laurie gone, Mama?' Alicia asked, her forehead puckering. 'He's gone wivout me.'

'He'll be back soon,' she told her. 'Papa wanted to show him something.'

'But I wanted to see it as well,' the child pouted. 'Why couldn't I?'

'You and I will do something special,' Beatrix told her. 'What shall it be?'

'I'd like to go and see Granny Mags,' Alicia said. 'I'm going to bake a cake; she said that I could, but we'll have to take Amby because he'll cry if we go wivout him.'

The children are close, she reminded herself as she put on her jacket and hat. I must try to keep it that way. Charles and his sister don't appear to have anything to talk about, whereas Thomas and I always did, even though he used to tease me. I wish he were nearer, she thought, as she always did when she had a confidence to impart. There are things I can't tell him in a letter, for he wouldn't understand; and I can't possibly write and tell him that I'm afraid of my husband.

Mags was delighted to see them; she only occasionally called at Old Stone Hall now that it had a permanent housekeeper, and when she did come it was mainly to see her sister Hilda.

It seemed that the last time they had called on Mags she had indeed promised Alicia that they would make cakes on her next visit, and she didn't let the little girl down. She got out her baking bowl and together they mixed little cakes or fairy buns as Mags called them, and when they came out of the oven Alicia spread sugar icing on top of them, on herself and on Ambrose who wanted to help, whilst her mother and Mags spoke in low voices.

'He's a well-adjusted lad,' Mags murmured as Beatrix spelled out her fears about Laurie. 'He'll probably settle very well.' She sighed. 'But I don't understand why well-off folks send their bairns away to school just when they're getting to an interesting age. I wouldn't have wanted to miss out on their growing-up years; nor would I have wanted anybody else influencing them. Learning their letters and numbers I understand, but 'meaning of life and behaviour should come from their parents.' She sighed again. 'But then, some might say I'm just a countrywoman with no learning and so I am, but what I do know is 'difference between right and wrong, and that's what we – Luke and me – taught our bairns, our Edward and his sisters.'

She looked up at Beatrix and saw the tears on her cheeks. 'Now then, ma'am. He's had a good beginning. I dare say he'll manage very well.'

Beatrix heard the carriage wheels as tea was being served. Aaron drove the clarence round to the stable block at the back of the house whilst Laurie flew in through the kitchen door and up the back stairs into the hall, shouting out for her.

'Mama! Mama, where are you? Come quickly. Oh, there you are.' He grabbed her hand as she appeared. 'Come on, I want to show you what Papa has bought me. He said it was a late birthday present and an early Christmas gift.'

A six months late birthday present, Beatrix considered, but she smiled with relief that he was home and
said nothing, and then the front door swung open and
Charles appeared. 'Oh, we must have tea first, before
we show Mama,' he said to Laurie. 'Come along.' He
led the way to the sitting room. 'Ring the bell for more
tea, Alicia.'

Alicia folded her arms. 'What else do we say?'

Her father looked at her. '*What?*'

She looked at him pertly, and he gasped and then
laughed. 'If you please, Alicia,' he said obediently,
hanging his head.

She nodded at him, slipped off her stool and pressed
the bell on the wall. 'We must always say please and
fank you, mustn't we, Mama?'

Beatrix glanced at Charles; to her relief, he seemed
amused. 'Of course we must.'

CHAPTER THIRTY-EIGHT

Laurie was thrilled as he showed his mother and Alicia his pony. 'It's a Shetland,' he said. 'And the lady at the stables said he'll grow a thick coat in winter so he never ever gets cold, but in any case he's very – erm . . .' He looked at his father.

'Hardy,' Charles said, and Beatrix was pleased that he was taking an interest.

'Hardy, yes,' Laurie said, jumping up and down. 'I think I might call him that; it seems like a good name if that's what he is. Aaron said he'd teach me to ride and how to groom him.'

'For the time being,' Charles clarified to Beatrix, 'I've told the stable lad to walk Laurence round on the pony's back with a leading rein until he gets used to the rhythm, and then we'll find someone to teach him.'

'He could practise in the paddock where the goats are,' Beatrix said. 'Goats are supposed to be good company for horses, so I understand,' she added, knowing that Charles didn't really like her to know too much about animals, or anything really, but she had learned so much about so many things since coming to live here and she wanted her children to learn too.

Aaron took Charles to the station early the following day and on his return asked Mrs Gordon if he could have a word with Mrs Dawley. She made him take off his boots and cap and wait in the hall until Beatrix came down. She smiled at him standing in his socks and clutching his cap, and asked him if Mr Dawley had caught the train all right.

'Yes, ma'am. I like to tek him in good time so's he don't miss it. I, erm,' he shuffled his feet, 'I know that Maister said I should tek young Master Laurie on 'leading rein round 'orchard or paddock and I will for 'first time, cos 'pony's got to get used to him as well as 'other way round. But I learned to ride when I was about his age and I think he'll be fine if I tek him out on 'road to one of 'other fields. I'll run aside of him to mek sure he doesn't tummel off. Will that be all right, ma'am?'

'If you're sure, Aaron?'

He assured her that he was, and as Charles had also bought a new riding jacket, cord trousers and a hard hat for Laurie, the little boy was eager to put them on and have his first riding lesson.

He had been out for half an hour, Alicia had gone up to the nursery for her alphabet lesson with Miss Andrews and Ambrose was playing with the nurse. Beatrix sat down in the study with a cup of coffee, and was preparing to look over the accounts when the front doorbell pealed.

'I'll get it, ma'am.' Dora was just crossing the hall, and went to the door. Beatrix heard her voice. 'Good morning, ma'am. Please come in; Mrs Dawley is right here.'

Rather early for calling, Beatrix mused, and opened the study door wider, to see her sister-in-law standing in the hall and several large trunks on the doorstep.

'That stupid driver!' Anne bellowed. 'He could at least have brought the luggage inside.'

'Anne! Hello. How – how nice to see you.'

Charles's sister glared at her. 'I'm glad you think so!' She gave a deep exasperated sigh. 'I'm pleased that I didn't inherit this place. I thought I was never going to get here. You're in the middle of nowhere.'

'Actually, we're not,' Beatrix answered. 'But come in, come in do.' She took her through to the sitting room, nodded at Dora to get someone to help with the luggage and arrange refreshments, and invited Anne to sit down. She was pleased that the sun was streaming through the windows, a fire was burning in the grate and there were vases of flowers and greenery gathered from the garden dotted about the room. It looked very welcoming.

They hadn't met since Beatrix and Charles's wedding day and Beatrix hadn't missed her in the least. She searched for something to say.

'You're very welcome, but what are you doing here?' she managed. 'Have you come to see the house?'

'No, I haven't,' Anne said loftily. 'Our parents brought us, Charles and me, when we were young. Father wanted us to meet the old uncle. Charles was supposed to make a good impression on him, except that he didn't, and I was brought' – she waved a hand in the air – 'because I couldn't be left, or something.'

She looked about her, at the good furniture, the lovely curtains, the comfy cushions on the sofas, for this was where Beatrix and the children gathered at the end of the day, not the elegant drawing room upstairs. 'It looks a lot better than I remember it. This must be your taste: it certainly isn't Charles's.'

Beatrix said nothing. Coffee and biscuits were brought and she murmured to the maid to ask Cook to set lunch back by half an hour.

'Why have you never visited before? You've been invited.' Beatrix served the coffee. She was prepared to be polite to her husband's sister, but no more than that until she was told of the reason for her presence.

Anne shrugged and sipped her coffee. 'I didn't want to. I thought the whole thing abhorrent. The *grand* arranged wedding! The honeymoon abroad! Paris, was it? What a farce.'

'Three days in the Lake District,' Beatrix corrected her, and thought how rude she was. 'Charles brought me here and went back to London a couple of days later.'

Anne's eyes shifted sharply to Beatrix and she frowned. 'What? Left you here on your own?'

Beatrix nodded as she recalled that day, which now seemed so long ago. 'Yes,' she said softly. 'Quite alone until a neighbour called and then went to fetch his young nephew to stay with me so that I wouldn't be nervous.'

'I can't believe that Charles would sink so low,' Anne muttered. 'Did you expect that when you agreed to marry him? Was it part of the bargain that you'd look after the house whilst he continued his cavorting back in London?'

'Bargain? There was no bargain,' Beatrix said sharply; she could see no reason to be pleasant to this disagreeable woman. 'Charles brought me and my mother to look at the house; he said I should see the house first before I decided – about marrying him.

'And I loved it: the house and the garden, the wood and the estuary running along its edge, and I saw the possibilities. But . . .' She paused. 'I was young and a dreamer and I thought there would be love too.' She was almost thinking aloud, and when she looked up at Anne she saw that she was gazing at her with her lips parted as if she had never seen her before.

'So it wasn't just because of the money that you agreed to marry him?'

'Money? I haven't seen any money. I knew that Charles would receive a large sum when we had a son, but I haven't seen any of it, and besides,' she said hotly, 'I keep the accounts. Every penny that is spent on the house and the servants, the children, everything, is accounted for; including the farm. Charles doesn't ever question the expenditure, which is on his behalf in any case, but I don't have a personal allowance.'

Anne put down her cup. 'I'm sorry.' She seemed almost contrite. 'It's true that I hadn't expected you to be as young as you were when we first met, but I had you down as being of the same ilk as Charles. Covetous beyond the point of greed.'

Beatrix gasped. She was lost for words, but Anne wasn't.

'When he said he had found a young woman who had agreed to marry him, I thought that you'd agreed on the basis of him giving you a good allowance to spend as you wished; not the house, of course, because only a male can inherit it. He said that our father and yours had agreed the terms of the marriage.'

'My father was misled,' Beatrix said. 'He thought he was doing his best for me.' She thought of her much-loved children and the lovely old house; had her unhappiness in the marriage been a price worth paying? Yes, she thought. It had.

When the luncheon bell rang Alicia came running down the stairs and Laurie appeared, flushed and excited about his first ride. Both children were introduced to their aunt, who seemed rather bemused by them, before Laurie was sent to wash his hands and face and Ambrose was brought down to sit in a wooden high chair and have lunch with them as he always did.

'What about *Children should be seen and not heard*?' Anne asked cynically. 'Charles and I never ate with our parents until we passed our twelfth birthdays.'

'How do children learn manners if they are not taught by example?' Beatrix said. 'And I like to know about their day and if they've enjoyed it.' She helped Ambrose, putting his child-sized cutlery into his hands and spearing a sliced carrot with a fork for him. 'You still haven't told me why you're here. Shall I ask for a room to be prepared? Are you staying?'

'Please. If I may,' Anne said quietly. 'I've been very rude – I apologize. And I'm sorry if I've thought ill of you in the past, but my excuse is being brought up to mistrust everyone.'

She forked a small piece of meat into her mouth and chewed thoughtfully, then swallowed and paused, looking first at the children and then back to Beatrix.

'If I might take you into my confidence, Beatrix? Yesterday I ran away from home. I am in my mid-thirties!' She gave a cutting laugh. 'I caught a train from London early yesterday morning. I hadn't thought of coming here until I arrived in Hull, which was my planned destination as I didn't think it would occur to my parents to look for me there.'

'Why?' Beatrix asked, a tremor of humour in her voice. 'Why have you run away?'

Anne licked her lips, and for a moment Beatrix thought she looked sultry and rather attractive with a gleam in her eyes and much more animation than Beatrix had ever seen on the two occasions when they had met.

'I too have come into an inheritance. One of my father's sisters. The only one who actually spoke to us,' she added grimly. 'I used to talk to her when I was growing up; I could ask her things that I couldn't ask my mother. She was a single woman with her own property and she named me as the sole beneficiary in her will. My father knew I was in it but he expected that there would be others who would benefit too, but when Aunt Frances died I went to her lawyers and instructed them not to send any letters home and told them I would call on them for the details. I also requested them to set up an account with another bank, not my father's. I don't trust him. I knew that he would harass me into buying shares or investing in companies in which he had an interest.' She sat back in her chair and smiled. 'I haven't told anyone else about this, Beatrix, so I hope you feel supremely privileged!'

I couldn't count her as a friend, Beatrix mused, although perhaps I understand her better now than I did. 'You haven't explained why you've come to Yorkshire. Or why you've *run away*,' she added.

'Oh, no, of course I haven't, have I?' Anne took a satisfying breath, and looking at the children, who were busily eating, she lowered her voice. 'I'm catching a ferry from Hull to Holland tomorrow evening and thought I'd rest here rather than at the hotel I stayed in last night, and your coachman could drive me to the dock. There'll be a hired carriage waiting for me in Rotterdam to take me to a railway station where I shall catch a train to Paris. I'm meeting an old friend who lives there and I'll stay with her whilst I decide what to do with the rest of my life.'

She paused, her mouth tensing, her eyes narrowing. 'I have been pressured all my life, since I was fifteen years old, to find a good – meaning *rich* – husband.' She lifted her chin. 'Hah. The things women have to put up with; no expectations of being able to choose a life for themselves. But now,' she glanced defiantly at Beatrix, 'thanks to my aunt I have the freedom to choose for myself, and that will *not* include a husband or playing nursemaid to my *beloved* parents as they slip into their dotage, which is what they expect me to do.'

CHAPTER THIRTY-NINE

'Oh, Bea! I have something to tell you.' Rosetta called one sunny morning in May, just before Laurence's seventh birthday when Beatrix was feeling particularly low at the thought of his going away to school. Charles hadn't given her any information, even though she had asked him several times; he'd simply said he would let her know when he heard.

'Come in,' she said to Rosie. 'You're a sight for sore eyes. I'm tired of my own company.'

'Is Charles still away?' Rosie shed her jacket. She'd driven over in her pony and trap. 'I haven't seen him at all this year.'

It was only ever by chance that when Rosie called Charles was here on a short visit.

'Yes,' Beatrix said. 'He is.' She was sure that people who knew her or saw her frequently must be wondering about her absent husband, and, she thought, there would be rumours spreading.

'Mm!' Rosie pressed her lips together. 'It's such a lovely time of year. He must be very busy if he's missing it; the trees are in full blossom and some of the petals are falling like snow. I love spring. The ditches are full of cowslips and primroses, and the hawthorn – the May tree, Mother calls it – is in flower and smells wonderful.'

'Charles wouldn't notice,' Beatrix said dully, and thought that the only thing he ever wanted to know was whether the estate was in profit.

Rosie sat down and heaved out a breath. She seemed buoyed up about something. The two young women were good friends, very easy in one another's company; they were never formal.

'What is it, then?' Beatrix smiled at Rosie's expression, one that showed she had something to share.

'I'm in love,' Rosie whispered, even though there was no one to hear. She clasped her fingers together. 'I have met the most perfect man!'

'Really? Who is he?' Beatrix was beginning to think there was no such person.

Rosie had fallen in love several times since Beatrix had met her, but the emotion had never lasted. The chosen suitors seemed to fail on various counts within just a couple of weeks, the main problem being, it seemed, that they had thought her extremely wealthy and had disappeared on urgent business when she had told them the lie that she wasn't and that there was no expected dowry.

'He's a friend of my Wiltshire cousins; they came on a visit for a few days and brought Esmond with them. He's lovely, Bea,' she said on a sigh. 'We both knew from the minute we met. This is definitely *it*. The cousins have gone home, but he – Esmond – is staying on.

Mother likes him, Papa likes him. He's an artist,' she said ardently. 'And a musician; he plays the cello beautifully. He's never been to this part of the country before and he loves it.'

'Why didn't you bring him with you? I could have given you my assessment of him.'

'Because Papa has taken him off for a drive around the district; he wants to take a closer look at the estuary and then he's going to paint. He likes to paint landscapes,' she said dreamily. 'Or seascapes and riverscapes. And he's not after my money, not that I have any just yet.'

'You've talked about that already, have you?' Beatrix hid a smile.

'Well, only in general conversation. I always tell possible suitors that I haven't a dowry, and I also told him that I'd decided not to marry, and he didn't turn a hair and said he quite agreed with me and thought it wasn't really necessary if you loved someone; he said he had friends who had chosen not to marry and simply lived together.'

She saw Beatrix's astonishment. 'They're artists, apparently,' she rattled on. 'So they are a bit different; the wife, who isn't really a wife, paints miniatures and the husband, who isn't really, paints landscapes in the style of the Romantics, like William Turner. Do you know his work?'

Beatrix nodded. Sometimes Rosie took her breath away. 'So how long is he staying?'

'Oh! For ever,' Rosie said, as if surprised at the question. 'Mama says he can have one of the attic rooms and if we're both still of the same mind in three months then we'll pledge our troth beneath the apple trees in the orchard.' She heaved a great breath. 'I'm so happy, Bea. I can't believe it has happened so fast.'

Nor can I, Beatrix thought as she waved her friend goodbye. Can Rosie be serious? She had assured her that she was and had promised to bring Esmond to be introduced. 'People do take lovers, you know, Beatrix,' she had said as she left. 'Marriage isn't the only option as long as you're both committed to being faithful.' She had appeared to hesitate, as if she was going to say more, but then gave a little smile and said she must be going.

Could I have done that, Beatrix wondered? Would I have agreed to be married without the blessing of a man of the cloth to say it was legitimate? My parents would never have allowed it, I'm convinced of that; they would have felt shame, I know. She sighed and felt sad; would it really have made any difference? 'To love and to cherish,' she murmured beneath her breath, 'until death doth part us.' That hasn't happened in our marriage. No love, no cherishing.

It was a month later when Charles came again; he seemed to be remarkably cheerful and Beatrix guessed that he might be coming to give her news of Laurie's schooling. It will be bound to be the September term when he begins, she thought tearfully. I must prepare myself; I know that Charles won't change his mind, so I must accept it.

But she dared not ask him and neither did he mention the subject during the three days he was there. Even when he and Beatrix were alone, he spoke up on diverse subjects but never on Laurie's schooling.

Neither did he mention his sister, and she wondered if he knew what had happened and if he did, did he care?

On the morning of his departure Beatrix came down in her dressing robe to see him off. He was wearing his summer coat and a top hat, and turned to her, ran his finger down from her mouth and chin to the cleft of her breasts, and bent his head to kiss her lips. He had not come to her bed and she had felt great relief as she hadn't wanted him to.

'By the way,' he murmured. 'The rules have changed at the old school. They're not taking boys until they're eight now, so our precious son will be home for another year. I expect he'll be very disappointed, but he has his pony to distract him, hasn't he? He can take comfort in that, and a year will soon fly past.' They heard Aaron drive up in the carriage to take Charles to the railway station. 'Will you tell him?' he asked casually. 'Just as well I hadn't ordered his uniform. He'll have grown inches in another year.'

'I'll tell him,' she said breathlessly. 'I hope you have a trouble-free journey.'

He nodded, and turning on his heel he was gone. A minute later the carriage wheels were clattering over the gravel drive. She sat down on the window seat and watched as it continued along the long track and out of the gates.

He knew. He already knew that the rules of entrance had changed, and he chose not to tell me! Why? He knew how anxious I'd been. *Why* does he do this? She felt bile in her throat. What pleasure does he get from tormenting me?

Her own voice echoed in her head: *He does it because he can.* No other motive is required in Charles's reckoning. It's like taking a toy from a child and hearing him cry. It's like pulling the wings off a fly. He does it simply because he can.

CHAPTER FORTY

As Charles had said, the year did pass quickly and they were now in September. Laurie was doing well with his lessons, his tutor said; Miss Andrews had given way to a quiet and patient young man who taught Laurie French as well as arithmetic and English, and in between lessons if the weather was fine he took him outside, where they ran races across the grass for fifteen minutes before coming in to eat lunch.

Laurie was encouraged to eat his lunch in the schoolroom, so that he got into the habit of 'schoolroom mode', as Mr Greenwood called it.

'He won't be allowed to linger over his meals at school,' the tutor explained to Beatrix, 'not as he would normally do at home. He will have time to wash his hands and eat. When he has there will be a short break outside and then he will be back into the classroom to continue lessons.'

Beatrix nodded. Her own home schooling had been much more relaxed before she went away to school. It is time, I suppose, she admitted reluctantly, although I would prefer it if he were nearer home. She confessed this to Mags Newby one day, who replied sensibly that Laurie would probably enjoy being with other boys.

'Our Edward enjoyed being at school,' she told her, 'though he was only down 'road at Pocklington.' She gave a sudden laugh. 'He once walked home; twenty miles or so it is, but he hitched a ride for part of the way. He said he wasn't miserable at school but he fancied some of my meat pie and apple crumble. I'd cooked some that morning as it happened, so he ate it and then one of Uncle Nev's men drove him back in 'trap, cos Luke wasn't well that day.'

Beatrix was puzzled. It was expensive to send a boy away to school; had the Newby farm been doing well enough to justify sending Edward away to be educated? She had previously assumed that he'd gone to a local school until he went to agricultural college.

Edward came in whilst Beatrix was having a cup of tea with his mother. Mags had told her that she could come whenever she wanted to or if she felt the need to chat, and she often did.

'Your mother was telling me that you were at Pocklington School and once walked home because you missed her cooking!' she said, as Mags went to make another pot of tea for him.

'Aye, I did,' he grinned. He sat by the table and looked across at her. 'Have you heard anything more from Charles about Laurie's schooling?'

'Not yet,' she sighed. 'But I'm prepared, and so is Laurie.'

'He'll be going to Charles's old school, I suppose?'

'Yes, that's what he wants – what Charles wants, I mean.' She paused. 'Which is rather odd, as I'd understood that Charles didn't enjoy it; that it was a rather punishing regime.'

'I believe it was, in Charles's day, but it might not be now. Uncle Nev . . .' He hesitated. 'Well, I overheard him telling Ma, years ago, that the headmaster had been removed from his position. He'd been rather too heavy with the cane, and I think that Charles might have been one of the unlucky ones to feel the brunt of it.' He reached out and patted Beatrix's hand. It seemed to her that he always wanted to touch her. 'It won't happen now.' He smiled reassuringly. 'That was a long time ago. Don't worry.'

'I'll try not to,' she whispered. 'It's just that he'll be so far away. I don't even know where in London the school is,' she confessed. 'Just as I don't know where Charles's London house is.'

He frowned, but didn't comment as his mother came in just then with a tray of fresh tea and a ham sandwich for him, and he got up to take it from her and put it on the table.

Mags went out again to call for Luke to come in for a hot drink and Edward said, 'I don't know where the London house is, but I do know where the school is. It's not in London itself, but in Hampstead; you'll probably know it? I remember Charles telling me about it when I was a young lad. He boasted about being there, even though he hated it.' He reached into his pocket and took out a stub of pencil and a scrap of paper and scribbled down the name of the school. 'There you are,' he said jokingly. 'At least you'll be able to write to the little monster.'

She thanked him, and left shortly afterwards. She felt a sense of relief that at least she knew where Laurie would be. She knew Hampstead; all Londoners did. It *was* part of London, contrary to what Edward had said; it was one of London's most famous landmarks, a grassy heath set high above the city where the air was good, with natural ponds where people swam, woods and long walks, and not least the tremendous views over London.

She had often seen schoolboys running up there from nearby schools, and people flying kites. Laurie will love the area, she mused. I'd been worried that he might have been in the heart of London, all traffic and noise, when he is such a country boy. I'll write to Charles care of the bank and ask him to tell me what date he'll be starting. Laurie's my son and I need to know. It is my right, surely!

Charles didn't answer her letter but he arrived during the last week in September with a medium-size trunk and Laurie's new uniform packed in it. Laurie gasped when he tried on the knickerbockers and the red stockings for size. 'My legs will be cold,' he objected. 'I thought I'd wear long trousers now that I'm old enough to go to school!' The coat was a miniature version of a frock coat and beneath it he would wear a starched white shirt with a high collar. He scowled at himself in the long mirror.

Beatrix smiled. She thought he looked rather sweet, but then he put on the top hat and she couldn't help but laugh at her little boy in grown-up clothes.

'What?' Charles came into the bedroom. 'What are you laughing at?'

Beatrix put her hand over her mouth. 'Our little boy in a top hat!'

But Charles wasn't laughing, even though Laurie now had a grin on his face as he moved the hat to the back of his head and then over his eyebrows.

'*My* son will be a credit to my old school,' he said brusquely. 'It is not a laughing matter. He will be commended for the Dawley name or I'll know the reason why.' He seemed angry and she didn't understand. He had told her he hated his time at school and yet had been insistent that their son should go there. 'We leave tomorrow, so make sure his clothes are pressed and ready to pack.'

'Tomorrow!' she stammered. 'Surely not? A few days more to make sure we have everything!'

'Tomorrow!' He turned his back and headed towards the door. 'We leave in the morning.'

It was a later train than the one Charles usually caught; he had ordered a hired carriage to collect them at ten o'clock and take them to Brough.

Beatrix wasn't expected to travel with them; it would be only Charles and Laurie and his trunk, and a small travelling bag that Beatrix had packed with his personal things: underwear, nightwear and dressing gown and a favourite soft toy that he always took to bed with him. She had also tucked in a tin of biscuits that Cook had made especially for him.

'Do you think that the other boys will think I'm babyish if I take Jim with me?' Laurie placed the toy carefully at the top of his suitcase.

Beatrix was sitting on his bed, waiting to close up the suitcase. 'No, I don't!' She picked up the strange creature, which she had made from an old wool blanket and stuffed with rags. It had long floppy rabbit ears, two eyes of large brown buttons, a smiley mouth she had fashioned from red felt and a nose made from a wooden toggle which was stitched firmly with strong black cotton, but no legs or arms.

'They'll probably wish that they'd brought a favourite something, too, when they see yours. Anyway, it isn't a baby's toy,' she said firmly. 'Jim is a comforter for when you think of home.'

Jim was the name that Laurie had chosen when Beatrix had first made it for him when he was three and he'd tucked it under his arm and said his name was Jim.

'I could give him to Amby,' he said reluctantly.

'You could,' she agreed. 'But I can make one for Amby as I did for Alicia.' She could see that he was torn. 'Why don't you take him with you now and bring him home when you come back in the holidays?' She swallowed hard. 'Then you can decide whether he goes back with you or stays at home.'

He looked up at her and frowned, his smooth forehead puckered. 'How long am I staying at this school? I will be able to come home when I've learned everything, won't I? It won't take too long, will it?'

'Of course you'll come home.' A tear ran down her cheek, and Laurie wiped it away with his finger. 'I don't know how long it will take, Laurie. It will depend on how quickly you learn.'

'Then I'll try my best, Mama,' he said bravely, 'and come home as soon as I can. I wish you were coming with me.'

Alicia was waiting for him and put out her arms to give him a hug as he dragged his feet down the stairs. Then four-year-old Ambrose wanted a hug too and Charles, waiting by the door, said impatiently, 'Come on, come on, we don't want to miss the train.'

'Papa!' Alicia put up her arms to him and made kissing sounds. Charles looked down at her and Beatrix thought that just for a second Charles looked guileless, as if his blustering façade had been ripped away from him; he bent his head and kissed his daughter's cheek.

'Goodbye, darling Alicia,' he said softly. 'I'll see you soon.' He bent again and kissed the top of Ambrose's head, then turned to Beatrix, whose face was wet with tears, and gave her a peck on the cheek but didn't look her in the eyes. He climbed into the carriage and rapped the roof with his stick and they were off, with Laurie standing by the window, giving a wave, his mouth quivering.

Beatrix ushered the two children inside but stood on the doorstep trying to control her tears. Then she heard the rattle of the trap behind her, and turned round.

'Where are you going, Aaron?' Her voice was unsteady.

'Anywhere you like, ma'am.' Aaron touched his forehead. 'I thought it was quite a nice day for a short drive. Up to Brough and back mebbe? Tek a look at Brough Haven?'

She stared at him. Who had put him up to this? She took only a second to decide. 'I'll get my shawl,' she said, and dashed into the house. Dora and Mrs Gordon were both there. Mrs Gordon was buttoning Alicia into her coat and Dora was holding out a shawl.

Beatrix took it from her. She couldn't speak but wrapped it round her shoulders. She took Alicia by the hand and saw the nursery maid going up the stairs with Ambrose. She called her back. 'Amby can come too,' she said.

'I know all 'shortcuts to Brough, ma'am,' Aaron said as he cracked the whip above the pony's head. 'We'll be at Brough train station afore yon carriage is.'

They were there at the same time. She and the children were sitting in the trap on a piece of rough ground as the train steamed into the station. Beatrix stepped down, carrying Amby, and Alicia followed her; she saw a porter on the platform step on board carrying Laurie's trunk into a carriage and Laurie shaking his head when another porter bent to take his bag; she saw the figure of Charles moving about inside the carriage, taking off his hat and his coat and putting them on the rack. And then she saw Laurie come to stand at the window of the carriage and look out, straight at them. He smiled and waved and put his hand to his mouth to blow them a kiss as the whistle sounded, steam gushed from the funnel and he was lost to sight as the train, shrouded in smoke, pulled away.

CHAPTER FORTY-ONE

The grain had been harvested and the fields broken open to allow the animals in to graze, and by late October the meadows that had lain fallow that year were ploughed, harrowed and sown with winter corn.

Beatrix stood with Hallam watching the labourers and horse lads. It never ceased to amaze her as they all did what was expected of them without a single false move, all used to the continuous rotation of crops and animals that kept the land in 'fine fettle' as they called it, as their fathers, grandfathers and forefathers had been before them. Except it was different from how it had been, Edward had told her; he had described how some of the grandfathers had cropped their own strips of land to make a living and feed their families, but had lost them since the last Enclosure Act and now had to work for the bigger landowner.

'You'll have to decide what to do, ma'am,' Hallam was saying. 'And before Martinmas, or some of these men will start looking for work in towns and industry if we can't promise to keep them fully employed *and* give them local accommodation, which is in very short supply.'

'So what must we do?' she asked.

'Some of them have lodgings in 'villages, but it means a hike to work and back, and . . . well, I know we have some accommodation for the regulars, but I was thinking of that run-down old barn in the far field. It's mainly brick and boulders, but it's falling down and the roof's collapsed. It's doing nothing; it's not even good enough for an animal shelter, and the way things are going it'll end up as a pile of rubble, which would be a waste. So I thought we could rebuild it, if you're willing. We could use reclaimed bricks and some stone – I'll ask at the Hessle quarry – and make it into a farm-house, and put a hind and his wife in it.' He saw the crease in her forehead, and then it cleared.

'You mean a foreman?' she clarified, and he nod-ded. 'Yes, and then what?'

'The gable ends are steady and safe, and the area is big enough to make a goodly house; we could build an extension at the back to make into lodgings for 'labourers and regular horse lads, the idea being that the hind's wife would feed them, and you'd have to decide whether you'd pay for the men's keep as part of their wages or let the hind's wife charge them. Either way you'd keep the men here and they wouldn't slope off to the local beer house and get drunk. Particularly if the food was good.' He grinned.

She laughed. 'You're a marvel, Hallam. That is such a good idea. I think we should do it.'

'Should we wait for Mr Dawley's opinion before we start?' he asked.

'No,' she said firmly. 'There's no need. If we want to keep the men here, it's the only option.'

She needed something else to keep her mind busy. In the time since Laurie had left for school she had written to him several times but had received only one letter back from him, saying he was settling in and that no one had laughed at Jim. Another boy had wanted to bring a soft toy with him, he told her, but his father had said no.

Poor little boys, she'd thought. Making them grow up so quickly. She had written to her mother asking her to pay Laurie a visit, but had not yet heard back from her.

But it was Charles who was causing her some concern. He had come to see her two weeks ago for the first time since collecting Laurie; he looked fit and well and she was sure that he had been abroad again, for his blond hair was fairer than ever and although his skin hadn't burnt as it had previously, the back of his neck was red and peeling. She'd asked him if he'd been to see Laurie and he'd laughed.

'Of course not! Why on earth would I? He has to grow up, not be a spoilt mother's boy. My parents never visited me!'

'But he's only eight,' she'd protested. 'He'll be missing home. You'll bring him back for half-term, won't you?'

'Nonsense! It's hardly worthwhile disrupting him for only a week. He can stay on at school, boys often do.' He looked at her and narrowed his eyes. 'Are you feeling broody? Is that it, Beatrix?'

She'd simply glared at him and turned her back, but he'd reached out and grabbed her arm. 'Careful, dearest wife. I will bring the boy home when I'm good and ready. He's eight, as you say, and under my control, not yours. He will do as *I* say, not you. You have two other children to look after until such time as I decree otherwise. Ambrose will go to the same school when he's eight, so you have time to prepare yourself. You can choose a local day school for Alicia if you wish,' he'd added casually.

She'd felt nervous, afraid even; but his attitude towards Hallam and the men who worked for them was agreeable and he'd congratulated them on their good work over the year; the men had touched their foreheads or their caps and Charles seemed well pleased, and so he should be, she thought indignantly, as she put away the account books which he always examined when he came. She was sure now that his accounting knowledge was not as good as hers, for he only ever looked at the bottom line to see if they were in profit and by how much.

Charles never bothered to go and watch the workers, she fumed; not the men harrowing or ploughing, nor the women and sometimes children too who worked in the fields alongside them at harvest time, the women gathering and binding the loose corn into sheaves, ready for the men to make into stooks, the children raking the ground behind them. He really has no idea about the working of the estate and I think he doesn't want to know; he's not in the least interested. She often wondered just what he did with his time in London. Does he really put in so many hours at the bank?

He must have a mistress, she told herself once more, and I hope it is only the one, for I would hate to think that he has other women too; that would be quite abhorrent to me. Do I care, she thought irritably? I'm not sure I do. I hope she makes him happy, for it seems I can't. Whatever I do, I never seem to please him.

She had written to him, addressing the letter to him at the bank and marking it *Strictly Personal*, pleading with him to allow Laurie to come home for half-term; she wasn't even sure if a boys' boarding school kept normal term times. But there was no reply, and she realized that it was probably now too late.

She was at her desk when a letter came from her mother, and she seized upon it eagerly and tore it open. Her mother apologized profusely for the delayed reply, due, she wrote, to Beatrix's father and herself being struck down with heavy colds.

I dare not risk taking the cold to Laurence, she wrote. *We did however travel to Hampstead yesterday as we had both recovered, but found him to be in rather low spirits. He said he had stayed on at school when most of the other pupils had gone home for the half-term holiday, and he couldn't understand why he wasn't allowed to do the same.*

We were unable to explain this to him, but asked the headmaster for the reason, and he said it was on the express instruction of his father. We couldn't understand Charles's decision; we could have had Laurence to stay with us if it was not convenient for Charles to collect him, but we asked the headmaster if we might take him out for the afternoon to make up for his disappointment, and he agreed. Perhaps you would mention this to Charles when you next see or write to him.

Beatrix sat dumbstruck and trembling as she read the letter. Why? Why did Charles do that? What reason could he have to keep Laurie at school? If he wouldn't let him come home, at least he should have allowed him to stay with him in his London house; they could have visited museums or galleries, rather than leaving a little boy alone without playmates.

She sat and wept; the thought of Laurie's being left alone really hurt her. It's so cruel, she sobbed. Is Charles doing this to hurt me? He is succeeding if that is his intent. But why? What have I done – or not done – to displease him so?

She thought back to their early married days. I did everything I thought was expected of me: what more did he want? Yes, I was naive and innocent, but he knew that from the start: she remembered their first night together and the subsequent honeymoon in Windermere, when what she experienced was totally new.

There were very few tender moments even then, she thought, no sweet or gentle murmurings of affection. So was he disappointed with me? Was he expecting passion from an inexperienced girl? For that is what I was – I knew no other young men, not as potential husbands.

Dora knocked on the door. 'Can I get anything for you, ma'am?' She looked at her mistress's face, wet with tears. 'Not bad news, I hope, ma'am?'

'No one has died, Dora, if that's what you mean.' Beatrix took a handkerchief from her skirt pocket and wiped her eyes. 'I'm just missing my boy,' she snuffled, her voice breaking.

'I thought he might have come home,' Dora said. 'Don't children have a holiday halfway through the term? Country children have extra time off to help with the harvest – or so I'm told.' She flushed a little and Beatrix wondered who had told her that. *Does she have a young man? Though she doesn't get much of a chance to meet anyone.*

She shook her head. 'Charles said as it was only a short holiday it wasn't worth the effort of bringing him home – or something like that. But I would have liked to see him.' She blew her nose. 'I really miss him.'

'I bet Master Laurie would have thought it worth it.' Dora smiled. 'I would have gone to fetch him,' she offered. 'I know the London trains quite well now from when I visit my mother. Whereabouts is his school?'

'Hampstead,' Beatrix said vaguely. 'Somewhere near the heath, so I understand.'

'I could come with you, if you wanted to visit him, ma'am,' Dora suggested. 'Could you perhaps stay with your parents? Not that it's my place to ask,' she added quickly, as if realizing she might be speaking out of turn.

Beatrix gazed at her; she had thought of it often, but how could she explain to Dora that if she did so, and Charles found out, there was no knowing what he might do; and she was terrified of doing anything to make him angry enough to forbid her from seeing Laurie at all, or even ever again. *Am I becoming neurotic? Am I imagining that things are worse than they are? Is what Mrs Stokes is saying really true?*

They both heard the front doorbell and someone walking across the hall floor; muted voices, one of them Mrs Gordon's, and then the door closing again.

A tap on her door and the housekeeper opened it. 'Telegram, ma'am.'

She handed it to Beatrix and stood waiting with her hands folded, in case there was a reply.

Beatrix read it, and with her mouth parted as if she was drawing breath shook her head. Mrs Gordon turned to leave, but paused when Beatrix made a low moan.

'It's from my husband,' she whispered. 'Laurie has run away from school.'

CHAPTER FORTY-TWO

Alfred Dawley stepped down from the cabriolet in Judd Street. He reached up to pay the driver but gave him only half the fare. 'Wait here until I come back and I'll pay you double.'

The driver swore at him, but had no option but to wait or lose out on the whole cost.

'Fifteen minutes at the most.' Dawley patted his top hat firmly on his head as he strode off. He had never visited his son's house but knew exactly where it was and who lived there with him. Must take me for an idiot, he muttered beneath his breath. He's the idiot; never thought, did he, that I'd have him followed. Of course he didn't, not back then, full of himself he was, untouchable, as we all were when we were young. But he has never changed.

He doesn't know how much I know about him and his doxy, although he's stuck by her, I'll say that. Not like me. He gave a satisfied grunt. Don't keep 'em more than a couple of years; they get settled into their habits otherwise, think of themselves as a second wife, expect more than we can give. But Charles thinks he's clever, doesn't know that I know about him and the estate and how well it's doing, hah! And no thanks to him, but all to his clever little wife. He would have had the inheritance spent by now, but she's got her head screwed on right enough; whether it will do her any good in the long run is a different matter, of course, but she has at least given him a couple of sons.

Women, he thought, you're lucky if you get a good one. He sighed. As for my daughter, Anne won't take a husband, not now she's got money of her own. I should have known that the hussy would be off as soon as she got her hands on it; not a word to anybody, not even her mother, though come to think of it my dear wife might have put her up to it.

She didn't even give me a chance to advise her on where to invest her money, but went to some other bank; I'd have offered her a good deal given the opportunity. She's gone to France, or so I understand. She's probably living in a women's commune or something and smoking poppy.

Is this it, is this the street? He screwed up his eyes at the street sign. This is the better end, I suppose. It's not so good at the other end, though I think it's working people living there. Can't help their upbringing, I suppose.

There was a shiny brass knocker on the door and he rapped firmly. The doorstep was clean in spite of the soot in the air; the windows were too. He rapped again. A woman's voice called out, 'All right. All right, I am coming. Who is it?'

'Open the door, Maria, and I'll tell you.' He grinned. Knowing her name would fool her; she'd be curious, as all women were.

The key turned and the door opened a crack and he put his foot in. 'It's Charles I want. Is he there?'

There was a whispered conversation behind the door and impatiently he pushed it open and went in.

'Don't pretend you're not here, Charles. I know very well that you are.' He pushed past Maria, through the small lobby and into the parlour where Charles was standing in his shirtsleeves with his collar undone.

'Wh-what are you doing here, Father?' Charles spluttered. 'How did—'

'How did I know where you lived?' His father gave a grim laugh. 'I've always known. Ever since you first moved in. But don't worry, I've never told your mother or your wife. It's just as well I did know, for otherwise you'd be in a great deal of trouble. You haven't been in the bank for nearly a week – don't think I don't know – and there's been a telegram waiting for your attention.'

'I've been busy,' Charles spluttered. 'I've been going over the estate accounts; you've no idea how much there is to do.'

'Haven't I?' his father said acidly. 'Really! Well, I'm afraid they'll have to take a back seat for the moment.' He looked around the room as if searching for evidence of the hard work, but the place was tidy and neat, without anything out of place.

'The telegram,' he said, 'if you're in the least interested, is from the headmaster of your son's school, and presumably he hasn't got your address either as he sent it care of the bank. I opened it as no one knew where you were, only to read that *your* son, *my* grandson, has run away!'

'What! When? How . . .' Charles looked from his father to Maria, who had clutched her hands to her mouth in dismay and was murmuring something that sounded like a prayer.

'I don't know the detail, but I sent a return telegram saying you were away, but that I'd let you know immediately, and one to his mother in your name to tell her.'

'You shouldn't have done that!' Charles blurted out. 'You know how hysterical women can be! He's probably only hiding somewhere on the heath waiting to be rescued.'

'Oh, of course.' His father's voice was full of sarcasm. 'So that's all right then, is it? Doesn't matter if he's cold and wet and probably with total strangers! You're a fool, Charles, you just don't think. Anyway, I've been in touch with the Hampstead police and if, as you say, that's where he's hiding, he'll be found!' His lips curled. 'But I wouldn't put money on it,' he snarled. 'And I hope you'll be prepared to answer questions if he's found dead from exposure or worse.'

'This is his mother's fault,' Charles shouted. 'He'll be heading for Yorkshire. She put it into his head that he'd be unhappy and would be better at another school, and that will be why he's run away. He'll have imagined that he's not happy there and decided to go home.'

His father gazed at him steadily. 'And does he have money for the train fare?' he asked. 'Does he even know the way home?' He shook his head slowly. 'I don't think so. But I leave the problem at your door, Charles.' He put his hat back on his head and walked out of the room. 'Let me know the consequences.'

Charles picked up the glass he'd been drinking from and smashed it on the floor. 'Damn and blast it. He'll get a leathering when I find him!'

'Oh, no!' Maria moaned. 'You must not hurt him; he is only a little boy, isn't he? He will be frightened.'

Charles buttoned up his shirt. 'I'll have to go up to the school and find out what's happened,' he muttered. 'Father has probably got it wrong, dithering old buffoon.'

'But he said the 'eadmaster send the telegram and he told him that you are away.'

'I've just got back, haven't I?' Charles muttered and slipped on his boots. 'Fetch me my coat, overcoat and hat, quickly; don't just stand there dithering.'

'You want me to come with you?' Maria stopped on her dash towards the stairs.

'No! What good will that do, for heaven's sake? Give the school staff something else to chew over? I know what they're like. They might have different faces but they're all moulded from the same clay, believe me.'

Maria nodded and went upstairs to collect what he had asked for, but she had no idea what he was talking about.

Beatrix will get a piece of my mind when I see her; I'll catch the first train tomorrow. She will have planted the idea of running away in his head. I'll remind her that he's under my control now and if I wish I can remove him from her altogether. That's what that conniving woman, what was her name – Norton, that's it – that's what her husband did. Divorced her and took the children. He paid her back all right. Writing books about him that were obviously untrue.

'Maria,' he bellowed. 'Hurry up, woman.'

He whistled for a cab once he was on the main road but several went by already carrying passengers. He could have gone to the mews for the carriage but by the time he'd found the groom and he'd hitched up he could be halfway to Hampstead if only one of these blasted drivers would stop. Eventually one did, and he told him that he'd pay him double if he would get him there quickly.

He saw the cabbie's lips move, and guessed what he was saying. *That's what they all say.* There was a lot of traffic and Charles reckoned it would be an hour at least before they reached the school on the heath.

He rehearsed what he would say to the headmaster; he'd give him a lash of his tongue for not keeping small boys safe. A sudden image of Laurence's merry smile came to him and he quickly pushed it away. He hadn't been like that at seven, when he was sent to the school; he'd been scared of his own shadow, and he pushed that away too. He'd had to learn to stand up for himself very quickly.

It was a different headmaster, of course, but they were all from the same mould; he'd be another old buffer, handy with the cane and the use of dark cupboards.

He asked the driver to wait; told him that he'd be at least half an hour. 'But wait,' he snapped. 'Don't leave.'

'I'm not likely to, am I, guv? Not when I ain't been paid. This is my job,' he muttered as Charles headed towards the door and hammered on it. 'Waiting on rich fellas to cough up what they owe.'

A middle-aged woman answered the door and took him straight to the headmaster's study when he gave her his name. A dark-haired man a few years older than Charles was sitting writing at his desk; he rose and murmured his name, which Charles didn't register, and invited him to take a seat. He hadn't met him previously, having seen the matron and teachers from the junior school and told them he didn't wish to see the head of school as he was a former pupil and knew the school's history.

But he was taken aback; he'd been expecting a much older man, someone more like his own father, grey-haired and forbidding, and that was who he was ready to do battle with; he was prepared to impress him, to show him he should be honoured by his visit, for he was going to tell him that he ran the family bank and owned a Yorkshire estate.

But this man put out his hand and apologized profusely that they hadn't realized that Laurence was unhappy enough to run away. 'If only he had told us,' he said. 'Matron usually spots if any of the new boys are homesick, but Laurence must have hidden it well. I realize that you are often away on business, and I understand from the comments that were recorded in Laurence's file that his mother is unwell and not able to travel to see him?' His eyebrows rose a little. 'I, erm, met Laurence's grandparents towards the end of the half-term holiday, when they came to visit him. They didn't mention that their daughter – your wife – was frail, but said that she was very concerned about Laurence. They took him out for the afternoon and he seemed much more cheerful on his return.'

Charles was furious; the Fawcetts had no right to take him out without his knowledge. I might have agreed, of course, but they should have asked. This is Beatrix's doing, he fumed. Trying to interfere. Well, I won't have it. It's her fault that he's run away, molly-coddling him and making decisions that were not for her to make, and she has no right.

'Do you know who I am?' he exclaimed, standing up and almost knocking the chair over.

'Why yes.' The headmaster also rose, and when he was standing upright Charles realized that he was a good head taller than he was. 'Of course I do.' His eyes fixed firmly on Charles. 'But perhaps you didn't catch my name, although it is of course on the prospectus. Andrew Robinson-Gough. My brother Stephen was in your year.'

Charles flinched and felt the blood drain from his face. He would never forget that name.

CHAPTER FORTY-THREE

They had never been friends: Stephen Robinson-Gough had been a few months younger than him; an advantage, to Charles's mind, as he always preferred to dominate the younger boys in his year. But Stephen RG was never cowed by bullies as some of the others were.

He had enjoyed a steady family background, knew the difference between right and wrong, and was known to be an excellent scholar, as his older brother was too. He had few friends and didn't seem to mind that – he chose them carefully, and kept them – but the only time Charles had invited him and a few other students to stay at an estate in Yorkshire, which rumour had it he was in line to inherit, he had said yes.

And it was after this visit that Charles Dawley had been on the tip of expulsion from the school after being reported to the then headmaster over an incident where a local man was almost killed.

Charles's great-uncle had invited him to stay one weekend in early summer and suggested that perhaps some of his school friends might like to come along too. Charles jumped at the chance to show off his future inheritance and took the half-dozen four-teen- and fifteen-year-old schoolboys on a tour of the estate.

The weather was unusually hot and Uncle Nev had warned Charles not to go near the cattle, as there were some with calves that they would instinctively protect if they thought they were under threat. But Charles was bored with the countryside and suggested that they take a shortcut through the meadow and go through the woodland to the estuary just a mile or so away.

'Not a good idea, Dawley,' Stephen had said. 'We'd be better going down the drive. The cows will be rest-ing in this heat. If we disturb them they might panic, and there are a couple of men working down at the bottom end.'

'Farmer Stephen!' Charles had laughed belliger-ently. 'Do you know about cattle?'

'Not much, only what my grandfather has told me. He's a farmer and he's always said to be careful amongst cattle, especially if they have calves.'

Charles had shrugged. He wasn't going to be told anything by an insolent young braggart like Stephen RG. He climbed the fence into the meadow and called to the others. 'Come on,' he said. 'Unless you're scared of a few cows like our friend here. Everybody knows that cows are docile.'

He gave a *whoop* and some of the cows lumbered up from where they were sheltering beneath a clump of trees and stood staring at them. Charles strolled towards them and some of his companions climbed over the fence too; Charles hollered again and the oth-ers joined in whistling and shouting. The cows shifted, moving away from them, and the two men working on the bottom fence looked up.

'No, stop,' Stephen called. 'Don't.'

But Charles just laughed and began to run towards the cattle, waving his arms. The others followed, apart from Stephen and one other.

It was a sheer accident, he thought now as he stood staring back at Stephen's brother. It wasn't my fault. We were just having a bit of fun. Besides, the men ought to have got out of the way. They saw that the cows were stampeding and should have climbed over the fence; they just didn't move quickly enough. One was elderly; too old to be at work, really, and apparently incapable of climbing the fence, but the other man heaved him over and he crashed down on the other side. But it all happened so quickly that the younger man was trapped himself, and that was how he came to be trampled upon.

It might have blown over, Charles considered, if it hadn't been for tell-tale Stephen and his friend whose name he had forgotten, running hell for leather back to the house and alerting Uncle Nev, who, old as he was even then, had apparently run to the back of the house and shouted out for as many men as possible to come and bring planks of wood to use as stretchers to carry the injured up to the house; and Stephen it was who had spilled out what had happened, not only to Neville Dawley, but to his own father when he got home, who in turn told the then headmaster, who had seriously considered expulsion, not only of Charles but of some of the others too.

*

'Stephen!' he said nonchalantly. 'Was he in my year? Yes, of course he was. What's he doing these days?'

'Law,' the headmaster said briefly. 'But what about your son, Dawley? The police are out looking for him and we have notified the railway station in case he's decided to try to get home. It doesn't look good, either for the school's reputation or yours, but especially not for Laurence. We have his best interest at heart, and I will tell you now that we are very concerned.'

'And do you think I am not?' Charles said aggressively. 'I am extremely worried. With the best of intentions I left him in your care and you have failed him.'

He saw that his remark had hit home and felt vindicated.

He asked the cabbie to take him to King's Cross railway station and then wait for him again. He walked swiftly into the station and looked around for a policeman; there were generally some about and he found one by the ticket office talking to a porter, and told him about Laurence.

'We've already been informed, sir,' he was told, 'and the message has been passed down the line. If the little fella is travelling by rail, we'll find him.'

Charles nodded. 'He'll be in school uniform, I should think. Knickerbockers and red stockings.'

'Blimey,' the porter muttered grimly. 'There's no wonder he's run off if he has to wear that sort o' get-up.'

Charles didn't answer but turned away. The last train north had left so there was nothing to do but go home and plan for the next day.

'I'll catch the earliest train in the morning,' he told Maria. 'There will be at least two changes but it can't be helped. It has to be done.'

He sat for a while, planning and scheming, and came to a decision. 'What I'll do, if he's managed to get back to Yorkshire, is bring him straight back here. I won't tell the school immediately, I'll let them stew for a day or two, just to teach them to take more care of other people's children.'

'You will bring him here? To this house – to *my* house?' Maria interrupted. 'But I can't – I don't know what to do with children. You should leave him with his mama for a few days. She will be very worried.'

He stared at her. 'I don't really care if she's worried. She has no jurisdiction over him; no authority,' he explained, in case she didn't understand.

'But, she is his *madre*,' she maintained. 'She will know what is best to do. He will have been frightened if he has been alone.'

'Hey! This is *my* son we are talking about. Don't you know that English law says that a child over seven belongs to the father, not the mother?'

'But . . .' she faltered. 'She has given birth to her children, looked after them; the father only provides the seed to make them grow.'

He stood up. 'Don't argue with me! I'm telling you that in English law the children belong to the father, not the mother.'

'Then this is stupid country,' she pronounced. 'Why would the father want to take the child from its mother?'

He leaned towards her and took hold of her firmly by her chin. 'Because, my dear, he can! And what's more, women can't own property either, so think carefully, Maria, about what I am saying: for this is *not* your house, but mine, and I'm telling you that I will bring Laurence here once I find him.'

But Charles was not likely to find him if he was leaving the search until the following morning, for Laurie was already in Doncaster and fast asleep under a blanket in a corner of the stationmaster's parlour.

He was blessed with a good memory and had recalled that when he and his father had travelled to London they had changed trains at Doncaster. The most difficult part of his journey towards home was finding his way to King's Cross from Hampstead, for he didn't know London very well, even though he had made occasional visits with his mother, sister and brother to his grandparents' house. His grandfather was a fund of information on all kinds of subjects, and had books and maps which were very useful for a young boy with an enquiring mind.

After coming off the heath following an organized run, he had slipped out of sight of his companions. He had told only one of his friends in confidence that he was planning on travelling home at some time, but hadn't said when. That day had seemed most appropriate; it was a bright blue-sky day, and during their lunch break his form had been told they would go for a run on the heath that afternoon, and to change into their sports kit of knee-length breeches, white shirt, grey wool jumper and grey socks and not the dreaded red stockings. The perfect disguise, he thought gleefully, and as he left the dining hall for the dormitory to change had slipped two bread rolls into his pockets.

Keeping to the back of the pack, he'd run towards the cover of trees and watched as the rest kept on running, then about-turned and set off downhill into Hampstead village.

He hopped on a horse omnibus as it was pulling away and then jumped off again when it turned a corner, for the one thing he had forgotten was money and he had not a penny with which to pay the fare. A boy a few years older than him was coming towards him and Laurie stopped to ask if this was the way to King's Cross railway station.

'Might be,' the boy said, eyeing Laurie up and down. 'Who wants to know?'

'I can't tell you my name,' Laurie said, 'because I've run away from school, and I can't pay you anything as I haven't any money.' He pulled out the two bread rolls from his trouser pocket lining to prove it and gave the other boy one. 'But I need to get home.'

'Toff fella, ain't yeh?'

'I suppose I am.' Laurie sighed. 'But I can't help that.'

The boy nodded and raised his eyebrows. 'Next 'bus that comes along, just hop on, and if the conductor comes for your fare hop off again and catch the next one. They all end up at King's Cross, mate.'

'Aw, fanks, mate!' Laurie said. 'You're a pal.' He and some of his school friends had practised what they had thought was Cockney slang and he thought he'd try it out.

The boy grinned and slapped him on the shoulder. '*Fanks* for the bread, mate. I'll have that for my dinner.'

It took Laurie over an hour to reach the station, which was extremely busy, and he walked along several platforms before he reached one where a train was already standing with a head of steam and an indicator marked Doncaster. He hung about until he spotted a family of mother, grown-up daughter and three children of different ages and waited until they all climbed into a carriage. He hung about a little longer until he saw the guard with his flag and whistle closing doors. Laurie looked about him as if he were waiting for someone, then jumped in with the family just before the guard slammed the door behind him.

By the time the train reached Peterborough he was asleep, and only opened his eyes when the family got out at another stop and more travellers got on. He promptly went to sleep again, and didn't wake until the train slowed and then stopped with a screech of metal and he saw through the window that it was almost dark.

He sat up, wondering where he was, and heard the guard shout out, 'Doncaster! Doncaster! Change here for Hull.'

CHAPTER FORTY-FOUR

Beatrix was pacing the floor; she couldn't concentrate on anything but Laurie and where he might be. The whole household was upset. Dora had asked if she might take time off and travel into Hull to ask at the railway station there if a small boy had been seen. Beatrix had said yes, but the maid had come back with the answer that no one had seen him. She'd explained what had happened to the stationmaster and described Laurie's school clothes; she'd scoured the view from the train window in both directions in case he was walking, and had had the idea that perhaps they could put up posters.

Beatrix had shaken her head. 'He's probably still in London, Dora. How could he possibly find his way home from there? I'm so frightened for him.' Her voice wavered. 'I'm having such nightmares, thinking of where he might be – and with whom.'

She sent Dora to help the nursery maid with Alicia and Ambrose and asked Aaron to bring the pony and trap round to the front of the house; she felt that she must do something, though she didn't know what. She set off without even thinking about where she was

344

going, and as she might have expected she ended up at Mags's house.

She knocked and opened the door, calling, 'It's Beatrix, Mags. I'm so sorry; I think it's your tea time, isn't it?'

A man's voice called to come in and she found Luke Newby sitting by the kitchen fire in an easy chair with his legs and feet stretched out on a footstool.

'Sorry I can't get up, ma'am.' Luke Newby's voice was weary. 'My legs are troubling me today. I'm in a deal o' pain.'

'I'm very sorry.' She was apologetic over bothering him. 'Is Mags not in?'

He shook his head. 'She'll not be long. She went over to our Edward's place to tidy up. He allus tells her not to bother but she will insist.'

She was puzzled, not knowing what he meant by Edward's place. 'Can I do anything for you, Mr Newby? The kettle's simmering, I see; would you like a cup of tea?'

'Oh, aye, that I would, ma'am, if you wouldn't mind. I'm parched. Teapot and everything's in 'cupboard.'

'I know,' she murmured. 'I've seen where Mags keeps them.' She busied herself taking out the teapot and measuring the tea leaves into it. 'Are your legs worse on some days than others?'

'No, they're bad all 'time these days. There's no let-up. I can barely walk two steps sometimes.'

She made the tea and stirred it and put milk into his cup, as she'd seen Mags do, and handed it to him. 'I'm so sorry,' she said. 'It must be so frustrating for you. What happened? You had an accident, didn't you, quite a long time ago?'

'Can't hardly remember.' He gazed into the low fire. 'Got completely knocked out by 'cattle, but at least I'm still alive. Not like old Josh Atkins. That's 'last thing I remember, trying to heave him over 'fence. I wonder sometimes if it was me that killed him. Broke his back when he landed, poor old fella, or so it was said; he onny lasted a month after. Shock, I expect, and 'pain. He was a grand old man, still working even in his seventies.'

He sipped his tea and then asked Beatrix if she'd pass him a box from the top of the mantelpiece. He opened it and took out two tablets, which he popped in his mouth and swallowed with a mouthful of tea.

'I heard there was a stampede. Does that often happen?' she asked. 'Or were the cows disturbed by something?' She was thinking of their own herd.

'It can, especially if they have young with 'em, which these did.' He hesitated. 'It was probably unintentional, but as I say, I recall little about it. Seemingly there was a group of youngsters larkin' about; Uncle Nev was right upset about it.'

She gave a little nod at the affectionate term that everyone gave the old man. 'He saw what happened, did he?'

'No, he didn't.' Edward had come in unnoticed by Beatrix or Luke, who both looked up. 'Da was working for Nev Dawley. He and another man were repairing the fence.' His voice was like steel. 'It was Nev's cattle that ran amok, and one of Charles's friends ran to tell Uncle Nev and fetch help. I was pottering about in the stables and I went to get Ma.'

'Aye, well, that's enough about that.' Mags had come in behind her son. 'Ah, you've had a cuppa tea. Did you manage to do that, Luke? Well done.'

'Nay, lass, course I didn't,' Luke began, but Beatrix interrupted.

'I made it, Mags. I hope you don't mind? We were both parched, weren't we, Mr Newby?' Her voice cracked and broke. 'I needed to get out and talk to someone. Dora and Mrs Gordon are so helpful, but—'

'What's happened?' Edward broke in. 'Something has!'

'I should be getting home,' she muttered. 'Instead of being out hiding from what I fear.'

He took a stride across the small kitchen and took hold of her by her elbows. 'What?' he said. 'Tell me and I'll fix it. Is it Charles up to his tricks again?' He looked so angry that even Mags seemed alarmed.

'No,' she wept. 'It's Laurie. He's run away from school and I don't know where he is.'

Mags and Edward insisted she sat down and finished her cup of tea and she told them about the telegram from Charles. 'He – Laurie – had been upset that he hadn't been allowed home for the half-term holiday; my parents had visited him and he'd told them.' She began to weep. 'He must have felt that we didn't want him; my mother said he seemed very low-spirited, which is not like him at all.' She stood up. 'I must go home. There might be a message waiting for me.'

'I'll take you.' Edward stood up too.

'No,' she mumbled. 'Thank you, but I've come in the trap.'

'I'll take you,' he said again. 'I can walk back.'

There was no denying him, so she said goodbye without achieving what she had come for: a chat; a chance to spill out all her fears to Mags.

She could have talked to Edward, but she didn't; she didn't want to tell him about her terror of losing her son, or any of her children. Did Charles really mean what he'd said? Surely he didn't – how could he? But at least Alicia and Ambrose were safe for now. What was it Mrs Stokes had said – or was it Rosie who said it, or was it even Charles, when he warned her that she might lose her children, that they were not hers after they had passed seven? But right now all her fear was for Laurie.

Edward pulled in at the same spot where she had stopped to look over the meadows towards the estuary, and put his hand over hers.

'You can tell me anything, Beatrix,' he said softly. 'Tell me what you're afraid of and I'll try to resolve it. I said once before that if you were ever worried or unhappy you should come to me.'

I want to, she thought. I know I can trust him. She heaved in a breath and nodded in reply. I know that he wants more than I can give, but he won't ask, and I hope he doesn't for I can't trust myself to be strong.

He loosened her hands and picked up the reins again and sat for a moment, then he turned to her and gently kissed her cheek. She felt her heart pound and she gazed at him, her eyes moist. She didn't speak; she couldn't tell him that what he wanted she wanted too: to be in his arms where she knew she would be safe, and loved. But right now she wanted her son home and unharmed.

He smiled and she gave a trembling smile back. It was enough, for the moment; it was enough, just to know.

The stationmaster's wife sat Laurie by her fire and brought him a cup of cocoa and a warm scone. He thanked her and said yes, he was *very* hungry, in answer to her question, and thanked her again.

'So where are you off to, dearie?' she asked, sitting down opposite him. Her husband had asked her to find out what she could. 'Running away from home, are you?'

He licked his lips of crumbs and swallowed. 'No! I'm running *towards* home! I've run away from school; just for a few days,' he added in mitigation. 'It's not that I don't like it, but I miss home – and,' he said tearfully, 'I miss my mother, and my brother and sister; they're all at home, you see, and I'm not.'

'And your father? Where's he? Or perhaps you haven't got a father?'

'Oh, yes, I have a father, but I don't know him very well. He lives in London and comes to see us sometimes. It was my father who said I had to go to school in London.' He pressed his lips together, suddenly aware that he might be saying too much.

'Perhaps he wants to see more of you?' she suggested.

He shook his head. 'No, I don't think so,' he said. 'I think he doesn't want my mother to see me.'

The woman brought him a cushion and a blanket and said he could curl up on the chair and have a sleep if he wanted, for there wouldn't be any more trains until early the next morning.

'Poor little chap,' she said sotto voce when her husband came in and she told him what the boy had said. 'I think you should send him on the first Hull train in 'morning. He could mebbe get off in Brough; I gather he lives somewhere round there. Near the estuary, he said, though he didn't want to give too much away.'

'Aye, he does,' her husband agreed. 'I telegraphed London and they're aware of him. He lives in North Ferriby, according to his schoolmaster, and a message has come down the line that he's asked if we can make sure he gets safely home, and not to send him back to London. We'll have him dropped off in Brough and have someone take him from there.'

It was a very excited young boy who rolled up at Old Stone Hall's front door next to the driver of a Black Maria, the only vehicle that the local police station could spare that morning.

His mother, looking out of the window on hearing the clatter of hooves and wheels, was instantly terrified by the sight of the black vehicle and its uniformed driver, and fearing the worst drew in a sobbing breath. Then she saw Laurie sitting next to the driver and waving to her. She tumbled down the stairs and dragged open the door and saw the policeman help her son jump down, and Laurie ran into her arms.

CHAPTER FORTY-FIVE

Charles slept late and blamed Maria. 'Why didn't you wake me? You knew I had to catch the early train.'

'So it is *my* fault?' she said incredulously. 'Have I to do everything?'

'Yes, you damned well do.' He washed his hands and splashed water over his face. 'Well? Are you getting up?' She was still under the sheets. 'I'd like my breakfast before I leave, *if* you don't mind,' he added sarcastically.

She sighed and rolled out of bed, and rubbed her back. 'You kept me awake all night,' she grumbled. 'You were dreaming.'

He didn't answer her. It was true he hadn't slept well. His mind had been a jumble of thoughts and most of them were unpleasant: the school that he had hated, the pressure from his father to work harder at the bank; and the suitable marriage that he had made to become responsible as a family man according to his great-uncle's directives: the great-uncle who had considered him unworthy of inheriting the estate because of a schoolboy prank.

It had been his father who had convinced Neville Dawley that Charles would eventually become a responsible adult, and to this end he had contrived to search out a malleable young woman for him: someone innocent and well bred, who would look elegant by his side and overlook his other romancing proclivities; and, most important of all, would provide him with a son and heir who would fulfil the dictates of the will; and then she would become superfluous, being there only to give Charles an air of respectability.

Neither Charles nor his father had reckoned on the strength of character that Beatrix had, innocent and well bred as she was, so that in a remarkably short time she had not only proved to be an asset to the estate but made it more prosperous and profitable than ever before.

And now, he had thought as he tossed about, Laurence was lost who knew where. He would be heading for home, that Charles was sure about, but how would he find his way?

Maybe he is too young to be so far from home, he had admitted during his sleepless hours. Maybe he is too young to break the ties with his mother. I should have waited a couple more years, perhaps; sent him away from her when he was ten or eleven.

But he was determined that Laurence and eventually Ambrose would attend his old school. He was set on making a good impression there; he had decided that he would endow a scholarship or a bursary or something of the kind, so that his name, Charles Neville Dawley, would be set upon a board in the Great Hall and the humiliation of his own time there would be wiped off the slate.

It was unfortunate that Stephen Robinson-Gough's brother was headmaster, and unless Charles could discover something about him that would cause him to lose his position he would be there for a long time; after all, he wasn't much more than a few years older than he was.

He left without breakfast. 'Don't bother,' he told Maria. 'I haven't time to wait now.'

She was cooking eggs and laying out slices of ham but he needed to blame somebody for the lateness of the hour; she would consider the rejection a punishment and try to make it up to him when he returned.

'I'll be away for a few days.' He shrugged into his coat and turned to pick up his hat from the hat stand.

'Don't you want your beaver? I'll get it for you.' She put down the knife she was holding and prepared to run upstairs.

'No! Don't fuss, this one will do.' He patted the top of his hat and turned to go; then, relenting, turned back and kissed her cheek. 'Have you got money? Do you want some?'

She gave a little shrug. 'I will manage,' she said in a small voice, so he put his hand in his pocket and drew out some coins.

'Buy yourself some flowers,' he said, and was gone.

He didn't go directly to the station; there wouldn't be another train for over an hour, so he headed towards Paul's house, which was a fifteen-minute walk away in the same direction. As he put his hand on the knocker the door opened and a young woman came out. She dipped her knee and said good morning, and he gave her a knowing glance. Her face flushed, and he guessed that he had caught her leaving, having been there all night.

'You're a lucky beggar,' he said to Paul, who was still in his dressing robe. 'Pretty young thing you've just deflowered, I'd guess.'

'No,' Paul said, yawning. 'She's a regular. Needs the money.'

'I've been thinking that I might buy another house.' Charles sat down on the sofa. 'My father knows about Judd Street, and about Maria, damn his eyes. If I bought another I'd keep it for myself, and not let anyone move in permanently.'

'Not tired of Maria!' Paul shifted on his chair. 'You can't throw her out; not after such a long time!'

'No, of course I wouldn't. But she's getting older and I'd quite like a bit more excitement in my life. And talking of which . . .'

He told him about Laurence running away from school, and that he was on his way north to look for him. 'It's Beatrix's fault,' he said sulkily. 'She's making him into a pampered mother's boy. I'm going to have to do something about her. She has too much influence over him.'

Paul frowned. 'You're not thinking of divorce? That would ruin her, and you too, financially. The costs are tremendous, so I hear. It seems a terrible waste of money. And can you be sure that she has committed adultery? That is the only reason for divorce, you do realize? For you, of course; not for her.'

Charles fidgeted. Maybe he hadn't considered it fully. 'I'm not thinking of just yet, more in the future. Just working things out.'

'I'd leave it if I were you,' advised Paul, who seemed to have more of a grasp on the situation. 'It won't look good for either of you; you'd both be named in the press. They'd chase you and probably find Maria and that wouldn't be good for your reputation; *and*,' he went on, 'have you thought that if you told Beatrix to leave you'd need someone else to run the estate? Keep a tight grip on the reins, that sort of thing.' He laughed, and Charles thought that it wasn't in the least funny when he went on, 'That will cost you the salary of a general manager. Your wife presumably does it for nothing but a few gewgaws?'

Not even that, Charles reflected. Beatrix doesn't ask for much; nothing for herself, in fact. Perhaps I won't proceed with the idea of divorce, but I might drop a hint or two simply to keep her on her toes.

It was after suppertime when he arrived at the house. Beatrix was alone with sewing on her knee when one of the housemaids took his coat and hat and opened the door into the sitting room.

'Have you had any news?' were his first words. 'He apparently travelled as far as Doncaster, according to the King's Cross stationmaster.'

She gave a little gasp. 'Did you not receive my telegram? I sent it immediately Laurie arrived home. The police brought him in a Black Maria! Here we were worried to distraction and he'd had such an exciting time. I hadn't the heart to chastise him, I was so relieved.'

Charles gazed stonily at her. 'No. It must have arrived after I left,' he lied, realizing that she would have sent the telegram to the bank. 'So where is he?'

'In bed, fast asleep. I think he was quite exhausted. He said the stationmaster's wife in Doncaster looked after him during the night and then he was put on the first train to Hull and a police constable was waiting for him at Brough station.'

'I'll have a few choice words with him in the morning,' Charles muttered. 'I've been chasing all over London trying to find him.'

'Yes, you must have been just as worried as I was,' Beatrix agreed. 'He wouldn't have thought about the concern he was causing us; he said he was sorry if we'd worried about him and that he wouldn't do it again.'

'I'll make sure of that,' Charles said grimly. 'I've already had words with the headmaster. It won't do his or the school's reputation any good at all, allowing a small boy to run off. No supervision,' he added. 'Whoever was supposed to be in charge of him should be dismissed. Ring for coffee,' he said abruptly. 'I've had a very difficult journey.'

'Of course. I'm so sorry.' She put down her sewing and got up from her chair to press the bell, wondering why he hadn't asked the maid who let him in to bring a pot.

The maid knocked and brought in a tray just a minute later, and Beatrix suppressed a smile of satisfaction that the staff were well trained enough to know to bring refreshments as soon as Mr Dawley arrived.

She waited until he had finished his second cup of coffee and had eaten the warm buttered scone before she asked, 'What are we to do, Charles?'

He wiped his mouth of crumbs. 'About what? Laurence?'

'No,' she murmured, 'although the children are at the heart of it. I meant about us, you and me.'

'What do you mean?' he asked brusquely.

'About our life together; a life we don't have. Can we resolve it somehow? Could I perhaps bring the children during the school holidays so we could spend some time together at your London house, as it seems that you are too busy to come here very often? We could visit the galleries, show them the parks and the gardens and the lovely houses – perhaps even—'

'No,' he barked. 'The place isn't big enough; it's not a family house by any means.'

'Oh!' She was silent for a while, and then went on, 'What if we stayed at my parents' house? They wouldn't mind at all and they'd love to see the children. My mother certainly would, and I could bring them to the bank to see where you worked,' she continued, trying to rouse some enthusiasm when there was none forthcoming. 'Laurie would be interested; he has a good head for figures, even though he's a country boy at heart.'

Charles stared at her. She's taking control, he thought. This was not part of my plan. I was going to give her an ultimatum and here she is stepping in and making suggestions before I'm prepared.

'A bank isn't a place for children,' he said tersely, and it seemed as if to every suggestion she made Charles gave a negative answer. 'They would disrupt the running of the bank. I do believe you are becoming neurotic – unstable – disturbed even – to mention such a ridiculous thing.'

She was silenced. There seemed to be nothing else to say. A great chasm lay between them. An abyss.

'I suggest that I divorce you,' he said at last, completely ignoring his friend Paul's advice.

Beatrix was stunned. 'What? Divorce me! But . . . ? On what grounds?'

He took a deep breath, and then shrugged. 'Adultery is the only possible cause.'

She put her hand to her throat. 'How – how could you suggest – I have *never* been unfaithful. In spite of your rare visits and so many lonely days and nights there has *never* been – not – and with whom?'

'Really, can I believe that?' He gave a scornful grunt. 'A rich and attractive young woman, ripe for the plucking—'

'How *dare* you!' She rose to her feet, furious. 'Don't be so coarse. Keep that kind of language for your male friends if you must; do *not* bring it here to this house where our children live.'

'*My* children,' he reminded her. 'Don't forget you have no rights over them. Well, yes, the younger ones at present, but Laurence, no, no rights at all. I can remove them and you from this house whenever I wish.'

'Why? Why would you want to do that? I've brought them up with love and without your help; I have improved the estate since we married, made you more money than you ever had.' Her eyes narrowed. 'And have you thought of Laurence at all? He is heir to the estate. I think you should look at the will again and you will find that you must leave it to him in a desirable condition. If you let it slide, the will might be invalidated.'

She had no knowledge to support this statement; no proof that what she was saying was true, but neither did she think that Charles would have read the will in its entirety.

He stood up and faced her, then suddenly grabbed her slim wrist. A wrist that he could span between his thumb and forefinger. He looked down at it. So fragile. He could snap it quite easily. He compared it with Maria's. He couldn't span hers.

'We'll sleep on it,' he muttered. 'I will take advice from my lawyers, but I see no way out of this impasse. I told you all those years ago that I wasn't a farmer. I'm a city man, and as such I cannot spend time here.'

'Then don't,' she said passionately. 'Leave if you must and live your life as you think fit and I will run the estate for you and for Laurence and his brother and sister. Please don't leave it in jeopardy. I'm begging you, Charles. Don't do this.'

CHAPTER FORTY-SIX

She didn't sleep. She was on edge all night, listening for the sound of footfall; afraid that Charles might come to her room. She had left the door unlocked as always in case the children needed her during the night, as sometimes they did, padding from the room they still shared in three single beds, and she would often wake with one or the other climbing into bed with her. Or at times she would look into their room early in a morning and find them all in one bed; since Laurie had gone away to school this had happened frequently with Alicia and Ambrose.

But no one had come during the night and she was apprehensive that she had challenged Charles too far; given him an ultimatum that he would not condone. But what else can I do, she worried? I can't divorce him; the law is against me and all women in a predicament like mine. She drew in a sob. Neither can I risk losing my children, for again the law is against me, despite Charles's being an absent husband and father.

She wept into her pillow. I will apologize; ask him what he wants from me. She fell asleep again, an uneasy slumber in which she was constantly searching for children who were hiding from her.

She awoke at seven to a grey, overcast morning and a maid tapping on her bedroom door carrying a tray of tea and toast as usual.

'Should I take a breakfast tray to Mr Dawley, ma'am?' Ruby asked: yet another relation, a niece or a cousin of Cook's family who was being trained by Mrs Gordon.

'N-no,' she said. 'Let him sleep in. He had a long journey last night.' She didn't know why she should excuse her husband to anyone, let alone a young country maid, and yet she felt that she should. 'Thank you,' she said. 'I'll eat breakfast with the children this morning. They can come downstairs for a treat as their father is home.'

Except that he wasn't. At nine o'clock, as breakfast was about to be cleared away, she asked Ruby to knock on his door and Aaron drove round to the back of the house with a note in his hand for Mrs Gordon to give to Mrs Dawley, which she was about to do just as Ruby appeared to say that Mr Dawley wasn't in his room.

'He's probably been up since dawn and gone for a walk,' Beatrix said excusingly, knowing that that was the very last thing Charles would think of doing.

Mrs Gordon waited until the maid had left the room before she handed the note to Beatrix. 'Aaron is waiting, ma'am. He asked if he could have a word.'

'Yes, of course. Laurie, would you and Alicia entertain Amby in the nursery for ten minutes, please?'

'Yes, Mama; and then may I go outside? I'd like to see what's been happening whilst I've been away.' He chewed anxiously on his bottom lip. 'Will I have to go back to London with Papa?'

'Mm, not sure yet.' She smiled reassuringly. 'Papa and I have to talk it over. Have a discussion, you know.'

He nodded, and ushered his siblings out of the room in a very grown-up manner.

Aaron came into the room and apologized for disturbing her at breakfast.

'We've finished, thank you,' she said. 'Where have you been this morning?'

'I – I took 'master to Brough railway station, ma'am. He came round to 'stables at about half past six. I'd washed 'trap and was brushing 'pony down ready for putting him out to grass when he came and said he needed me to drop him off at 'station. I said I didn't think there was a train till eight, but he said he wanted to go anyway and he'd wait at 'station if necessary.' He seemed anxious, she thought. 'I had to wait with him, ma'am, as he said if there wasn't a convenient train I'd have to drive him into Hull and he'd go by a different route, Leeds or York, he said. But there was one after all. Then he gave me this letter to give to you. But what I wanted to say, ma'am . . .' He fidgeted, tapping his fingers together, and went on, 'He seemed to be in a bit of a state, ma'am, and I wondered if mebbe he wasn't well and I should have suggested that he came back here instead of travelling to London.'

Beatrix shook her head. 'No, he had to get back, Aaron, but thank you for the kind thought. He only came because he wanted to be sure that Laurie had arrived home safely after his escapade.'

How easy it was to lie, she thought, to make up a fantasy just to save someone's pride or self-esteem. But why would Aaron think that Charles was unwell? What had he been doing or saying to make Aaron so concerned, as if Charles would take any advice from a horse lad anyway?

She slit open the envelope when Aaron had left the room and read the letter. It was brief and to the point, and without any courteous address to her he had simply written in an uneven hand:

Beatrix. We have come to an impasse. I have had enough of your cold-hearted behaviour towards me and my children. I have left for London to consult with my lawyers who on my instructions will begin a lawsuit against you for divorce on the grounds of your adultery with other men. I will make preparations to remove the children as soon as I have made arrangements for their care.

Charles Neville Dawley.

Beatrix bent and put her head in her hands. She felt faint and sick and her mind was in a whirl. How could he say such a thing? How cruel. How shameful, when he knew it wasn't true. Would the lawyers, the courts, believe him? Did he have to prove it, or did the courts, all men, simply accept it as fact because he said so?

And the children? Where would he take them? Who would look after them? Little Amby didn't even know his father, hardly ever saw him, and Alicia . . . how could Charles look after a little girl?

Someone knocked on the door. She heard it open but she didn't, couldn't, lift her head.

'Mrs Dawley, ma'am. Are you all right?' It was Dora, faithful Dora who was not only a lady's maid but a confidante too.

'Ma'am? Are you unwell?' She bent down to peer into Beatrix's face and lifted her chin. 'Ma'am,' she murmured. 'What is it?'

Beatrix simply pointed to the letter that had fallen to the floor. Dora picked it up, and glancing at her mistress began to read. In a moment she sank on to a dining chair; not something she would normally do. 'He can't do this. Surely he can't.'

Beatrix lifted her head. 'It seems he can do whatever he likes.' Her voice was thick with unshed tears. 'He can lie and scheme and say *anything*, and my children can be taken away from me – not all of them, only Laurie at present, not Alicia or Ambrose as they're too young – unless . . .' she hesitated, trying to recall what she had read of the Custody of Infants Act, 'unless I am proved to have committed adultery.'

Dora breathed out a sigh. 'That's all right then,' she said.

Beatrix turned to her. It was a relief to think someone trusted and believed her, but she shook her head and whispered, 'I would still have to prove that I was innocent of the charge.' She put her elbows on the table and her head in her hands. 'What am I to do? The law leans towards the husband, and I have no money to put up a fight against him. Everything I have belongs to Charles; even the clothes on my back.'

'I don't know, ma'am. I've never known of such a thing.' Dora hesitated, and then stammered, 'It's, erm – that is, I'm probably speaking out of turn, but I know

– or think I know – something about Mr Dawley if it would help.'

Beatrix gave a wry grimace that turned into a sob. Servants always seemed to know more than one expected and it appeared that Dora would be no exception.

'If you're going to tell me that you've seen him with another woman on your occasional visits to London, Dora, no, it wouldn't help at all.' She cleared her throat. 'If he was seeing any number of women it wouldn't make the slightest difference; he can do whatever he likes, and according to the law of the land I cannot divorce him or do anything at all about it.'

CHAPTER FORTY-SEVEN

Charles sat with his arms crossed for most of the journey, glowering at anyone who made any attempt to come into his carriage when they stopped at a station. It was a slow journey, as there were many stops and two changes, and despite leaving so early it was almost three o'clock before the train pulled into King's Cross.

'I'm sick of this,' he muttered aloud, and a couple looked at him and moved away. Sick of travelling up and down. He shoved his ticket at the guard, who tipped his hat and stepped back. I'm going to see my lawyer and I'll find out what divorce will mean with regard to the will if I decide to sell. She must be wrong. It's too late. The estate is mine.

I will not have any woman telling me what I can or can't do. Then the thought came into his head that if he took Laurence away from his mother he would have to make arrangements for someone else to look after him; the school wouldn't keep him over the holidays.

Maria had already said no. Beatrix's parents? No. That would mean Beatrix would have access to him. My parents? *No!* I wouldn't let them look after a dog! Not that Mother would agree in any case. She doesn't like children; she didn't even like me or Anne, just thought us a nuisance.

Anne! He continued his contemplations. What about her? But no, she wouldn't. I don't know where she is, in any case; she took off in a hurry as soon as she received her inheritance, before anyone else got even a chance of a sniff at it.

He hopped on to a horse bus. Had he change? No, he hadn't. He hopped off again and was nearly run down by a cabriolet. He shook his fist at the driver and set off walking again, turning round every few steps to look for an empty cab. Those drivers always had change though they often were unwilling to give it.

He kept on walking, his temper worsening. So, it has to be Maria. Never mind that she doesn't know anything about children; that's a lie, he decided. She has brothers and sisters; she comes from a large family – ah! Maybe that's why she doesn't like them. Well hard luck, Maria, you're going to have to get used to them.

It might take time, of course, for everything to be completed; can I take the children away before the divorce? That might be inconvenient, especially with three of them. Could they attend nursery school, or would I have to employ a nanny? Perhaps it would be easier to only take Laurence.

Thoughts rolled around in his head like a bouncing ball but he reached no conclusion and his irritation increased.

He was nearly home; two more streets and he was there. He looked ahead. Two women in front, their gowns brightly coloured, both wearing gaudy shawls over their jackets. Maria? Yes, probably, and Bianca?

He heard them laughing. Jolly laughter as if they had heard something funny; happy laughter as if they hadn't a care, which they probably hadn't.

He didn't know Bianca well; she was the younger and to begin with he had been pleased as he thought she would be a good companion for Maria, but then he began wondering if Maria gave her money. She was inclined to be very generous, which he resented – it was his money, after all – although he didn't mind so much when he married Beatrix, as having Bianca to fill in the gaps and keep Maria entertained was very convenient.

But now he narrowed his eyes; they had been having a good time. They were both carrying parcels. Shopping, he thought; spending *my* money.

The two women parted company at the top of the street, bidding each other extravagant goodbyes. '*Adios, nos vemos pronto.*'

What was that? Goodbye . . . erm, see you soon, I think. In spite of knowing Maria so long, he had never mastered her language. His temper didn't abate. If she had been out shopping there would be no food ready and he was hungry, having missed breakfast and only managing to buy a small cake when he had changed trains.

He slowed his walk to allow Maria to get inside the house, and then rather than using his key he hammered on the door.

She had shed her jacket and shawl and she opened the door, greeting him with delight. 'Aah, darling, you are home already! I didn't think you would be here for another day or more.' She ushered him inside and took his coat. 'Did you find him?' She clasped her fingers together. 'Was he safe?'

'Who?' He stared at her woodenly, temporarily forgetting why he had left in such a hurry. 'Laurence! Oh, yes, cowering, and his mother protecting him. I'm going to bring him here. Make me something to eat,' he told her, 'and coffee. I've had nothing to eat all day.'

'Bring him here? No!' she said. 'He can't live here, not in my 'ouse. You know that. We have talked. And did your wife not make you breakfast before you leave?' She changed the subject. '*Tut*!' She clicked her tongue. 'I will make paella *pronto*.'

'Don't tell me what I can do,' he snarled. 'And I want something to eat *now*! Bread, beef, ham. I can't wait for paella.'

'All right. All right! Sit. I will be five minutes only. I take my coat and shawl upstairs. I have only just arrived home. Bianca and I—'

'Yes,' he snapped. 'I know. I saw you. You've been shopping!'

She smiled. 'Yes, you wait and see what I buy.'

'Later! I want food now.' He pointed to the stairs. 'Be quick.'

She cast a glance at him and turned, putting her coat and shawl on the stairs to take up later, and went into the tiny kitchen. She washed her hands under the tap and lifted the lid on the wooden bread bin, took out a loaf she had made the day before, and sawed a thick slice. Then she took another sharper knife and cut slices of ham from a joint in the meat safe, finally mixing a spoonful of yellow mustard powder with a drop of water in a small bowl to make a smooth paste.

She muttered, so that he wouldn't hear, '*Santo cielo. Que hombre!*' For goodness sake. What a man! She carried a plate with the food on it into the sitting room and placed it on the table, put a bundle of sticks on the fire to make a bigger flame, and went back to the kitchen to fill the kettle to make his coffee. As she stood up from putting the kettle on the fire, he grabbed hold of her by her arms. 'What did you say?'

She shrugged him off. 'When? I say nothing.'

'Yes you did. I heard you.'

She lifted her shoulders and her hands in an extravagant gesture. 'No! I say nothing. I make you food. Now I cook you dinner. I am your servant, yes?'

He lifted his hand and smacked her across the face, causing her to stagger and almost fall. She gasped and backed away from him, clutching her cheek. 'What I do? I do nothing!'

'You women are all the same,' he hissed. 'Always trying to get the better of the men who feed and clothe you, *and*,' he added menacingly, 'it is *not* your house. It is *my* house.'

She stared at him, her mouth open. 'What you say? I am here always for you. I cook and clean and share your bed and still it is not enough?'

He leaned towards her. 'No. It is not enough! I asked you, *what did you say?*' He spanned her throat with one hand and with the other grabbed her arm again. 'Do you not understand?' he roared. '*What did you say?*'

'I say nothing!' she shrieked. 'Get your hands off me!' With all her strength, she pushed him away so that, unprepared, he toppled backwards. Backwards so that he fell towards the fireplace, whirling his arms to retain his balance, but falling and hitting his head on the stone mantelpiece and crumpling into the hearth.

She sank to the floor and sat looking at him. What had happened? Why did he do this to her? She who loved and cared for him. Why did he attack her so?

She crept towards him on her hands and knees and saw that his hair was singeing from the hot coals. 'Charles! Get up.' She took hold of his feet and pulled him away from the fire, bumping his back against the brass fender. But he didn't flinch.

'Charles.' She patted his face. 'Charles! Wake up. Don't let us quarrel. Please. You know I do everything for you. You are my only love. Charles!'

She looked at her hand. It was sticky; sticky with blood. She drew in a breath. '*No*,' she gasped. 'No! Charles. Speak to me. Wake up.'

She rose from her knees and ran to the kitchen and seized a cloth, held it under the tap, and ran back to Charles and wet his face with it, squeezing the cloth so the water ran down his cheeks and neck. But still he didn't move. She put her head against his chest. Nothing.

She lay beside him, her arm across him, holding him, her face close to his. What must I do? Who can help me? They had lived secret lives. Few people visited them. Only his friend Paul, but she didn't know where he lived. Bianca, who came only when Charles was away. She knew no one else in the area. Charles had said that she mustn't invite anyone in when he wasn't there, and she never had; only Bianca.

The old man next door. He talked to her, and sometimes she took him bread that she had baked, or some leftover ham or half a bottle of wine, as Charles wouldn't drink yesterday's wine. But he was old. What could he do? How could he help her?

She put her head to Charles's chest again, but still couldn't hear a heartbeat. She put her fingers round his wrist. No throbbing of a pulse. She began to sob. 'Charles. Charles. What must I do? Please! Don't leave me, Charles. I don't know what to do.'

Using all her strength she pulled him up and put her arms around him, holding him close to pat his back, but he was heavy and she couldn't keep a grip on him. He lolled against her and she was frightened; she made the sign of the cross on her chest and let him down on to the rug, pulling him away from the hearth and cradling his sticky bloody head.

If I run for a bobby, will they come? Tears ran down her face as she sobbed. Will they think I have killed him? The thought terrified her. I am not an Englishwoman. Her sobbing was becoming unstoppable. They will put me in jail, or hang me. There is no one who will save me. Not Charles's father. He doesn't like me. I see it in his eyes. He knows my name.

Her thoughts and imaginings were becoming more and more muddled and eventually she stood up. She was shaking as she looked down on her lover. 'This is how you treat me after all these years,' she mumbled incoherently. 'I do everything for you. I am your wife and your mother. I take care of you always. And now you die.'

She began to back away as reality stepped in and her breath began to race. Her tears fell as if they would never stop, but now she was crying for herself and her fear and the predicament she found herself in. She bent and put her hand in his pockets, but drew out only coins, which she put into her own skirt pocket.

She backed away to the foot of the stairs in the small hall, closing the sitting room door behind her. She climbed the stairs to the bedroom they had shared, carrying the parcels she had brought in from shopping. The other tiny room was where she and Charles hung their clothes. A dressing room, Charles had called it. It was also where he kept money in a box which was locked with a key, and she knew where it was hidden. Charles had told her in case she ever needed money. He trusted me, she assured herself.

She dropped the parcels. They didn't seem important now, but she opened one and brought out a silk shirt she had bought for Charles and carefully hung it in the cupboard; she took a dark blue gown with a matching jacket from a hanger, and changed into it. She chose a three-quarter woollen cape and put that on. The skirt and blouse and jacket that she had been wearing she put into a large cotton shopping bag along with two petticoats and a warm shawl.

She unlocked the money box. It had coins and paper money in it: she took some out and tucked it into a cotton money bag that she fastened to her petticoat, and the rest she put at the bottom of a cheap carpet bag she had bought for its bright colours.

In this she left space for jewels. Hers, that Charles had bought her: rings and brooches, necklaces and earrings that might be worth money should she need it, and covered everything with a shawl and other items of clothing. She knew what it was like to be poor. She didn't want to revisit that situation. Now is the time, Maria, when you must look after yourself.

There, she thought. It is everything. She tried to hold back her sobs but she still hiccuped every second, and the tears ran down her cheeks as she closed the door behind her and crept down the stairs.

She hesitated outside the sitting room, undecided whether or not to enter; then she put down her bags and went in. He was as still as stone. She closed the door to the kitchen and then on reflection opened it again and took down a bottle of red wine from the shelf. Taking a bottle opener from a drawer she drew the cork.

She put her mouth to the neck and took a deep long swallow, then half filled a wine glass and took it into the sitting room. She sat down and considered, looking down on Charles. 'We have had some good times, Charles,' she murmured, speaking in her own language. 'You saved my life and I loved you for that. I think I helped you in yours, and I don't know who else could have or would have, for you are not an easy man; you are troubled, I think.' She gave a deep sigh. 'Maybe you are tiring of me, yes? I am older than I admit and you were very young when we met.'

She raised the glass to him, and then gently poured a few drops on to his lips and chin, sprinkled some on his shirt and upturned the rest on to the carpet, lowering the glass on to the stain.

I don't want anyone to think you were killed. I want them to think that you fell and banged your head, which is what you did, Charles. We shouldn't have fought, though it wasn't the first time.

She bent low and blew him a kiss. '*Dios te bendiga.*' God bless you. She crossed herself once more, and went softly into the entrance hall. She hesitated again. Through the small square of glass at the top of the outer door she saw that dusk was drawing in. She took the key from the shelf and put it in her pocket, pulled her shawl over her head, picked up her bags, opened the door and closed it behind her, leaving it unlocked, and stepped into the street.

It was drizzling with rain and just for the briefest second she wished for the warmth of her own country, but she shook her head. She had been safe here. Here she would stay.

Looking through the curtain of the house next door, the old man saw her leave. Where's she going? It's almost as dark as night. She rarely goes out in the evening except with *him*. He liked Maria. She was kind to him; but he didn't like the man she lived with. He often heard him shouting at her, as he had heard him tonight.

He turned away and closed the curtains on the night.

CHAPTER FORTY-EIGHT

Beatrix paced the floor. She had been awake again most of the night, and couldn't settle to anything. She had risen at five o'clock and written a letter to the headmaster of the Hampstead school to tell him that Laurence had been found and was safely home again.

She said that Laurence was sorry for having worried everyone so much and had promised that he wouldn't do such a thing again; and had added that either she or her husband would write again with a decision as to whether he would be returning to school. She had sealed it and left the envelope on her dressing table for Dora to take down.

She could hear the chatter and laughter of the children, but the sound seemed surreal, as if they were in another time and space. Is this how it will be if Charles divorces me? Will I only hear the sounds of my children's voices in my head?

How can he do it? Who will he accuse? The only men I see are the men who work on the estate, and Hallam. Surely Charles wouldn't think – no, he couldn't. She cast around in her head for acquaintances whom Charles, in his anger, might indict.

There was no one . . . except – perhaps – Edward. He is the one he might choose. Charles will know how he helped me when I first came here. She gave a throaty sobbing cry as she thought of Edward going to fetch Aaron to be with her during her first week of marriage, so that she wouldn't be alone. A marriage without a husband present. What would the courts make of that?

'Nothing.' She spoke aloud. It will be a court of men. She thought of the good men she knew who would judge her fairly. Her father, even though he had made a huge mistake in introducing her to Charles. Her brother Thomas: oh, if only he were here. His letters were few as yet. Hallam would be astonished by the question, though he would probably be fair; and Edward of course, regardless of his dispute with Charles; his father, Luke, who seemed to bear no grudge against anyone in spite of his misfortune.

Why am I thinking like this? I feel as if I am preparing for battle, but who is the enemy? Charles! What have I done to cause him to make such an attack on me?

After reading Charles's letter the previous day, she had replied immediately, pleading that they must talk and that she would do what she could to repair the rift in their marriage.

I swear on the heads of my children that I have never consorted with any other man . . . and had faithfully kept their wedding vows, and then sending the letter as urgent mail addressed and underlined to *Mr Charles Dawley only. Strictly private and confidential.* She had thought of sending a telegram but didn't want anyone but Charles reading it. He would see the letter the next morning when he went in to the bank.

Except that Charles didn't go in to the bank and his father, Alfred, eyed the letter waiting on Charles's desk. He thought he recognized Beatrix's handwriting on the envelope and wondered if Charles had actually travelled to Yorkshire to look for the boy. *He might at least have let me know.*

By midday he was becoming extremely annoyed with Charles for taking more time off, and decided that a serious meeting was called for. If Charles didn't conform he would call a board meeting and have him removed. He had the power to do that.

'One last chance,' he mumbled. 'But of course he won't care; he never wanted to join the family firm anyway, and now that he has the estate and all the profit that is coming in, he'll care even less.'

However, he didn't want the other directors to know just how little Charles did to earn the prestige of being second in command. *Even though he won't ever be in my position, I care about our standing in the banking world, so I will go once more to see him and give him a final warning. Three months only to turn himself around or he's finished. He must resign.*

Brusquely, he asked one of the clerks to send for a cabriolet, picked up the letter and slipped it in his briefcase, put on his top hat, and half an hour later was rolling along in the direction of Judd Street. He asked the driver to wait near the top of the street as he had done before, but this driver had a sharp tongue and insisted that he paid him first.

'If I get a fare, guv, I'll take it,' he told him. 'But I'll drive back this way and if you're waiting here I'll pick you up. My time is money, you know!'

'Please yourself!' Alfred was affronted. 'I'll be half an hour at least, but if you can afford to turn it down that's all right by me.'

He paid him for the single ride and turned to walk down the street. 'Who does he think he is?' he muttered. 'Doesn't he know who I am? He picked me up at the bank, for heaven's sake!'

The old man who lived next door to Charles's house was standing by his gate, nodding to people walking by and passing the time of day with some of them, but Alfred didn't acknowledge him in any way. The old man turned to look at him before stepping back inside his own house.

Alfred hammered on the door and waited; then he knocked again, noting that the door rattled against the frame but not the chain. He put his hand on the knob and turned it; the door was unlocked. He knocked again, and pushed it slightly.

'Charles!' He opened it wider. 'Where are you? Maria! Are you there?'

Nothing. No sound, no voices, no smell of wood smoke or coal fire or cooking. He stepped inside. How foolish of them to forget to lock the door. Where had they gone in such a hurry that they forgot, especially in a neighbourhood such as this? It wasn't as if Charles hadn't a lot to lose. Alfred had an obsession with locking doors and windows in case of burglars.

'Charles? Maria?' For such a bullish man, an unexpected sense of propriety made him baulk at entering

379

someone else's property, even though it belonged to his son.

He pushed open the sitting room door. Everything seemed neat and tidy, though the room was rather dark and he noticed that the curtains were closed; and then he saw a pair of feet attached to two legs and vaguely thought it was odd to lie on the floor when there were comfortable chairs to sit on.

And then he saw the rest of the figure lying so still. A body. And it was his son. It was Charles lying there, dried blood on his face and caked on his fair hair and what looked like blood on his shirt.

Alfred made a stifled sound and he wasn't sure if he shouted, but he backed out of the house and ran to the low iron gate, and then he did shout. '*Help!* Help me, someone. Fetch the police, somebody; help me! There's been a fatality. My son. *My son is dead!*'

Alfred went to the house next door and rattled the knocker, but no one answered. Maybe the old man's deaf, he thought, and then he saw a young lad open a door further down the street and walk towards him.

'Hey,' Alfred called to him. 'Can you run?'

The boy looked at him warily and nodded.

'Run to the nearest lock-up and find a policeman, will you? Tell him – tell him someone's died.'

The boy seemed more interested. 'Who?' he asked.

'Never mind who, just run. Sixpence when you return with one.'

'No point in running, is there, if somebody's dead?'

Alfred jingled coins in his pocket. 'Are you going or not? I'll go myself if you won't.' I'll have to lock the door if I can find a key. Can't leave the door open now.

'Yeh, all right.' The lad seemed to have a change of heart and set off at a lope until he reached the main road, where he slowed his step.

Alfred sat on the low garden wall with his head in his hands. What am I going to do? His chest felt tight, breathless; reality was crowding in on him. What do I say to his mother? What do I tell his wife? I barely know her. Will she have hysterics? What about Maria? Is this an accident, a murder? Is anything missing? Money? Jewellery?

He turned to see two people walking down the street towards him but they passed him by without even glancing at him. Should I have stopped them? Will that lad come back?

Then he saw the boy and two policemen coming towards him, their distinctive tall hats and shiny buttons on their tailcoats immediately recognizable. He signalled to them to hurry, and they quickened their steps.

'Yes, sir,' one of them said. 'What is your difficulty?'

'My difficulty, constable, is that my son—' His voice broke. 'My son is lying dead.' He pointed a finger over his shoulder to the door. 'Inside his house.'

Once Alfred had established that the police would now take over, he hired a cabriolet for the day and went first to a post office where he sent a telegram to Beatrix, asking her to come to London as urgently as possible as there was disquieting news regarding Charles, and suggesting he meet her at her parents' home the following day.

Next he called back at the bank and put the manager in complete charge, saying he would be away for a few days but offering no further information; and finally, bracing himself, he was driven home to tell his wife the news, knowing that he would get the blame.

The bobbies, or peelers as they were sometimes known, called on every house in the street and vicinity to ask if anyone knew the man who had lived as their neighbour. No one did, not even the old man who lived next door.

'No, sir,' he said. 'Seen him coming an' going, but he never stopped to pass the time o' day. Reckon he had a bob or two, though; always dressed smart. City gent, I'd say. A wife? Not as far as I know. Never seen him wiv anybody. Bit of a loner. Sorry I can't help you further.'

CHAPTER FORTY-NINE

Beatrix opened the telegram and her fingers shook as she read the message. What disquieting news? What is Charles up to now? Has he told his father that he is going to divorce me and take the children away?

But why would he do that? There was no love between him and his father: quite the opposite in fact. She rang the bell for Dora. 'I have to go to London immediately, Dora, and I'm taking the children with me. Will you check the train times, and if there's one this afternoon we'll catch it. I also need to send a telegram to my parents to say we are coming, so will you ask Aaron to come and collect it and take it to the post office for me?' She wouldn't say much, just to expect them to arrive late.

'I'll pack a suitcase, ma'am. Will you be staying long?'

Beatrix shook her head. 'I don't think so, just a day or two. I've received an urgent message from my father-in-law.' She looked at Dora. 'He says to come immediately. You'd better come with me.'

'Yes, ma'am.' Dora had had every intention of packing an overnight bag of her own and travelling with her; the state of mind her mistress was in, she wouldn't think of letting her travel without her, especially if she was taking the children. 'I think there's a train at about four o'clock. We should be in good time for that.'

'Am I going back to school, Mama?' Laurie asked her glumly when she told the children they were going to London; he'd hung back when Alicia and Amby scampered off to choose a toy to take with them.

'I'm not sure yet.' She dropped a kiss on the top of his head. 'I need to speak to the headmaster first. Don't worry.'

'I can't help it,' he mumbled, pressing his lips together. 'I'd hoped to have a little longer at home.'

'I know,' she said softly. 'Papa and I will talk about it and come up with a solution.'

It was late when the train pulled in. They had changed trains in Doncaster and Laurie had looked eagerly about to catch a glimpse of the stationmaster, but didn't see him. On the next train all three children fell asleep, as it was long past their bedtime, and on arrival at King's Cross they had stumbled unsteadily out of the carriage. A porter immediately took charge of the luggage and even carried a sleepy Amby as he headed towards the cab rank to order transport to Russell Square.

'Soon be at Grandpapa and Grandmama's house,' Beatrix told Alicia, who put her head in her mother's lap in the cab and clung to her hand. 'Then a warm drink and off to bed.'

She was glad she had brought the children with her; she had felt uneasy about letting them stay at home without her in case Charles was plotting some ruse to collect them whilst she was in London. He's right: I am becoming paranoid and feel as if I must watch them all the time, but it's only because of his threats.

'What has happened?' her mother asked, after they'd seen the children safely into bed, her father had retired to bed too and Dora had gone to her old room.

'I don't know,' she confessed. 'I received a telegram from Charles's father asking me to come to London immediately as there was disquieting news about Charles. He's coming here tomorrow. Charles's father is, not Charles. Mama, I must tell you and you must try not to be upset, even though you are bound to be. Charles says he is going to divorce me and take the children away.' Her voice trembled, and a small sob escaped from her lips.

Her mother stared at her, aghast. 'On what grounds?'

'The most disreputable allegations, which are simply not true! I dare not even say them.' Beatrix put her head in her hands and wept, racked with sobs. 'Charles seems to think I'm neurotic and unstable, but I think he's the one who is.'

Her mother leaned towards her and patted her knee. 'I have not the slightest notion why Charles would do this, but I will believe you above any other. You were always an honest child; I can't think that you have changed so much. Come, come. We will get through this, whatever it is.' She sat back in her chair and pondered. 'All our hopes and dreams for you seem to have disappeared, and I don't think you've been happy for quite some time.'

'I'm happy with my beautiful children and my home,' Beatrix took a deep breath, 'but I believe that I have married the wrong man. I don't think that Charles has ever loved me, which was what I wanted most of all. I was a seemly young woman, one who would be suitable to his position; perhaps that is the requirement for all rich gentlemen. Love doesn't come into it. Never once has he said he loves me.' She sighed. 'Ah, well. We will see what tomorrow brings.' She wiped her eyes. 'If it is more bad news, we are at least safe here with you and Papa for the time being.'

'Of course you are,' her mother said softly. 'Always.'

In her own former bedroom and the bed she had slept in ever since she could remember, it was as if she had shed her responsibilities and become a carefree young woman again, and she slept accordingly. But she stirred early, wakened by the noise of traffic and the raucous sound of voices, and for a few seconds she wondered where she was and why she couldn't hear the cry of gulls and wildfowl overhead.

What will today bring, she wondered? Will Charles come with his father, and why did his father send the telegram? She sat up, suddenly struck by a thought. What was the wording again? Disquieting news! What does it mean? Is Charles ill and can't send his own message?

Her father couldn't shed any light on the matter; there had been nothing in any financial paper, no run on any bank as far as he knew.

'I'm assuming everything is in order with your accounts? You would probably have heard if – ah, but no, of course you wouldn't,' he muttered.

And of course she wouldn't, she railed silently; even though she had looked after the estate accounts for years, she was a woman after all and wouldn't have the wit to understand them.

'We'll have to wait until Mr Dawley arrives and hope that he brings Charles along too,' she said. 'I do hope he isn't ill.'

Then she realized that if he were ill he wouldn't be coming anyway, and with that the doorbell rang.

Alfred Dawley was offered coffee, which he accepted, but then he suggested that Beatrix might like to take a small glass of brandy, for he had some bad news to impart.

'I wouldn't,' she said firmly. 'I rarely drink spirits, especially not at this time of day, and I would rather you told me why you have asked me to come all this way. Will you please tell me where Charles is and why he isn't here?'

She saw him visibly pale, and his hand trembled as he put down the coffee cup.

'I regret,' he said, 'to tell you . . . this isn't at all easy . . .' He wasn't a man known for delicacy or sensitivity, and Beatrix frowned at his faltering.

'To tell you that yesterday . . .' He took a breath before continuing, and held his hand to his chest as if he had a pain. 'Charles sustained a serious injury, and was found dead at his London house.'

Beatrix clasped the chair arm. 'No! No! What are you saying? How do you know? Who – who found him?'

Dawley lowered his head. 'I did. He hadn't come in to the bank in the morning, nor the day before—'

'The day before he was in Yorkshire, with us,' Beatrix heard herself say. 'He caught the early morning train back to London. Mama, will you ring for a jug of water?'

Her mother rose from her seat, pressed the bell on the wall, and came to stand close behind Beatrix's chair, putting her hand on her shoulder. Her father had also risen to his feet.

'And you found him – how?' he asked Dawley.

'The door was unlocked; I'd knocked several times and realized that I could open it. I went in and called for him or Maria,' he mumbled. Realizing what he had said, he looked up at Beatrix and added awkwardly, 'The – the woman who cleans for him.'

Beatrix, distressed, turned her head away. 'I am aware that he has – had a mistress, although I didn't know her name.'

'It was nothing,' he insisted. 'It didn't mean anything—'

'I'm not interested in hearing about it,' Beatrix said, her voice wavering, 'but I would like you to accompany me to the police station and then to the place where Charles is lying.' She turned to her mother, her face white and her voice breaking. 'Mama, will – will you take care of the children, please?'

It was Dora who knocked and opened the door in answer to the bell, and Beatrix had the strangest sensation of having stepped back in time. She felt incapable of choosing the words she required. 'Will you send in a jug of water and – and then bring my warmest shawl; the – dark one. It seems that I have to go out and – and I would like you to come with me.'

'I will come with you,' her father said, and to Dora, 'Please bring me my coat and hat.'

'Papa . . .' she stumbled over her words. 'There's no need,' she began again, but her father interrupted.

'There is every need,' he said firmly. 'You must have a family member with you in case there are documents to sign.'

Alfred Dawley opened his mouth to say something but closed it again, seeing by Fawcett's expression that his mind was made up.

They drove to the police station where Dawley said he had reported the death, and Beatrix and her father were taken into a small room and given details of where Charles was found and the evidence that had caused the police to conclude that his death was accidental. He had fallen, perhaps unsteady on his feet as they had found an almost empty bottle of wine; and there was blood on the mantelpiece where he had hit his head and sustained the blow that killed him. There didn't appear to be anyone else involved, the police sergeant said, and no one had come forward with information. He appeared to live alone, according to his neighbour. Then, as the mortuary where Charles lay was only a short walk away, a constable accompanied them, and Beatrix asked to see Charles alone, for she couldn't accept the news without seeing him for herself.

He looked so peaceful and handsome, the only injury the fatal blow on the back of his head. 'This is how I will try to remember you, Charles,' she murmured. 'How you were when we first met. You were, or appeared to be, without anger or rancour. What was it that had enraged you so? What gave you such anguish that you had to inflict it on others? I could have loved you.' Tears began to run down her cheeks. 'But you were not open to receive that love.'

She bent and kissed his forehead. 'God bless you,' she said. 'Rest in peace; your travails are over.'

CHAPTER FIFTY

Beatrix went back to her parents' house to plan. She felt shaky and incredibly shocked, but realized that she must keep her wits about her. The time for weeping would come later. She decided that she would stay in London until the next day and then take the children home; she would return the following day and stay quietly at her parents' house until Charles's funeral. Her father-in-law had said he would attend to the organizing of it and send the letters of invitation. Beatrix would not be expected to attend in person, but, she thought, I might. It will be the last duty I will carry out for him.

She asked her mother if she had a black gown that she might wear for the next few days, until she could order garments from Peter Robinson's General Mourning House for herself, and Mrs Fawcett suggested a black bombazine wool and silk gown and a veil that she had bought following her own father's death. She was a little plumper than her daughter but they were a similar height, and though the gown hung a little loosely on Beatrix she thought that if she bought a black wool cape to wear over it it would be quite appropriate.

But her mother produced a black cape too, one that Beatrix had never seen before. 'You don't have to attend the funeral, Beatrix,' she told her. 'Widows are not expected to.'

'But I want to, Mama. I consider it fitting. Charles was my husband, even though we had some difficulties in our marriage. I care not a jot for society's conventions on who should do what and when.'

The children had not yet been told; Beatrix said that she would wait until the next morning when she would begin wearing her widow's weeds. Today she would borrow her mother's cape and visit Charles's mother in Hampstead, and then make two more calls.

Charles's mother was wearing full mourning dress when Beatrix and Dora arrived unannounced just after luncheon. When the maid answered the door she was wearing a black armband, and told them that Mrs Dawley was not at home because of bereavement.

'Yes, I know,' Beatrix said, stepping inside. 'Please tell her that Mrs Charles Dawley is here to see her.'

Dora waited outside the parlour door when Beatrix was shown in. Mrs Dawley was reclining on a sofa, but sat up immediately and exclaimed at Beatrix's normal dress. 'Did your mother not explain to you how things should be done? You must not be seen in public as you are dressed now or you will be disgraced!'

'Mrs Dawley!' Beatrix sat down without waiting to be invited. 'I have just come from my husband's side after his sudden death. I do not need to be told by my mother or you or anyone what I must or must not do. I am a grown woman, mother of Charles's three children. *They* are my full concern, and I do not wish to upset or alarm them, so I will not wear mourning until I have explained to them, in words suitable for their young ears, what has happened to their father. I have come to give you my deepest condolences on the loss of your son – my husband.' She stood up. 'I bid you good day.'

She spoke to the driver of the waiting cabriolet, gave him details of their next destination, and took a huge breath as she climbed aboard. 'Well, that went very well, Dora,' she muttered as they sat down. 'I rather think that Mrs Alfred Dawley will welcome this interlude in her boring life, when she can write to her friends on black-edged notepaper telling them of the sad sudden death of her only son – as if she had cared for him,' she said bitterly, 'when she surely had not.'

Dora gazed at her. It wasn't her place to comment; her mistress, however, turned to her. 'You think I'm being unkind, Dora?'

'No, miss – erm, sorry, ma'am.' She put a gloved hand to her lips. 'A slip of the tongue, ma'am. It's because we're back in London and staying in Russell Square.'

Beatrix nodded. 'I know; I feel strange too. Even though I've been to stay with my parents often, this time seems different, as if I'm a different person.'

'Which you are, ma'am,' Dora answered. 'And ready to stand up for what you believe in.'

'Yes,' she murmured. 'You're very astute, Dora. I am ready, but I've been thrown out of kilter by Charles's death.' She paused; in a weak moment she had shown Dora the letter that Charles had left for her on his last visit to Yorkshire. Then she added, 'But by his death he has in some aspects saved my life. A life without my children I could not in the least have contemplated.'

They were up on the heath, passing ponds and clumps of woodland, and the driver pulled into the drive of a mansion, a building surrounded by trees and a lush green lawn, and drew up outside an imposing front door. Beatrix made a *humph* in her throat. It looked fine from the outside, and not at all as grim as she had expected. 'Have you been up here before, Dora?' she asked.

'Don't think so, ma'am. I've been up on the heath, but not this bit. It's massive, isn't it? Miles of it.' She looked back and sighed. 'What a lovely place to live. The Lungs of London, we were taught at school. It's where Londoners came to escape from the plague in days gone by.'

'Indeed.' Beatrix was about to pull the bell rope when the great door opened and two schoolboys appeared. Both immediately gave a short bow and one of them asked if they could be of service.

'I haven't an appointment,' she said, 'but if possible I would like to speak to the headmaster. It is rather important.'

A matronly woman bustled along the hall behind them and the boys moved back to allow Beatrix and Dora inside. Beatrix gave her name to the housekeeper, who asked her to be seated whilst she discovered if Mr Robinson-Gough could see her.

He was free and she was shown into his study, where on introduction he said how very nice it was to meet her and asked if he might offer her refreshments, which she declined.

'Are you well now, Mrs Dawley? Restored to good health? And how is young Laurence?'

'Laurence is very well, thank you, and is here with me in London, but as for me, I have been lucky enough to have always enjoyed good health, especially since living in the country.' She gazed at him and thought him a very pleasant and personable man. But he seemed puzzled. 'Have you been told otherwise?'

'A misunderstanding, I'm sure,' he said evasively, and sat down again. He seemed rather embarrassed, but then asked, 'Can we expect the pleasure of having Laurence back with us?'

She was completely thrown. She had been sure that she would find harshness and bleakness here, but there appeared to be neither. Yet Charles had hated it, even though he had wanted Laurie to come. Why?

'I think I will have a cup of tea after all, Mr Robinson-Gough,' she said. 'I have several things to discuss.'

'Gough will do, Mrs Dawley.' He smiled. 'Robinson-Gough is rather a forkful to swallow, I admit.' He shook the bell on his desk and she relaxed.

She told him of Charles's sudden death, and that she had come to London only the day before completely unaware of it. He was stunned and shocked and offered his condolences; he told her that although Charles had been an old boy of the school he hadn't known him himself, but his brother Stephen had been in the same year. He didn't think they were close friends, but Stephen had once visited the Yorkshire estate at Charles's invitation, along with several other students.

'Stephen has always had an enquiring mind,' he said. 'He hadn't been to Yorkshire before and that was possibly why he accepted the offer.' He hesitated slightly before adding that his brother had been captivated by the county and had made subsequent visits. 'So much so,' he added, 'that he married into a Yorkshire family and subsequently set up a law practice in York. He specializes in property and estate matters and the custody of children; he was most impressed by Mrs Caroline Norton's writing. No doubt you have heard of her?'

Beatrix nodded, and breathed in; a subject close to her heart, of which she now had no need. 'You must give me his details, Mr Gough.'

They parted company with Beatrix saying that she would consider sending Laurie back to the Hampstead school; but not yet, she said. 'We must get over this dark period in our lives, and for the present I wish to keep my children close by my side.'

Dora was waiting on a small sofa in the hall, having been offered tea and biscuits, and dipped her knee as the headmaster escorted Beatrix out.

'One more call, Dora,' Beatrix told her as they walked towards the cab and its driver, who was sitting on a wall patiently waiting, 'and I might need your help with finding an address somewhere close to Judd Street.'

Dora looked up so sharply that Beatrix marked it. 'What?' she asked once the carriage moved off. 'Do you know it?'

'My mother lives at the bottom end, ma'am. I cut through from Judd Street when I go to visit her.'

'Is that the way we went when I visited her with you all those years ago?'

'Yes, ma'am,' Dora mumbled. 'It is.'

When they got to the top of the street, the cab driver slowed and Dora pulled down the window to give him directions. 'It's this end,' she told Beatrix. 'The better end. My ma lives at the other end.'

How does Dora know where I'm going? She knows something, but she's keeping it to herself.

Dora knocked on the roof and the driver slowed the horse; she opened the door and helped Beatrix down, calling to the driver to wait.

'It's a little further on, ma'am.' Dora's face was white.

'You saw him, Dora? You saw my husband here?'

Dora hung her head. 'Yes, ma'am,' she whispered. 'And someone else.'

She opened a gate to one of the terraced houses; the path led through a small patch of garden with a few rose bushes and shrubs of lavender and bay and pots of herbs. The door was closed.

'I'm going inside, Dora. I have Charles's key.' Beatrix opened her palm to show her the iron key. 'It was given to me at the police station. Sit in the carriage if you wish.'

'Yes, ma'am.' Dora turned and went back to wait.

There was no need of the key. The door was not locked and Beatrix stepped quietly inside. There was a smell of beeswax and lavender and something else, faintly exotic. She looked up the narrow staircase and saw that the stair carpet was well brushed; she opened the door into what she thought would be the parlour and saw a bright fire burning and brasses gleaming by the fire. Two small sofas had silk shawls draped over the backs and soft plump cushions.

She listened. She could hear a clattering of dishes coming from a door at the other end of the room and a voice. She listened but couldn't hear the words, and pushed open the door and saw a woman, much older than her, with a mass of dark hair streaked with white, and her hands in a bowl of soapy water.

She turned and they looked at one another and Beatrix, with a catch in her throat, said, 'Maria?'

'*Si.*' She dried her hands on a towel. 'M-Mrs Dawley? I am – I am cleaning the 'ouse for you. I – I have a key. I will give it back when I finish.'

Beatrix saw a slow trickle of tears running down Maria's face. She knows about Charles. Do they – did they live here together?

'May I sit down?' Beatrix went back into the parlour and sat down anyway, and Maria followed her. The enormity of what had happened suddenly hit her and she bent her head: so this is the other woman in Charles's life. She looked up. 'Is someone here with you? I thought I heard someone talking.'

Maria shook her head and patted her chest. 'I – I was talking.' Her voice was hoarse. 'I clean my kitchen and talk to Charles. I ask him – I ask him why we quarrel? Why was he angry with me?' She choked back a sob. 'He want me to look after his children – *your* children – and I say no, I cannot.'

She sat down on the opposite sofa. 'He fell,' she said. 'He hit me when I say no, and I hit him back and he fell over.' She pointed to the mantelpiece. 'He fell and hit his head.' She began to sob. 'I try to help him.'

She held her hands palms uppermost and looked at them, bending her fingers. 'There was blood. I wash it off but he had gone; so quick,' she whispered. 'I never think that death come so fast.'

Tears ran swiftly down her cheeks and overflowed down her chin and her neck and she brought out a handkerchief to pat them away, a handkerchief with a red flower embroidered on it.

So it was hers; Beatrix thought, but she doesn't seem to have the guile to think of planting it in Charles's pocket. So him then, to torment me? Or simply by chance? And so perhaps after all she was the only one?

'How long – how long have – have – had you known Charles?'

'Oh, a long long time. He was just a boy. He finish at university and come to Madrid for 'oliday with 'is friend for a good time.' She wiped the tears which flooded her eyes. 'I was what you call *sirvienta* – a maid in hotel. I was very unhappy and he made me smile.' She gave a watery smile. 'Then he come back, he look for me and bring me to England. He was good to me.'

Her face creased and she looked very sad. 'He say to me that it was our house. Mine and his, but then he change his mind and said it was not mine, that it was his. He say that women cannot have houses.'

Beatrix nodded. Her relief that Maria had been the only other woman was profound. 'He was right. There are rules. It's the same for all women. But some-times . . .' She had a sudden thought. Maria has been faithful to him all these years and what is she left with? Nothing. It's the same for me. Old Stone Hall is not mine. It belongs to my eight-year-old son. 'Sometimes,' she said, 'the rules can be changed.'

She got up to leave. 'Maria, Charles's funeral will be held very shortly. Will you stay in the house until then and take care of it? Keep it safe, and then I will come back and talk to you again. Please?'

Maria nodded, her face awash with tears. 'I will stay until you come. I clean it for you and I will remember Charles. My dearest love.'

CHAPTER FIFTY-ONE

Early the following morning, Beatrix dressed in the black gown to travel back to Yorkshire, and as she did so she realized her life would be changing once more.

When she came down to breakfast, the children were already eating theirs and were dressed ready for the journey. Laurie looked at her, and putting his head on one side asked, 'Why are you wearing that strange gown, Mama? I don't like it very much.'

'I don't either,' Alicia said. 'I like your blue one best.'

'I like it, Mama,' Amby said contrarily.

Beatrix sat down at the table with them. 'Well, first of all, Laurie,' she said, 'it is not polite to comment on ladies' apparel, so I'd like you to remember that.' She sighed. 'I don't like it very much either, but your grandmama has very kindly loaned it to me for this particular time, which I will explain just as soon as I've had my cup of coffee.'

'Sorry, Mama.' Laurie hung his head. 'I didn't mean to be rude.'

'I didn't mean to be either,' Alicia piped up. 'But I still like the blue one best.'

Beatrix hid a wan smile; this was meant to be a serious time, and the children had to be taught. She drank half her coffee. She didn't want anything to eat. Her appetite had disappeared.

'There's a reason why I'm dressed in this way,' she began, 'and I want you to sit very still and listen whilst I tell you what has happened and why we are going home again today.'

She told them only that their father had had an accident from which he hadn't recovered and had died. The children sat quietly, as she had told them to, and only Laurie asked a question when she finished speaking.

'Does that mean I won't have to go back to school?'

'You will have to go to school, but I haven't yet decided where. Perhaps you would like to come to the Hampstead school when you are older and spend the weekends here with Grandpapa and Grandmama?'

Laurie nodded his head. 'Yes, that would be all right,' he said brightly. 'There's a wooden board in the Grand Hall and there are quite a lot of Dawleys on it.'

'Are there?' she asked. 'I hadn't noticed.'

'Yes. Papa is on it and Grandpapa Alfred and some others, someone called Neville and – I can't remember any more.' He gave a deep sigh. 'I'd quite like my name on it.'

'Come here,' she said, and put out her arms to give him a hug. 'We've plenty of time to consider.'

'I want to as well,' Amby butted in. He always wanted to be the same as his brother and sister even if he didn't always know why, and so he and Alicia had a hug too.

As they dressed in their outdoor clothes, Dora came in carrying black armbands for the children to wear on the sleeves of their coats. 'Look,' she said, and showed them her sleeve, also with a black band.

'Oh! I'd like one on mine, please,' Alicia said. 'Laurie and Amby can have them too, and then we'll all be the same.'

Beatrix kissed her mother goodbye and told her she'd see her the next day; her father was travelling with them and would escort her on the return journey. Her mother remarked that Beatrix would be worn out with all the toing and froing, but Beatrix claimed that she wouldn't be. She asked Dora if she would like to return to London with her the following day and visit her mother; she said that she would and asked if she might be permitted to attend the funeral. Beatrix agreed at once – she would be glad of Dora's support.

'Papa,' Beatrix murmured to her father when they were alone, 'when we return tomorrow, would you seek out or write to Charles's father and tell him that I don't want too much ostentation at the funeral? No plumes on the horses, or long scarves on the mutes. Charles wouldn't like it and neither do I and there is no one we wish to impress.' Her father raised his shaggy eyebrows and said that it might be too late for that, but Beatrix insisted. 'We've several days yet before the ceremony. Time enough for him to cancel instructions if he has already issued them.'

They caught an early train, and as they travelled homewards Beatrix made numerous notes, but uppermost in her mind was the need to speak to Charles's solicitor regarding his will, and what was to happen about Laurie and the future of the estate.

It was an odd homecoming, with much to plan. First of all Beatrix asked Mrs Gordon to come to the study; the housekeeper had of course guessed that there had been a death on seeing Beatrix arrive in mourning dress, but not that it was Mr Dawley who had died. She offered her sincere sympathies and said that she would inform the other servants.

'I'm returning to London tomorrow and leaving you in charge of the household, Mrs Gordon. I will be away for a few days, at least until after the funeral service, but I will come home as soon as I can. Would you ask Aaron to come in, please, and I'll send a note to Mrs Newby and her husband. They've known my husband since he was a boy.'

She knew that Mags, on a word from her, would send the news around the district. She would also write a note to her friend Rosetta so that she and her parents would know the circumstances that would preclude her from socializing until the mourning period was over.

Mrs Gordon assured her that she need not worry about the household or the children, and within no time at all all the servants were wearing black armbands. Beatrix spoke to the nursery maid and gave her strict instructions about the children, and told her that she must speak to Mrs Gordon if she had any worries.

Within half an hour of Aaron's departure on his errand, Mags appeared at Beatrix's door in tears and wearing a black shawl. 'I'm so sorry, ma'am. So very sorry for your loss. I wish he had been here with us and not in London; his passing might have been easier on you.'

Beatrix thought of the desolate Maria and how much worse it would have been for her if Charles had died elsewhere. Then she thought that if Charles had been at home with them he wouldn't have died. At least now, with what I have in mind, Maria above all others will have fond and loving memories of him. I have so very few; I cannot claim to have more, for it would be an untruth.

She took a deep breath which she hoped Mags, sitting across from her, would think was one of sorrow, but was in fact a sense of reprieve that her children would now be safe in her hands. I did not wish for Charles's death; never would I wish that for anyone. She felt choked with tears and regret, and wondered if his death would have been bearable if there had been love in their lives to remember, rather than strife.

Mags stood up to leave. 'I've told Mr Newby,' she said. 'He is not able to come himself, but he sends his condolences. I've told Edward too, and that you are leaving for London again tomorrow. I'll look in on the children if you'd like me to?'

'Thank you, dear Mags. I would like that. It is such a comfort to know that you are near at hand and that you feel real sorrow at this sad time.'

'It's time to put away hard feelings, ma'am.' Mags wiped her eyes on the corner of her shawl. 'Should mebbe have been done with many years ago, but some old memories tend to linger, I'm afraid. God bless you, Mrs Dawley, and your bairns.'

She let herself out of the room, leaving Beatrix wondering what she was actually referring to.

Dusk was gathering as Beatrix opened the front door, stepped outside and went down the steps. Bats were swooping across the front lawn and she looked up as a skein of geese honked and whistled as they flew down the route of the estuary, making a dark V formation in the evening sky.

The children were in bed, tired after their early morning travelling, and Beatrix, tired and emptied out with shock and melancholy, felt the need of solitude and cool evening air on her skin to ease a lingering headache. She was wearing a white cotton cap as was the custom for widows when indoors; preferable, she thought, to the black bonnet and veil that she had worn on their journey.

She heard the rattle of wheels on the gravel and turned. Who was calling at this hour?

Edward was driving the trap and Hallam was with him. Both men got out and each put his hands to his chest.

Edward spoke first. 'It's late, ma'am, but I understand you are leaving again in the morning, and I – we – wanted to give you our deepest condolences on hearing of Ch— the loss of your husband.'

She nodded her thanks; his manner was formal and he could almost have been a stranger offering his sympathy, apart from that little slip of the tongue over Charles's name. Then Hallam said almost the same thing, except for using 'Mr Dawley', and assuring her that everything would continue as usual in her absence.

Beatrix made an appropriate reply, and to her surprise Hallam went on to ask if it would be permissible to call at the kitchen door to have a word with Miss Dora. She saw the uncertainty on his face as he said, 'I thought that perhaps she'd be travelling back with you to London, ma'am.' A faint blush caught his already ruddy complexion.

'She is,' she said, 'but if you're quick' – she pointed over her shoulder to the front door – 'you will find her downstairs in the sitting room.'

'Thank you, ma'am.' With a quick bow, he ran up the steps and opened the front door.

She turned to Edward. 'Have we a burgeoning romance here?'

He smiled briefly. 'Yes, I'm sure so.'

'I won't know whether to be glad or sorry,' she said softly. 'I would be lost without her. She came as a maid to my parents' house when she was fourteen. I'd forgotten she's only about four years younger than I am.'

'What happened?' he asked quietly. 'To Charles.'

She swallowed. No one else had asked about the circumstances. 'An accident. He caught his heel on a rucked carpet and fell backwards and hit his head on the mantelpiece.' She heaved a breath and put her hand to her throat as she embroidered the detail. 'It was instantaneous.'

'I'm so very sorry; that must have been dreadful for you.' His concern was genuine. 'Were you there?'

'No,' she whispered. 'I wasn't. I received a telegram from Charles's father asking me to come at once. He said that there was disquieting news, but gave no indication of what the news might be.'

His lips parted. 'And you went alone?'

She shook her head. 'With Dora and the children. I – I didn't know what the news would be,' she stammered, not knowing how to explain and realizing that she couldn't. 'I – I didn't – I thought it might be something else entirely, which is why I took the children with me. I – didn't know what to expect. But he – Charles's father – came to see me at my parents' house. So I wasn't alone when he gave me the news. I . . .' She paused. 'I went to see Charles. It was the only way that I could believe that he was – not here any more.'

He reached for her hand as she touched her throat, but gently she pulled it away.

'I can't think of – that is . . . ' she closed her eyes momentarily, 'I can't think of anything more than getting through the next few days, Edward, and what else – what other developments – they might bring. My position with the estate,' she looked back at the old house and sighed, 'well, I don't know what will happen until I see the contents of Charles's will.'

Edward frowned. 'I don't understand. Surely Laurence will inherit when he reaches twenty-one. I recall—' He stopped. 'I was going to ask,' he went on after a moment, 'if I might represent our family at the funeral service, and Hallam would like to represent the estate. That was our reason for seeing you before you left for London, as well as to offer our commiserations.'

'Thank you,' she said on a grateful sigh. 'I would appreciate that very much indeed.'

CHAPTER FIFTY-TWO

Beatrix wrote to Maria advising her of the date and time of the funeral; she was quite sure that she would want to attend, and as the funeral service was to be held at the church of St George where Beatrix and Charles had been married, which was not far from Judd Street, it would be easy for her to be there if she wished.

The day was dull and cold, and all the men at the service, which was attended by many of Charles's friends and bank officials, turned to stare at the young widow on her father's arm with Dora in attendance. Edward and Hallam sat near the back, and behind them a woman dressed completely in black with a black mantilla that covered her face and head.

At the graveside everyone stood in silence as the sounds of the London traffic continued unabated. The horses that had pulled the cortège were decked out in tossing feathered plumes; the mutes who had walked in front of the draped carriages wore long white scarves wrapped around their top hats in express opposition to what Beatrix had requested, and waited patiently to escort the passengers on the return journey.

'Can't do it, I'm afraid,' Alfred Dawley had said to Beatrix's father when he had passed on Beatrix's request for no extravagance. 'Not done to have a plain funeral,' he went on. 'Not for people in our position, and besides, his mother would have been mortified,' and he was probably left wondering why Fawcett had turned his back on him and walked away.

After the burial, when Beatrix had scattered soil into the grave she stood aside in a state of unreality, inclining her head as mourners came to greet her, mumbling platitudes, and wishing she could return to the safety of her parents' house. One of the mourners was Charles's friend Paul, who unashamedly shed tears and said he could not yet believe that his friend had gone.

Others whom she recognized had visited their home in the days when Charles had invited them to summer parties, but she could not recall their names; there were clerks representing the bank, and Edward and Hallam hanging back to speak to her. Edward was wearing a black frock coat and top hat which completely unnerved her, and Hallam was neatly dressed in a dark cord jacket and bowler. She thanked them for coming.

Alfred Dawley, who was also receiving the mourners, wore a black cloak fashionable for funerals in a previous decade, and a very tall black top hat which was trimmed with a 'weeper', a long trailing hat band; he turned to her when she had finished speaking to Edward and Hallam and said she was on no account to worry about anything, and that he would handle all the details of Charles's will and those of the estate which would come to Laurence when he came of age.

'That is most kind,' she murmured sweetly, and set to tell a white lie. 'But I have already notified my solicitor of Charles's demise and he will come to visit me at home as soon as I am able to receive him.'

'Will he?' He seemed quite taken aback. 'He's here. Parkinson! Has he not introduced himself?'

'Parkinson? No, that is not the name. Robinson-Gough; do you remember him? He was at school with Charles. Highly recommended. His offices are in York, so much more convenient than London.'

She turned back to where Edward and Hallam were standing and said to her father-in-law, who seemed to have been thrown into disarray by her comment, 'May I introduce our farm manager, Simon Hallam, and you will perhaps know Edward Newby.'

'I don't think so.' Alfred Dawley tipped his hat to Hallam and then turned to Edward. 'What was the name again?' he asked rather brusquely.

'Newby,' Edward responded. 'You perhaps won't remember me, I was only a boy when we last met, but you'll remember my father. Luke Newby, a good friend of Neville Dawley.'

Beatrix watched as an expression of unease crossed Alfred Dawley's face; why would he be uncomfortable about that?

'How do you do. If you'll excuse me,' Dawley stutteringly made his apologies, 'I need to speak to some other people,' and Beatrix watched as he hurried over towards a man dressed very soberly in black and wearing a watch and chain, which he looked at several times, as if he were anxious to be gone. She saw Alfred Dawley say something to him, and the man frowned, shook his head, and scanned over to where Beatrix was standing.

She glanced about her; a woman was standing by the graveside, covered completely by her black garments; her shoulders were shaking. Beatrix's father was in conversation with Edward so she stepped across to speak to the woman, who had to be Maria, for there were no other women present.

When she approached her, Maria stepped back, her head bent. 'I am so sorry. I should not be here, but thank you, thank you for allowing me to come.' She gave a great sob. 'I am so unhappy. I cannot bear to live without Charles.'

'But you must,' Beatrix said in alarm. 'You must stay in the house to preserve his memory.'

Maria shook her head. 'I don't belong here. I am a foreigner, yet I can't go back to Spain.'

'Maria! Will you trust me? I will try to do my best for you, but I can't do it now, not whilst I am in mourning. Meanwhile, this is what I want you to do. Tomorrow you must find a locksmith and have the locks changed on the door. Ask to have two keys made, one for you and one for me. Do not give them to anyone else. Do you understand? Two keys only. One for you; one for me. Do not give a copy to anyone else, not even Charles's father. Ask them to charge it to me.'

'They will ask for the money in hand.' Maria lifted her veil and wiped her eyes. 'Everyone does.'

Beatrix sighed; she really wanted to go home, or at least to her parents' home. She spotted Edward looking her way and discreetly signalled to him.

'Edward,' she whispered. 'Do you have any money with you?'

He gave a small smile at the odd question. 'Some,' he said.

'Would you kindly give this lady enough to pay a locksmith to change a lock and supply two keys, and I will pay you back when next I see you.'

He nodded and took out a notebook and purse and gave Maria a crown. 'It won't be so much, sir,' she choked.

'With the change you may buy yourself a new bonnet,' he said softly.

Beatrix blinked away tears; how kind he was. The few simple words opened up her heart as they seemed to do for Maria, who dipped her knee, tears streaming down her face as she lifted her veil to wipe them, turned to Beatrix and dipped again, and walked away.

Edward gazed at Maria's back as she walked towards the gate of the graveyard and shook his head before offering his arm to walk Beatrix back to her father. He knows who she is, Beatrix thought. How does he know?

He told her when she asked. He had seen Maria by chance when Charles had brought her to look at the house; he didn't believe they had gone inside but only looked at the exterior. 'I was making fast a window cord when they came,' he said briefly. 'She wouldn't have remembered me.'

She told her father that she was ready to leave and the thought came to her that never would she have imagined she would need her father as much as she did now. She felt as if she were drowning in matters out of her control: the London house, Charles's will, and most of all her son's estate, which if she had to fight for it would need all the strength she could muster. Why she felt threatened, she couldn't put into words, but it had been triggered by Alfred Dawley's smooth suggestion that she was not to worry and should leave all the legal details to him.

When they returned home, her father invited her to come into his study and her mother sent in a tray with coffee and a plate of bread, beef and ham. There was still a lingering trace of tobacco smoke, but it was not unpleasant as her father had given up his pipe, her mother had put up new curtains and changed the cushions and the room had a fresher smell than it once had.

By the time they finished talking Beatrix had a headache, but they had discussed all the considerations that were worrying her, and with her father's reassurance that they could all be attended to she went upstairs and slept for two hours, but awoke wishing that she had brought the children with her, for she was missing them and their chatter.

Her father returned home the following lunchtime after several successful visits to various people to ask advice on her behalf and sending a letter post-haste to the York lawyer Stephen Robinson-Gough, requesting a meeting at the home of his daughter Mrs Beatrix Dawley ten days hence, for Beatrix had embroidered her words to Alfred Dawley when she claimed she had already arranged a meeting with her solicitor; it was actually still on her reminder list, waiting to be actioned.

He had made one call at his former bank, where he spoke to the present manager to confirm a query, and was pleased by the welcome he received, to know that he was still held in high esteem; and another to the office of Parkinson, Charles's former solicitor, who appeared at an inner door of his chambers just as Ambrose Fawcett was enquiring for an urgent appointment.

Parkinson invited him to come into his office as his next appointment was late, and as he later explained to Beatrix, who had come again to his study, he seemed a decent enough fellow who had looked after the matter of the estate well, in spite of some difficulties with Charles's father which naturally he didn't divulge.

'He explained that he couldn't give me any details, which was as I expected,' he told Beatrix. 'But what he did confide was that if Charles had made a will, he hadn't asked him to take instruction; and as far as he could ascertain, and he had pressed Charles on many occasions, there wasn't one.

'A remarkable lapse, I would say,' her father mumbled, 'but one that might make it easier for you in the long run, as you will automatically inherit. Had he made a will and left the estate to Laurence then you would have been the property custodian.' He had a very serious expression as he continued. 'This makes you a most desirable target for any Tom, Dick or Harry in need of a great deal of money, for if they can persuade you to marry them you will have to give it all up to them. You will need advice from Robinson-Gough to clarify.'

He paused before opening the door for her. 'I must confess that I hadn't given enough consideration to the fact that the system is very unfair indeed towards women.'

CHAPTER FIFTY-THREE

Dora asked if she might take the morning off to visit
her parents and Beatrix said yes, of course she could,
and to stay the whole day or overnight if she wished.

'I'll stay for the day, ma'am, but come back before
supper. My ma and pa have a routine and I wouldn't
like to bother 'em, even though they'll be glad to see
me.'

She deserved to have time off, Beatrix thought;
she's forever at my side, taking care of my every whim.
She glanced out of the window shortly after she heard
Dora's footsteps on the stairs and the bang of the
front door, and saw Hallam crossing towards her from
where he must have been waiting by the gardens in the
square. Dora took his arm.

Ah, Beatrix thought. Is he going to ask for her hand?
How lucky I've been to have her. Will she now be leaving me?

She dressed in the black cape and a black bonnet
that her mother produced out of a cupboard. Mrs
Fawcett had shrugged her shoulders as she handed it
to Beatrix, and murmured that it was as well to be prepared. Her father had ordered a cab and they set off,

probably in the same direction as Dora was heading, she surmised.

Maria was in and busily cleaning the inside of the windows when they arrived at the door. 'This is my father, Maria,' Beatrix told her. 'Might we have a few words?'

Maria took a sharp breath and put her hand to her chest, but Beatrix assured her that there was nothing to worry about. Her father took a seat and said how very nice the house was and indeed it was, Beatrix considered: every surface was polished, the cushions were plumped, and the hearthrug, which she noted was new, had been well shaken.

'We want to ask you if Charles kept any papers here; official papers, I mean.' Mr Fawcett gave her a reassuring smile.

'Oh, yes, he did. He said so that his father didn't see them; he did not trust his father always to do the right thing. You may come upstairs and I show you where he keep them.'

They followed her up the narrow staircase and into a very small room that looked as if it was used as a dressing room, for there was a chest of drawers, a very large wardrobe, a mirror on a stand and a tall filing cabinet.

'I know where is the key.' She smiled proudly. 'I am the only one who knows, not his father, no one else. Please, you close eyes.'

They both did as they were bid and each heard the clang of the drawer as she opened it. 'There,' she said. 'You can open eyes now.'

The bottom drawer of the filing cabinet was open and they saw several files neatly contained within it.

'May I?' Beatrix's father asked politely, and she nodded.

'They are yours now, I think?' she said to Beatrix, who replied that yes, they were, or at least her son's, but he was too young to understand them.

'Ah, yes. Charles say to me that the old house and the land would one day belong to his son.' She shrugged. 'He tell me that he doesn't want it; it was his father who say he must have it.'

Beatrix glanced at her father as he took out several files, then she turned back to Maria and said, 'Could we trouble you for a pot of tea whilst my father looks for the papers we need? And I wish to speak to you about this house.'

Immediately Maria was apologetic over her lack of manners and led Beatrix downstairs to sit down whilst she made tea. When she had done that and taken a cup upstairs to Mr Fawcett, Beatrix said, 'You have a lovely home, Maria. May I call you Maria? I don't know your surname.'

'I use Garcia,' she said softly. 'It is my mother's maiden name, not my 'usband's or my father's. I don't wish to use them. My 'usband is not a good man.' She gazed at Beatrix. 'I would like it if you call me Maria.' She paused for a moment, and then said, 'I loved Charles always, and although he marry you he say to me that it is what the English do, but he still love me and care for me.'

Beatrix nodded and agreed that was possibly true, and thought that Charles probably did love Maria in his way, although not enough to give her his London house. 'We have ascertained Charles's wishes, and one of them is that although you will not own this house and therefore cannot sell it, you may stay in it for as long as you live. If you decide to marry or live with another man, however, then there will be rent to pay.'

'I will never marry,' Maria said determinedly. 'I cannot, as my husband is still alive in Spain, but may my friend Bianca come and live with me? Like me she is alone, and we can grow old together.'

'Yes, she may, but only one friend, no more than that. I will ask my solicitor to send you the particulars and someone will visit once a year to check if any repairs are needed. But you will always be notified that they are coming.'

'Thank you,' Maria said. 'I understand. I am very grateful.' She leaned forward, and raising Beatrix's hand planted a kiss on it.

Her father came down with some of the papers and said he thought he had everything. 'There is a list of jewellery here,' he said to Maria. 'Perhaps what he has bought you over the years?'

Maria paled. 'Yes,' she whispered. 'For me, Charles said, for if he wasn't here, and if ever I needed money I could sell.'

'Then you must insure it against loss or theft,' Mr Fawcett advised. 'Don't just keep it in a drawer for burglars to find.'

Her face cleared. 'Thank you,' she said. 'I will do that.'

They left her then, and as they stepped over the doorstep Maria pressed the new door key into Beatrix's hand. 'You are very kind and beautiful lady,' she said softly. 'You are kinder than I expected. Charles was very lucky to marry you.'

'Thank you,' Beatrix said, feeling quite moved by the other woman's sincerity.

'Did you find a will?' she asked her father as they bowled away in the cab.

'Not exactly,' he said. 'But a letter of intent which I think will be enough; it was written some years ago. June 1852.'

'After Laurie's birth,' she said, a tear sliding down her cheek. 'What does it say?'

'It says,' and he harrumphed as if he too was caught out with emotion, '*My beautiful wife has given birth to my son and heir just as I asked her to. The estate will go to him when he comes of age. Until then I will take care of him to the best of my ability, but if I should fail, then I know that she will not, as she is as capable as any woman I know.*'

CHAPTER FIFTY-FOUR

Beatrix spent another week with her parents and then felt that she wanted to go home.

'My need to be with my children exceeds all else,' she told her mother. 'I can grieve in my own home and I can't think of any reason why I shouldn't travel with Dora as usual.'

Her mother agreed with her. 'Your sense of loss will perhaps be less in your own home as Charles spent so little time there,' she suggested.

'Yes.' Beatrix thought that she was right. But, she pondered, that was Charles's choice. I know now that he didn't want the estate; he already had the life he wanted with Maria, and given the opportunity he would have sold it and lived on the proceeds. It was his father who wanted the prestige of the inheritance, and I believe his influence over Charles was paramount for most of his life.

She was pensive for a moment and her mother didn't interrupt her musings. That was why Mr Dawley chose a wife for him: someone who would bear him children; give him an heir so that the Dawley line would continue. Her thoughts drifted on. It will continue, she thought, but without any influence from Alfred Dawley. I will make sure of that.

'Mama,' she said, 'when Charles and I married, I saw you speaking to a silver-haired gentleman outside the church. I noticed him particularly as he was rather handsome, and I've wondered who he was. A relative, perhaps?'

Her mother was silent for a moment; then she murmured, 'An old friend. Someone I knew when I was young.'

Beatrix waited. It seemed a poignant moment before her mother spoke again, looking down at her clasped hands.

'He was the man I wanted to marry, and who wanted to marry me.' She sighed. 'My parents didn't think he was suitable and his parents didn't think that I was.' She gave a sad little smile. 'We kept in touch even after we both married other people, until your father retired and then it didn't seem right or possible, but I invited him to your wedding in order to say a final goodbye.'

Beatrix swallowed, unsure of her feelings; perhaps she shouldn't have asked. Kept in touch? What did that mean exactly, and did she really want to know? 'Was he your lover?' she asked quietly.

Her mother shook her head and gave a hint of a smile. 'No. We both felt we wanted to be, yet neither of us could take that step. I think too that if we had, we might have lost the magic of the idea of love. We were young: in love with the idea of being in love.' She looked up. 'But your father has proved to be a loving and reliable man, and I'm not sure if Anton would have been so faithful.'

Anton, Beatrix mused. Even his name seems exotic, but I'm glad that the decision was, after all, the right one. Thomas and I have had the security of it.

Dora was wearing a pretty engagement ring on her left hand when they travelled home, and had said to Beatrix, when she asked if she would be leaving her, that she wouldn't be going anywhere for quite a long time, providing her services were still required, and Beatrix said that of course they would be.

They had arrived to a merry welcome from children, dogs, housekeeping staff and her good friend Mags, who, she considered, was almost like a second mother to her.

I can begin to live again, she thought, and although I must do so quietly for a few months yet, wearing my mourning in Charles's memory, and not at home to visitors, the best thing I can do is continue with my usual activities and see to the needs of the estate and the workers: then I must proceed with all the official paperwork, and to help me with this I will have Stephen Robinson-Gough, who seems, at least by his correspondence, to be an efficient and caring man. She would also ask for his assistance in moving the estate finances away from Dawley's private banking company into the Hull branch of her father's former bank.

It seemed, when the earnest, friendly York lawyer called to see her, that not only did he know Charles, he also knew Edward, although he didn't say how. Edward satisfied some of her curiosity at least when he said that Stephen had been kind to him when he was a boy of ten and had met him on the occasion of Stephen's visit to the estate at Charles's invitation.

'And?' Beatrix asked. 'How was he kind?'

Edward brushed away the question. 'It's a long story. I'll tell you some other time.' And he would not be moved on the point, which increased her curiosity even further.

Her friend Rosie, disregarding the not at home rule, called to see her and quite disarmingly, forgetting that Beatrix was in mourning, told her in great delight that she and Esmond were going to be wed after all.

'It will be in the spring and the clergyman has agreed to marry us in the orchard as we had planned; I don't want this little one to think,' she patted her belly, 'that she or he is illegitimate, as I am, although Mama says that perhaps she and Papa might marry after all, as Papa doesn't have a head for accounting and is quite lazy and wouldn't in the least know how to claim her property, any more than Esmond would in time to come. Besides,' she added, 'I have to learn to trust.'

Recovering from the shock of learning that her friend's parents were not married, Beatrix hid a smile. How wonderful to be not in the least caring about proprieties, or what anyone else thought. But would society break down if we all did whatever we wished? There must surely be some order in life.

The weather was darkening as winter approached. The sky was heavy with cloud and constant flocks of waterfowl and over-wintering birds flying in from the Arctic; golden plover and shelduck searched the mudflats for a source of food. During the daylight hours, the workmen mended fencing and prepared the ground for the following spring, and womenfolk filled their cold larders with meat and game to last them over the winter, alongside bottled fruit picked from the summer crop.

On Christmas Day Beatrix went early to church wearing her mother's black cape over her gown so as not to upset any of the congregation, for she had now abandoned her black wardrobe for grey, trimmed with black crêpe. It was time, she thought. Christmas Day wasn't ever going to be a quiet one with three boisterous children eager to play with their presents.

Her parents came to stay and brought news that Thomas's wife had given birth to twins, a boy and girl, Sean and Alaina. Their letters had crossed, for Beatrix had written to her brother at the same time to tell him and his wife of Charles's untimely death.

Although Laurie spoke of his father sometimes Alicia rarely did, and Ambrose didn't remember him at all. Beatrix tried to rectify this by talking to them all about Charles, but the younger ones simply looked at her blankly as if they didn't know who she meant.

She walked a lot during that winter, when the frost hardened the ploughed ridges and left a crystal cloak over the trees and hedgerows; one day her feet had taken her down the woodland path to the gate at the edge of their land, where she could see the strong current in the estuary carrying the flow of dark, brackish water on its journey to the sea, and she vowed that come spring she would accept Edward's suggestion that she should go with him to Holderness and visit his sisters and see for herself where the estuary waters emptied into the sea.

He had told her too of the phenomenon of the island in the Humber mouth that was once beneath the waves and was now the best corn-growing area in the land, after being reclaimed over the last century and now boasting of farms, a school and a church. One of his sisters, a farmer's wife, lived there, and Beatrix had often thought that she would very much like to see that strange place, but as a married woman she could not be seen out with a single man. Such restrictions were now irrelevant, although she must be careful not to appear flighty.

She had breathed in deeply and relished the silence, broken only by the whispering of the wind in creaking leafless branches, the call of birds and the cackle of waterfowl, and thought that in spite of all that had happened between her and Charles she had her children, a beautiful home and a wonderful landscape.

What more could she want? She gazed over the estuary towards the narrow banks of Lincolnshire and the low shadowy rise of the Lincolnshire Wolds beyond, and thought that to have someone to love her would be the most wondrous thing, for she had plenty of love in her heart, and now that the property was entailed to Laurie and could not be sold or handed on except to someone within the family, no one could be accused of marrying her for her wealth. Was that still a possibility? Edward had been a prospect, but he had not given any sign since Charles's death.

As spring neared she accepted Edward's invitation to visit his cottage, and took the children with her for form's sake.

'It's hardly a cottage,' she said, when they drove up to the front door in Edward's trap. It was a substantial four-bedroomed house, originally built of brick, with extensions of stone and boulders brought, he told her, from Holderness shores.

It was set higher up the hill than Old Stone Hall and had an open view down to the estuary. Next to the front door and beneath the window was a long wooden bench, where she imagined Edward would sit at the end of a working day, with perhaps a tankard of ale in his hand.

'This is a lovely little house,' Alicia declared, jumping down from the trap before Laurie and Ambrose. 'I'd quite like a little house like this,' and the three children went off to explore the orchard and garden whilst Edward invited their mother to look inside.

It lacked a woman's touch, for it was devoid of cushions, paintings or flowers, but, she thought, it breathed Edward's personality: leather armchairs and comfy sofas, a large open fireplace, and views from the windows of the land sloping down towards the estuary. She sat down on the sofa and he asked if she'd like a cup of tea.

Beatrix shook her head. 'Not yet,' she said. 'I'd like to know how you came to be here and are not still living at home.'

'This was originally our home. It was still a cottage when we all lived here, my sisters and me and Ma and Da.' He sat down next to her. 'That was before Da was injured.'

'That must have been a very difficult time for you,' she said softly.

'It was, but most of all for Da; he knew he wouldn't be able to work as he used to. I wasn't there when it happened; Uncle Nev had sent me to look for something in one of the stables. I was always at his house at the weekends and holidays and mostly made myself useful, helping Da, who was foreman, or anybody really. That day was very hot, and Da, who is an excellent carpenter, had gone down to the bottom field with old Josh Atkins to help him mend a broken fence. Then I heard someone shouting out for help and Stephen Robinson-Gough came running into the yard, although I didn't know who he was back then.' He took a breath before he continued. 'He shouted that the cattle had stampeded and someone was injured and to fetch help, and I knew immediately that it was Da or old Josh and I ran like the wind to fetch Uncle Nev.'

He blew out his cheeks. 'Nev was furious. "I warned them," he was shouting. "I told them not to worry the cattle." He knew that it must have been Charles and his friends who had tormented the cows who were with their calves in the bottom field. I ran first to tell my mother and then down to the field where some men were rounding up the cattle and others were running to the fence with makeshift stretchers.' He blinked, and his voice croaked as if it had happened only yesterday. 'And then I saw them lifting up two bloody bodies and I thought they were both dead.'

It was as if he had bottled up the scenario for ever, and I suppose he has, Beatrix thought, and gently put her hand over his to comfort him.

'They carried them into the house and someone went to fetch the doctor. Alfred Dawley was having a nap on the sofa,' he went on in a calmer voice, 'and Uncle Nev rounded on him, saying he wasn't fit to have a son if he didn't teach him the difference between right and wrong, and I heard him threaten to disown Charles. I didn't know if he could do that; the estate had always belonged to the Dawleys, but it was soon afterwards that he sold Da a goodly piece of land with the cottage where Ma and Da live now.'

'Sold it to him?' Beatrix queried. 'Was he able to afford to buy it?'

He nodded and said. 'For a peppercorn. In other words, it was a concealed gift. Compensation, I suppose, to make up for Da's injuries, for we all knew that he wouldn't do physical work again. He also gave Josh and his wife a pension for life, but the old lad only lived for another month or so after the stampede and his wife died five years later.'

He smiled at her and stroked her hand, which he was now holding. 'And now,' he said softly, 'I'm going to tell you a love story which will explain why Uncle Nev had always been such a special friend to the Newby family.'

CHAPTER FIFTY-FIVE

'Uncle Nev was a great friend of Da's father Joe,' Edward began. 'Even though they were from very different backgrounds. I didn't know my grandfather; my father was only just out of school when he died, but seemingly Uncle Nev had promised Grandad Joe that he would always take care of his wife and son and he did, right to the end of his life.' He looked at Beatrix with a twinkle in his eye. 'Can you guess why?'

Beatrix blushed. 'You said it was a love story, so I suppose he loved your grandmother?'

'Exactly. He did. Apparently – or so my mother said, for Nev had confided in her after she and my father married – he had fallen in love with Grandma Amy as soon as he set eyes on her, but he was a great friend of Joe's and would never betray that trust or their friendship. After Grandad Joe died he waited for the right time to declare his love for Amy, but she refused him, and even though she said she loved him as a friend she couldn't break her marriage vows. So poor old Uncle Nev never did marry. He remained faithful to Amy, and thought of us as family. Ma said that when Grandma Amy died – and she was old by then – he was heartbroken and valued the friendship of the Newbys even more, even my sisters and me.'

'Did he never consider leaving your father the estate rather than the Dawleys?'

He shook his head. 'He was an honest fellow, and I believe that apart from that one time when Charles played havoc he felt honour bound to keep it in the Dawley family.' He was silent for a while, still holding her hand, and then placing it to his lips he said softly, 'And I'm pleased that he did, as otherwise I would never have met you.'

Gently she pulled her hand away. 'You know that I'm still in mourning?'

Edward nodded. 'I fell in love with you when you came to Old Stone Hall as a young bride,' he murmured. 'I saw you dancing on the lawn in the moonlight. You were like a sprite conjured up out of the mist, and you captivated me completely.'

She raised her eyebrows. 'I remember. I went outside and danced beneath the moonlit sky.'

He gazed at her and tenderly touched her cheek. 'Will what happened to Neville and Amy happen to us? Will I love you for ever and for ever you'll say no?'

She closed her eyes. She could hear the children's voices outside as they sat chattering on the bench under the window. 'My children—'

'Will have a father,' he said softly. 'I'll love them as if they were my own.'

'Yes,' she breathed and smiled, so full of happiness she couldn't believe it. 'I know that you will, but what I was going to say was that I wouldn't want their reputation to suffer because of their mother's improper behaviour.' She leaned forward and kissed him. 'How long will you wait?'

He gathered her into his arms, breathed in her scent and nuzzled into her hair, and whispered, 'For ever.' He smiled and his eyes glistened as much as hers. 'Until next spring?'

'I love you,' she murmured, and he caught his breath.

But it couldn't be the following spring, she thought as she tossed beneath the covers in her bed that night. Even though he had waited so long. He had waited when there had been no hope; only Charles's death had made his declaration possible. But she wasn't the innocent girl she had been when he had watched her dancing in the moonlight.

Could she be that girl once more? Would she ever find herself again? She wasn't a rebel like Rosie's mother Hannah Stokes, who abided only by her own guidelines and did what suited her. Nor was she a woman like Caroline Norton with influential friends, even though she would fight like a tiger for her children if they were ever threatened.

And then there was Charles: would his memory always haunt and hurt her? She closed her eyes and from out of nowhere recalled the party when her father had announced their engagement. *Shall we run away from this charade?* Charles had asked her. Yet he was already committed to Maria, and very obviously that commitment had been strong and he would never have left her.

She opened her eyes and sat up against the pillows. Poor Charles. He'd been forced into a marriage that he didn't want. His father, and generations before him, even the holy Neville Dawley, had played their parts in ensuring the Dawley line continued as it always had.

It isn't only women who must obey the rules, she concluded. True, Charles wanted the money and prestige that the inheritance would bring: that greed too was running in his blood; but it hadn't been entirely his fault and she felt, as in honour bound, that she must at least mark his life and death for the full period of her mourning.

She threw back the covers, slipped out of bed and into her slippers, reached for her dressing robe and crossed to the window. She looked up into the midnight-blue sky as she always did and saw a waxing crescent moon and uncountable stars, and then looked down on to her beloved garden, her eyes drawn to the gleam of the statuary in the moon's slender light and the new flower beds that were now rimed with silver frost; and then she saw him, gazing up at her.

She fastened the belt of her dressing robe and drawing the hood over her head went down the stairs and unlocked the front door.

She went down the steps and Edward came towards her. 'I couldn't sleep,' he explained.

'Nor I,' she answered. 'I have to ask you to wait a little longer.'

He nodded; it was as if he had expected it, as if he had come especially to hear the words she was saying.

'Forgiveness?' he said, then murmured, 'I understand. It's only right and proper. It's who we are. I said I would wait and I will.'

'We'll wait together,' she said softly. 'Until the time is right.'

He took her hand in his and drew it to his lips, and with his other he embraced her waist and drew her close, his cheek touching hers, and together they danced beneath the moon's silver light.

ACKNOWLEDGEMENTS

The Victorian House by Judith Flanders, Harper Perennial, 2004

Various internet sources for information on Mrs Caroline Norton, writer and social campaigner.

To my editor Sally Williamson; copy and production editors Vivien Thompson and Nancy Webber and the whole of the dedicated Transworld team, I thank you all.

AUTHOR'S NOTE

I have read often of Mrs Caroline Norton's remarkable life, which has influenced my thinking of Victorian women whilst writing fiction of that period. She was a society woman, a social reformer, a lady, in fact, born into a grand though penniless family.

She had many powerful and influential friends including important political figures, such as Lord Melbourne, who were drawn into her continuing chronicle, upsetting the powerful in Parliament as she strove for the right of women to control their own lives and to consider their children as belonging to them as much as to their husbands.

In 1837 she filed to the courts on The Natural Claim of a Mother, following her husband's decision to remove their children from her care, as was his right at that time.

August 1839. The Custody of Infants Act was made law, giving custody, after court petition, to the mothers of children under seven, providing they had not been proven to have committed adultery. In 1873 the Act was changed to allow access to or custody of children below the age of sixteen.

1858. Marriage and Divorce Acts became law. Women could petition Parliament for divorce on the grounds only of their husband's incestuous adultery. Prior to this, women could not divorce their husbands under any circumstances, though men could divorce their wives.

Caroline Norton wrote several books including a novel based on her own experiences, *A Story of Modern Times*, which drew much acclaim. Alas for her, her husband took their children to Scotland where the custody law did not apply and she never saw them again.

A Place to Call Home
by Val Wood

Ellen thought she'd always live in the remote, pretty coastal village where she grew up. After all, her husband, Harry, works on a farm where he's guaranteed a job and home for life.

But when the old landowner dies and the couple and their young children are forced from their cottage, the future is suddenly bleak. Rather than stay – and starve – in the countryside they love, Harry sets out to find a job in the factories and mills of nearby Hull, and Ellen must leave behind everything she's ever known to follow him and build a new life for her family on the unfamiliar city streets.

The road ahead is full of hardships and challenges. But with love and determination, they make the best of things, forging friendships with other newcomers and refugees; even helping them to succeed in their new surroundings.

Then tragedy threatens Ellen's fragile happiness. How much more can she sacrifice before they find a place to call home?

A Place to Call Home is available in paperback and ebook now

Four Sisters

by Val Wood

Hull, 1852.

Matty has had to care for her three younger sisters
ever since their mother's death ten years ago.
She and the girls' beloved father have worked
hard to keep the family together and now it's
time to celebrate as Matty turns eighteen.

But their joy is short-lived when tragedy
suddenly strikes and their father disappears
on his way to London.

The sisters have no way of knowing what has
happened to him – only that he hasn't returned
home. With little money left, they're now forced
to battle life's misfortunes alone . . .

Four Sisters is available in paperback and ebook now

Praise for *Following Ophelia*:

"Sophia has conjured up a world as alive with colour and texture
and beauty and rebellion as the paintings that she references…
I was utterly engrossed from first page to last."
Perdita Cargill, author of *Waiting for Callback*

"This is Bennett's first historical fiction title, and she does a wonderful job
with the glamour, scandal and dresses of the period."
Fiona Noble, *The Bookseller*

Praise for *Love Song*:

"…perfect for anyone dreaming
of living the rock star life."
S Magazine, Sunday Express

"I loved this book! Funny, romantic
and smart, *Love Song* is a total treat."
Cat Clarke, author of *Undone*

"One of the funniest, most touching
romantic YA novels ever, smart and warm."
Amanda Craig, author and journalist

"For anyone who ever fell in love with a pop star,
Bennett helps bring that dream to life."
The Sun

"A really entertaining, well-written,
feel-good contemporary."
The Bookbag

"This fun, feisty, fabulous
novel is a total blast."
Heat

"Bliss in
book form."
Sister Spooky

"I flew through it; hot boys, tantrums and
a delicious peek at life in the fast lane of fame."
Melinda Salisbury, author of *The Sin Eater's Daughter*

"*Love Song* is like a chart-topping hit:
fun, thrilling and totally addictive."
Maximum Pop

"An uplifting love story."
The Telegraph, Best YA Books
of 2016

"I've loved all of Sophia's books – she writes teenage reality
with such honesty and generosity and style."
S

"Nothing co   ulsive read.
story I've r   spell."
*Serena   or of *Crush*

Following Ophelia

To Katie.
Telling this story together has been such a joy.
Thank you.

STRIPES PUBLISHING
An imprint of the Little Tiger Group
1 The Coda Centre, 189 Munster Road, London SW6 6AW

A paperback original
First published in Great Britain in 2017

ISBN: 978-1-84715-810-9

Text copyright © Sophia Bennett, 2017
Cover copyright © Stripes Publishing, 2017

A CIP catalogue record for this book is available from the British Library.

Printed and bound in the UK.

2 4 6 8 10 9 7 5 3 1